THE DEFENDERS' APPRENTICE

AMELIA SMITH

ISBN-13: 978-1-941334-13-3 (paperback)

ISBN-13: 978-1-941334-15-7 (ebook)

Published by Split Rock Books

Cover and book design by the author

The title font is Canto Brush Open, and the text is set in
Starling Book, both by The Font Bureau.

Cover image is a detail of "Landscape with the Flight into
Egypt" by Pieter Bruegel the Elder, ca. 1563.

Table of Contents

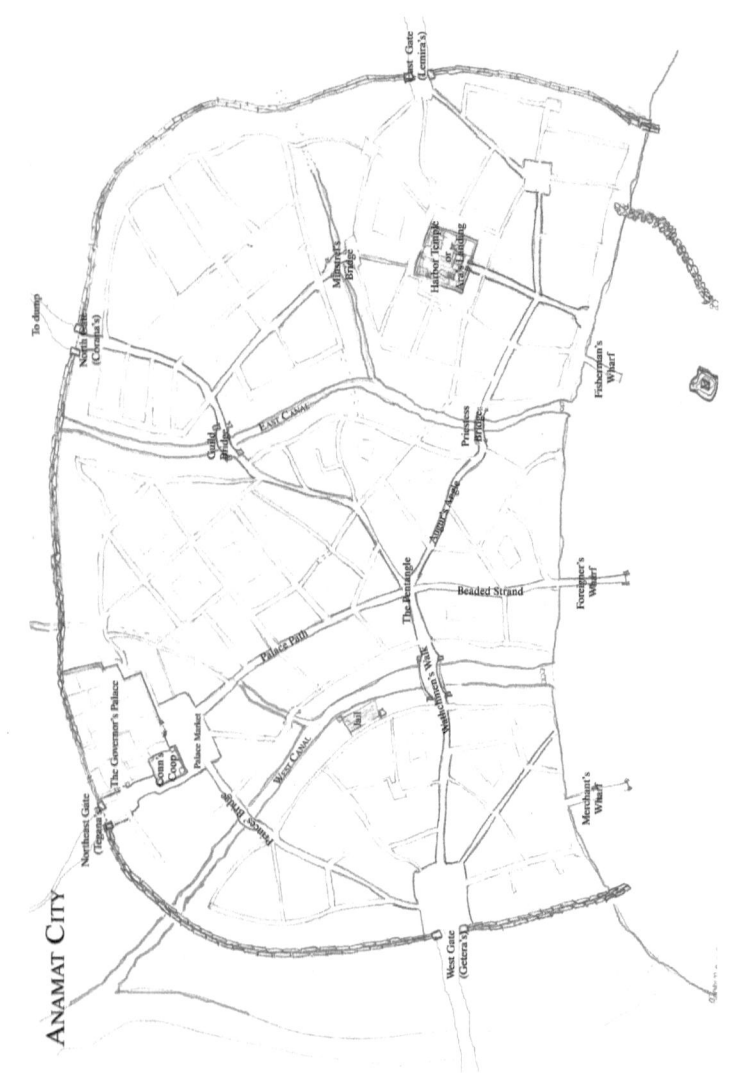

ANAMAT CITY

Theranis

land of the dragons

Seiganum

Teganum

Onarun

Naramun

Anamat

Lemirun

Slaradun

Galamun

Helanum

Getedun

Kiralun

Tiadun

Chapter 1

The pale fire tongues of the dragons' realm flickered away as the warmth of the rite receded into the offering place, into the earth. The heat between their bodies flowed into the place where he could never follow. Thorat gazed up at the eggshell dome as he reached out to run his hand along Iola's smooth back. The trance was leaving her, too, leaving them alone together as themselves, at last.

"I'll send for tea," Iola said.

Instead of answering, Thorat pulled her closer. They had so little time together.

She draped the red robe around her shoulders to go out to the garden to summon her attendant. When she danced, that robe became a river of molten fire, but now it was just very fine clothing, separating him from her and reminding them both of her calling. As ambassadress, she had dozens of petitioners, princes and guild masters, wealthy merchants, the governor. He'd come to bring the Defenders' offering, but he wished that he could come just for himself, to be friends again, even ordinary lovers.

When she returned, she went to a quiet alcove, far from the altar where he lay. He pulled away from the last thin traces of dragonfire and went to sit beside her, holding hands, human again. When he edged closer, she pulled away and turned to face him, letting only their feet touch.

"Tell me: what news do the Defenders bring this year?"

"We haven't been down to the shrine yet. I should have waited until after that, but Sunna said that you wouldn't be able to see me after tonight," Thorat said. "There aren't enough of us to go to all the gates every year, either, but those we saw were quiet." The worst news wasn't news at all. They hadn't had a single new apprentice in years. Dragonsight was dying out, and the Defenders with it.

Iola nodded. "The princes tell me that the dragons guard their own gates now, or so they must be doing, to keep the foreign miners away."

"I don't know what keeps them away, but I'm fairly sure it's not the princes."

"Surely, they wouldn't let their trading partners steal the heart of their lands."

Was she so isolated here that she believed that? "At least the foreign miners can't find the gates on their own, so there's that much to keep the dragons safe, even when we can't go," Thorat said.

Iola looked down at her hands and frowned. "Unless a priestess helped them."

She was not utterly ignorant of what was happening beyond her marble walls, then. A long moment stretched between them, and he was about to reach out to hold her hand when she spoke again.

"Who is the Enatel?" Iola asked. "He can't be dragon-blind, so why does he send you rather than come to me himself?"

Thorat hesitated. It seemed hard to believe that after all these years, she still didn't know who the Enatel was, but he'd seen no reason to tell her, and apparently no one else had either.

"Of course I want to see you, more than I want to see anyone else, I really do." She bit her bottom lip. "It's only that I wonder."

Thorat took a deep breath. There was no reason not to tell her. "The Enatel is a woman now, even though she's Enat's heir, so of course she can't come." Sovara was a thin, gray-haired woman who had nothing good to say about priestesses in general, stealing offerings meant for the dragons, lazy in their luxuriant temples.

"She did send our offering, though," he said. "She made it herself."

"She could come to me," Iola said. "The rite is not dependent on the petitioner's sex, you know."

"It isn't? I don't think she knows that. I'm sure I didn't." He didn't much like the thought of Sovara lying with Iola, though it wasn't as bad as the thought of the governor heaving over her, understanding nothing.

"Most priestesses aren't willing to draw from another woman as they would from a man, if they even know how, but you're right; I would rather see you, while we can," Iola said. "Show me now: what did she send?"

Thorat handed her the package and she leaned against him as she unwrapped it. She smiled with appreciation as she held it up to see, a double-edged blade, wider than most, with an intricately worked handle.

"A dragon-grooming dagger. How lovely," she said.

There was a quiet clatter of cups and plates as Iola's attendant set the tea tray down outside. Iola brought it in and placed it on a low table between them. She poured Thorat a glass of wine, then filled her own cup with tea. She reclined, her raven hair flowing down over the crimson robes and alabaster skin. He reached for a cake.

"The Aralel wants me to retire, but I can't," she said.

"Why not? You've been ambassadress a long time now; what is it, five years?" Most ambassadresses didn't last nearly that long. The journey to the dragons' realm wasn't easy for a human, but then, Iola was closer to the dragons than anyone else he'd ever met.

"Six years. This will be my seventh descent."

"There must be dozens of priestesses who'd want to be ambassadress, despite the danger."

Iola shook her head. "Dozens of foolish, dragon-blind girls. It's not that there aren't enough; it's just that they're not the right ones. A few of them might survive one voyage, but no more than that."

"I wouldn't think it would be so hard to find priestesses." The Defenders couldn't find apprentices with dragonsight, but that was different. After all, his order wasn't supposed to exist, while the priestesses offered wealth, power, and as many of Theranis's best cakes as a person could want, every day. They were very good. He took another.

"The oracles say that there's a scrappling this season who might be fit to journey to the dragons' realms. There was one last year, but they missed her. I hope they don't miss her again this year." She looked up at Thorat. "You're out on the streets. If you find that girl, the one with dragonsight, could you bring her to me?"

"I'll do what I can," Thorat said. "Anything for you."

Iola half-smiled. "They all…" She stopped herself, but Thorat knew that he'd said something foolish, something that made him sound like just another lust-addled petitioner. He drained his cup.

"If you retired, you could leave the temple," Thorat said, another absurd idea. The only place retired priestesses went was to the hills, and there were bandits in the hills, lawless, violent men. He shuddered at the thought.

Of course, Iola laughed. "Not yet, not yet. Besides, I'll be a creature of the temple and the dragons as long as I live." Her face shone in the lamplight. It was true, but that didn't make him want her less.

"Darna and Myril left the temple, didn't they?" Thorat said, as if Iola were like them.

"They never wanted to be priestesses, not as I did. I am this." Iola indicated the room around her with its rich carvings, draperies, jewels, and the offering place. It was foolish to try to imagine her in a mountain hermitage wearing fiea-ridden furs.

In the outer courtyard, a bell rang.

"I told them, no more tonight," Iola said, sounding suddenly tired. She grasped Thorat's hand, then wrapped her arms around him. He held her, wishing that the moment could go on forever.

"It could be the new Slaradun prince," she said, pushing him away. "It would be good to have some taste of Salara before I see her again. In any case, you have to leave. After Midwinter, come see me as soon as you can. Promise it. Swear it."

"I will. I do." Thorat let her pull him back into the bath chamber, the way he came and went in secret. "Be safe; be well," he said, though it didn't seem like enough. "Send my love to the dragons."

Iola glanced to the outer doorway, then ran back and kissed him, full on the lips.

"Now go!" She pushed him toward the secret passage.

Thorat hurried away before any more foolish pledges of love could fall from his lips into that unforgiving splendor.

§

Eppie woke under the still-cool shade of the bridge. The traffic of feet and carts grew noisy on the bridge above and the sun beat hot on the canal bank. The others were still sleeping beside her. She sat up carefully, not wanting to wake them yet. Mist rose from the canal in delicate feathers, fading into the air. The dragonlet—if she was not only a figment of Eppie's imagination—hid in the crevices between the stones, her green scales blending with the moss-green rocks and twining into the earth, as dragons were said to do.

"Hey, lazybones," Eppie whispered, prodding one of the sleeping boys.

"What?" Squid grumbled.

"It's morning."

"'Course it's morning," he said. "I'm going back to sleep."

Squid had gone to the taverns the night before to pick pockets and look for an apprenticeship. Mostly to pick pockets, though; that was what he usually did when he wasn't fighting. Eppie was nearly his equal in both pursuits – pickpocketing and fighting – but he was better known. Probably that was just as well. Squid left a trail of confusion in his wake, like ink, like the darkness he disappeared into. If he'd ever had another name, it was long forgotten.

"They'll run out of bread," Eppie said.

Squid half sat up. "I don't need the temple hens' bread. You go."

He rolled over as if to go back to sleep while Eppie wormed her way out of the blankets. Squid was always grumpy in the morning, but today he was more talkative than usual.

"D'you think the dragons will kill her this year?" he asked.

"The ambassadress? I don't know," Eppie said. "Do you think we'll get real apprenticeships?"

Squid shrugged. "I got a lead. I might go on that Ganatean trader; able-bodied seaman, they'd call me."

Eppie hesitated. Squid was prone to bragging, but he'd never come close to getting an apprenticeship before. "That could be all right," she said, thinking of sailing the seas. "I've got nothing. D'you think I could join up too, be a sailor?"

Squid shook his head and sank back down under the blankets. "Not for a girl. They don't have girls on their ships, not as sailors anyway. Just as cargo, they say."

Eppie shuddered.

"Go on to the temple," Squid said. "You know they'll take you, and at least you'll eat. Otherwise, there's the foreigners' brothel."

Eppie shuddered at that as she walked away. No one wanted to go to the foreigners' brothel, over by Merchants' Wharf. There was no dignity in it, and you didn't even learn to read. In a way, though, it might be better than the temple, where the walls seemed to close out every sound of the outside world, where the silence stifled everything, and where she'd never seen a dragonlet, not that they showed themselves often by the docks, but she'd glimpsed them there sometimes. In any case, she didn't want to go to the temple, but Squid would never understand why. She could talk to him about almost everything else, from fighting to scavenging and which of the green-knees would last the season, but never about the dragons. Like most people, he didn't see them, and he thought that those who did must be drugged or just crazy.

Eppie followed a side street around to the back of the temple to get her share of festival bread, keeping to the shade as she went. In two days' time, the ambassadress would go to the dragons again, maybe forever. On that morning, she would see Anara again, and could look at her without worrying. She always did, at festival times, and then she wouldn't have to pretend not to see, since everyone else would be pretending that the *could* see, for a change.

Behind the houses, the white marble walls of Ara's Landing stood closed to the outside world, unbroken by windows or ordinary doorways. The temple was self-contained, like an egg, indifferent to the fate of anything outside its walls, except that they did give bread to the scrapplings, the Children of Anara, until they found their work or else fled back to the dragon-forsaken provinces. That suited Eppie fine for now.

The temple's towers reached high above those closed-in walls, their gilded roofs shining above the city. Eppie looked up at them, as she always did when she was close to the temple. She told Squid that she thought the watchmen went there, looking for scrapplings trespassing on rooftops, but he said that was ridiculous, which of course it was. The priestesses would never let a watchman so deep into the temple. The truth was more ridiculous, or would be to Squid. Once, she'd seen Anara there, and not even at a festival time. As far as Eppie knew, the only other person who saw dragons anymore was the ambassadress, and she was hardly an ordinary person. Sometimes, guildsmen or soothsayers claimed to see Anara as a shadow at crossing times, when everyone was drunk, but no one believed them.

Even without Anara spreading her wings over the gilded towers, the temple was beautiful. It was as big as the governor's palace and far outshone the columned shrine that the Cereans were building to their philosopher gods at the far end of the harbor, facing away from their brothel, of course. The dragonlets seemed to shun the temple despite its beauty, as if Anara didn't trust it any more than Eppie did.

She joined the pack of ragged scrapplings outside the back gate. There were young ones from the near provinces and a few others she'd seen the year before or the year before that, newly returned to the city, trying their luck with the guilds again.

"Hey, Eppie," one of them called. "What are you still doing here? Not an apprentice yet?"

"Shut up, lapper," Eppie said. "I bet you're going home to your mama again this year, too." She hadn't, not once, even though it was only two days' walk to her home village.

Sure, she'd been tempted that first winter, but she wanted to stay in Anamat, not get stuck back home, herding goats, with no chance of anything more.

The priestess at the gate let the scrapplings in one at a time, counting them, measuring them. She turned away three of the older ones. Eppie willed herself to look smaller. She wore boys' clothes, and so far, the priestesses hadn't seemed to notice that she was a girl underneath. She was starting to wonder how long that could last, but her tunic was shapeless enough to cover her for now. She slipped through the gate with the rest, some two or three dozen of them, and shouldered her way to the front of the crowd.

A red-robed priestess sat beside the old one who tended the oven. She looked sadly at the scrapplings. "It seems to me," she said to the elder priestess beside her, "that when I was on the streets, there was enough for everyone."

"Now, now," the elder said. "You're not as old as all that. When I was young, the guilds even begged for apprentices, none of this nonsense about fees you had."

Eppie stared despite herself. Imagine, the guilds begging for apprentices!

"It's true, my son," the elder said to Eppie. Then she winked. "But you're here for the bread, and maybe the ambassadress's blessing."

Eppie's face fell. "Oh. Is that today?"

"Of course it is," said the younger priestess, who was rather beautiful, if a bit weary-looking. "We seek our novices, but you—" She looked into Eppie's eyes. "You're not a boy, are you?"

"Not gonna be a priestess, either," Eppie said.

"We'll see about that." With that, the younger priestess sashayed away, winking back over her shoulder in a way that Eppie didn't like at all.

§

After early training at the sword hall, Thorat found that he couldn't fall back asleep, even though he knew that he should rest. It was the morning before Midsummer Eve, and Iola would be blessing the scrapplings. Hoping for one more glimpse of her, he took a walk back down to the temple. Ragged youngsters crowded the street. The land was drying up, and the people were getting poorer, especially the scrapplings.

"Why go now?" the gate priestess was saying to one scrapping. "She is almost here for the blessing. You could find an apprenticeship."

The scrappling shrugged. "I don't need her blessing. Anyway, the guilds all say they don't have room for our kind."

Thorat wondered how true that was. He had to spend a great deal of time away from Anamat, but it *had* been hard to place their last apprentice in the swordsmiths' guild, despite the Defenders' long clandestine association with them.

There was a stir in the courtyard as the ambassadress emerged. Iola stood on a small stage, veiled in silk and incense. Through it, even from outside the temple, he could still see that she glowed with what they had shared together, the heat of the earth, the glory of the dragons. A gong sounded. Thorat bowed his head and began to pray.

"O great ones, who rule the bounty," they began together.

Out of the corner of Thorat's eye, he noticed a small movement. The scrappling had slipped the key away from the priestess on guard and was opening the gate, just wide enough to squeeze through. Thorat turned his attention back to the ceremony. Even the scrapplings who had been left on the street outside paused in their scuffles. They listened, even if they didn't know the words well enough to speak the prayer themselves.

"For Anara's wings bring sun and storms,

Her tail sows marvels in its wake,

Across the seas and in the –"

Thorat's sword hand moved refiexively to stop the fingers reaching for his pocket. He twisted the wrist before he even looked to see who the pickpocket was.

"Ow!" the scrappling said.

It was the same one who had just left the temple against the priestess's orders.

"Stay," Thorat commanded. The scrappling tugged, but he had a firm grip on the wrist. The prayer droned on and he mumbled along, tightening his grasp now and then to keep the pickpocket near.

As the prayer drew to a close, the novices surrounding Iola rang a chorus of bells. Thorat looked up into her eyes. Every time he saw her felt like the first time they had met on that mountain path, the first time he had come to save her. His heart yearned to do it again, to save her forever.

The thief slipped out of his grasp. Iola wasn't supposed to be looking at him, anyway, wasn't even supposed to know him. Thorat grabbed at the twice-escaping miscreant.

The scrappling would have gotten away, but just then, a dragonlet scurried along a wall, and he – or she – stopped to watch. So did Thorat. The dragonlet's crossing gave him just enough time to reach the pickpocket and grab an arm. Thorat watched the dragonlet go. A look of confusion crossed the scrappling's face.

"What are you looking at?" the scrappling demanded.

Thorat studied the face, dirty and thin. The scrappling had short, ragged hair, and was a little too tall to have no whisper of hair on the upper lip, if this were a boy, but too sharp and awkward to be a girl. But then, some girls were sharp and awkward.

"I believe I was looking at the same thing you were," he said.

"I wasn't looking at nothing!"

"I think you were," Thorat said.

"You can't arrest me," the scrappling said. "You're not even the watch. You're just a palace guard. Governor's toady."

Thorat sighed. He hated even looking like the governor's toady even when it was only for a day or two at Midsummer, and he hadn't officially been hired. It stopped people from asking questions—stopped most people, anyway. The youngster squirmed.

"No, I can't arrest you," he said. "You should be more careful whose pockets you pick, though. I'm just a poor guardsman. Besides, I used to be the best pickpocket in the East Market."

The scrappling snorted. The gate was open now, and the ones who had gotten their share of festival bread were hurrying out to take cover in their own corners of the city.

The dragonlet reappeared, dancing along the roofline of the building opposite, one of the weavers' warehouses. It glinted red and gold, dancing on the red-brown tiles of the roof, then disappeared. When Thorat looked down, the scrappling was still following some motion there with her—or his—eyes.

"Is it still there?" he asked.

"What?" the scrappling said. "Let me go!"

For a moment, their eyes met. He knew, they both knew, what they had just seen. "I believe that only a very few of the priestesses would have seen that," he said quietly.

"I won't be a priestess," the scrappling said.

"Can't be, or won't?"

"What's it to you?" she said.

"Nothing much," Thorat said. "But if you don't want to be one, you'd better find something else to do, and soon."

One of the red-robed priestesses was talking to the one at the gate, pointing at the scrappling girl whose wrist was locked in his grip.

"I've got to go," the girl said, pulling away.

"I have work for you," Thorat said. "Meet me at the top of the first bridge over the east canal at sundown." A worried look crossed the girl's face for a moment, quickly replaced by affected nonchalance. She nodded, and he released her. She ran full tilt toward the east canal, her festival bread held tight against her chest.

"I have an aunt who needs help with her housekeeping," Thorat shouted after her, not that she would believe him.

§

Eppie didn't even feel like detouring to the east gate to pick pockets. She'd been caught. No one ever caught her. If she was getting that clumsy, maybe she *should* let the governor's guardsman turn her over to the watch. She couldn't believe it. It was common wisdom that you couldn't pull off every heist, that they'd get you sooner or later and send you back to the provinces or lock you up in jail, but for three years, she'd dodged them all. Three whole years and a few moon-rounds, and she'd dodged them all, until now.

A stupid palace guardsman had caught her. But he wasn't just any guardsman. He saw dragonlets. He'd even seen her seeing a dragonlet. It made no sense. *No one* saw dragonlets, and if anyone were going to see them, it would be a priestess, or a soothsayer, or someone like that. Maybe a valley farmer, at festivals. Certainly not the governor's thug. Worse, he'd wanted to meet her there, on the very roof of her home shelter. It was as if he'd known, as if he could read her mind.

Eppie scaled down the rocks and hid in the shadows to eat. The others had all woken while she was away and had gone off to do their begging or thievery for the day. Even the dragonlet was nowhere to be seen. Dragonlets didn't like midday; they preferred twilight and rain. Eppie found the water jug in a cranny in the stones and took a swig. It was a bit stale but not too bad. The festival bread more than made up for it. Eppie bit into the soft dough, tasting an apricot, spices, and honey. If only she had some tea, it would be perfect.

As she ate, her heartbeat calmed. The water shimmered dully in the heat, and a few scraps of kitchen garbage drifted down toward the harbor. Under the surface, a fish swam. Above, the road across the bridge was quiet. Flies buzzed. Everything was just as usual, but that man, that stupid guardsman, had seen her in a way that no one else had seen her, and he was coming to get her. She felt that she ought to get away – he'd caught her trying to pickpocket him – but where would she go? She knew well enough that she couldn't go on the foreigners' ships, even without Squid telling her so. She wouldn't go back to Lemirun, that was for sure, and of course the guilds wouldn't have her. Whatever the guardsman was offering, it had to be better than the silence of the temple, the suffocating silence of it, the absence of the dragonlets.

Now that she was a little calmer, a little safer, now that she was alone, she could think. The man was quick and he could see dragonlets. He was handsome, too, with shining brown hair and clear eyes, crinkled at the corners as if always ready to laugh. He was the kind of man that girls gazed at wistfully, especially girls who weren't pretending to be boys so they wouldn't get pulled in to the temples or worse. At least the priestesses had their dignity and the power of the dragons to strengthen them. A man didn't go to a priestess to feel his own might; he came to honor hers, or at least that was how it was supposed to be. But because men didn't see dragons, didn't know what they were coming to honor, they mostly just leered and spilled their seed anyway. No, she did not want to be a priestess. She'd rather fetch water and sweep floors for that guardsman's aunt, or whatever it was he wanted her for. She could do worse.

§

Chapter 2

In all the wide city, the bridge was the one thing that always seemed the same. Between the training hall and his assumed role as a guardsman, Thorat had to stay mostly to the upper part of the city, even when he was in Anamat, so this place still felt like it belonged to his scrappling days. The row of stone houses shading the canal was bright in the afternoon sunlight, even as the whitewash peeled away from some of them. Thorat leaned over to watch his dark reflection in the canal waters. Down on those banks, he'd spent every night of a too-short season curled around Iola in sleep. They'd been scarcely more than children, but they'd bonded as surely as if they'd been lovers, more surely in some ways.

Now she shared her magic with the world, with the princes, and they didn't understand it. What if they could see her truly, could see the dragons for what they were again? The world would dance to that mystery once more, and she would be even further out of reach to him than she was now. There was no going back. For one thing, they were too old to camp on the streets anymore. For another, he could smell the cold remains of a fire. Someone else was camping under the bridge.

A trumpet sounded from the top of the soothsayers' hill, and he turned to see that one of the princes was coming to make his petition, to lie on Iola's altar so that she could carry his unfelt offering to the dragons' realm. Thorat stood at attention and saluted the prince's train as it passed, Enomaean horses bearing the dragons' gifts, as if horses didn't hate the dragons. The moment his back was turned, someone climbed up the canal bank and landed soft-footed on the bridge beside him.

"Why did you want to meet here?" the scrappling girl demanded. He was sure now that she was a girl.

"It's where I used to camp, the trading season that I was on the streets."

"Just one season?" the girl asked.

"That's how it used to be." Thorat looked over his shoulder. It was bad enough to linger on the bridge alone but much worse to have a conversation there. Their voices would carry up the canal, even up the streets.

"Follow me," he said. The girl followed close behind him as he climbed up the soothsayers' hill.

At the next corner, he turned to her. "How long have you been in Anamat?"

"Dunno," the scrappling said. "Three years or so."

"And no apprenticeship yet?"

"The guilds all say they're full, don't have enough work for the journeymen even, with so many foreign goods in the market, and them not taking so many of ours away."

"I'm sorry we didn't find you before," he said.

"We? And why?" the girl said with a sneer. "I do all right. I got my trade."

"Picking pockets isn't a trade."

"It is," she said.

Thorat shrugged. He turned off the main street at the next square, leading the girl into a long alley between houses. It was so narrow that a bridge connected two of the buildings above their heads. A short distance later, counting the houses as he went, he opened a wooden gate and walked into an even darker passageway, which dipped into a tunnel under a house.

Behind him, the girl hesitated.

"Don't worry," he said. "You're safe enough here. See?"

Ahead, a dragonlet's eyes flickered in the darkness, then disappeared.

"Maybe," the girl said. After a moment's hesitation, she followed him through the gate, closing it behind her.

The underground passage was only five strides long, then the light of the sunset sky shone in from above. Three broad steps led up into a sheltered courtyard bounded by the kind of tall, well-kept houses that merchants and elder guildsmen favored, except for one that seemed to be abandoned. A ramshackle stair leaned against its outer wall, running all the way up to its attic story.

The girl had stopped. She looked around, puzzled.

"What's wrong?" Thorat asked.

"I've never seen this place before," she said. "I thought I knew every inch of this city."

Thorat laughed. "I thought I did, too."

"Yeah, but I've been here a while," she said.

"Not as long as some. Come meet my...my aunt."

"Sure, your aunt. Right."

§

If Squid was going to go off sailing, there really was no reason to stay under the bridge, and since the guilds wouldn't have her, it was either this or the temple. Eppie followed the mysterious guardsman, still wondering what could possibly be mysterious about a guardsman. She didn't have much to lose. She might get a roof over her head. He wasn't leading her to a brothel or the fallen temple. Those were down by the harbor and a lot easier to find than this place, whatever it was.

At the top of the stair, he told her to wait on the landing. A pair of potted geraniums bloomed there, as if whoever lived here cared more for the flowers than for the staircase. She had a pretty good view out across the city. Eppie reckoned that she was about halfway between the governor's palace and the East Canal bridge, where she lived. It was a residential quarter, not far from the metalsmiths' guilds, and across the East Canal from the Chroniclers' guildhall. She traced the rooflines to try to figure out how they'd gotten there.

"You won't be able to find it that way," the guardsman said from behind, startling her. "Come in, but give me your name first."

"They call me Eppie or just scrapper. Who are you?"

"Thorat," he said, "or just 'you there, guard!' I often prefer it that way."

Eppie nodded. "And this aunt of yours?"

He didn't answer, just pulled the curtain aside and motioned for her to enter.

Eppie had been expecting some kind of cramped apartment with a low ceiling. Instead, a short set of stairs led down to what might have been the next-to-top story of the building except that it was open all the way up to the roof beams. It was a vast hall, as big as a temple sanctuary but plainer and dustier, lit by the sky's fading light coming through broad slits under the eaves. As Eppie's eyes adjusted to the darkness, she saw a glimmer on one of the side walls, metal reflecting the light of a lone torch. A row of swords hung there, a whole rack of them perfectly polished, at odds with their dusty surroundings. A barred set of double doors at the far end of the room looked like something out of a temple, too, but there were no priestesses there. If there were, it would have smelled better, like incense, not like dust and sweat and rot.

Someone coughed. Eppie turned to see old woman as she emerged from a back room behind a grimy curtain. A beam of light from the windows threw ridged shadows over the wrinkles around her squinting eyes. Her hair seemed to reflect the light in bursts, then fade back to reddish gray. She peered at Eppie for a long while, saying nothing and puffing on a curved pipe. She was smoking some sort of bitter, medicinal-smelling herb. The old woman was wearing boys' clothes like hers, only a little less ragged. She beckoned for Eppie to come closer.

Eppie stepped forward, measuring the distance between them with her eyes. The old woman had a wildness about her, though mostly she looked like any other old woman: creaky knees, wrinkled hands, and sharp eyes.

"Thorat says you see dragonlets," the old woman said. "Do you?"

"I don't always." Eppie let the words out slowly. What kind of person thought that it was good to see dragonlets, that it didn't just mean you were crazy? "I don't see what that has to do with anything. He said you need help with cleaning or something."

The old woman shook her head at Thorat. "Is that what you told Anot, too?"

Thorat shrugged. "That was a while ago. I thought I'd be more careful this time."

"Careful is never enough." The old woman turned back to Eppie. "Can you fight?"

Eppie nodded. She could lay claim to some distinction in that field. "I'm not the best in the city, but I'm close."

The old woman chuckled. "We'll see about that."

Something flew up into the air between them, though Eppie hadn't seen the old woman, or Thorat, move. She caught it – just a small chunk of firewood, nothing more.

"Good enough reflexes," the old woman said to Thorat. "You're right about that much."

"I wouldn't have brought her if I didn't think there was a chance."

"A chance of what?" Eppie said. Outside, in the falling night, she was missing the best pickpocketing of the year. "What is this place?"

"It's a training hall of sorts, but our requirements are different from most," the old woman said.

Thorat nodded. "Some of the guardsmen at the palace and in the princes' keeps learn just enough swordplay to ensure they can get the taxes from the farmers, but some of us train more, under teachers like...like this one."

"I've met some of them," the old woman said. "That's not a flattering comparison."

"My apologies, Your – Master."

The old woman grunted. "We are a training hall, but we don't brag of our existence in the marketplace, or anywhere. If you tell anyone that you've been here, I will not hesitate to hunt you down and silence you."

Eppie took a step back. "But how?" she wondered aloud.

"You don't want to know that," Thorat said.

"I do, though."

The old woman laughed. "You'll have to find your way back here, then. If you can't, there's no sense telling you more." She took Eppie by the arm and looked into her eyes. After a long moment, she nodded approval, then thrust Eppie away so smoothly that Eppie didn't even realize what was happening until she landed on her back halfway across the fioor, winded but uninjured. How did those old arms have such strength in them?

"Come tomorrow, then, if you can find us again," the old woman said. "We can teach you to fight. After that, we'll see."

"I don't need to learn to fight," Eppie said. She bested Squid half of the times that they sparred, and he was the best fighter in the southeast quarter of Anamat. She did all right, just like she did with her pickpocketing, but she'd never thrown someone halfway across a room, not like that.

The old woman just laughed. "You don't know how to fight. There's more to it than catching blocks and not breaking apart when you land on your ass."

"I'll be back," Eppie said.

"We'll see," the old woman replied. "Now get out of here before I change my mind."

"Go on, now," Thorat said. "Maybe we'll meet again tomorrow."

Eppie bowed clumsily to both of them and ran up the stairs. She paused on the landing and listened.

"I don't know about this one," the old woman was saying.

"What else do we have?" Thorat said.

"Nothing, or only a little more than nothing."

"A bit more than nothing."

Eppie felt sure that if she lingered any longer, they would find her there, so she hurried back to the bridge. On the way, she lifted a large bead from a country tanner's pocket. It stank of dyes and lye, and she bought a whole loaf of festival bread with it, plus a jug of ale at the corner tavern. When she got back to the bridge, Squid and three new scrapplings were crouched beside the sputtering campfire, poking at it with sticks.

"Who are they?" Eppie asked him.

"Bunch of green-knees. I told them they had to get out of here, but then the watch came by. Are they gone yet?"

Eppie shrugged. "I didn't notice. I brought some bread. You got anything?"

The green-knees leaned forward. Eppie could practically see their mouths watering. They were just scrawny kids from the provinces, their tunics in rags already. They shook their heads.

"You can't live on nothing," Eppie scolded them. "It's Midsummer, best begging of the year."

"We just got here," one of the green-knees said.

"All right, here, have some bread. There'll be more tomorrow at the temple. What do you have?" she asked Squid.

He held his hands out. "I got nothing. I spent the day at the docks, getting the lay of the land for that ship. I'm going tomorrow."

"You really are going, aren't you?" Eppie said.

Squid nodded.

"Well, I got enough to share," Eppie said. "And I'll be going too."

"Where to?" one of the green-knees asked eagerly.

"Nowhere much," Eppie said. "I got a job cleaning, big house."

"Ha!" Squid said. "The only thing you know how to clean is the lint from peasants' pockets." He leaned toward her, reaching for her pocket with a strange, blank look in his eyes.

"Who'd bother with a peasant?" Eppie said, latching onto the insult, which galled her but wasn't as unsettling as the suddenly predatory look in Squid's eyes. He'd gotten like that once or twice before, but then he'd been normal again. Picking pockets had to be better sport than dusting out an old attic, even if it was full of swords. She reached for familiar ground. "Wanna fight about it?"

"Yeah." Squid backed off so he could get to his feet, and they squared off across the open space. The green-knees backed away under the arch, watching as the two older scrapplings circled each other. Eppie and Squid knew every inch of the space, every dip and bump in the ground, where the bridge arched too low to walk beneath and where the wet stones would be slick on the edge of the canal bank. Eppie let

Squid land the first punch – almost. Then she tried to grab his wrist, something like what that guardsman, Thorat, had done to her at the temple. She wrestled with it and he straightened up, then bam! He was on the ground and she punched him lightly on the ear for good measure.

"Ow," Squid complained as he reached up to wrap an arm around her to help himself up. "You take that round."

"Only fair," Eppie said. "You're the one who got the apprenticeship. Here, have some ale."

§

The next morning was Midsummer Eve. Eppie left Squid and the green-knees still sleeping and set off to find the place that Thorat had led her to. She found the right alley – she was sure of it – but as much as she looked, she couldn't find the right gate. Every one she tried opened onto a small garden or to laundry hanging in an alley. She paced up and down. The streets were garlanded with flowers. All the princes in the whole land of Theranis had gathered at the governor's palace for their annual council, while every peasant, merchant, and guildsman had come to celebrate the ambassadress's crossing by dancing around the bonfires until dawn. It was the best pickpocketing of the year, but there she was, pacing up and down an empty side street, wondering where in all the realms that gate had gone.

After a while, she gave up and went scavenging. By the time the gates reopened after midday, she'd found a heavy blanket with a hole burned in its middle and a broken-lipped clay jar. She carried them back to the bridge, where she found Squid collecting his things into a rough bundle.

"What did you get?" he asked.

"Just this." She set down the jar and blanket.

"It's not much."

"So, what'd you get, then?" Eppie asked.

"This and that," Squid evaded. "I don't really need much, since I'm getting on that boat." He settled his bag of loot under his head and closed his eyes.

Eppie tried to sleep too, in preparation for the night's vigil – no one slept on Midsummer night – but she just couldn't. She kept thinking about Squid's stash of loot resting under his head, just near her, purses and coin and credit notes. Would he really get onto a ship? She probably would, if she were Squid, if she were dragon-blind and a boy. At least she was in Anamat, though. Better than being back in Lemirun, herding her older sister's goats with no future to call her own. Her sister was probably married by now, maybe with a baby or two. She wondered if they even kept the Midsummer vigil there any more.

Eppie got up. She would just have to stay awake through the night somehow. Meanwhile, there were purses to be snatched, at least for one more day, before she fell into whatever new life was waiting to trap her. She set off toward the front of the temple, tempting fate. What if the priestesses saw her? She could run faster than they could, couldn't she?

In the wide avenue before the temple gates, a group of men waited to be admitted for their audiences with the priestesses. Others sat in the nearby taverns, playing dice to try to raise their pile of beads high enough for the gate priestess's approval. A crowd of half-drunk men should be easy pickings. Still, most of the trade beads and foreign coins in those pockets were meant to be offerings for the dragons, and it didn't seem right to take them, even if the priestesses kept more than their share.

Sounds of the ceremonies inside drifted out over the walls, a gong being struck, drumbeats, singing. Eppie wandered away, up toward the palace. The palace hill temple was far less devout. Eppie had certainly never seen Anara on those towers, or even any dragonlets on the nearby walls.

When she arrived, a chorus of priestesses was dancing just inside the temple's main gate, chanting and playing on small drums.

"Bring your beads, bring your silks, bring the fire of your heart, lay it out, pave the way, join in the rite, send her to the deeper realms, let the dragons welcome her for all you have given." "Her" obviously meant the ambassadress, and she was at the harbor temple, not here, as even a petitioner would know.

Eppie scanned the crowd for fools. There were plenty to choose from. At the far corner of the square Eppie spotted an especially tall man wearing an embroidered cape. He cast a sharp eye at the scene around him and frowned.

"Come," he snapped at his page, who was a sickly-looking boy about her own height. Eppie sidled over in their general direction and crouched behind a donkey cart. She paid no attention to the two half-wit bodyguards who marched behind the prince and his page.

The page boy skittered along beside the prince, glancing around, nervous under his master's shadow. He wouldn't last a minute on the streets of Anamat. He'd get beaten up and wind up washing dishes at some tavern for the rest of his life. He was carrying something very carefully. Not carefully enough.

As the prince's group approached her hiding place, the priestesses' music changed, and the page boy turned his head to gawk. Eppie's hand slid out and relieved him of his burden. By the time he looked back, she was halfway across the square, leaning casually against a baker's oven, hidden in plain sight. Na's blood, but that was easy!

"Kinner!" snarled the prince. "I have told you..."

Kinner—that must have been the page's name—had stopped in his tracks, looking bewildered. He shrank away from the prince.

"Where is my purse?" the prince screamed at him.

Even the priestesses seemed to miss a beat. Every head in the crowd turned to look at the prince and his too-small retinue. It was a good time to leave, before the watch was on her tail. Eppie slunk off into the shadows. At the last moment, she glanced back at the page. He was crying. She hesitated. That prince would probably have one of the half-wit guards flog him. It wasn't his fault that he was dazed by Anamat – everyone was.

The watch would be on this bit of thievery before she could say "Na's blood," so Eppie snapped back into motion and ran down an alley, over a garden wall, up a shed and onto a rooftop. She crawled over the tiles and dropped onto a narrow path along the bank of the west canal. She found a hole in the rocks and hid. The moments dripped by. She listened. No sounds of pursuit. She knew her trade well, even if that guardsman said that picking pockets wasn't really a trade. He knew as well as she did that it took some skill. She leaned back against the rocks and steadied her still-too-noisy breath.

Soon, she was as quiet as the rocks, but it would be safer to wait a little longer, and waiting would give her a chance to see what she'd snatched. Whatever was in the purse felt solid, a faceted ball ridged on one side. Even through the thick fabric of the purse, it felt warm, alive. Eppie puzzled with the complicated knot for a while. It kept her still while she waited for the watch to blow past. She could just about hear Squid's voice in her head, saying, "What's wrong with a knife?" but the cords were thick, and the undamaged purse itself might fetch a few middling beads.

She had just about finished unraveling the knot when the watch came along. She could hear them from a good ways off. There were two of them on this loop. They thundered along the canal path on their boots, muttering the usual lines:

"Quiet!"

"What's that over there?"

"Just a dog."

"Cursed scrapplings."

"We should send them all back to the provinces. Jail's too full already."

It was as if they'd forgotten that half the city watch had been scrapplings once too, all boys, of course. Even if she could have, that was one trade Eppie would never take up: the watch were her enemy. Soon they were gone, on up the canal.

She leaned a little bit out of the darkness to get some light on the last twist of the knot so she could pull the purse strings open. Inside, she found a few credit notes and bills, one from the weaver's guild, another from the swordsmiths. She couldn't read the marks, but she recognized the seals. A smaller purse inside held beads, about as many a prosperous journeyman might carry, not much for a prince. She transferred those to her own pocket. Finally, there was the heavy thing, wrapped in its own bag of purple-dyed glove leather. She'd never seen leather dyed purple before.

It was time to move on, to get back to the bridge for a last evening meal with Squid, but it would be the work of moments to open the bag. She untied the knot, pulled the strings, and looked in.

The stone within glowed faintly, even in the daylight. It was set in a casing of silvery metal and was heavier than she would have thought something so small could be. On the side of the casing opposite the stone was the seal, the deeply ridged pattern she'd felt through the two bags. A prince's seal. Now, what was she going to do with that?

Eppie put the seal back into its bag and the bag back into its purse. She retied the strings as they'd been, bundled her find into her small sack, and set off down the canal to find

Squid. After all, what good was getting a handful of the prizest loot in Anamat if Squid sailed off before she could brag?

A crowd swarmed along the waterfront, people staking out their places for the morning's spectacle, for a glimpse of Anara as she flew back down to the dragons' realm. Eppie joined the throngs, flowing along the sand. Squid never claimed a space there. Instead, he wove in and out, making fools of everyone. This year, he would be off at sea with the foreigners who fled before Anara made her yearly appearance, fearing the dragon's curse if they breached Anamat's seasonal ban on trade. It was Theranian tradition to stay in place during the waning year, to care for the harvest, to safeguard the ambassadress in her journey under the earth. Even the scrapplings honored it. Only minstrels and messengers traveled during the half-year when the ambassadress was with the dragons.

An Enomaean boat was tied up at the second dock, heavy in the water, its sailors checking the ropes, readying the ship to sail away. She saw no sign of Squid there, so she moved on. A Cerean boat lay at the next dock, and sure enough, Squid was perched on its bowsprit. She ran up the dock alongside.

"You're really leaving?" she asked, shouting over from the dock.

"Hey, there! Sure am!" Squid said triumphantly.

"I got something to show you."

"Hang on." Squid looked to make sure that no one important was watching him, then tiptoed back along the rail to where he could jump onto the dock.

"What've you got?" he asked, sitting down and dangling his legs over the lapping water.

"Prince's seal," Eppie whispered. She loosened the purse strings so that he could see but not touch it. It glowed, even in the sunlight.

"Wow." Squid looked at it appreciatively for a long moment. "Was it hard to catch?"

"Nah," Eppie said. "Watch was pretty fast on my tail, though. Lost 'em quick enough."

"Sure," Squid said. "What are you going to do with it? You can't hardly sell it, can you? I mean, everyone'll know what it is and they'll have you in the lock-house faster than you can take the money."

"But..." He was right. "I can keep it," she suggested.

"I got a better idea," Squid said. "You give it to me, I'll take it to Cerea, and I can sell it there and bring you back half the coin. You can swap the Cerean coin for Anamat trade beads, and we'll both be rich, and not in the lock-house."

It made a certain amount of sense, but she knew he'd take more than his share, and she didn't like the thought of selling the seal over to Cerea, somehow. Eppie slipped it back into her pocket. "I'll think about it," she said.

"Got no time for that. We sail at midnight—foreigners don't want the dragon to catch them." He rolled his eyes, as if he didn't believe in curses—or blessings, for that matter.

"You coming back?" Eppie asked.

"I dunno, we'll see," Squid said. "Maybe see you next trading season?" He had that look in his eyes again, but it was gone before she was sure of it. He jerked his thumb toward the shore, toward their canal as he sprang away from her. "Here comes the watch! I have to get back on board!"

With that, he jumped back onto the ship. Eppie checked to make sure that he hadn't slipped off with anything of hers, then she sprinted the length of the dock, dodged through the crowds on the sands, and disappeared again into the back alleys. She found herself on the west canal once more and sidled along its banks until she reached the first bridge, where she strode back onto the main street as if she'd never stolen a thing in her life, and whistled on her way back toward the east canal bridge.

At the next square, she hesitated and changed course. She was going to look for that hidden courtyard again.

§

Chapter 3

Sovara paced in front of the shrine doors, pausing occasionally to stare at the thick wood as if her gaze could drill straight through to the image of Anara within. This was not a temple – it was a training hall – but it had far more in common with the dragons' temples than any other swordmaster's salon, including a sometimes-resident priestess, who was late again, as usual. Thorat looked toward the entrance in the midst of Anot's complaints about the provinces.

"I don't see why Ferrent didn't come back. Surely, the charms of Kiralun can't be so wonderful. I know I can't ever wait to get back here when I'm stuck in the provinces," Anot was saying.

"To get trained up again because you haven't kept up with your drills?" Garren said.

"I do keep up with them, but it's not the same as training with you," Anot said.

"That much is true," Thorat agreed. "I know I never get any better when I'm away. I wish I could stay here more, too."

Raina clucked. "You wouldn't if you were stuck here. It would only torment you; you'd want to be doing something." Raina was a valley farmer two decades or so older than Thorat, the mother or foster mother of a houseful of children of varying ages. Her house was also a way station for the

Defenders, a place to leave messages and to fill their bellies before they reentered the city after a journey to the provinces.

"That's right," Garren agreed. "It's quiet here in the waning year." Garren never went anywhere either. He kept a close eye on the comings and goings in the West Gate market from his sweets shop there. He also probably stayed because he was the second oldest of the Defenders, after Sovara, and so it was generally assumed that he would be the next Enatel.

Soft footsteps on the stair announced Sunna's arrival. She entered with a flurry of hastily changed robes and incense, then ducked under the stair to change again into a plain guardsman's tunic. At heart, Sunna was a Defender more than a priestess, but as a practical matter, she spent most of her time at the temple. The temple had food, which was always in short supply at the training hall, and Sunna kept them all apprised of what was happening among the priestesses.

"Sorry I'm late," she said from under the stairs. "The ambassadress made me promise to go looking for that suitable scrappling the oracles told her about. Of course I couldn't find her."

Thorat's stomach sank as Sunna peeked out at him. "Did she ask you to look, too?"

"I told her I'd do what I can, but –"

"If the girl you brought here is the one the ambassadress is looking for, you'll just have to tell the Most Blessed One that we need her more, and try to keep it from the Aralel," Sovara said.

"You found the girl?" Sunna asked as she came out. "If you did, I'll have to tell the Aralel."

"You don't have to tell the Aralel anything," Thorat said. "It's Iola who wants her."

Sunna shook her head. "And I'll have the Aralel to contend with in the meantime. She'll have it out of me in no time."

"You can keep in that much; it's only for a season," Thorat said. "Besides, I'm not sure this girl is the one Iola wants. All I did was find a scrappling who was looking at a dragonlet while trying to pick my pocket. She's not very priestessly." He hoped that she wasn't the one Iola wanted.

"She can fight a little, and she might even see dragonlets better than most of us," Sovara said.

"Still, I hope it's not that one the ambassadress has her eye on," Sunna said.

"I don't like the idea of being at odds with the temple over an apprentice," Garren said, "but Sovara's right: we need apprentices more than they need new priestesses. A person can't defend what they can't see."

Thorat wondered, sometimes, how so many seemed willing and able to attack the invisible-to-them dragons. For the most part, they didn't do it directly. As he'd learned long before, the Defenders had once stood guard over the dragons to remind the dragon-blind where the border lay, to be a visible force for the dragons so that the winged ones didn't drain their strength from the land by fighting foolish people.

"You can't be a very good priestess without dragonsight, either," Sunna said.

"Men seem perfectly happy with inadequate priestesses," Sovara said dismissively. "The temples can make do with what they have, and it only matters if this girl can find us again. I'm not sure that she will be able to."

"She has to," Anot said. "I can't have been the last apprentice."

Sovara ignored him. "It's time to go down. Take your swords."

"She's been in the city for years," Thorat told Sunna as they moved toward the shrine doors with their best swords in hand. "The temples have had their chance to claim her, three years of chances, she says. I don't know how no one has spotted her yet." Curses, though. He suspected now that the scrappling *was* the one that Iola wanted, but if he handed her over to the priestesses, Iola wouldn't even see her until after Midwinter. By then, she could have had a half year of training with Sovara. He could tell Iola about Eppie after she returned from the other realm. Surely, she could wait until then—after all, she would be with the dragons.

The Defenders gathered in a gap-toothed circle to prepare for their own small descent to the ancient inner shrine. Sovara sat closest to the shrine door with Garren at her right hand and Raina to her left. Anot, Varin, Sunna, and he completed what was left of the circle. They sat with their best swords at their sides, waiting. Ferrent and Harron were missing, still out in the provinces. Even counting the absent ones, there were only nine of them. Not enough.

"We may be ghosts to everyone outside this training hall," Sovara said, "but one Defender can do the work of a dozen ordinary guardsmen or a hundred foreign invaders, because the dragons work with us."

No one needed to point out that they couldn't do the work of a hundred ordinary guardsmen, or a thousand invaders, no matter how subtle their skills. If only the ghosts of the Defenders from generations past could fight beside them, blade for blade, ghostly or not. They would all be nothing more than ghosts soon unless more joined their ranks.

Sovara opened the doors of their upper shrine with its image of Anara, wings spread over her offering bowls of gleaming bronze, filled with water, earth, and wood. As Sovara sounded the gong, she sprinkled incense onto the coals in the brazier. The smell of cedar filled the room, cedar that

Thorat had brought down from the high pass out of Teganum last season. Sovara, the Enatel, placed her hands on the floor of the shrine nook and chanted a series of notes. She struck the gong and pushed down with all her weight, making a panel of the floor slide aside to reveal a long stair spiraling down into the darkness, into what had been the heart of their long-forgotten temple, now buried ignominiously under a cobbler's shop and a rarely used storeroom belonging to the swordsmiths' guild.

Sovara lit a torch and lead the way down the stair, dank and moldy from its long darkness. Thorat wondered if any of those long-ago Defenders had died here, if their ghosts guarded it, and what other ghosts might haunt this almost-forgotten place. There were probably ghosts of men and cats and maybe even dragonlets, if those had ghosts, if they weren't as immortal as their dragons. Long-dead voices seemed to whisper to him through the drip of condensation, the shuffle of someone in the house on the other side of the wall, and their own footfalls going down and down into the earth.

At the bottom, Sovara placed her torch in a wall bracket, lighting the vaulted chamber where the rock crust between the worlds thinned to almost nothing. Here was a plane of living rock, not the still, inert stuff that made up the ground around them or the buildings above. It lay in darkness except when they came to it twice a year, at the crossing times. It was even closer to the dragons' realm than the ambassadress's chamber. It, too, was made of stone, but there the similarities ended. Where Iola had splendor and light, clean white marble and silk, the Defenders had a rough cave in the earth, neglected, dark, and cold.

The torch threw off just enough light for them to see each other's faces. They gathered, facing the one smooth stone wall, and then—through some magic that Thorat could still only guess at—Sovara pulled the veil aside. The rocky face of the wall flickered to life, colors pulsing dimly beneath the surface, then growing out like twisting veins, like the trunk and branches of a tree, like the world tree insignia that still branded half the craftworks in Anamat, even if its significance had been forgotten by all but these few.

Each branch, each color, bore the mark of a dragon. Anara flared bright, her flame tended by Iola and the other true priestesses of Ara's Landing. Na's thread was a dim white, strong but far away, running straight up from the chamber's floor to its ceiling, central, yet remote and untouchable. The other threads were harder to pick out. Their positions, colors, and strengths seemed to shift with each half-year, sometimes moving clearly from one position to another, sometimes leaping across from one half of the map to the other, even as their realms stayed steady in the world above.

"There's Tegana," Thorat said. He'd been to Teganum, and the dragon's color seemed familiar to him. It was also the province where Iola had been born. "And Onara," he said, indicating the yellow branch coiling beside Tegana's purple, neighboring realms still touching in their mirror world among the dragons.

"Lemira," Sovara said, reaching toward a pale green part of the tree.

The others found the traces of all the realm dragons in turn, one after the other, until they were left with one dim, fading thread. That last one belonged to Tiada, the dragon of the southernmost province.

"Tiada," Sovara said. "Her thread is fading. One of us must go to her."

They all lay their swords in front of their knees and prostrated themselves before this window into the dragons' world, which sometimes told them where they must go. When they rose, the chamber was dark again except for the flickering light of the torch in its common wall sconce.

Thorat was glad that they were together. He had faced the shrine alone, as they all had, keeping vigil there through Midsummer night after the first year of his apprenticeship. That was how the dragons tested the new Defenders, and not all of them passed. Some saw nothing and were sent away with the drink of forgetting, while others saw too much and gave way in the darkness, or so Thorat had heard. They came back from that long night with their minds all but erased by the dragons, returning as madmen, destined for the hills and Na. He shuddered at the thought – not of Na, but of those who worshiped the wild dragon, the dragon who tolerated no permanent building on his untamed lands. Those bandits had almost killed Iola once.

No one spoke until they were back in the training hall above and Sovara had closed the trapdoor. The last of the incense smoked in its bowl while sunlight slanted in under the rafters. They said a brief prayer together, then closed the doors of the upper shrine.

Sovara looked around the circle. "One of you must go to Tiada, to see her if you can and make contact with Ferrent in Kiralun. Thorat?"

Thorat's heart sank at the thought of another year in the provinces, probably not returning to the city until Midsummer was on them again, or maybe even longer if something held him there, as it had Ferrent and Harron, but he accepted the Enatel's command. He'd seen the thin thread of Tiada's energy, what was left of it. He would have to find a way to protect it until the dragon could heal herself from whatever harm had befallen her. He wished he'd thought to ask Iola if the Tiadun prince had come to make his offering.

"Tiadun's prince didn't come to the Most Blessed One this Midsummer, or last year either," Sunna said, as if she'd been thinking the same thing.

"You should have told us last year," Sovara said.

"He's not the only one, and sometimes the Most Blessed One forgets to tell me. They say that Slaradun's prince is too old and frail to travel across the mountains for Midsummer councils, and his son didn't take his place, so he wasn't there either. Naramun's prince sent a cousin. The rest make their visits brief, and only Galamun, Helanum, and Coradun have princes who seem to heed the dragons' messages."

Sunna had left the governor of Anamat out of her tally. Parnet was eager enough to enjoy Iola's body even if he was blind to the true significance of the rite.

"We'll have to go to all those places," Sovara said.

"I could go as a minstrel and see all of them," Thorat suggested. He had seen the prince of Tiadun and didn't look forward to even pretending to serve him.

Raina guffawed.

"It's not a bad idea," Garren said.

"Except that Thorat's too old to be a first-year minstrel anymore and he hasn't learned half the ballads," Sovara said. "He would look like a fool. Besides, whatever's happening in Tiadun may take some time to untangle."

Sunna sighed. "Darna might know something useful. She has a connection to Tiadun. You should talk to her before you leave Anamat."

Darna had come into the city with Thorat when he'd first arrived, leading their little group of one-season scrapplings with her swinging cane and keen sense of direction. She *had* hailed from Tiadun, but that had been many years before, and she'd had no occasion to return to the province, nor did he think that she would want to.

"I expect you to find a place with the Tiadun prince's guard by sunrise," Sovara told him. "You can put yourself forward as a tournament fighter for the Midwinter games."

"Yes, Your Grace," Thorat said, knowing that Sovara hated the antique honorific that went with her position.

"What about Harron?" Raina asked. "Who will go to him?"

"You have crops to tend," Sovara said. "We need you here to alert me if there's anything amiss in Anara's farmland."

"There are gardens in the temple, too," Sunna said.

Raina shot her a grateful glance. Harron was Raina's old lover, and the father of two of her children, or so Thorat suspected. Raina obviously missed him.

"That's different," Sovara said. She turned to Anot. "You can go to Onarun and visit Harron in Teganum along the way. That way, we'll have two in the north, two in the south, and the rest of us here in Anamat."

The arrangements would have to do, Thorat saw, but meanwhile, there was still a little time until the night's revelry began in earnest, so a few of them picked up swords and began to spar, while the others gathered around Garren's basket of bread. Anot slouched against the wall, stitching up a hole in his scabbard with the training hall's good needles. Thorat and Sunna faced off. He parried, stepped back, parried again, and then with a flick of the wrist, Sunna's sword was flying wide over her head, barely in her grip.

"Ouch!" Sunna shook out her wrist as she brought her sword under control again. "What was that?"

"Trick I learned from one of the other guards last season," Thorat said. "Want to see?"

"How are you two going to stay awake all night after spending the whole day sparring? That's what I'd like to know." Anot yawned.

Sovara stepped away from the wall. "Show us that again."

Thorat and Sunna faced each other again. Sunna lowered her sword in slow motion and Thorat twisted, the tip dipping lower than usual. Sunna's sword spun to the side again. Sovara stepped in to take Sunna's place, but just then, there was a clatter on the stairs outside and they all turned to look. She'd made it back. Thorat muttered a prayer of thanks before she even appeared.

The scrappling girl came in looking slightly flushed and winded from the climb up the stairs. At first, he thought that she'd been drinking already, like half of the rest of the city, but then he sensed that something else was amiss.

Sovara returned Sunna's sword to her, eyes fixed on Eppie. "What's that in your pocket?" she asked.

"I...umm..."

Anot stopped sewing. "Is this the scrappling apprentice you were talking about? She's a little thief. She got a bead out of my pocket last Midsummer. I remember," he said, scowling at Eppie.

"She's faster than you, then," Garren pointed out. "That's not a bad thing."

"You'd have been a thief too if we hadn't pulled you off the streets right away," Thorat said.

"Sorry," Eppie said, backing toward the door. "I'll just go, then..."

"No, stay," Garren said. "I've seen you for years. I never guessed that you had dragonsight. When our old apprentices came, I could always see it."

Eppie shrugged. "Don't like people thinking I'm crazy, that's all." She was good at hiding, better at it than most of them. It was pure luck that he'd found her at all – that, and taking every chance he could to see Iola.

Sovara stepped up to Eppie and held out her hand. "Give it to me," she said.

"I don't know what you're talking about," Eppie said, not very convincingly.

"You have a dragon stone, or something very like it, in your pocket, and it's out of place," Sovara said. "It doesn't belong to you."

Eppie continued to edge back toward the stair.

"I advise that you give it to me," Sovara said. "It must be returned to its rightful place."

The girl tensed as the Enatel stepped up to her, too close for comfort but not yet touching. She reached into her tunic and pulled out a purse far too fine for a scrappling or even for a middling-prosperous merchant. Eppie handed it to Sovara. The moment the offending purse was out of her hands, she turned and started running.

"Stop her," Sovara commanded.

Thorat sprang up and started running barefooted after her. The girl was on the landing when he started moving. She was halfway down the outside stairs before he was out of the door, and he didn't catch her until they were halfway through the hidden passage out of the courtyard.

Eppie pulled to break free. "Let me go," she said. "I don't want to go to jail!"

"To jail?" Thorat laughed with such surprise that he almost let her go. "We wouldn't take you there. We need you here too badly."

"Why do you need me? No one needs me. Just let me go."

"We do need you," Thorat said. "Besides, this could be the best apprenticeship in Anamat, if you don't mind being a bit hungry. If you really like to eat..." He glanced in the direction of Ara's Landing. They would take Eppie, disheveled as she was. He could take her to Iola; that was what Iola would want.

Eppie shuddered. "No, thanks. I don't like to eat that much."

"Then you'd better come back upstairs with me. I can't let you go free now that you've found us. If you want to go, you'll have to talk to the...to my aunt first."

"She's not your aunt; anyone can see that," Eppie said, but she turned back and walked across the courtyard with him. One of the neighbors was bringing in her potted plants in case the revelers brought their riotous dance that way, though there was no clear way for them to get in. She ignored Eppie and Thorat as they passed, almost as if they were invisible.

"You should have gotten an apprenticeship years ago," Thorat said as he climbed the rickety stair behind her.

Eppie shook her head. "Easy for you to say. There's none to be had unless you're Anamat-born, and even then, it's mostly trading ships or the temples, but even the priestesses don't take many, not the real priestesses."

"They never did. It was only one from each realm, I heard," Thorat said. He wondered what realm she'd come from and if she would ever go there again. He'd still never returned to the village where he'd been born.

Back inside the training hall, everyone had gathered around the suspicious purse.

"So, there's definitely a dragon stone in there?" Anot asked.

Sovara nodded.

"We can just cut the cords," Varin suggested.

"Inelegant," Sunna said.

"Crude," Garren agreed.

"But quick," Raina said.

Sovara took the purse over into the brighter light at the base of the stairwell, where Thorat stood guard behind Eppie, wondering if she would try to run again.

"I can untie that," Eppie offered. Sovara handed her the purse.

"No running, now. You'll wear out poor old Thorat," Garren said. He'd sensed her hesitation too, but Eppie, intent on her work, seemed not to hear him. Her fingers flashed over the cords, and in a moment, the knot was undone, the purse strings loose, and a bundle of credit and debit notes fell onto the floor.

Sunna picked them up and scanned through them. As a priestess, she could read better than the rest of them. Garren could do his figuring, but Thorat, Anot, and Ferrent couldn't read at all. Eppie took a purple leather pouch out of the purse and began to unweave its knot.

"This is Salara's stone," Sovara said before Eppie had finished drawing it out. "One of us needs to return it to the prince of Slaradun or one of his minions before dawn, the sooner the better." She was not speaking to Eppie but rather to the other Defenders.

"They sent out an alarm in the palace market early in the afternoon," Varin said. "They had the whole watch out looking for it."

They needed an apprentice, but running afoul of the princes? That, they didn't need.

"Well," Sovara said, "it has to get back somehow."

"But... But why?" Eppie said.

Sovara frowned. "It's a dragon's stone. It belongs to Salara, in her realm. It's as if you stole it from her."

"But I didn't. I wouldn't do that. I just took it off that boy, the prince's page. I was stealing from... Well, I didn't even know at first that he was the prince. I didn't mean to steal from a dragon, and I can't see how this is the same at all." Eppie glanced back toward the stair and Garren moved around to join Thorat in blocking her escape.

Sovara took a deep breath. "The prince belongs to his dragon, whether he knows it or not, and so does this. It is merely entrusted to his care. At least, that's what we believe. Whether the prince understands it or not doesn't matter. This goes back to Slaradun with him, one way or another."

"Should we hand it over to the watch?" Anot suggested.

Garren snorted. "They'd be as likely to sell it on to Cerean merchants as to return it. And they're slow, not quick enough to get it back to the prince by morning, even if they don't take it for their own purposes."

"They're not that bad," Anot said.

"They can be," Sunna said. Thorat had heard of some of the false priestesses running afoul of the watch lately. Sunna had more sympathy for them than he would have thought, but then, what was the difference between the priestesses of Ara's Landing and the ones at the street-corner shrines, really? So few of them were true priestesses any more.

"In any case, it's too much risk to leave it to someone else," Sovara said. "Thorat, girl, you find a way. Come back here after the ambassadress's flight, and without that." She threw it to Eppie, who froze.

"I have no idea how to –" Thorat began, but then he had a thought. "Come on," he said to Eppie. "I have a friend who you might say specializes in this kind of thing. We'll find her."

"Tie that knot again before you go," Sovara told Eppie. She watched as Eppie worked. When the cords had been knotted exactly as they had been, Eppie handed the purse to Sovara, who then gave it to Thorat for safekeeping.

"Keep yourself to the shadows if you can," she said.

"Yes, ma'am." Thorat thought he caught a glimpse of a smirk on Eppie's face. She did know how to keep to the shadows, at least. That would serve her well.

§

Eppie followed Thorat out onto the streets. Evening had fallen, and the denizens of Anamat, young and old, were building up piles of scrap wood, old furniture, cloth, anything that would feed a fiame, to burn through the shortest night of the year. Taverners and their one-night servants rolled barrels to the sides of the streets, setting up temporary stalls ready to refill any empty tankard.

After a short walk, Thorat turned onto a back street beside the planners' guild and mounted the stairs to an empty room. He cursed under his breath. "She's not here," he said. "One more place to look, and if she's not there, at least Myril will be."

"Who's Myril?"

"A friend of mine, a chronicler. We were scrapplings together. We camped under that bridge where I met you yesterday."

"You'd trust them with this?" Eppie asked.

"Of course I would. They wouldn't be friends otherwise."

"I wouldn't give it to my friends," Eppie said. Squid could be counted on to fence a piece and give you a share, but not necessarily a fair share, just what he thought you'd take.

"There used to be more honor among the scrapplings," Thorat said. "More honor everywhere."

Eppie doubted that, but she followed him on anyway, back across the East Canal and up to the fortune-tellers' hill. The orange moon was rising up over the harbor, shining through the gaps between the buildings. Thorat took a narrow set of stairs up to a landing for a second-story apartment. A sign over the stair showed a steaming cup and a pair of plants, an advertisement for herbs and simples.

Eppie stopped halfway up the stairs. Something about this place felt different, and after a moment's refiection, she realized what it was. She hadn't been inside a proper house since she'd left her home village. She'd been into taverns and had made forays into shops, and had sheltered from downpours on temple porches, but this felt different. The sword hall where Throat had taken her didn't feel like a place where people lived either. This place smelled of cooking and cleanliness and maybe even needlework.

Thorat turned back when he reached the landing. "Come on."

"I can't," Eppie said.

A sound on the street outside spurred Eppie to action—a troupe of priestesses from one of the lesser temples, coming to find new scrappling girls and lure them into marble-walled cages. She went on up. From the doorway, she could hear two women's voices. Taking a deep breath, she gathered her nerve and went in.

It was the warmest, most welcoming room she'd ever seen. Two women sat by the window in a pool of lamplight. The one closest to the lamp, leaning against the wall, had dark hair. She was tall and sturdy-looking, comfortable. Eppie had seen her on the street and crossing the bridge many times, going to and from the harbor temple. On a rare venture up the palace hill, she'd also seen the dark-haired woman in chronicler's robes, near the governor's palace. The other woman was sitting almost in her lap, looking out onto the street and fidgeting as the comb worked its way through her tangled red hair. She was a guildswoman too, though Eppie wasn't sure which guild she belonged to. She'd seen the red-haired one from time to time, and all she knew about her for sure was that she walked with a stick, hunched over, and that she didn't look like easy pickings.

At first, Eppie thought the women hadn't heard them enter, though Thorat had made no effort to be quiet.

"Hold still, will you?" the dark-haired woman said.

"I'm sure it's good enough. It's not as if I'm looking for a suitor," said the red-haired one. She turned to look at Thorat.

"We saw you coming up the street," she said. "I heard you saw Iola. What took you so long to come visit us?"

"I've only been here a few days," Thorat said. "I've been busy, and I have to leave again soon."

"Where to this time?" the dark-haired one asked.

"Tiadun."

The red-haired woman jerked up, pulling away from the window and ruining her friend's careful braiding in the process.

"Hold still!" the other one said. "I'm sure he's not looking for you now."

"Actually, I am looking for Darna," Thorat said.

Eppie wanted to say something. How could Thorat not see that they weren't talking about him?

"Myril, Darna, this is Eppie. She needs help with a... reversing a theft. Of course I thought of you."

Darna guffawed. "I can't say I thank you for that. It almost killed me last time."

"You've brought something?" Myril asked Thorat, looking pointedly at his pocket as if she could see through the wrappings, too.

Thorat sat down on a stool near her and took out the purse. "Eppie here lifted this off a prince." He held out the purse.

"Off his page," Eppie clarified. "It was just walking by."

"Rich pickings, but it's got nothing to do with me." Darna said.

"It belongs to the Slaradun prince," Thorat said. "It's his seal."

"With a dragon stone in it," Myril said grimly. "Interesting. He feels Salara's presence enough that he won't carry the stone himself, but he refuses to go to the ambassadress."

Thorat took a deep breath as if to say something but then just shook his head. Myril seemed to know a lot more than what she'd been told, which made Eppie uneasy, and a little bit curious, too.

"You're the only person I know who's returned a dragon stone after it was stolen," Thorat told Darna, who frowned at Eppie.

"It was Anara's stone, and we're in her realm, and she helped. I don't know Salara, and we're not in her realm."

"But that one was on a Cerean ship, in a blinding box, while this one is in your hand," Thorat said as he placed the purse in Darna's hand. "Salara probably hasn't even noticed its displacement, but she will if it isn't on its way back to her realm in the morning."

"So, what would you have me do?" Darna asked.

"Return it to the prince," Thorat said.

"Why can't she do it herself?" Darna said.

"It would be easier for you," Myril said. "You have an invitation to the feast, and this one? They'd never let her past the gates, not looking like that."

"I can't think of a good line for how I came across it," Darna said.

"Will you do it?" Eppie asked. "I can come up with a line. Let me think about it."

Myril finished off a braid and offered Eppie a piece of bread. "Eat this," she said. "You'll think better on a fuller stomach." The bread was festival bread, from the temple if she wasn't mistaken. She could never have too much of that, but it didn't usually help her think. Still, she hadn't eaten since morning, and she was hungry.

She paced back and forth across Myril's chamber as she ate. Thorat had helped himself to more tea and was watching her, which didn't help.

"Does anyone owe you beads?" Eppie asked Darna suddenly. "Maybe a lot of them?"

Darna looked at her and nodded. "Not really, but I could think of someone who might, maybe a foreign merchant who asked for drawings and, when I delivered, said he would bring me payment today, and then he brought this. He's sailed already, of course, or will have sailed by the time midnight strikes at the palace and I finally discover whose purse this is. Yes, that would do. An excellent idea."

A settled guildswoman who still understood how things worked. Eppie nodded. "That's the story, all right. I might even buy it."

Darna smiled at her. "You wouldn't."

"No, but a prince probably would."

Myril shook her head. "I don't think so. Eppie will have to do this herself. We'll clean her up, and she can go to the palace as your servant."

Eppie froze. "I don't think that's a good idea," she said, just as Darna said, "I don't need a servant."

"It's what you need to do," Myril said.

"What, are you an augur? Your sign doesn't say that you are."

"I try not to do divinations where common sense works just as well."

Darna snorted. "You shouldn't do them, then, even if the Aralel asks."

"She hasn't asked lately," Myril said, trying to pick up the dropped threads of Darna's now re-disheveled braid. She pulled an oiled comb through Darna's curls, which flattened them and made them almost manageable, tied off the last braid, and turned to Eppie.

"Your turn now."

§

Chapter 4

Thorat muttered something about going up to the palace to secure his hire, saying that he would meet them at a tavern up the hill after midnight. He abandoned Eppie with the two women, who hauled her off to the baths, where they set about scrubbing every trace of the last three years off her skin, leaving her pink and uneasy in new clothes that made her feel like a stranger to herself. It was Midsummer and supposed to be the time of change, but still she couldn't feel at ease in her guise as a respectable young citizen of Anamat. Not even Squid would recognize her, let alone the watch, never mind the prince of Slaradun, who probably hadn't even noticed her.

Eppie followed Darna up to the palace with the prince's purse lodged tight beneath her belt, practically burning a hole in her side with its presence.

"That thing does glow," Darna said as they climbed the hill. "Good thing they're all dragon-blind up there."

At the palace gates, the guards let Eppie pass without a second glance. She looked back at them for a moment but Darna jerked her forward.

"Don't look at them like that," she said. "Look like you belong here, like you do this all the time."

Eppie nodded. That was something she should have known without being told. She checked to make sure that the seal was still in her pocket. It was, and it was humming a bit.

Milling noblemen and their horses filled the outer courtyard. It was said that the horses went mad if they saw a dragon or even a dragonlet. Eppie had never seen so many in one place. She didn't see any dragonlets, either, but wouldn't have expected to see them in the palace, not even on a festival night.

Darna led her between two buildings, along a sort of quiet side street. Doors opened onto one chamber after another. There was a lot a person could loot in there: lamps, ropes, cloth, glass. There were guards everywhere, too. The stone bumped against her side. How would she find the Slaradun prince?

They entered a large garden with a bubbling fountain at its center. Around the edges, paths led to nooks where the noblemen and their entourages could converse unseen, their voices shielded by the fountain's splashing. A group of minstrels gathered at one side. Darna nodded a greeting to them as she passed. The scent of roses and herbs filled the air. A nobleman and a woman ambled out of a lamplit chamber and into the garden, trailed by a page and a serving woman.

"What entertainment have we tonight?" yawned the nobleman.

"Only some poor minstrels," one of the minstrels said.

"Shall we go out later to see the dancing?" the lady said, ignoring the minstrel. She pulled her partner away and into the hall.

"Who's that?" Eppie whispered.

"A chieftain from Coradun and his mistress," Darna said quietly. She looked around. "We might as well wait out here."

"Where are the other guildsmen?"

"We're all supposed to go in the other way," Darna said as she settled onto a bench behind a rosebush as if she were perfectly at home there. Eppie tried to look at ease, but she didn't feel as if her servant act could hold up to any kind of inspection. At least it was dark.

A prince arrived, trailed by a dozen hangers-on. Eppie could spot the prince not only by his clothes but by the way the others bunched around him, angling to get closer yet careful not to jostle him. They were all very finely dressed, with jewels dangling from their necks and wrists – none of them dragon stones, though, as far as she could tell.

"Onarun," Darna told her in an undertone.

A noisy laugh erupted out of a nearby doorway. Someone drew the curtain aside and two men stood silhouetted by torchlight. Darna froze, her breath growing fast and shallow.

"Next year, brother, I promise you," one of them said. He slapped the other on the back with what could only be menace, and they disappeared into the banquet hall again.

"Who was that?" Eppie whispered.

Darna just shook her head. "Time to go in and face them," she said, as much to herself as to Eppie.

A prince, attended only by a page and two guardsmen, strode into the courtyard. Eppie knew immediately that it was the Slaradun prince. He stood a head taller than his guardsmen, and no one seemed to be courting his favor. He was paying far more attention to his surroundings than Eppie was comfortable with, as if he were looking for a thief – that would be her – to take vengeance on. His page glanced nervously around too, peering into the shadows as if some monster might be lurking there.

Before the prince reached the middle of the courtyard, one of the minstrels got up on the stage and set his harp in front of him.

"I begin," the minstrel intoned, "with the ballad of Ara and Enat." He adjusted his tuning one last time and cleared his throat. As he struck the first chords, a few idlers came out of the banquet hall to listen. The Slaradun prince paused, as if he were considering whether or not to stay. The minstrel sang:

> *The long wave bore their craft to shore,*
> *away back in the days of yore.*
> *This newfound land, green at ev'ry hand,*
> *bloomed with powers of the dragons.*
> *And so they came, to this land unnamed,*
> *on the wind-swept raft of Connat.*
> *But none dared go where dragons flared,*
> *only fair Ara and brave Enat.*
> *The first footfall rang through the earth*
> *to summon great Anara.*
> *Ara heard the dragons' word,*
> *and with her Enat followed.*
> *The dragon touched the earth as much*
> *as you or I upon it.*
> *The strong chief's son, he was undone,*
> *but Enat was claimed for Anara.*
> *Now dragons know where Enat goes,*
> *and Ara's heirs grace the dragons' ways.*
> *They make our land to flourish.*
> *So has it been, since they crossed the sea,*
> *and made our lives 'midst dragons.*

As the first minstrel played his closing chords, Eppie struck on an idea. "Wait here," she whispered to Darna. "I'll be back."

"Don't steal anything," Darna warned as she slipped away.

The Slaradun prince and his guards were standing very close to their bench, with the page boy closest of all. Eppie steadied her breath as well as she could and tapped the page on the shoulder.

"Where are the privies?" she asked him. It came out in a squeak, but he didn't seem to notice her nervousness. The prince glared at his page, ignoring Eppie.

"Quiet, Kinner," he growled.

The page looked back and forth between Eppie and the prince's indifferent back.

"Sorry," Eppie whispered.

He put his finger to his lip and beckoned her to follow him. He led her to the adjacent edge of the garden as another minstrel struck up a tune, this time with the harpist accompanied by a tambourine and a flute. They were noisy.

"You need the privies?" the page, Kinner, asked.

Eppie nodded.

They were standing in one of the doorways now. "They're all the way down there and through the practice yard and the stables," Kinner said, pointing down a corridor to the left. "There are a lot of guards and I'm always afraid they're going to poke me with a sword just by accident, even, but there's a chamber pot down the hall here that you can use, just past our rooms." He jerked his thumb to the right.

"Which are your rooms, then?" Eppie asked, not quite able to believe her luck.

"Just over there, the third door and then the next two after it. Who are you?" he asked, "I've seen you before, I think."

"Just a kid from the city, sort of. I don't think..."

"Well, my name's Kinner," he said, "and I'm from Slaradun. I can read and write Theranian script and I'm learning Cerean and Ganatean when we get back to the keep."

"Cerean and Ganatean," Eppie echoed. She couldn't imagine why anyone would want to learn those unless they were traders. And why would he think she wanted to know? "Are you training to be a merchant?"

"Oh, no, I'm just a page," Kinner said, "but my mother says I might be a keep steward someday, if the prince favors me."

"Huh. Listen. I really have to go to that chamber pot."
In the torrent of his chatter, Eppie had forgotten the
directions. "Where is it again?" she asked.

"Oh, it's just down here; I'll show you." Kinner started
off down the corridor. "I only just got to the city the day
before yesterday," he said as they walked. "It's as bad as
people say, all full of thieves and murderers. We've been
pickpocketed, even," he said.

Eppie said nothing, but he didn't even pause for a
response.

"I don't want to meet the murderers, but the prince
wants me to go find the s...the thing that was stolen, and..."

"Are these your rooms?" Eppie asked casually as they
walked.

"Yes, so as I was saying, they all say the city is so
dangerous, and it is, but I didn't know how beautiful it would
be," he said. "If it weren't for the thieves and murderers, I'd
want to see it all!"

"This is it, right?" Eppie said. She could smell the
chamber pot.

"I'll wait for you," he offered.

"No," Eppie said, too quickly. "I'll be fine; I can find my
own way back." She hurried in and tried in vain to pass water.
The page paced outside. It would look too suspicious if she
left the purse there.

Kinner was still waiting there when she emerged. "I have
to go, too," he said. "Wait for me?"

"Uh...I guess," Eppie said. She took a few steps away
down the hall. She didn't want to hear him pee.

She slunk back down the hall to the door of the prince's
apartment, breathing as quietly as she could, listening. From
inside she heard the sound of someone shifting from one foot
to another, the heavy leather strap of his new sword belt
creaking. The rooms were guarded, but there was no one else

in the corridor, and the guard hadn't noticed her yet. She untied her pocket and set the seal in its bag next to the door, in a shadowed corner just under the folds of a half-drawn curtain. Someone was bound to find it there by the time the night was out, she hoped. She was back at the chamber pot's closet by the time Kinner emerged.

"They say the feast is going to be amazing," he said as he came out. "I thought I was eating well at the keep, but I never knew what I was missing. I can't believe all the foods they have here. I even had a fruit that they said came all the way from Ganat; I don't even remember what it was called."

"Mmm," Eppie said. They were passing the door. She tried very hard not to look at it.

"What's that?" Kinner said, bending down to look at the purse.

"What's what?" Eppie said.

"Who goes there?" the guard barked. He opened the door, stopping short when he recognized Kinner.

"What are you doing here?" the guard demanded.

"Nothing," Kinner squeaked, "just—" He gestured to the chamber pot's closet.

Kinner had picked up the purse. Even in the dimly lit corridor, his sudden relief was clear to see.

"Give that here," the guard said.

"But the prince will want it."

"I found it," the guard said, as if that would make it so.

"When?" Kinner asked.

"None of your business," the guard said. "Stay here, keep watch."

Eppie backed away. "I have to go," she said. "I have, that is, I'm helping a lady... I have to go."

She sprinted away, brushing past the guard. The moment she reached the garden, she slowed to a casual stroll. She circled through the rosebushes' shadows back to Darna's hidden bench.

"You sound like a winded horse," Darna whispered. "Calm yourself."

Eppie gulped and nodded. She tried, really she did. The guardsman was crossing the garden, purse held high in triumph.

The prince snatched it from him and untied it with impressive dexterity. Eppie must have missed some trick to the knot, but she was glad she'd at least figured out how to retie it.

"Where did you find this?" he demanded of the guardsman.

"I have a cousin in the city, and, uh, he has some connections with people, thieves..."

"You're lying," the prince said.

Darna nudged Eppie, who shrugged. "Should we go inside?" Eppie whispered. Darna didn't move.

"I am not," the guardsman said. "How much is missing?"

The prince frowned. "Not much," he said. He measured out a handful of beads, not the best of them, either, from what Eppie could see. "Take that for your trouble," he said, "and please resume your post. Where is my page?"

"Watching the rooms, Your Highness," the guard said with a bow.

"Idiot!" the prince hissed. He shoved some of the beads at the guardsman. "Take these. Do you suppose that child could stop a thief?!"

"No, Your Highness. Thank you, Your Highness." The guard backed away, stammering.

The prince tied the purse onto his own belt and nodded to his two flanking guardsmen. "Now, that's settled," he said, satisfied. "I suppose we should go see this feast."

He swept into the hall, trailed by his guards. Kinner scurried across the yard and into the hall a few moments later.

"I think we'd better go in too," Darna said at last. "Keep your head down. That's what servants are supposed to do. Besides, you'll hear more that way."

Eppie was not at all sure that she wanted to hear anything, but she certainly didn't want to be noticed again. Darna leaned on her arm, steering her around the periphery toward a table thronged with guildsmen and merchants. A gong sounded, and the mingling citizens and noblemen dropped their conversations and went to stand in their appointed places. An army of serving girls and pages swept into action, bearing heavy trays of meat, casks of ale and wine, and baskets billowing with bread. Eppie's stomach grumbled.

Darna took her place at a bench. "Stand behind me and make sure no one poisons my wine while I'm looking the other way," she said.

Eppie stiffened, but Darna was smiling, so perhaps she was only joking.

"I'll pass you food when I can," Darna assured her. "There will be plenty at the end, too. Good thing you've done your errand already."

"Mmm. Maybe I should go now," she said.

Darna shook her head and turned to greet the merchant sitting beside her, an old dealer in metal goods from up by the northeastern gate. They'd clearly known each other for a long time, and they chatted amicably in between interruptions from their fellow diners. As the feast went on, Eppie's feet began to tire from trying to stand so still and trying not to be seen. She grabbed a passing hand pie and a piece of cheese to calm her rumbling stomach as a priestess appeared and chanted out the names of all Theranis's realms.

Some time after that, Darna turned as if to speak to her, but then she froze in mid-motion. Eppie followed her gaze.

One of the other noblemen was talking to the Slaradun
prince. He had red hair. Another man stood beside him,
scowling. They looked as if they might almost be twins – it
was hard to tell which was older – but one of them was fit and
lean while the other tended a bit toward pallor and paunch.
The leaner one wore his beard like a Cerean, as many of the
noblemen did. The paunchy one pointed across the hall and
his companion nodded, frowning. As the paunchy one set off,
the other leaned in and whispered something to the Slaradun
prince.

Darna busied herself with her food as the man walked
by, keeping her head down and muttering half-replies to the
garrulous tailor seated beside her.

"They say the curtains in Enomae are so thin and fine, a
cooling breeze passes straight through them."

"Is that so?" Darna said, then took another very large
bite out of her meat. She chewed it slowly. The other red-
haired man disappeared into the throng. The Slaradun prince
said something to his page. The trumpets sounded again.

"Dancing already?" Darna said.

"It will be dawn before you know it," the merchant said.
"Will you join us in the dance?" He gestured an open-handed
invitation to the cleared space at the center of the hall.

Darna only shook her head and picked up her cane. The
merchant nodded and went off, presumably in search of a
more willing and able dance partner. People were getting up
from their seats, some carrying their flagons and glasses,
others gathering into dance formations. The minstrels tuned
their instruments.

"I think it's time we left," Darna said. She pushed the bench
back and let Eppie help her to her feet. She winced and clenched
her teeth as she got up, and Eppie was going to ask if she was
alright, but Darna was already steeling herself to set off. They
waited for a path to open through the crowds, then headed to the
doors. Darna paused once to pluck a stray crumb from her cloak,

but Eppie thought that it looked as if she were just making sure that the two red-haired noblemen were far away.

§

Once they were out on the streets, Eppie looked back over her shoulder. "Who were those two?" she asked.

"I don't know what you're talking about," Darna said flatly. "Come on, let's see if there's any ale near here."

There had been plenty of ale, not to mention wine and liquor and cakes, back in the governor's feast hall. Out in the market square, a bonfire flared, revived again and again by revelers feeding it broken benches and bits of scrap wood. A drummer began to play, not half so expert as the ones inside. Another joined him, and so did a scrappling who had gotten his hands on a clay flute. A man with a metal pot and a cooking spoon added to the din. Dancers circled the fire. Something exploded and a young woman leaped away, giggling, only to be caught by a tall man. They rejoined the circle arm in arm, dancing their ring around the fire with the others.

Darna steered herself and Eppie into a back alley, which led to a low-ceilinged tavern even more crowded than the market square outside. Darna used her cane to beat a path through to the stairs. The tavern's upper room had a window that opened onto the neighbor's not-too-steep roof. Darna climbed out onto it, cane and all. She gave Eppie a bead to pay for the ale, which Eppie retrieved from the taproom below, still feeling like a stranger to herself in her new, clean tunic. Once she was back out on the roof, though, she forgot her self-consciousness. They had a view from the palace's front courtyard all the way down to the harbor.

"How did you find this spot?" Eppie asked. She'd never found such a good view from this far up in the city.

"I know all the best places," Darna said. They looked out together in silence for a while. "What will you do now? Join the priestesses?"

"Not if I can help it," Eppie said. "Thorat said he has an apprenticeship for me."

"Does he? With what guild?"

"Uh, well, it's more of a servant thing, I think?"

"I wouldn't think you'd make much of a servant, but it's a freer life than being a priestess, at least." Darna paused. "There he is now." She pointed to a man ambling around the bonfire, headed indirectly for the alley. She drank half her ale in a single long gulp. They sat in silence until Thorat appeared.

"Errand completed?" he asked.

Eppie nodded.

"Good, it's out of our hands now." Thorat looked over his shoulder, back into the tavern. More revelers were in the square now, and others had started to move down to the harbor. Thorat pressed a middling bead into Eppie's hand. "You go get another ale," he said. "I'm tired."

Eppie went, wondering what it was that Thorat had to say to Darna alone. She didn't think that they were lovers, but she wasn't sure. It was too noisy to eavesdrop, anyway.

§

Thorat yawned, feeling a little guilty at his pretense of being more tired than the prospective apprentice. The girl had led the watch on a chase halfway across the city all afternoon, then by all appearances, Myril had scrubbed her to within an inch of her life. She looked like an entirely different creature now, very respectable, possibly too respectable to be a Defender.

"You made the scrappling get more ale?" Darna asked.

"She's not a scrappling anymore; she'll be an apprentice."

"An apprentice what?" Darna asked. "That girl's too scrawny, and too female, to be a guardsman, and I don't know what else this sword hall of yours does, except that Sunna goes there too, and it lets her come and go more than any of the other priestesses. What is it?"

"Don't badger me about it." Thorat trusted Darna, but he was also sworn to secrecy.

Darna sighed, exasperated. "Myril knows, and she won't tell me."

"She didn't hear it from me. I can't imagine anyone else would have told her either."

"I think it's something she read in a temple scroll. She didn't say anything, exactly, but I can tell that she knows whatever it is you won't tell me."

"She can't know much," Thorat said. "Listen, though. I'm leaving for Tiadun in the morning, going to guard for the prince there and maybe fight in the tournaments. I know you came from there. I was hoping you could tell me something about it, or about Tiada, really."

"I can't, not really," Darna said. "I was a child when I left, but even then, Tiada was a shy dragon. I rarely saw her, and when I did, it was only in glimpses, in the distance. I'm not like Iola." She sounded bitter, even though he knew that she'd never wanted to be a priestess.

"What about dragonlets?" Thorat asked.

"There were dragonlets," Darna mused, "but not many, and only in the woods, I think. I'm sure it's just a province like any other. The keep's a dark, miserable place, and the villages aren't much better. I haven't been there since more than ten years ago, but I can't imagine that it's changed much."

"Have you heard anything since?" Thorat asked. He'd heard rumors of bad blood between the prince and his brother, but the noblemen of Theranis always seemed to have family squabbles.

"I did hear a rumor that there was a foreign priest there," Darna said. She seemed as if she were holding something back, but he wasn't sure what.

"What kind of priest?" Cerean tutors were commonplace now, but actual foreign priests never stayed, fearing the dragon's curses.

"Enomaean."

Just then, Eppie reappeared with the ale.

"Ah, there you are!" Darna said, obviously relieved by the interruption. Thorat took his ale and busied himself with drinking it while Darna turned to Eppie.

"So, you're not going to join the temples," she said. "You do learn to read, and the food is good."

"I just don't like the place."

"Not even Ara's Landing?" Darna asked, slowly.

"No. I mean, it's pretty, the temple, but it feels so empty."

"I know what you mean," Darna said. "I never wanted to join up, myself, but they tricked me in, and I was there for a few years."

"But you got out? I didn't think they let anyone out."

Darna shrugged. "They used to let some go all the time, but not so much now. It's a good thing I didn't come along a few years later, fees paid or not."

"Fees?" Eppie asked.

"The princes and chieftains used to send their daughters to Ara's Landing to learn to read and write and dance. It's the proper education for a keep mistress. They've only just recently stopped, but the Galamun prince sent his daughter a few years ago, and the one from Coradun came just last year. They won't go through initiation, though, I don't think."

"Was it...empty?"

Darna nodded. "I never saw a dragonlet there, not inside the temple. I don't think they come there. It's as if the priestesses' offerings flow down inside the walls but nothing comes back up unless you count the plants in the gardens, but those...well, they're just not the same."

"No dragonlets in the temple?" Thorat said, more loudly than he'd meant to. He looked over his shoulder into the tavern, but no one seemed to have noticed his outburst.

"I never saw them, and Myril didn't either," Darna said.

"Surely, Iola must have."

Darna shook her head. "She didn't say that she did. She would have. She always said when she saw the dragons or talked to Anara."

"Who is this Iola?" Eppie said.

"She's the ambassadress," Darna answered. "She was a scrappling with us."

"Oh." Eppie stared out across the city, as if it had never occurred to her that the closed-in yet exalted ambassadress had once been a scrappling too. Thorat thought that Iola had been as unsuited to scrappling life as Eppie was to being a priestess. Still, he couldn't fathom that there might not be dragonlets in the temple. He would have to ask Iola about it when she returned. If she returned.

"Let's have our toast to the ambassadress, then go on down to the harbor. It's getting late." Darna said. She looked as though she were gazing into some kitchen fire from long ago. Over the eastern hills, the stars were just beginning to fade, out beyond the swirling smoke and bonfire sparks.

As soon as they all drained their jars, Thorat helped Darna back through the window and they were off, clattering down the tavern's back stairs and picking their way over the night's wreckage in the alley and the streets.

Eppie stuck her hand into the fold of her tunic. "I have three small beads' change from the ale," she said.

"Keep it," Thorat told her. "You might need it. I know I could have used a few small ones when I was an apprentice."

Ahead of them, the crowds were getting thicker. He let Darna take the lead.

It looked as if every soul in Anamat was packed along the beach and in the harbor-front squares, their shoulders and elbows jostling for space as they waited for the dragon to fly. Thorat could see over the sea of heads in some places, but Eppie and Darna were much shorter than he was. He put a hand on Eppie's shoulder so that he wouldn't lose her. "Follow Darna," he said. "She'll know where to go."

Darna elbowed and cane-whacked her way through the crowds and around behind a low harbor-front workshop, hardly more than a thatched shed. She stepped over a pile of manure and into a back alley, where a stairway appeared. There hadn't been anything there a moment before.

Eppie inhaled sharply. "I never saw this place."

Darna turned and gave her a half-smile. "I told you I know all the best places."

At the top of the stair, a flat stretch of wall surrounded the two-tree orchard of a townhouse. The wall was wider than it needed to be, wide enough to walk or stand on comfortably, and it gave them a fine view across the harbor. The seawater gleamed darkly in the rising light of dawn, punctuated by the tower on Anara's Island. That tower hid the dragon's gate to the other realm, and from this vantage point, it was straight in front of them, sketching a line toward the fading morning star.

As the sky grew brighter, dozens of red- and purple-robed priestesses processed down from the temple. Drums rolled a tattoo at the water's edge, where the ambassadress emerged from her curtained palanquin. Thorat willed her to turn to see him, but she didn't. Instead, she lavished her blessings on the crowds closest to her. He could see the curtain of her blessing, the glow of it, just as he could see the trail of light Anara left in the sky sometimes, burning through the clouds.

There were no clouds this morning. Iola stepped onto the barge, a long, dragon-shaped vessel poled by masked oarsmen, a fraternity that was so secretive that the Defenders who lent them an oar had no idea where the raft was hidden. Once they reached the island, Iola hurried into the tower to meet her dragon. There were people who believed that the ambassadress didn't go anywhere at all, but rather that she lived in some kind of drugged trance inside the temple for the whole of the waning year. But Thorat knew, and Iola knew. She knew the paths to the dragons' realms, as did the others who had made that journey before her. Thorat wished that he could be by her side, or at least guard her at the gate, but he could not pass for a priestess, and Anara could only carry one.

A gong rang out across the water, stilling the hubbub of the crowd. The dragon emerged from her tower, red and golden in the rising sun. Anara stretched her wings.

Thorat's heart ached for Iola. She was a slender streak of crimson clinging to Anara's back. Seeing her there, he ached for the dragon, too, wishing that he could fly with those wings rather than stay earthbound. He watched them until priestess and dragon plunged back into that passage where no man could follow and live.

§

The dragon exploded from her realm beneath the earth, flashing translucent, crimson, golden. She arched up into the sky. Eppie had never seen Anara so clearly before. She'd seen the dragon at other festivals, and sometimes even in between, but never like this. This time, she didn't need to look over her shoulder to see who was watching her, watching the sky, whether they would pick her pockets or think that she was dragon-touched, crazy. For the first time, she was with people who understood and who could see the dragon too.

Squid had always doubted the existence of the dragons, as if there were no proof that they moved through the air, that they shaped the lands and made the harvest strong. At the beginning, she'd soon given up trying to change his mind. She'd learned to keep those thoughts to herself. No one wanted to be thought a fool, but now she thought that if either of them were a fool in this, perhaps it was Squid, not her. The dragon was far too vivid and real to deny now that she could look without fear of being discovered.

The two people with her this morning had no doubts that the dragon existed either. It was strange that she'd never thought the older denizens of Anamat could see better than the scrapplings. She had been on the streets a long time, thinking that the whole world was dragon-blind, or that the price of vision was to be locked away inside temple walls forever, subject to any petitioner who paid at the gate, and to be separated from the dragonlets. She was glad that Darna understood that too.

Far away on the horizon, she could just see the sails of a foreign ship. Perhaps it was the one Squid sailed on, and good riddance to him. She stopped short of hoping that he wouldn't return, though, because he had been a friend of sorts, but she was glad that she would be able to walk into this new life with no ties to old acquaintance of any kind, just as she'd walked alone into the city.

Beside her, Thorat and Darna were still looking up at the dragon. Eppie let the sight fill her eyes, the wide blue sky, the red-winged and golden body of Anara. For a moment, she thought that the ambassadress looked down, thought those eyes locked gazes with her own. In that moment, she longed to feel the dragon's curving scales against her chest. She wanted to wrap her legs around that fiery form, the life force of the city, to feel that heat in her core.

Anara fiew on, back down to the dragons' realm, and soon there was nothing to see but the clear blue sky and a single swallow winging across the rising sun.

§

Chapter 5

Thorat trudged across the Anamat valley with the rest of the hired blades at the back of the Tiadun prince's procession. At the border shrine, he turned to look back at Anamat one last time. Anara and the other dragons were under the earth now, having their own councils, so he would only say farewell to the valley, to try to see her presence in the ripening fields and orchards, in the swift-flowing streams and blossoming gardens. He wished for the hundredth time that day that he could stay in the city, among friends.

They would cross this thin reach of Na's realm by nightfall and camp on the edge of Galamun. The year of a hired guard fell into several parts. At Midsummer, there was the hiring in Anamat. While the princes gathered for their councils, their masters-at-arms watched the guardsmen and chose their mercenaries for the year to come, preferably including some who would compete well in the Midwinter games. The Defenders excelled in these games, but it seemed wiser these days not to win the top place, to avoid being offered a permanent place in a prince's retinue.

Once hired, the guardsmen traveled to the keep with the prince and his court. The march to Tiadun would take almost ten days altogether, crossing two spurs of Na's mountains and two other realms along the way. Thorat's fellow mercenaries were mostly former scrapplings who had taken up employment as palace guards or other armsmen; some had come from other prince's keep towns, too. Few of them had great skill as swordsmen, but most were tall and muscular – intimidation worked better than force when it came to persuading peasants to pay tax.

Thorat became popular in the camp because he was willing to sing and knew more songs than most, but the men wanted mostly bawdy songs, not the long ballads of the dragons that he had worked so hard to learn during his year as an apprentice minstrel. After he'd failed his first-year minstrel examinations, Sovara had tried to place him at the swordsmiths' guild, but they'd been loath to take on an apprentice with no family connections in Anamat, and one who had already failed at another guild. So, Thorat had begun his rounds as a common guardsman, usually in the provinces, one keep after another, listening and watching for the ever-distant dragons.

They passed through some fine countryside, but Thorat had little opportunity to eavesdrop on the prince. The prince and his brother rode side by side on their Enomaean horses at the head of the column, with the prince's nephews a short distance behind. The prince's consort had stayed at the keep rather than make the journey to Anamat, which was unusual. "Perhaps she was expecting an heir?" Thorat wondered aloud. But the Tiadun men told him no, it would not be likely. She and the prince were barren, and she was old for that now.

Thorat stayed alert for signs of bandits as they crossed the mountains. There had been none in the low hills between Anamat and Galamun, but he'd seen smoke from a campfire as they crossed through the wild country into Getedun. In the border hills of Tiadun, the hill bandits had made visible tracks beside the main road, and it looked as if they'd carved out places to ambush unwary travelers. He made a note of those spots in case he might have to come this way alone later in the year with only his own sword for defense.

As they came over the last ridge of hills, Thorat made an excuse to hurry ahead to make his offering at the border shrine of Tiadun. His fellow swordsmen teased him for his piety.

"There's not even a serving girl there, let alone a priestess," one said.

Thorat shrugged. "It's my habit to make offerings at the borders. The dragons have guarded me so far."

The man marching beside him rolled his eyes. "You do like those old songs. D'you know any of the ones come over from Enomae?"

"I don't," Thorat said. "What are they, for horses?"

That got a laugh, at least.

"Careful with that, man," said one of the men from Tiadun, taking him aside. "Our prince here hosts a priest from Enomae. But go ahead; make your offering quickly and get back to your place. Throw in a prayer for the rest of us while you're there."

Thorat climbed up the steep side of the road to the bandits' narrow path. He double-timed his step, jogging to the front of the column. One of the prince's bodyguards looked up at him, setting a hand on his bow. Thorat held up his open hands and gestured to his weapons. He had only a sword visible, no throwing spear or bow. He also had a knife hidden in his leggings, but he had no intention of harming the prince, and the bodyguard seemed to recognize him.

A group of women had gathered at the shrine, women in fine red robes – so much for the man who said that no priestess attended this shrine. Drawing closer, though, Thorat could see that there was no place for them to shelter there. Farther down the road, donkey carts carried their tents. Thorat paused on the slope above the shrine. It was only a columned porch, with no inner room for a priestess to make the Great Rite out of sight of the road. Still, it would have a statue of Tiada and a little shelf for travelers to leave offerings of bread and incense, which bandits would steal as night fell.

The leader of the women stepped forward. She was tall, about fifty years old, with gray hair and a straight back. She ran forward to greet the paunchy prince, smiling with unfeigned delight. Thorat caught a glimpse of the prince's face just then, too. His usual constipated mien shifted away and his face lit up with the look of a man in love.

The prince swung down from his horse and embraced his mistress. The train of horses, courtiers, servants, and fighting men stuttered to a dusty halt behind them.

"Can we not go on?" one of the prince's nephews complained. He was a young man, not a child, and shockingly uncivil.

His father, the prince's brother, only said, "Patience." It was a milder reprimand than Thorat would have expected.

The prince, oblivious to all this, wrapped his arms around his mistress and kissed her.

"Gallia," he greeted her. "Ride with me?"

Gallia looked downhill to her own horse. She waved her horse's handler away and took the prince's hand with a smile.

"Did you –" he began.

"It is accomplished," Gallia said, "though I don't like it."

"But the priest is happy with it?"

"As happy as he'll ever be," Gallia said. "Farseer is a grim god."

The prince glanced nervously about and shushed her with another kiss.

"I'll go take the dragon-blessed bread to the guardsmen," Gallia said. "I'll be riding with you in no time." Her eyes sparkled, and she smiled again at the prince before going back to her women to take up her share of the bread. The prince stood starry-eyed, distracted by his happiness at rejoining his mistress.

Thorat made a hurried, whispered offering at the shrine. He hoped that Tiada could hear him, away as she was under the earth, but if she didn't, well, at least he had tried.

§

They entered the keep's main yard just after sunset the following day. Torches burned in the feast hall, but where they should have burned brightest, on the temple porch, there was nothing. Or rather, there was something, but the space looked oddly empty. Thorat felt wary, but the other men around him stopped to stare, so he did too.

The entrance to the temple had been walled over. On the porch, in the place where a priestess should have danced, stood a broad, dark table, more like a kitchen table than an offering place. Behind it hung a tapestry, a broad banner with a man's image painted on it, a man with an eagle's head. Thorat gaped, but then the priestess came at last, followed by a foreign man wearing a cape of silvery gray fur, his oiled hair dressed into a sort of spike. He, like his god, was birdlike, though probably too old to be swift in flight. Thorat let his left hand rest on the hilt of his sword, as if he could use it to cut the foreign god's invasion off at the neck. What on Na's earth had they done with the temple?

The prince and his mistress joined priest and priestess on the porch, and it was the keep mistress who spoke first.

"Welcome to Tiadun," she said. "The feast awaits. We live here with the blessing of Tiada, who rules the earth, but we welcome also the lord of the skies, Farseer." She nodded to the Enomaean priest. "Farseer's shrine is here for the prince and any who choose to join him. For those who follow the dragons, our priestesses await in their temple, but its entrance now faces the town, to be better open to all."

The prince smiled, his gaze fiitting over the silent guardsmen and servants. They seemed stunned, or maybe they were simply indifferent to this strange god in their midst. Thorat heard no murmur of outrage except in his own mind. The prince's brother and nephews stood on the porch steps, also measuring the crowd through narrow eyes, more calculating than nervous. They had expected this. They were seeking a way to turn it to their advantage.

The priest of Farseer stepped behind his altar and raised his arms, as if to invoke the god, but the prince shook his head. The priest frowned.

"We will conduct our sacrifices to Farseer at sunrise, his most favored time of day," the prince announced, finding his voice at last. "We will show him our gratitude for our safe journey here. Meanwhile, the feast, and if you will –" He tilted his head toward the priestess.

The priestess stepped forward. "I greet you in the name of Tiada and all the great winged dragons who give life to this earth. Come bring her offerings, and she will feed you with the power of the earth."

As Thorat made his small obeisance with the rest of the men, he saw, out of the corner of his eye, the prince doing the same. He also saw the Enomaean priest take a staff and tap the prince in reprimand. The keep mistress, scowling, strode away before the men rose from their bows.

The prince had turned his back on the dragons.

§

Outside of the small circle of noblemen who lived in the prince's tower, the men of Tiadun mostly kept to the old ways of the dragons, insofar as they kept any faith at all, which wasn't saying much. They gave small offerings of bread and wine when they wished for some small thing, and when fortune favored them, or they hoped that it might, they took their beads to the priestesses to make their part in the Great Rite. Sometimes, they went only went to satisfy the urges stirring in their loins, or that is what they said in the barracks beside the stables. Still, every morning when they went out to train, they saw the foreign god's beady eyes staring down at them from the old temple porch, which smelled of the fading blood of sacrifice. The priest looked down on them hungrily.

If the other men felt as uneasy as Thorat did under Farseer's gaze, they were at pains not to show it, nor did any of them rise at dawn to greet the prince's newfound god with the blood of voles or other furry creatures. They marched past the makeshift shrine on their way out to train in the fields and as they came back in from the mess hall beside the kitchen at the back of the keep. After they had been following this routine for a full moon-round without incident, and without any sign of Tiada or her dragonlets, Thorat sat down to his stew and bread one day and turned to the man beside him.

"Would you pass the salt, friend?" As he spoke, he looked up to find that it was not a fellow guardsman beside him. It was Farseer's priest.

"With pleasure." Despite his foreign accent, or possibly because of it, the priest's voice was smooth and mellifluous. He handed Thorat the salt bowl. "And with Farseer's blessing," he said.

Thorat accepted the salt, not sure what else to do.

"I wonder that none of you men have come to join in the dawn sacrifices," the priest said. "Farseer is a warrior's god, the lord of the sky. Why would you prostrate yourselves to women and the cold earth, when Farseer brings the sun's blessings?"

"The sun may shine as it will," said the man on the priest's other side, "but the crops need the rain, too, and our Tiada brings that in its season."

Thorat chewed his now-too-salty meat, wavering about whether or not to join in this debate.

The priest smiled. "But your dragons live under the earth. They cannot rule the sky. They are bound by these small mountains, while Farseer, a great god, strives to fly across the seas and higher peaks than these."

"Our dragons fly in the sky, too," Thorat said. "They bring both the rain and the fair weather."

"Ah, but they are creatures of earth, are they not?"

"And why shouldn't they be?" Thorat said.

"They may be what they are," the priest said, "but a warrior's way should be pure and high, unsullied by the scent of women and earth."

The priest reeked of scented oil, but it was not enough to cover the tang of blood that wafted after him.

"What about blood?" Thorat asked.

The priest's smile broadened, but his eyes shifted as he chose his words. "Is blood not the work of the warrior? Man cannot stop the earth from pushing up her fruits, but he can choose which live, and weed out the impure. Your dragons will not stop your weeds from growing."

"Is Farseer a god of farmers, then, too?" the man to the priest's other side asked. He was a Tiadun man, and had a family in a nearby village.

"He is a god of warriors," the priest said.

Another man leaned in. "They say that Enomae is dry and barren, suited to nothing more than grazing animals like your horses."

"It is a pure land," the priest said, "a subjugating land. We rule a country larger than all of Theranis. These petty farms of olive and grape bind your people down to the earth." He made it sound like a pitiable fate.

"To enjoy our wine!" another man chimed in.

The priest's smile faded, and he mumbled something to himself in his own language, something that Thorat could not think was friendly.

"So," Thorat said. "Does Farseer seek to subjugate our dragons?"

The priest looked at him through narrowed eyes. "No, there is honor among the taloned gods, I think. They would be allies."

"Would they?" Thorat asked. "And what of the gods of Cerea?"

The priest made a sour face. "The Cereans make gods in their own image," he said quietly. "Their gods are as petty and grasping as their merchantmen." The rest of the men had taken up some other conversation and were ignoring them.

That much matched with Thorat's own estimation, from the little he'd seen. "He is interesting, this god of yours," Thorat said.

"He is more than interesting," the priest said, his eyes brightening again. "I would like to speak further of him with you."

That was not quite what Thorat had had in mind. He nodded absently, and it seemed that the priest took that for assent. In the coming days, though, the priest refrained from hounding him but only smiled his oily smile when Thorat passed his way. Thorat was glad when the first harvest came a half-moon later and he had to set out with a troupe of guardsmen to collect taxes from the villages. He could put the keep behind him for a little while, and perhaps he could discover some signs of the dragon in the villages.

On the first night out on patrol, he asked one of the Tiadun men about the prince's newfound religion.

"How long has the foreign priest been here?" Thorat asked.

"This one?" the man said. "He's only been here since last Midsummer, but there was another one before him."

"And another one before that," another man chimed in.

"Altogether, it's been... Well, I'd say it's been seven or eight years since the foreign priests started coming."

"And before that were the Cerean tutors, since before I can remember."

"Ah, but you're young," said the man in charge of their group. "I remember the first one that came. People used to say that he stank like a kitchen, he wore so much oil."

The other men laughed.

"We're used to them now, though, I suppose."

"Calar and his sons still keep Cerean tutors. They even still go to the rite sometimes."

"Who wouldn't?"

"The Enomaean did once; now he won't."

"He's an odd one, all right."

"Shush. He's the prince's right hand."

"I thought the keep mistress was that," Thorat said. At least she still left offerings to Tiada; he'd seen her do it more than once.

"She's more like his brains," said someone.

There was a long silence.

"I think we'd best clean up before bedding down for the night," said the man in charge. "We've the donkeys to feed, too."

They left it at that, and Thorat didn't raise the topic again. At least the townspeople honored no foreign god in Tiada's place.

The same seemed to be true in the villages. The temples were there, but their porches were dusty, neglected. In one village, the temple doors were barred and locked, as if no one lived there at all. Thorat saw a pair of priestesses along the road and when they arrived at the next village, where the

temple looked slightly less derelict, but there, too, the doors
were barred. The fields all around were dusty with a late
drought, and though the harvest was enough to stave off
hunger, there was little surplus. The farmers handed over their
tax, heads bowed with resignation.

Thorat was beginning to worry that Tiada had faded
away entirely when at last they reached one village where the
temple was a little less neglected than the others had been. He
paused for a moment to look at it, and as he looked, he
thought he saw a dragonlet flicker by. When he turned to
look, it was gone, of course. The priestess came out and
barred her doors to the prince's tax collectors. He wondered if
she was one of the ones who kept the offerings rather than
handing them on to the dragons. If Tiada had been strong,
then any weak service might have been enough to sustain her,
but she was fading: the harvest was thin, and after that one
dimly seen, possibly illusory dragonlet, Thorat saw was no
sign of her anywhere.

§

Back at the keep, in between rounds of tax collecting,
Thorat longed to be on the road again. The closest he came to
freedom each day was his patrol on the walls, where at least
he could see beyond the cold gray stone enclosing him,
trapping him in with everyone else in the keep. No wonder
Darna had been so anxious to escape the place. He wondered
what Iola's home village had been like, far away in the north
of Theranis. She had only told him that it was in the
mountains, small, and poor. Everything was poor beside
Anamat and its temples, which was the only other world she'd
known. From the small watchtowers that flanked the main
gate, Thorat looked out at the farmland beyond the little
town, fine farmland to have given such a poor harvest. In the
southern part of Theranis, the early winter the rains were

light, the sky blue and dry. The golden autumn grain had been gathered in and low winter grasses rippled in the fields.

At the midday watch change, Thorat decided to take his bread from the kitchen and go out walking for the brief interval before their afternoon training, rather than take the usual midday rest. He followed the main Anamat road, then cut across the fields of new winter wheat. There was something about the earth under his feet that felt fiat, even fiatter than it should have been in the height of the winter's day. It wasn't a time when a dragonlet would come out, even if there were any to be seen. Tiadun should have been a fine place, but no one in the keep smiled. Even the birdsong fell fiat, muted.

Before he could properly clear his head, a bell clanged from the temple's tower, announcing the end of the midday rest. Thorat doubled back along the western side of the keep, coming in through a muddy bit of pasture beside the stables and hoping that his absence would not be noted. It had been, though. The guard captain met him at the barracks' door.

"Which of them are you spying for?"

"Which of who?" Thorat said stupidly, his thoughts still away with the sparrows. Even as he asked the question, he knew what the captain had meant – the prince or his brother. Before he could stumble back over his words, the captain shook his head.

"You're quick on your feet but none too clever. Stay in the barracks unless you're on patrol or out on training."

"Yes, sir," Thorat said with a bow.

As the captain walked away, he muttered, "Good with a tune, too. Should've thought he'd have more sense."

Thorat looked up at the arch of blue sky and despaired. No one seemed happy here, neither in the keep nor in the villages, but maybe he only saw the worst of it. No one ever was happy when the tax collectors came. The prince and his

Enomaean priest made grim offerings to their bloody god, as if it were somehow better than dancing and baking bread for an absent dragon. The prince and his brother Calar circled each other like cats spoiling for a fight, and when the prince's nephews came to the yard to practice their sword work, they eyed each other warily. He never saw much of the keep mistress. For all he knew, she might have been a good woman and one of Tiada's own, but she did not make her presence felt. The priestesses turned their backs on the keep. What dragon wouldn't fade when her prince turned to praise to a foreign god?

Occasionally, the prince's nephews paired off against some of the common soldiers, and when Thorat had his turn against them, he discovered that they were actually quite skilled with their blades, that it wasn't all flash and bluster. He kept his own moves straightforward and predictable, taking the measure of the two young noblemen. He learned that they'd spent a season training with a well-known swordmaster in Anamat, a man known for his efficient footwork and feints. Thorat took care to keep his best techniques to himself, but even so, he won a bout against one of them. He could best most of the other hired men without much effort, despite the guard captain's dim view of his intelligence.

When the time came to set out for the border of Kiralun and the Midwinter games, Thorat was not surprised to learn that the captain and the prince planned to set him against Kiralun's champion from the year before, a hardened warrior from Anamat with a scar on his cheek. Ferrent—Thorat's fellow Defender, the one who hadn't returned last Midsummer—had a scar on his cheek. The prospect cheered Thorat as nothing else in that dragon-forsaken keep had done all season. He would see his fellow Defender again at last, and with swords crossed, too.

The walk up into the hills lightened his mood. Looking back at Tiadun Keep on the edge of its rocky bay, it had the appearance of an ideal situation for a keep, with the bowl of the countryside easing down around it. Having been there, though, he felt that the craggy mountains seemed more welcoming. Thorat walked with the other guardsmen in a less defensive spot near the middle of the train, just in front of the lumbering oxen and donkeys that carried tents and provisions for the hundred or so noblemen, hired swordsmen, and servants. Two priestesses led the way, swinging censers. Behind them, the keep mistress, the prince, and his brother walked side by side. They brought no horses, as the games were ostensibly held in honor of the dragons, so the long train of walking men and a few women felt much more like a proper religious observance than anything Thorat had seen since leaving Anamat.

The Enomaean priest and the prince's nephews stayed behind at the keep, which seemed odd. Thorat would have expected the nephews to take part in the games, but perhaps they didn't want to risk being beaten by a commoner. Or else they had another reason. In any case, they were missing a lovely walk, through the rolling pastures and into the frosty pass. In the mountains, Thorat felt as if a dragon might come along after all, and with the prince's men armed for the tournament, they had nothing to fear from bandits.

They reached the pass on the afternoon of the second day of their stately march. The mountains at the peak of the pass dipped down to form a broad natural arena with a stream on either side. The party from Kiralun had arrived already, their coral-and-white tents dotting the far slopes, their donkeys and oxen grazing. The invisible border where the two realms touched was marked by a single shrine, or rather two shrines side by side under a single roof. The shrines themselves were in full view of the camp, and priestesses from each realm would sleep there, saving their blessing for the champions of the games.

Thorat slept better that night than he had since arriving in Tiadun. Iola would be winging her way back from the other world, too, and that meant that even if she were in Anamat, she would at least be on the surface of the earth again.

After breakfast the following morning, Thorat was told that the games would begin at high noon, and that he would be in the first round. He grunted and nodded, as if were all the same to him. The morning dragged by, but at noon, Ferrent and Thorat faced each other at last, their leather vests and arm guards strapped on carefully, wooden practice swords in hand.

"By Anara's wing," whispered his old comrade in arms. "It's good to see you."

"And you, too. I hear you were last year's champion," Thorat said, circling. "Is that why you couldn't come back to Anamat?"

"They wouldn't let me go. Besides, I know too much." Ferrent kept his eyes on Thorat, but they were both aware of the many eyes watching them.

"I don't know enough," Thorat countered.

"Then maybe you should win," Ferrent said. His eyes narrowed. "I can't, not this year."

One of them had to lunge, so Thorat did. Ferrent knew this dance. He parried and struck. They circled again.

"Your turn," Thorat said, and Ferrent went in so that it would look like he was going for a killing stroke, or at least a winning one. Thorat obligingly fell back, then charged ahead.

"Meet me behind the shrine at midnight," Ferrent said. "You take this round."

"And you, tomorrow's."

They fought in earnest then, holding back no more than they would have in training under Sovara's watch back in

Anamat. Their temporary comrades-in-arms cheered and hooted, booed and applauded. They drew out the fight.

"You've gotten rusty," Thorat said. He flipped Ferrent's sword up and it careened over his head, flying up through the air and landing just short of the princes' stand. Ferrent threw his hands up in defeat, and their fellow armsmen cheered.

§

Thorat closed his eyes, pretending to sleep until his fellow guardsmen were either drunk or asleep. When midnight was nearly upon them, he crept out of his shared tent and staggered out onto the high meadow. A lone stand of tall, dark pines shaded the shrine, keeping the moonlight off it. The trees also blocked any view of the hill behind it. Thorat affected a bit of a stagger, hoping that no one would notice him or, if they did, that they would think he was as drunk and only going to piss.

He staggered over to the pines, hoping that the priestesses were sleeping too. After a short while, he heard the call of a night bird – Ferrent's signal. Thorat followed the sound to where Ferrent leaned against a tree trunk, looking up the mountain slope. He got up at Thorat's approach and embraced him.

"What news of Anamat?" Ferrent asked as they both sat down again, this time facing down hill in case anyone wandered their way.

"It's much of the same, but even fewer of us than last year," Thorat said. "You didn't come, and neither did Harron. Raina's beside herself over that, as you can imagine."

"And our Enatel?"

"Sovara's the same as ever," Thorat said. Then he thought about it. "Her hair is getting grayer."

"Garren?" Ferrent asked.

Thorat thought of Garren, always smelling of yeast and honey. "He's well, or was at Midsummer. I miss him, and it's only been half a year. Miss his bread, really. I still can't get past his guard."

"I never could either," Ferrent said. "So, we're down to..."

"Nine," Thorat said, "if you and Harron return, and then maybe ten if this new apprentice makes it through."

"An apprentice? That is good news. I hope he doesn't mind Sovara's diet of smoke and water."

"She," Thorat corrected. "She'll manage, I think. She's been a scrappling for years, used to finding her own food, but it's complicated. The ambassadress wants her for a priestess."

Ferrent cursed softly. "The ambassadress can have any girl she wants! We need apprentices more than the temple needs more wh – I'm sorry. I've been out here too long. I should go back, but there's a woman now, and she has a farm and she wants me to stay." A breeze whispered through the pines above, letting in a little dappled light from the setting quarter moon.

"You haven't told her why? About us?" Thorat asked.

Ferrent sat in silence for a while, listening to the wind in the trees. "Would you?" He didn't wait for an answer. "I haven't, but I've wanted to. No, never mind, you wouldn't be tempted by an ordinary woman, would you?"

"Sovara sent me with the offering this year," Thorat said. "So, no."

Ferrent looked away from Thorat. "Once a year, even if it's the ambassadress. That's not often enough to be with a woman."

It might not be enough, but in those hours with Iola, Thorat felt whole, even outside of the rite. It was enough, as long as it lasted, and any other woman would pale in comparison. No one of them could be enough, not even many of them. He would rather only have Iola, even though he couldn't touch her more than once or twice in a year.

"There's something else," Ferrent said. "It's closer, more urgent. After our bout, I had a message from your prince's brother, Calar. He asked me to meet him just after nightfall by the edge of the camp. He was dressed in a dark but common cloak. He wants his brother killed."

"Na's blood!"

"Well, Tiada's first," Ferrent said.

"I haven't seen the dragon," Thorat said. "I doubt they have either. Did you hear that the prince has an Enomaean priest?"

"I hadn't. In that case, I might take the brother up on his offer, but I don't like it."

"The job, or the foreign priest?"

"I don't like either of them, but if the prince has turned his back on the dragon, he should be replaced. Do you think his brother would be better?"

Thorat shook his head. "He doesn't keep a foreign priest, but I don't like the man. The prince seems to be a bit of a fool, but he doesn't try to make the others in the castle follow him, and the foreign priest is not as bad as I would have thought. He seems to think that his god and the dragons can live in peace with each other."

Ferrent snorted at that. "What about the prince?"

"He's distant but not unfair, and no crueler than anyone else in the keep. The priestesses still have their temple, and I haven't heard the prince blaspheme against Tiada, despite his Enomaean priest, though his nephews are another matter."

"That's better than his brother, then. Calar offered me a large land grant and five priestesses of my choosing if I saw that the prince was killed some way or another, far from his own hand."

"And what did you tell him?"

"I told him that the priestesses weren't his to give," Ferrent said, shaking his head. "And do you know what he said? He said, 'I'll be able to do what I like when I'm prince, with half a Cerean fleet at my back. You'll have your priestesses, or if you'd prefer, I'm sure I can get some Cerean slave girls. I've heard they're much more pliant.'"

Thorat gaped. "And?"

Ferrent let out a long sigh. "He seemed sure that I was just holding out for a better offer. After all, I'm just a hired blade; why would I object to regicide if the pay was good enough? But even without the offer of the priestesses, I wouldn't slay any man unprovoked, much less a prince of the land. It would be one thing if he had wronged me and wasn't a prince, or if we were in battle, but there's no call to war here."

The moon had sunk behind the mountain, and they could barely see each other. "I wouldn't do it either, but there are men who would, lots of them," Thorat said, shaking his head. "Any fool can see that the prince and his brother are at odds, but I didn't realize it was a killing feud."

"It seems it is," Ferrent said grimly. "I wonder why the prince doesn't have his brother sent away."

"I don't think he'd be so determined," Thorat said. "Calar's two sons are strong young men, some of the strongest fighters in the keep."

"Apart from yourself. You've gotten better."

Thorat shrugged. "I could get better yet if I could stay in Anamat to train."

"So could I." Ferrent sighed. They sat in silence for a long moment. "It's a wonder the boys don't do the job themselves."

Thorat considered that. "They could do it. I wonder why they stayed back at the keep instead of coming to the games."

"Up to no good, if you ask me," Ferrent said. "Send word to me if you need help."

"Only if the dragon is threatened," Thorat said. "That's what Sovara told me. I plan to keep to that, but you should go back to Anamat as soon as you can."

"I'll go in full spring," Ferrent said. "I'd like to enjoy a few more moons with my – but you don't need to hear me praise her. I suppose I'll see you on the field in the morning."

"Most likely," Thorat said. Ferrent had a lover. He would have felt jealous, but he couldn't imagine wanting that life, on a farm, in a village, forever exiled from Anamat. Even the endless round of guard duty suited him better than a farmer's life, because at least it allowed him into the ambassadress's realm once or twice a year.

He embraced Ferrent and they went their separate ways. Their bout the following afternoon gave them no chance to converse, but they both managed to avoid taking the prize, acting as if they'd drunk too much the night before. Thorat set out for Tiadun Keep again, knowing only that his fellow Defender was still nearby, and that Calar had even fewer scruples than he'd thought.

§

When they rounded the pass out of the mountains and had their first sight of Tiadun Bay, Thorat saw that fratricide was only part of Calar's plans. A whole merchant fleet lay at anchor, not a single ship of it Theranian, and from the glint of sunlight on something aboard the largest ship, they might be armed for war, too. Thorat, having taken second place in the tournament, walked beside the captain of the guard, near the prince.

As the bay came into view, the prince stopped in mid-stride and turned to his brother.

"What is the meaning of this?"

"I thought to please you, brother," Calar cooed. His voice carried, though.

"It does not please me," the prince said.

"Nor me," Gallia added. She stood beside her prince, staring Calar down.

"You are fools to oppose this," he said more softly.

"I am the prince and ruler of this province. I say they must go!" The prince turned to his captain of the guard. "Send a man ahead with my orders. The Cereans must go."

The captain hesitated.

"Go, man!" Gallia said.

Calar held up his hand. "Stay, hear me out. They have come a long way. Would you refuse these guests the hospitality of our keep?"

Gallia looked very much as if she would like to. "They are out of season."

"They gave word that they would not land until after Midwinter dawn, even though they say that they do not understand how our land can close itself to trade for half the year. Come ahead with me," Calar said, putting an arm around his brother's shoulders.

They walked ahead down the hill, going far enough that no one else in the party could hear what arguments Calar whispered to his brother, and what weak rebuttals gave way to his persuasion. The fact was that the Cereans were already in the harbor, so they must trade, of course, and it would be uncivil to turn them away from the shore when they had braved the risk of winter storms to come so far. Thorat looked for the flicker of a dagger, but Calar would not bloody his hands in full sight of the court.

When the prince and his brother returned, the captain of the guard bowed to the prince. "Shall I send a man ahead?" he asked.

"I suppose not" the prince sighed. "We will meet them ourselves."

§

The Cereans landed with picks and shovels. They built a makeshift barracks on the shore, a dwelling of logs and roughly split shingles. Thorat considered whether to send for Ferrent. On the one hand, he would need someone at his back when the foreigners went to the hills to seek Tiada's gate, to rob her crystallized blood from the land. On the other, Ferrent had been approached to assassinate the prince. If he came, Calar would assume that his offer had been accepted and that Ferrent was his to command. No, better to send to Anamat for help first. With a little luck, Garren would come, and then they could send for Ferrent. Sunna or Raina could be formidable too, when they weren't too wrapped up in their priestessing or farm-wife duties. Varin was a solid swordsman, though not as strong as Garren or Anot. Sovara would stay there to tend the shrine, but she would know what to do.

He sent his message off to Anamat with the first merchant caravan of the season and waited.

§

Chapter 6

Eppie spoke hardly at all that autumn. Silence conserved her energy: the training was hard even on the days when Garren and Raina did not come. On those days, Sovara forgot to eat, leaving Eppie to forage her own food as she had when she was a scrappling. Silence let her watch, and imitate the movements of the sword. Silence saved her from awkward excuses when she could not match those movements. Besides, there was no one to talk to most of the time. Sovara stayed mostly in her small room at the back of the training hall, muttering to herself or tinkering with bits of metal. She seemed almost wary of her new apprentice, as if unsure that Eppie would last beyond the season.

Still, when they all gathered, it felt too good to be real, bowing together before they began training. In the morning, light slanted in under the rafters so that the roof looked as if it might fly away. The shrine doors hid a statue of Anara, taller than a man, with her wings spread wide. The statue was golden and so lifelike that Eppie half expected it to shake out its wings and fly away. It was magic, and she did not speak for fear that the dream she'd stumbled into would disappear before her eyes, landing her back under the bridge without this strange fellowship gathered around her.

The people in the training hall were an odd bunch, and their purposes seemed obscure to Eppie: Who could defend the dragons when the dragons were so much more than people, and mostly invisible? No one who could see the dragons could possibly think to attack them, and for those who couldn't see them, indifference to their fate seemed more likely than attack. And yet, they said that they defended the dragons. They taught Eppie their fighting techniques, which would have been enough to keep her with them even without their shared secret. All her life, Eppie had had to hide the fact that she saw dragons, but everyone else in the training hall could see them too. She didn't have to hide that part of herself when she was with them. If they had other secrets still to keep, that didn't bother her any more than Raina's chattering, maternal advice did.

Outside of the training itself, Eppie's duties were simple enough. First thing in the morning, she had to bring in water from the neighborhood water spout, then she dusted and swept. Sometimes, it was only herself and Sovara, but most days at least one or two of the others came: Varin, Raina, Garren, or Sunna. Thorat, Anot, and the two she hadn't met were away from Anamat, looking for their lost comrades or the provincial dragons. Later in the day, Eppie ran errands for Sovara, delivered messages, or collected wood for the fire. In the evenings, Raina and Garren brought enough food for a small evening meal, but between the training and the lack of a hot dinner at midday, she was always hungry.

For Sovara, training seemed to stand in place of eating. That was the first secret that bothered Eppie: what did Sovara eat? She was an old woman and thin as a rail but strong and energetic. She only seemed to nibble at the evening meal when they had it and didn't miss it when they did not. She seemed to subsist on nothing but well water and pipe smoke.

Autumn passed in a blur of days. In the first month, she grew thin and wan, but after that, Garren and Raina began to find excuses for her to come to their places at midday, so she went to Garren's bakery or Raina's farm most days, ate, and stuffed her pockets with bread or fruit to ease her midnight hunger. She grew stronger. She'd still never get inside Garren's guard or Raina's, but sometimes she could glimpse a gap in the less-polished technique of Varin or Sunna, on the rare occasions that the priestess joined them. Sunna's presence puzzled her. She was a priestess, and those who trained in the sword hall were as devoted to the dragons as anyone, but they never seemed to have anything good to say about priestesses in general. When Sovara spoke of priestesses, her mouth wrinkled around as if she'd eaten a lemon.

Midwinter came, and Eppie watched the shrine light up from within as the dragons coursed back to the surface, Anara foremost among them with the ambassadress riding on her back.

§

One midday, not long after Midwinter, Eppie found herself peeling onions in Raina's kitchen, the sharp smell of them gouging into her eyes.

"Don't wipe your eyes," Raina warned. "You can't do that in battle."

Eppie nodded. She'd heard the advice more than once before, but she didn't mind the repetition. With Raina, advice came like a comment on the weather, a casual bit of conversation you could take or leave, nothing like the swift strike of Sovara's words in the midst of the real training, or Garren's, for that matter.

Sovara's nagging cough had deepened, and she sent Eppie out to Raina's farm almost every day, even though there was little farm work in winter, with the endless gray skies and rain, sheeting rain, drizzling rain, threatening rain. She sat in Raina's kitchen, helping with the midday meal while it poured down outside.

"Raina?" Eppie said.

"What is it?" Raina rested her spoon on a spot of crusted broth beside the bubbling pot and gave Eppie her full attention.

"When I was out scrapping, there was this one time I just about got jabbed with a knife. I don't know how I could've gotten out of it if the other scrapper hadn't dropped the knife because the watch was coming, but with all these disarming techniques Sovara's been teaching me, I thought I would have figured it out by now."

Raina considered. One of the boys came in from the yard. "That tunic's still too dirty," Raina told him. "Go brush it off again."

"Where did he jab you?" she asked when the boy had gone out.

"Here, near the gut," Eppie pointed.

"And you did what?"

"Scooted back."

Raina pensively picked up a kitchen knife. "That's not a bad first reaction," she said. "Then what?"

"Like I said, he dropped it. I just got my foot out of the way in time, then we all ran off."

"How did he get you, like this, or like this?" Raina illustrated a sideways swipe, and then a jab with the blade up.

"Like that, but with the blade down," Eppie said.

"Well, then, you could..." Raina began. There was a disturbance at the doorway and she set the knife down. A very young man staggered in, his cap and ragged tunic soaked with mud, with tired shadows under his eyes.

"Is this the Gone Duck Inn?" he panted.

"Some call it that," Raina said. "What's your business?"

"I got a message, from a fellow in Tiadun." The young man coughed.

Thorat was in Tiadun. Eppie's heartbeat quickened.

"Come in, then; sit down," Raina said, as if nothing were out of the ordinary. "Eppie, get this young man a cup of water." She took him by the arm and offered him a stool beside the fire. Eppie brought his water while the children peered in from the back porch. Raina shooed them away and refilled the messenger's cup.

"The drake's egg is in the cuckoo's beak,'" the messenger relayed. "I don't know what it means. Some guard, journeyman by the look of him, gave me three big ones to bring you the message, though, so it's gotta be important." He looked around skeptically. "You sure this is the 'Gone Duck Inn'?" he asked.

"Sure as we're having chicken soup," Raina said as if nothing were amiss. "You're in luck, too; it's almost mealtime."

The messenger grinned. "I'd pay three middlings for some stew right about now!"

"It won't be that much," Raina smiled, but her fingers fidgeted with the ladle, and she flicked her eyebrows up at Eppie, jerking her head. "I just need to get another bowl from the larder."

Raina pulled Eppie outside as she went, digging her fingers into Eppie's arm. "Go," she whispered. "Get into the city and tell Sovara and find all the others. Everyone must come tonight."

"Is it Thorat?" Eppie said.

Raina nodded. "Probably. In any case, he's sent word and that means he needs help." Eppie's stomach rumbled. Raina shoved a dry bit of bread into Eppie's hand and shooed her toward the road. "Hurry, now."

Eppie took one last, deep breath, inhaling the smell of the soup she hadn't tasted yet, then pulled her cloak over her head and ran, keeping the old bread tight against her grumbling stomach until she crawled through a culvert and out into the alley behind Garren's shop.

§

Garren told Eppie to go to the temple to get Sunna while he went to Sovara, and he sent her off with a piece of nut bread and an apple, which she downed as she scuttled across the city. The West Market's scrappling gang were still her habitual enemies, but they only scowled at her now rather than blocking her way and starting a fight. She could take any of them now if they came at her one at a time, but three or more would still be hard. They saw the difference in Eppie even though she still dressed more like a scrappling than a respectable apprentice, maybe because she wasn't weaving through the crowds, looking for pockets to pick anymore, and without her own pocket to pick, she was beneath their notice.

She rounded the corner of the fortune-tellers' street and her old home bridge came into view ahead. The canal ran sluggish and brown underneath it and an old bit of brush had washed up just downstream. She could see a bit of ash blowing out from under the bridge, but there was no fire. Surely, it hadn't been abandoned? As she crossed the bridge, she heard a whisper of voices underneath and the sound of someone breaking twigs into kindling. The gate bells rang, announcing the end of the midday rest. Eppie hurried on to the temple's back gate, where a stern old priestess in dark green robes glared at her from the gate house.

"What brings you, scrappling, to our door?" the gate priestess asked.

Eppie didn't correct her. Better that they think she was still a scrappling. "I have a message for the priestess Sunna," she said.

The gate priestess held out her hand. "Give it to me," she said.

Eppie looked wide-eyed at her. "Oh, no," she said. "I have to tell her myself. Talking, you know."

"You should learn to write," the priestess said slowly. "You're of novice age."

Eppie shook her head. It wasn't the season. The priestesses only took novices at Midsummer, didn't they? "I have to tell her myself."

The priestess frowned. "Come inside and wait," she said. She fit her key into the lock and swung the gate open just far enough for Eppie to slip in sideways, then locked it behind her, pocketing the key. The priestess indicated a bench beside the gatehouse, along the wall and sheltered by a narrow tile roof just wide enough to shade the bench in summer or to keep most of the rain off if the wind wasn't gusting. Eppie, dripping, sat down and shivered as she waited, her muscles shaking with the long run. She finished off the nut roll and bit into the apple.

She hadn't been inside the temple's back courtyard since the morning before Midsummer eve, the day when Thorat had taken her by the wrist and propelled her into this new life. Then, the courtyard had been thronged with hungry scrapplings and visiting priestesses in varying degrees of finery, from plain red robes worn at the hem to fine-woven cloaks embroidered with images of their realm dragons. Now, the priestesses were inside, keeping out of the rain. Eppie closed her eyes for a moment, and when she opened them, another red-robed priestess was coming across the courtyard, headed straight toward her. It was not Sunna.

Eppie got to her feet and bowed, a man's bow. When she looked up, the priestess had her lips pressed together in a strained smile, and her eyes crinkled with amusement.

"Sunna's messenger?" the priestess asked.

Eppie nodded. "I need to see her myself. Can't she come?"

"No," the priestess said. "She and I are attending the ambassadress. The ambassadress sent me to fetch you."

"Oh. No." Eppie edged toward the gate.

"Or is your message not so important, then?" the priestess asked.

"It is, but – but I can't go in there. I have to go on. I have other messages to deliver."

"Stay," the priestess said. "The ambassadress wishes to see you. I promise that she will not keep you long."

Eppie peered at her. "You can't promise that, can you?"

The priestess shook her head. "Not quite, but on my honor as Lenasa, princess of Galamun and as a peresi, I swear that you will not be held here against your will."

Eppie made no effort to disguise her doubt.

"I assure you, none of us are."

"You can just leave?" Eppie asked.

"Most choose to stay. There are advantages to being here." She eyed Eppie's ragged clothes.

Eppie looked back at the rainy street outside, to the place where she'd waited for bread so many mornings. "I guess I'll come, as long as you're sure I can go again," Eppie said. "I guess I don't have much choice."

Lenasa of Galamun nodded. "Come then." She led the way into the inner parts of the temple, to places Eppie had never wanted to go. She did not want to go now, either, but Lenasa—out of arrogance, bravado, or some subtle priestessly sense—never so much as turned around to see if Eppie was following, though Eppie kept her footfalls light and nearly silent. She'd learned to walk quietly as a pickpocket, and Sovara had taught her to become more silent still, but the priestess went on as if absolutely confident that Eppie was behind her all the way.

Lenasa led her on through the immaculate temple, past walls painted with dragons, landscapes, flowers, and birds.

Golden lanterns and polished sconces shone. It was dazzling. No wonder so many girls wanted to be priestesses, even though they were trapped in this gilded prison with their hypocrisy and their sweating petitioners. The priestess had seemed earnest in her assertion that they were all free to leave, but if that was true, why didn't they? It couldn't be only the clothes keeping them there, could it? Then again, there was the food, and they had company. Thorat's friends Darna and Myril had left the temple, and Sunna came and went all the time, but they all seemed different, not like the other priestesses with their vacant eyes and fine robes.

The corridors were deserted. Where were they all? Lenasa stopped and waited for Eppie to catch up.

"Wait here." She gestured for Eppie to wait at a nook in the wall, then went ahead and looked around the corner. She waved Eppie forward, ushering her onto a colonnaded walkway surrounding a rose garden with a fountain at its center, then through a gate in the short end of the courtyard. They entered the ambassadress's realm.

Eppie felt the air shift even before she saw the dragonlet. The garden was nothing like the rest of the temple, nor like anything she'd ever imagined. It was neither farmyard nor wilderness, not ornamental either, not like the rose garden just outside its gates. The ambassadress's garden seemed to hold every type of herb in Theranis, growing even in winter, not that Eppie would know them all, but this was far more than she'd ever seen in one place, or possibly all together in her life. She didn't need to be a farmer to see that this was no ordinary garden. A dragonlet sat at the base of the fountain, solid as could be, looking straight at her with its golden eyes. The dragonlet stretched its wings and preened. This was not like the rest of the temple.

"Come," Lenasa urged. She couldn't see the dragonlet; Eppie was sure of it. "Let's not keep the ambassadress waiting. She's ordered tea and cakes for you."

"But I'm not staying!" Eppie said. The dragonlet disappeared. It couldn't want her to stay, could it? Then she saw it again up on the wall, in the direction of what had to be the outside of the temple. Good.

"At least stay for tea," said a clear, bell-like voice. Eppie turned to see who had spoken. She'd been so preoccupied by the garden and the dragonlet that she hadn't looked at the building, which was like a small temple itself, set at the center of the garden. The ambassadress stood on its steps, unmistakable even without her festival finery on, with her clear, pale skin and black hair. Her eyes, though human, carried echoes of the dragons.

"You look just like they say you do," Eppie blurted out.

"Who says?" the ambassadress asked with a gentle smile.

"The minstrels. In the songs." Eppie said.

"Come in out of the rain," the ambassadress said.

Eppie approached cautiously. "Where's Sunna?"

"She's inside," the ambassadress said. "She may yet have to replace me someday, so we've been talking. So few of the younger priestesses can see the dragons these days. Come in."

The walls of the ambassadress's garden surrounded them, and the temple's walls circled those. One more set of walls would make no real difference, and she could smell the tea inside, the hot baked cakes and honeyed scones. Eppie went on up the steps and into the shelter of the porch roof.

Sunna was sitting on a bench inside the building, scowling as usual. "I could have gone out to her," she grumbled. "Before your time, we wouldn't have let anyone in here, not even the other peresi."

"I remember that," Iola said, "but isn't it more important that we all come together, now that there are so very few?" She smiled at Eppie. "What do you think of my dragonlet?"

"It's the garden's dragonlet, not yours, isn't it?"

The ambassadress smiled. "Very good. Come, you must be so cold in those wet clothes. That bench is warm."

Eppie suppressed a shiver and stayed standing just inside the door. The bench was warmed by the heat of the dragons' realm, or else by some other magic she didn't know.

"I can find you a dry, clean tunic," Sunna offered. "Not priestess robes, unless you want them."

"I'll just keep these on," Eppie said. She wrung a drip from the hem of her damp tunic. It was none too clean, and the mud ran onto the white tiles at her feet. She should just get her errand over with and go, before the clean heat lured her in and she forgot the will to leave this place. "You need to come tonight," she said to Sunna. "Thorat's in trouble. I think he needs help."

The ambassadress startled. With sudden clumsiness, she grasped Eppie by the arm. Her touch was very warm. "What trouble?" she demanded, her voice suddenly harsh.

Lenasa was no longer in the garden, as far as Eppie could see. Sunna put a hand on the small of Eppie's back and pushed her the rest of the way through the door into the ambassadress's chamber. It was unimaginably gorgeous. Eppie gawped at the high-domed ceiling while Sunna led her to the dragon-warmed bench and put a cup of tea in her hand.

"Tell me," the ambassadress said.

Eppie looked to Sunna.

"It's all right," Sunna said. "You can tell the ambassadress – at least this one, there's no telling about the next."

Eppie's tea was honeyed and tasted like a summer meadow in the sunshine. She inhaled its steam and drank before answering. "A message came to Raina's, something about a bee... No, wait, that wasn't it. Let me remember."

"Was it about a bird?" Sunna prompted.

"An egg!" Eppie said. "In a cuckoo's beak."

Sunna closed her eyes. "Na save us."

Eppie reached for one of the cakes and ate it whole. It was the most delicious thing she'd ever eaten, even better than festival bread.

"What does it mean?" the ambassadress asked Sunna.

"The cuckoo. Cereans," Sunna said. "And he's worried about them. He's summoning us, as many of us as can come."

"You'd better go, then," the ambassadress told Sunna.

"It's up to the Enatel who goes," Sunna said. "And I'd rather you didn't tell the Aralel anything yet. We don't know enough."

The ambassadress bit her lip and nodded, looking cowed. "Whatever is best for Thorat." Eppie gaped. Sunna, who was always late and not even very good with the sword, had just given the ambassadress, the most honored priestess in the world, an order? How could that be? And the ambassadress looked as if this were quite correct and to be expected.

Then the ambassadress turned to Eppie. "I'd like you to join us in the temple," she said. "You have vision."

"I'm no priestess," Eppie said, practically spitting out the last crumbs of the bun. "I can't. I don't want to."

"We need you here."

Eppie shook her head, even as she reached for one of the small sweets on the tray. "You don't. What would I do here, pick the petitioners' pockets?"

"They don't wear their pockets in," Sunna said.

"They empty them out for us willingly, but of course not," the ambassadress said. "We need you so that you can fly to the dragons when I cannot anymore. There is no one else suitable, except perhaps for Sunna."

"And I'll be too old soon," Sunna said.

Eppie looked around at he luxuriously appointed chamber, the woman sitting in front of her, the sweet in her hand. None of it seemed real. "What makes you think I could do what you do?"

"The oracles have seen you. They've searched for you. So few can see the winged ones now. You must have your part to play."

Eppie shook her head.

Sunna turned to the ambassadress. "The Enatel might not be willing to let her go."

The ambassadress sighed with frustration. "I can hardly persuade her if she won't come to me."

"She doesn't like the temple," Sunna said.

"Neither do I," Eppie said.

The ambassadress reached for Eppie, but then let her hand drop. "Go help Thorat, then. You cannot fiy this year in any case; you're not ready."

The idea of flying to the dragons' realm seemed worlds away from the grasping gate priestesses with their talk of offerings. It seemed closer now that she was sitting across from a woman who had gone there, but no less strange.

Sunna took Eppie by the arm. "Let's go. We can talk about this later."

"I don't think I'll change my mind," Eppie said, but it was so warm and dry in the Ambassadress's realm, not to mention dazzling. If she were asked again if she were hungry or cold or tired, or even if she'd just seen Anara fiy, she might want to go, to become what the ambassadress was, even if it meant being trapped inside the temple.

"You really have to consider it," Sunna said, "but I won't tell you what you need to do, just that it's not all bad." She led Eppie into the private bath chamber attached to the ambassadress's quarters. It was another shockingly beautiful place, but Sunna seemed unaffected by it.

"In here," she said, showing Eppie into one of the small nooks surrounding the bath. She lifted a marble grille from the back of the nook, revealing a narrow, dank tunnel behind it. "You're here now, so you might as well know. If you told anyone, you do know what would happen."

Eppie nodded. "I'd have to take the drink of forgetting."

"And no one wants that," Sunna recited.

The ambassadress watched them from the doorway, leaning against a marble column carved with twining vines.

"Do come back," she said. "And send my love to Thorat."

Then she turned and ran away, into the outer chamber. Eppie thought that she heard a sob, but she wasn't sure.

§

They emerged a short while later onto the banks of the East Canal, somewhere upstream of the bridge. It was still raining, a fact that Eppie had hardly noticed while she was in the ambassadress's domain with its bubble of a roof and the heat of the dragons' realm coming up through the floor.

"You won't be able to get back in that way unless you're invited," Sunna said. "That grate locks from the inside."

Eppie raised an eyebrow. "But someone might be able to pick the lock, wouldn't they?"

Sunna shook her head. "Would you try?"

"No," Eppie said. "But I do wonder why no one ever finds it."

"It's hidden," Sunna said. She gestured to the bank behind them. Eppie could no longer see the opening. "Dragonlets do it, I think. I'm not sure how." Sunna took a deep breath. "You'd better go up to the palace and get Varin. I'll see you back at the training hall."

Some place up beyond the rain and clouds, the sun was setting. Eppie ran through the darkening streets, glad of the temple's food keeping her belly warm even as her sandaled toes grew cold and numb. She reached the palace gates gasping for breath and with her stomach knotting around the hastily eaten meal.

The guard on duty at the gatehouse looked down at her.

"Varin," she said. "He's a guard here. I have a message for him. Can you send him out?"

"Tall, thin fellow?" the guard asked. "Bit of gray in his beard?"

Eppie nodded.

"You got his medicines from the temple?"

Medicines? Eppie thought.

"Uh, no. I just had a message."

The gate guard rang a small bell, and a young serving girl appeared from an inner room. "Take this scrapper to see that young guard what just twisted his ankle," he said. "And make sure he don't steal nothing."

Eppie opened her mouth to protest but thought better of it. It was just as well that the palace guards still thought she was a boy, even if the priestesses could see her for a girl.

The serving girl said nothing as she led the way into a long, low barracks, a warren of semi-partitioned rooms and bunk beds. They looked scarcely more comfortable than the training hall floor, and the building stank worse, of men and sweat. Or rather of more men and more sweat. She found Varin lying on a bench beside a fireplace right at the center of the building, his ankle clumsily bandaged and resting up on a stool.

"Someone here to see you," the serving girl said. She hurried out.

Eppie couldn't see anyone else, but with the low, thin walls of the barracks, anyone might have been listening.

Varin sat up. "Eppie!" He smiled, wincing with pain as his foot slipped off its perch. "Cursed rock in the training grounds turned my ankle. D'you think you could send for a healer priestess?"

Eppie shook her head. "That looks like it hurts, but no, I came with another message. Maybe I should just leave it." She lowered her voice to a whisper. "We all have to meet at the hall tonight. Raina says it's important, a message from Thorat."

"I can't even walk!" Varin said, exasperated.

"Should I send a healer-priestess, then?" Eppie asked. *Sunna?* she mouthed.

Varin nodded. "I'll try. Maybe she could take me to the temple to heal up," he said with a grin.

Eppie rolled her eyes. "I'll send for her, or for one of them, I mean." She looked behind her. "How do I get out of this place?"

Varin gestured in the direction Eppie had come from. "Go more or less straight and out the first door you see. You'll be able to see the main gate from there. And come back with that healer-priestess, would you? I might need someone to carry me."

§

Eppie lumbered up the steps to the training hall with a jug of ale and a loaf of bread on her back and a good-sized pot of stew in her hands. They'd assembled long after dark, and their neighbors around the courtyard took no more notice than usual of their comings and goings. At first, Eppie had wondered why they never pried into the secretive nature of the training hall, but they genuinely seemed not to notice it.

As soon as they were all there, Garren had sent her to get a meal from Ink Pounders, a tavern halfway to the northeast gate. Now she was back. At the top of the stairs, she paused to readjust her load. The night sky shed a dim light, but it was enough to alert her to the sudden change before she plowed headlong into the barred door where the door curtain usually hung. Eppie set down her burden and pushed against it. The way in to the hall was barred from the inside.

Why had they shut her out? Garren hadn't sent her as far as he would have if he didn't want her to come back, and it was an ordinary enough errand. They'd sent her out for dinner other times too, including Midwinter night, when everyone was there. Eppie sat down and tore off a lump of bread. She chewed it, thinking, but she'd eaten so much at the temple earlier that she wasn't even hungry. She climbed up onto the railing and shimmied along a ledge on the outer wall to where she could look through one of the gaps under the eaves. The hall was deserted, silent.

Through the next opening she could see that they'd left the shrine doors open and a fire offering burning. Smoke from the incense clouded the now-familiar yet still breathtaking statue of Anara. It also veiled a black gap in the floor before the shrine, a hole which Eppie had never noticed before. When she thought about it, she did remember that the wood made a square there, but she'd thought that maybe the fire bowl had tipped over, that it had just been replaced. She had a good grip on the sill beneath the eaves, but her toes and fingers were starting to feel the strain of clinging to the wall. As she started to edge back to the landing, she saw Varin emerge from the hole in the floor, leaning heavily on Sunna.

"We'd better open the top," Varin said. "I'm starving."

Sunna rolled her eyes. "Wait until we close the well, at least."

Eppie scuttled back and dropped onto the solid landing just in time to hear Sunna come up the inner stair and lift the bar. Sunna grunted as she pulled the door back to its usual position flat against the wall.

"What are you still huffing for?" Sunna asked her. "I thought you'd be back ages ago."

Eppie didn't answer, but her hands shook as she picked up the pot.

Sunna took it from her. "You go on down," she said. "I'll come back for these things."

Eppie hesitated. "Are they going to send me to the temple?" she asked.

"I doubt it. No one here bows to the ambassadress, apart from Thorat. We need you here, but you're an untried apprentice. There are things you're not ready to know, or to see."

Eppie wondered if that included the hole in the floor, but Sunna kept talking before she could ask.

"There's a lot I don't know, a lot that none of us knows. Right now I want food and ale."

"Hurry up!" Varin called from below. "If I could walk, I'd have gone down to the tavern and been back again already!"

Eppie picked up the ale and bread and hurried after Sunna, her hands no longer shaking.

Inside, the shrine doors had been closed and the Defenders were gathered around the table at the back of the hall. Varin rested on a bench, while the others stood. Sovara paced the length of the hall, back and forth. Raina hurried to help Sunna and Eppie with the stew, and Garren took the bread from her, to set it on the table.

"No oil?" he asked Eppie.

"No, I forgot it."

"I have some in the back," Sovara said. She ducked into her room and rustled around for a while, returning with a glass ewer of remarkably fine workmanship.

"That looks like the ambassadress's own!" Sunna said.

"It's not," Sovara said, and left it at that. "Let's eat."

Sovara, to Eppie's surprise, filled her flagon with ale and sopped up some of the olive oil with a piece of bread. The others followed suit, and no one said anything more until Sovara had finished her bread and tipped the last of the ale down her throat.

"I've heard rumors that the prince of Naramun has been making deals with Cerean traders," she began. "Now Tiadun appears to be, also. We can't be in both places at once."

"We can scarcely even be in one place," Garren said, shaking his head. "I would go to help him, but – "

"Not you," Sovara said. "You need to be here in case something happens to me." She coughed, but she managed to contain it before it made her double over.

"And you can't, not with that cough," Raina said.

"I have to tend the shrine, but you could go," she suggested to Raina.

"Varin would be the logical choice," Garren said. "He's still young enough to make the journey easily, and he was at Lemirun, too."

"But with that injury, you're worse than useless," Sovara said. "What do you say, Raina?"

Raina was quiet for a moment. "I'd have to find a new wet nurse," she said.

"Is your babe still too young to leave?" Sovara said.

Raina sighed. "You've never had little ones."

"I think you might be the best choice even so," Sunna said.

"It might take me a while, maybe a half moon, but by the time Varin is healed up enough to walk, I might be able to. Why don't you go?"

She looked at Sunna, who looked at Sovara, who said nothing.

"I'm supposed to tend the ambassadress. And besides, I'm pregnant."

Sovara struck her jar down onto the table with a thud. Eppie stared at Sunna. Priestesses weren't supposed to get pregnant. As for the Defenders, swordplay hadn't stopped Raina, at least.

"What?" Raina said.

"That was careless of you," Sovara said. "What use –"

"I can still stand watch here at the gate," Sunna said, "and I'll be in the temples and find out what their diviners have to say."

There was a brief silence.

"We should send someone right away," Garren grumbled. "Am I the only one who's able to walk now?"

"At least someone should bring him a charged sword," Sovara said.

Eppie looked up from her bowl of stew. "I could go," she offered. "I could go if you promise to let me back."

Sovara looked at her. "You'll never be ready for the trials if you stop your training now."

"I can start again as soon as I get back."

"*If* you get back," Raina said. "It's too dangerous."

"No more so for her than for the rest of us," Varin said.

Sovara frowned. "She won't have a sword, though."

"I won't?" Eppie said.

"No," Sovara said. "You'll have to carry it but not touch it. You're not ready to handle a charged sword."

"A charged sword?"

"She's not even ready to know what a charged sword is," Sunna said. "But there's another problem with Eppie."

They all turned to look at her.

"It's not her fault," Sunna said, "but the ambassadress wants her for a priestess."

Sovara laughed at that, a strange and unfamiliar sound. "All the more reason to send her. The old hens can't get the girl if she's in Tiadun."

Eppie ventured a question. "Why do you dislike the priestesses so much?"

"I don't mind Sunna, but the Aralel...well, it goes back a long way. We are about the same age." Sovara had a faraway look in her eyes, a younger look. "In any case, I suppose you'll be the one to go, though I can't say I think you're ready."

Eppie teetered on the edge of saying that no, that Sovara was right, that maybe she wasn't ready, that she'd stay. Then, in the back of her head, she remembered how sad the ambassadress had looked, saying, *Send my love to Thorat*, as if her heart were breaking too. Eppie could go, so she would.

§

Chapter 7

That night, Eppie dreamed of Ara, the first priestess, golden and twice as large as life, wrapped in the gauzy red of the peresi. The dream Ara touched Eppie with her silken hand, stroked her until she trembled with desire. "Come to me," Ara said. Eppie looked down at herself and saw that she was robed in Anara's colors, fiowing like the dragon. "Come back to me," Ara said. Eppie felt the temple walls wrap around her like an embrace, enshrining her body with chains of a new hunger. She looked to the distance, to the hills. Was that Enat there, sword in hand, or was it Thorat?

Eppie woke in a sweat as the sky was just beginning to brighten. She took a practice sword down from the wall and swung it in a fiurry of cuts, striving to drive away the ache of longing from the dream. She cut, cut again, more furiously, turned and cut some more, the sword slicing through the morning air in steady, sharp arcs.

Sovara emerged and leaned at the entrance of her nook, watching.

"I had a dream," Sovara said as Eppie raised her sword. Eppie stopped. She held her position and listened to the Enatel. "The dragon Tiada spoke to me in my dream. She said that the land is dry, that you are young, not dry. She thinks that you should come, being young and not dry."

Eppie blushed and let the sword drop, nothing like a proper cut. She set it back on its rack.

"The dragon doesn't know me."

"We've all been to places where the dragon didn't know us. Of course, most of us were older then, or at least better trained. I don't know what good you could do if it came to a pitched battle there. I hope it won't, but the last time it did, only a few of us walked away. Varin was an apprentice then. He was one of them. Maybe the dragons guard apprentices, but I don't know. It's only that there are so few of us."

"It's all right; I'll go."

"I'd rather the priestesses didn't get you, but life is better than death. I wouldn't blame you for changing your mind."

"I don't want...that. I don't want that either," Eppie said, but not as surely as she would have said it the day before, or even just before the dream. Ara called her. No, she wanted to say no, even to Ara herself. If she stayed, and Thorat didn't come back, or if the dragon were killed – if that was even possible – then it would be her fault.

"What would you do if Tiada asked you to stay?" Sovara asked her.

"Do they do that?"

"Not usually, but they rarely speak of apprentices, either," Sovara said. "It will be strange to be without an apprentice again. I think that I may have forgotten how to teach you new ones." It was as close to an apology as she was likely to get. "I'd gotten used to the lack of apprentices; I don't think we looked hard enough for you, to miss you for so many years. I was too wrapped up in my own work, refining my own technique."

Sovara rarely said so much at once. "It's all right," Eppie said. "I've learned a lot."

Sovara shook her head. "The last time we had to defend a gate, the Enatel died. I would go myself – maybe I should – but Tiadun is a long way off, and if both Thorat and I died, there would be no going on."

"What about Garren, and Raina, and the others? I thought that Garren was your...the one who would be Enatel."

Sovara shook her head. "Garren is a good man, a good Defender, but he can't be Enatel. In truth, I was surprised to be chosen over him, but then after I was chosen, it made more sense. People like him too much; he can't go so close to the dragons, even if he isn't blind to them. He used to be a better swordsman than I was, too, but now I can't tell anymore. I'm not sure I should be the Enatel, but I feel now that I need to stay alive until Thorat is ready. I'd like for you to stay out of the fight, but try to keep him alive, too."

"I will if I can."

Sovara ducked back into her nook and came out a little while later, carrying a long dagger.

"You're making progress with your sword work, but you're not ready to refine it on your own," she said. "Besides, carrying a practice sword would slow you down and make you more conspicuous. This knife will have to do. You've done some knife practice, maybe enough that having a handy blade is better than going empty-handed."

She also got Eppie a bag, a flint box, and a heavy string of beads. She belted the knife around Eppie's hips and stuffed a spare tunic into the bag, then took the last of the bread from the night before and threw that in on top. She took Eppie by the shoulder and led her out the door.

Eppie felt a sudden panic rise in her gorge at the thought of leaving Anamat. She froze on the threshold of the training hall and looked back.

Sovara shrugged. "We all have to go out there, sooner or later; it's just that for you, it's sooner. I'll ask Tiada to let you return and hope she can hear me."

That wasn't much reassurance. Out on the street, Sovara turned into a hidden passage that Eppie had never found before. Sovara looked like a limping old lady, but she quickened her pace there just as she did on the training floor, making Eppie jog to keep up.

The city streets were quiet and foggy in the early morning. The roads out of Anamat would be cold and still mostly empty this time of year, hard walking with no fellow travelers to share the watch for bandits in the mountains. The dark city felt comfortable and reassuring against that prospect. They came to the back of the swordsmiths' hall, still quiet with the sleep of night.

"Wait here," Sovara said as she slipped in through a back door. Soon, she returned with a sleepy master swordsmith at her side.

"We need to have the sword on its way as soon as possible," Sovara said.

The master swordsmith nodded. "It's just emerged, in back. You should have a look at it before you carry it all across the land."

"Sovara said for me not to touch it at all," Eppie said.

"If you see it first, you won't have to go poking around to satisfy your curiosity. Come." He led them into the workshop. In a back alcove, the sword lay on a smooth wooden table. A massive gong hung beside it on ropes fading into the rafters. The sword was as good as Sovara's but newly forged.

Out of the corner of her eye, Eppie saw Sovara nod her approval. She felt irresistibly drawn to the sword.

"Don't," Sovara warned. "You'll have your own in time if all goes well." If all didn't go well, having a sword like this would be the least of her worries.

Sovara and the swordsmith stood on either side of the weapon. Sovara touched a burning ember to a bowl of incense and fanned its smoke over the sword. Together, Sovara and the swordsmith murmured an incantation. They sounded the gong, and as the sound resonated through the hall, they slipped the sword into a fitted sheath that they wrapped in plain linen, followed by a blanket of coarse wool.

"There she sits, there she rides," the swordsmith said.

Sovara handed the bundle to Eppie while the swordsmith fashioned a leather carrying strap and wrapped it on over the blanket.

"Remember, leave it wrapped until you give it to Thorat," Sovara warned again. "And send Thorat our regards, our best wishes, and any news you can give." They were walking out through the torchlit workshop now, back out into the early dawn. The sky had brightened only slightly, and the streets still slept.

"All right, off you go." Sovara shooed Eppie out the door with a crack in her voice and a gentle push.

Eppie strode off into the morning fog, one foot in front of the other.

§

As she walked out of the city's gates, she felt a strange feeling come over her: liberty. She had a knife at her belt, a sword on her back, and a pocket full of beads. The watchmen fell away behind her, the ones who had dogged her every move for more than three and a half years, always hoping to catch her red-handed. She had slipped past them all, and now only the empty open road stretched ahead of her, and an errand to the far reaches of Theranis.

She'd scarcely been outside the city's bounds since she first arrived, when she was so much younger. The farthest she'd been was Raina's farm and the city dump. Anamat had become her whole world since she'd come in from a little village on the border between Coradun and Lemirun. It was in the mountains, near Na's country. Eppie had been a second-born daughter, and so condemned to go to Anamat. People in the village talked as if it were such a curse to leave that place, rather than a blessing. She hadn't missed that village once since her very early days in the city, when she hadn't yet figured out how to win her daily bread, how to pick pockets, and how to stay out of sight.

Here on the road, there was hardly anyone to even see her, no need to creep through shadows and alleyways. Before she was halfway across the valley, she found herself whistling a sea chantey she'd learned long before, and a shepherd's tune after that. At nightfall, she found a tavern and bedded down in the barn out back. In the morning, she set out once more, and if she felt a little lonely, the sadness was only a distant counterpoint to the thrill of setting out to see more of the world, escaping the walled confines she hadn't even realized were holding her back. A few oxcarts rumbled past her on the road, headed toward Anamat. Beyond a nodded greeting, she ignored them. She bought bread, cheese, and dried fruit in the last village before the mountains and slept that second night in a small lean-to behind the border shrine on the edge of Galamun.

She crossed Galamun in two more days without incident, and on the sixth day, she reached a crossroads in Getedun at dusk. She slept under a dense bush there and in the morning filled her waterskin at the spring. She crossed out of Getedun into the mountains, leaving a token offering at the border shrine when she paused there at midday. She hadn't seen Getera, but she did spot a dragonlet darting into the rocky barren lands near the border.

She expected to reach the border of Tiadun well before sunset, but this spur of mountains was broader and steeper than the ones she'd traversed so far, from Anamat to Galamun and from Galamun to Getedun. Dusk found her in a rocky, dry crevasse with no water or shelter in sight. An owl cried out. She knew that it was only an owl, but it spooked her as if it were the voice of travelers gone by, a ghost waylaid by bandits.

On Eppie's way to Anamat, in her thirteenth summer, she'd met a band of bandits, toothless women and filthy men with animal pelts for clothes, who seemed never to have heard of spinning and weaving. They'd called out from the cliffs above, inviting her to join them, saying that in Anamat she would find only sorrow, hunger, and corruption, that theirs was the pure way of the dragons, and that she would come to them at last. The oldest of the women, gnarled beyond ordinary aging, had cackled after her, "Come to us, dearie, and see Na, the greatest dragon, face to face!"

Eppie had run. She'd only seen Corana up until then, but she'd heard that Na was no friend to humankind, though maybe Na favored these wild men and women with their pelts and their weathered faces. They had all looked very old indeed to her young eyes, old and frightening.

Now, with the sun gone down over the peaks and the sky getting darker, she thought of them again. The moon was a long way off from full, and she didn't know for sure if she was any closer to Tiadun than she'd been at midday. Perhaps she'd wandered off the path and into Na's country, bandits and all. The trail was broad enough, but it was rocky, and the ravine the road ran through was getting dark. There was a bit of vegetation on the slopes above, so when Eppie found a narrow track leading up, she climbed it to see if she could get a view of what lay ahead.

She found a small ledge partway up the slope, a comfortable-looking spot of grass just about big enough for a house cat to curl up on. It might have served as a decent perch in broad daylight, but it was far too small and narrow to serve as a bed. What's more, it seemed to be the terminus of a narrow path leading further up into the mountains. Eppie readjusted the sword on her back, took a last swig of the water she'd taken at the crossroads that morning, and followed the trail a little farther.

From the top of the ridge, Eppie could see the dusky land sloping away in all directions. To the west, it flowed up into the sunset, into the heart of Na's country. To the southeast, it reached down, the mountaintops narrowing into a point that jutted out into the sea. Behind her, to the north, Eppie saw the green forests of Getedun, its pines lush even in late winter. Ahead, to the south, lay Tiadun.

Tiadun, Eppie presumed, was a province like any other. She'd seen Coradun and the border of Lemirun in her youth, and in the past few days, she'd traversed Galamun and Getedun. Anamat was different, not a province but the center of the world. As she looked down at Tiadun, she felt a strange stir in the wind, a ripple in the light over the south-sloping fields. She felt that she could sense its soul, that she could feel the presence of Tiada the dragon, as alive as Anara. As she watched, the sunset clouds rippled, wings breaking through them. The dragon flew, her body orange in the sunset sky, her blue wings stretching up to the emerging stars.

Eppie was so entranced by the distant winging dragon that she didn't hear the man approach until the rope was tightening around her neck.

She pushed her hands up and threw it off, whipping around to face her attacker.

"Quick," the man said. "You'd be good in a fight."

Eppie backed away, wary of the steep slope behind her. "What's it to you?"

"Where are you going?" The man was a bandit, dressed in furs, just like the ones Eppie remembered from her long-ago trek to the city. She would have been able to tell that he was a bandit even if she couldn't see him, from the reek of him.

"I'm not staying here," she said.

A woman appeared on the path below, blocking Eppie's return to the main trail.

"I say you are," she said.

"I got a package to deliver to Tiadun Keep," Eppie said. She drew the hunting knife out of her belt and let it rest in her hand, hoping that the sight of it would be enough to discourage the bandit man from laying hands on her again.

"Don't be taking the dragons' magic to their enemies," the bandit woman said.

"Who said anything about the dragons' enemies?" Eppie wondered if she could push past the woman. She might be able to manage it, but these were the first people who had surprised her in years – apart from Sovara, and from Thorat when he'd caught her – and certainly the first on her journey to sense the sword's magic.

"They're all enemies of the dragon, down there at the keep," the man said. "The prince worships that eagle-headed god from Enomae, his brother is fallen in with Cerean philosophies. There isn't a good man among them."

Eppie looked in the direction of Tiadun Keep, but she could scarcely make it out now in the falling dark.

"You won't get there tonight, anyways," the man bandit said. "Sup with us."

The two bandits flanked her, so Eppie let them lead her farther along the path. In the dark and unfamiliar terrain, she probably wouldn't get far before they caught her again. After a short walk, the trail arrived at a bowl in the mountains, a small, grassy valley with a spring at its southeastern edge. It looked like about half a dozen bandits were camped there, all gathered around a fire with a spitted roast cooking over its coals.

"Welcome to Na's knee," the woman bandit said. "You'll stay here the night. We'll keep you safe from the prince's men."

"I'm not worried about the prince's men," Eppie said.

"You should be," the man said. "Shouldn't she?"

One of the forms around the fire laughed. "Should," he said. There was something odd about him. Even in the gathering dusk, his stare looked wall-eyed. Eppie edged away.

"Don't mind him; that's just Forlan," the woman said, taking Eppie by the arm and bringing her forward again. "He had the drink of forgetting. Not much use now."

The lumpish man called Forlan made a grunt. Eppie forced a bit of a smile. How did these bandits know about the drink of forgetting? The madman didn't seem hostile, only unhinged, unpredictable.

"I'm Vigda," the woman said. "Once a priestess, never again, not in the lowlands. What's your name?"

"Eppie. And I've no plans to be a priestess anywhere."

Another of the men around the fireplace spoke. "She see Tiada in the sunset?"

"She did," said the man who'd stopped her on the trail.

"How could you tell?" Eppie asked, startled.

"Kendet there can tell. We don't like the dragon-blind walking in our hills."

Eppie edged away, even though she had mostly given up on the idea of fleeing. The bandits were bigger and stronger than she was, and they knew the terrain. She was also just a bit curious. "Isn't nearly everyone dragon-blind?" she asked.

"Down below, yes," Vigda said. "But you're in Na's country now, and we've a leg of mutton. Come and eat."

The offer of hot food was too good to turn down, especially with night closing in. She hadn't had a really hot meal since the night before she'd left Anamat. The tavern stews were always tepid, and though the bread on the road was tolerably good, it was not hot leg of mutton. Vigda passed Eppie a drinking skin full of wine that she put it to her lips. She didn't drink, though; she was still too wary for that.

"You're too old for a scrappling," said one of the men.

"I've been to Anamat, been there for years," Eppie said. "Plenty of scrapplings as old as I am these days."

"And you're carrying some magic," Vigda said. "Doesn't smell like priestess magic, though."

"I don't know," Eppie said. "I just got a job to carry this where it's going."

"If you give dragons' magic to the foreigners, Tiada will find you and rip you in her claws," the man said.

Eppie considered the distant form of Tiada she'd lately seen on the horizon. "It's not for foreigners. Besides, I'm just a messenger."

"Let her be, Larn," Vigda said. "Now let's have our meat."

As the bandits portioned out the roast, Eppie wondered if the dragon would attack a person for such a betrayal. She'd never heard of it happening, and perhaps that was why the foreigners were coming in now. She wondered too what Vigda believed the dragon could do, but they were all dealing in half-truths around the fire. They were wary of her, too. She sure wasn't going to tell them about the ceremony with Sovara and the sword maker. That could have imparted magic, but the magic in the blade, if there was any, must also have been something in the process of making it, something she truly didn't know. The important thing was that she had to get it to Thorat without touching it herself, and without letting anyone else get a good look at it, either.

Eppie and the bandits fell to eating as the night darkened. The wine skin went around again and again, and none of them seemed to notice or care that she didn't drink. Larn, who appeared to be the leader of the group – unless Vigda was – licked his fingers noisily as he polished off the last of his piece of meat.

"Now, girl, a song for your supper!" he said.

Eppie was still eating. "I can't sing," she said through a full mouth.

"Sure you can sing better than Forlan there," the other bandit said. His name was Gran, and he was a little younger than the others. "Anyway, that's the price, so you've got to do it."

Eppie swallowed her meat down and at last took an actual swig of the weak and acidic wine. A song, badly sung, was a price she could pay willingly. She'd thought they would ask for other things and was glad that they hadn't, at least not yet.

"I only know the Ballad of Ara and Enat, and a few sea chanteys," she said.

The bandits muttered among themselves.

"Let's see what you make with Ara and Enat, then," Larn said.

Eppie cleared her throat and began to sing.

The Ballad of Ara and Enat was well known, one of the first songs taught to apprentice minstrels, who came into their trade knowing one version of it or another, as most people did. During the Midsummer festival, the new minstrels came out to show off what they'd learned in their first apprentice year, and the full version of the ballad could be heard on every street corner. Some, bombarded with rotten produce, never returned to try their hand at loftier ballads, and left for other guilds or lesser work. Others either put in a better showing or were immune to the discouraging thwack of spoiled peaches. Later verses of the song told of Ara fleeing into the hills to follow her dragons, and Enat following, begging to be at her side. Eppie had heard it a hundred times or more, but she really didn't sing much, and she stumbled over the words and the high trilling part at the end of the chorus. She was worse than the worst of the apprentice minstrels, but she'd given them no illusions that she'd be better.

As her voice slid into the final note, the bandits raised a muted chorus of appreciation.

"An honest try," Vigda said after they'd quieted.

Larn grunted and turned to Eppie. "So, what do you think? Did Enat really follow Ara into the hills, or was he just looking for dragons too?"

"Well, I don't know," Eppie said. "I mean, I always thought he was following her. That's what the song says."

"Or does it?" asked the one called Kendet. "Just think on that."

Eppie had a reply half-formed, but a sudden need to yawn interrupted her thoughts. She shook her head.

"Leave her be," Vigda said. "Can't you see the poor girl's tired from all her walking?"

"I'm all right," Eppie said. "I s'pose it was a long walk today, though."

"Rest up, then," Larn said. "We'll talk more in the morning."

Eppie dimly wondered what there was to talk about as she lay down, wrapping herself in her cloak. Through her half-closed eyes, she could hear the bandits arguing.

"I wouldn't follow any priestess," one of the men said.

"Ah, but it was Ara, and they say she was devoted to him."

"Nonsense. A priestess can't devote herself to a man. She's a dragon's creature or nothing, and if there's one thing we know, it's that Ara was a true priestess."

"And that there are none anymore."

"Unless the ambassadress is."

"Sure as I once served Tiada, you'd never make it past the gate priestess up there in Anamat to find out, not none of you."

"As if we'd try. Those city priestesses are as bad as the Cereans say."

There was more grumbling, but before they said much more, Eppie was fast asleep.

§

Eppie woke with a start, her bladder bursting and her feet half numb with cold. She heard a loud snore from one side. The bandits had all fallen asleep around what was left of their fire. Far away, the eastern sky was brightening, and it was bitterly cold.

Her first thought was to go to the bushes and attend to her call of nature, but the nearest stand of bushes was halfway across the valley, a short distance downhill from the far side of the camp. She gathered up her cloak, belted on her knife, and only then noticed that her bundle, the precious sword, had slipped out of her reach.

Or maybe "slipped" wasn't the right word. It had been taken. She picked up her sandals and tiptoed as lightly as she could around the slumbering, snoring bandits, all reeking of sweat and wine, not to mention their unwashed furs. They would not waken if she slipped away now, alone, but she had not been a thief on Anamat's streets for three years only to let bandits steal the first thing of value that had been entrusted to her.

Vigda and Larn lay beside each other under a single fur cloak. Eppie crouched and peered closely at the cloak as Larn's snoring breath carried it up and down. Yes, there was something between the two of them, tightly guarded. She collected her wits, focusing her mind on this one task—to slip a hand in between the two bandits and to come back out unfelt, holding the object that now lay between them.

An owl hooted. These mountains were lousy with owls. Vigda rolled closer to Larn, mumbling incoherently, sleep-talking. Eppie stuck her cold hand in her armpit to warm it. When Vigda had stilled again, Eppie crept forward and wormed her hand in as gently as a whisper. She took hold of the sword – still in its familiar wrappings – and drew it out again. She had only just tucked it under her cloak when Forlan sat up and looked straight at her.

"Where ya going?" he asked with a yawn. He seemed more awake, more aware of what was happening around him than he had the night before. He still wasn't quite right, but the wine had worn off.

Eppie shrugged and gestured toward the bushes.

"Awlright," he said, lying down again. "Jus' don' go too far."

Eppie nodded. "I won't," she whispered. Nowhere was too far, as far as she was concerned.

She scurried to the spring and ducked behind the first bush she came to. Looking out through the leaves, she could see all of them still lying there around the fire, their gentle chorus of snores floating up into the gray morning air. Forlan had turned away from her. His blanket rose and fell in a gentle, sleepy cadence as if he had not woken at all. With any luck, he wouldn't remember that she'd spoken to him.

Eppie filled her waterskin, then followed the frigid stream downhill. When it crossed a path, she turned back in the general direction of the main road from Anamat. Although she looked back over her shoulder at every turn and every long straight stretch, too, she neither heard nor saw signs of pursuit all morning. She wondered if they were still sleeping, if they were letting her go, or if they were following, hoping to catch her unawares when she slept. She came to a village shortly before midday, and the taverner there told her that it was only a day's walk to the keep, but too late already to make the distance before nightfall. Eppie bought a meal from him and begged a place to sleep in the hayloft. She slept through the evening and the first part of the night, setting out again at dawn before the village woke.

§

Chapter 8

The last stage of the walk to Tiadun Keep led through farmland and small villages made up of thatched houses in moderate repair, their gardens roughly turned under in preparation for the spring planting. Eppie kept her head down, trudging along under the light gray skies.

The keep stood on a small hill beside a broad, open bay, with the small town spilling down the slopes around it. There were slate- and thatch-roofed houses, a water mill, and the chimney of a smithy. All in all, it was probably about the size of one of Anamat's market neighborhoods. Down by the harbor, Eppie spotted a long, new building like the merchants' warehouses back in Anamat. Even from the road, she could see the headdresses of the Cerean and Enomaean sailors lounging under its eaves, with their boats rocking on the bay.

Thorat's message had hinted that there would be Cereans, but it jarred her to see so many of them in the hinterlands of Theranis. Foreigners were supposed to stay in Anamat's merchants' quarter. Eppie entered the town, willing herself to look as small as possible, but she needed to present herself at the keep's guardhouse to find Thorat. She straightened her back and walked up to it, hoping that she didn't look too ragged to be allowed in.

"State your business," said the guard on duty there. He was big but sleepy and inattentive.

"I got a message for a guard here," Eppie said, in a nervous, childish voice. "Name of Thorat."

The guard yawned. "That new fellow from last Midsummer?"

"I don't know," Eppie said.

"If you're bringing an offer from another prince, you can save your breath. The prince wants to keep him right here."

"No, no, it's just news from...of his family," Eppie said, inventing it as she went along.

"If that's so, he's out on patrol in the town now. He'll be at the evening meal. You might as well wait in the kitchens. Go 'round that way."

He pointed her around the keep wall. She considered going back out to look for him, but the day was growing late already and she was hungry again.

As she rounded the first sharp corner of the keep's outer wall, she was surprised by the sight of a temple porch. She could see a priestess waiting in the shadowed doorway, watching. Eppie scurried past, looking back once. Yes, that was the temple, or at least the keep's shrine, but it seemed out of place there in the street. She'd never been in a keep town, but she'd heard that the provincial princes liked to have their towns' priestesses within keep walls. These weren't, not quite.

She smelled the kitchen before she saw it, the odor of onions and grease blowing out over the town. She entered the scarcely guarded back gate and soon found the servants' mess hall, where she sat down to wait.

A moment later, someone shouted at her.

"Hey, there!"

Eppie jumped up, so startled that she almost toppled the bench. She turned to face the person who'd shouted at her. She couldn't believe her eyes. It looked like Squid, of all people.

"Eppie? That *is* you!"

"Squid?" she said. "What are you doing here?"

"I should ask you that, I've been here for ages, since just after Midwinter. I got traded to this Cerean crew, and they've been down at the harbor, but I mostly sit around here at the keep to see what's going on, report back to the captain, that kind of thing. Besides, food's better here. I can't say I like Cerean sailor food yet."

Eppie sat back down and narrowed her eyes at the boy she'd shared a fire with for three years. He looked different. Had sailing for the past half-year changed him so much? "You're a spy for the foreigners?" she asked.

Squid shrugged. "More of an interpreter, kind of a translator, but I guess you could call it that." He reached for the bundle on her back. "What you got there?" he asked. "Looks like a sword."

"I –" Eppie stammered. "I – D'you remember how I said I got that servant job?"

"Sure. You're not still doing that, are you?"

"Well, the lady I was working for, her nephew's a guardsman here and his...he inherited this from his father. I'm just delivering it, then I go back to Anamat." Even naming the city seemed to bring it closer, as did Squid. She felt a wave of homesickness.

Squid looked away. "I don't know when I'll see Anamat again. You should see Calandria, though; that's the big city in Enomae. It's twice as big as Anamat, maybe three times. It's got all white marble, all the way down to the docks, not just the temples, and it's – Well, it's a sight to see. D'you really want to go back to boring old Anamat?"

"Anamat's not boring," Eppie said, "but the walk here sure was." She had to say that something was boring, to match Squid's world-weariness. It was just the provinces, after all.

"Come down to the shore with me," Squid said. "You can deliver your message later, or maybe my captain would buy that sword you're carrying for more than they're paying you, if it's a good one. He'd probably like you if you weren't a girl."

Eppie detected a trace of a grimace.

"He might like you even so," Squid added quickly. "And better for me. I get a bonus for brining on more sailors."

"What, can't he keep them?"

Squid looked toward the outer door. "Say, what ever happened to that, um, that interesting thing you picked up last Midsummer?"

Eppie had to think to realize what he was talking about the prince's seal. She could hardly admit that she'd let it be returned to its rightful owner.

"I hid it," she said.

She was spared from further interrogation by the arrival of small patrol of guardsmen, followed by a pair of serving girls carrying a loaded bread board.

"Out of here, boy!" one of the maids said to Squid. "Get your masters to feed you."

Squid fiashed her his most charming smile. "Ah, but I'm here now, and your bread is fresher." He said it lightly and raised his eyebrows. He made as if to pinch the maid's bottom, which she whisked out of his reach, getting a chuckle from one of the guardsmen. Even the affronted maid smiled. Eppie had forgotten how charming he could seem, especially with the new scrapplings, how they always wanted to follow him around. She'd been immune to it for years, she'd thought, but now she wondered.

Eppie spotted Thorat out of the corner of her eye. He was at the back of the group of guardsmen, looking tired and less well kempt than he'd been at Midsummer. He saw Eppie, and for one unguarded moment, he relaxed and almost smiled, then he shook his face back into an apathetic scowl, mirroring the weary expressions of his fellow guardsmen. He looked right past her. Eppie stood to let the guardsmen take their places. She waited until Thorat sat, then tapped him on the shoulder.

"Excuse me, sir," she said.

"Yes?" he said, looking rather blankly at her.

"Sir, I have a message for you, from your aunt."

He knitted his brow, as if puzzled. "From my aunt, you say?"

Eppie took the package from her back. "She says you've inherited this," Eppie said.

"This?" Thorat said, taking the sword from her. "But what of the house? What about the farm?" He'd set the wrapped sword down on his lap as if it were of no interest to him.

Eppie shook her head, genuinely befuddled. "I don't know. I s'pose you'd have to go find out yourself."

The serving maid plunked a bowl down in front of Thorat. "You want me to bring some for your messenger?" she asked him.

"I've come a long way," Eppie said hopefully. She could see that the maid was eager to have her out from underfoot, dusty as she was and lacking Squid's charm.

Thorat gave the maid a nod and gestured for his companions to make room for Eppie on the bench. They did so, but in such a way that she had to sit two men down from Thorat, making any conversation impossible, and the maid went off to get another bowl, looking unhappy with the extra guest. Another group of guardsmen ambled in, filling up the rest of the benches. Squid, bowl of soup in hand, came up behind Eppie.

"Eat your grub, then come on down and see the ships with me," he invited. "It's a grand sight."

"Sure," Eppie said. She turned her attention to the bowl and bread in front of her and ate, making herself as small as she could between the armed guardsmen around her.

"Is that a sword?" Thorat's neighbor asked.

"This?" Thorat said. "If you can call it that. It was my father's. I don't know why they'd have sent it to me unless my older brother were gone, but I heard nothing of that."

"Your older brother get the farm, then?" one of the other men asked sympathetically.

"That's what I always expected," Thorat said. "It's why I'm here soldiering, like anybody."

That statement was greeted with general nods.

"But my brother should have gotten this sword, too. It's not much of one, just a farmer's sort of a sword."

"Aren't you going to open it up and look?"

"No need," said Thorat.

Eppie marveled that he could be so dismissive of it. He knew that what was inside was no crude farm implement, but his carelessness of it, and of her, seemed to dissuade his fellow guardsmen's halfhearted curiosity.

"What I'd like to know is if I'll need to turn farmer," Thorat said.

"That'd be a waste; you're a fine swordsman."

"I wouldn't mind having a house of my own."

"The guard captain wouldn't like you to leave now, with all this going on."

"With all this going on, I'd rather keep my skin safe on a nice quiet farm in the north!" Thorat said. "I have all my limbs and I don't mind keeping them. I think I'll take my leave."

"You can't," said one of the men.

"Of course he can," said a smooth-voiced man who appeared to be the leader of their patrol. "That's the law. If a man has a farm, he must farm it."

"And if he thinks he might, he'd best get there before planting season is come and gone," said another man. They'd all grown up on farms; most people did.

The others nodded and gave affirmative grunts. Thorat downed his stew and got up from the table. "I'm off to give my notice!" he said cheerily, then swept out of the room, ignoring Eppie, with the precious sword dangling from his hand as if it were worthless.

§

Thorat held the sword as casually as he could manage under the table, but if any of the men had so much as a whiff of vision, they would spot it for what it was. He ate his soup quickly, ignoring Eppie and hoping that the other guardsmen would take no notice of her either. Why had they sent *her,* of all the people in Anamat? She needed training, not to be sent out into the hinterlands to face foreign incursions and maybe even a battle. If she was slaughtered, it would be his fault. He should have sent for Ferrent, who at least knew his way around with a sword. He was still only one province away in Kiralun. He could be summoned, but not to the keep, not with Calar still looking for him.

As Thorat took his leave, he noticed that the Cereans' young Theranian informer had been staring at Eppie, staring as if he expected something of her. He hadn't known the girl long, and he hoped that she would be sensible enough to avoid that boy and his employers. He left them anyway. He had to pretend that she was only a messenger who meant nothing to him, and that the sword Sovara had sent meant little more.

Normally, Thorat went through the inner part of the keep to get back to the barracks, but a man who'd inherited a farm would ordinarily make a visit to the temple to give thanks. He didn't have enough beads or Cerean gold to pay for the Great Rite, but now he had a reason to give a small thanks offering at the temple. Besides, he wanted to talk to the priestesses before he left. They kept to themselves and made a desultory showing at public occasions, two pale women who seemed resigned to their displacement. None of the men from the barracks went to them, preferring to visit some of the townswomen they met in the tavern, or to take up with the serving girls in the keep. Although the prince had not forbidden the worship of the dragons, anyone could see that it was frowned upon, and Thorat was trying to pass unnoticed as much as possible. Besides, he didn't sense the dragon's presence in Tiadun Keep or in its sad remnant of a temple.

Now he climbed the broad, hastily constructed stair to the temple porch. The steps were already going out of plumb, with crooked gaps showing between the marble facing stones. They'd been swept but not well, and ashes and dirt dulled their polish already. The curtain across the entryway was tattered at the hem and its dragons faded as Tiada herself.

Thorat sounded the bell and waited. At length, a priestess came, the younger of the two. She was about Thorat's own age. She looked distracted.

"What brings you, petitioner, to our gates?" she asked fiatly.

"I come to give thanks to Tiada for my inheritance, and to ask her blessing on my journey."

The priestess nodded and ushered him in. She held out a hand for beads.

"I don't have enough for the Great Rite," Thorat said.

"No?" The priestess looked suddenly more awake. "Then why come?"

"To give thanks to the dragons for their bounty."

"Oh. I see. Come through to the hall, then," she said. "We had a public shrine there, and it's still there."

A narrow corridor led past two small offering chambers and around an empty bath, which was not fed or heated by the dragon's springs, and thus rarely used. The older of the two priestesses looked out from her chamber, and the younger one nodded to her.

"Blessed one," the younger priestess said. "Bring cakes and wine for the offering."

The other priestess gave Thorat a quick look-over, then went to get the cakes.

In the dusty hall, now at the back of the temple, Thorat took his place before Tiada's shrine and said his silent prayer. The tapestry honoring Farseer hung just on the other side of the wall, the foreign god's bloody altar set up where the priestesses should have danced. The dragons were not bloodthirsty, even if they did sometimes take sheep who wandered away on their upper pastures.

The older priestess returned, so Thorat left a few beads on the altar and went to take wine with the priestesses.

The younger one seemed tongue-tied, but at least the older one remembered what was supposed to be said to a lesser petitioner.

"Is there anything you would ask of the dragons?"

"The blessing on my journey, and..." Thorat looked between the two of them. They would be unlikely to say anything about his requests, even in a lesser temple like this. Priestesses were a secretive lot. "I would like for Tiada to show herself to me," he said.

"But you've only been here since Midsummer!" the older priestess exclaimed. "No one has seen Tiada in years. I saw her in my youth, but not in many years."

Thorat turned to the younger priestess. "And you?"

She shook her head. "I saw her when I was a child, I think, and dragonlets, at least before I came to the temple here, but that was years ago."

"And not in the town, never in the town," the older priestess said with a sigh. "Tiada shuns this keep, even before

Farseer came –" She made a warding sign. "Even when only the Cerean tutors were here, she did not bless the prince."

"Shh!" the younger priestess said. "The princelings will be here."

"They are not princelings," said the older priestess. "They are only his nephews. They do not rule us yet, even if they'd like to, no more than we rule them."

They both looked at Thorat. Maybe they weren't so good at keeping their petitioners' secrets. They didn't look at the sword that Thorat held across his lap. He could feel its power stir, but only dimly, so very, very dimly, and the priestesses clearly couldn't sense it at all.

A knock sounded on the wall.

"What's that?" Thorat asked.

The older priestess put a finger to her lips then beckoned him to follow her. "Your audience is over," she said as they hurried back to the makeshift entryway. "Blessings of the Great Ones go with you."

Thorat hoped that she'd at least meant to say her abrupt blessing with some sincerity, even if she was no longer sure that Tiada existed. He was beginning to doubt it himself.

§

Eppie polished the last drops from her bowl with her bread crust. Thorat's snubbing of her had been very convincing, so convincing that she wondered if he'd been feigning at all. At first, she'd thought that he had only been trying to diffuse any interest in her or the sword, but then she wasn't sure. In any case, the other men ignored her, not counting Squid. When she'd dallied all she could stand to, she got up and went out through the kitchen. Smoky torches gave the keep kitchen a gloomy feel despite the bustle of maids coming and going. Outside, it was getting dark.

"Excuse me, miss," Eppie said to one of the maids. "I'm just a messenger, but I need a place to bed down for the night."

The maid narrowed her eyes at Eppie. "You with that boy who's with the foreigners?"

Eppie shook her head. "No, it's just that I met him before, in Anamat," she said. "Didn't know he was here. I'm just a messenger, and not for the foreigners, either. What do they want here, anyway?"

The maid gave her head a little shake and swatted at the air. "It's no business of mine," she said. "You can bed down in the barn, but try for the end over the oxen. Those Enomaean boys are over the horses, and I wouldn't trust them around my little sister, and I dare say she's nearly as tough as you."

Eppie mumbled her thanks as the maid hurried away. She didn't know how to find her way through the keep, so she went back out the way she'd come, hoping that the front gate wasn't closed.

Squid was waiting for her at the kitchen door.

"Took your time," he said.

"I was hungry," Eppie said. "Getting the lay of the land, too. What do you know about this Enomaean god?"

Squid hurried her away from the kitchen before he answered, down through the seaward side of the town, where a few houses stood close together on the short side of the hill. The foreigners' new warehouse was on flat area down near the shore. It was so new that Eppie could smell the fresh-cut pine of its planks.

"No one on my ship gives much blood to Farseer," Squid said as they cleared the last house. "They're mostly Cereans, and they have an altar back in Calandria where they give gold. That's all their Cerean god cares about, gold, though they say that dragon stones are just as good, maybe better. That's why they're here."

"But the stones belong to the land."

"And who does the land belong to?" Squid said. "The prince, right? The prince's brother, who's next in line for the throne anyway, says that the prince can trade whatever he likes."

"But did the priestesses agree?" Eppie asked.

Squid laughed. "You're so up to your neck in Anamat that you can't even see how none of these men even go to the priestesses except like they're going to a whore. They don't care what their women say. In Cerea, only men can sacrifice gold to the god, one light face and one dark face, he has, the two-sided god, they call him, and they don't even give him a name. They have a whole philosophy, they call it, whole schools which are like their temples to keep the god's light face on them and turn his dark face to their enemies. In case you wondered, that's us, the two-faced god's enemies. The dragons too, if there's anything left of them."

Squid seemed not to notice Eppie's stony silence as he babbled on.

"I got a coin about the god when I joined this ship; the navigator gave it to me for luck. It's worked so far, only one hungry night and then a big feast the next morning to make up for it. I tell you, you should join on."

"But Squid, I'm a girl," Eppie pointed out. "It didn't matter on the streets of Anamat, not the way we lived, but surely the Cereans would notice. You said that was no good to them."

They were coming up on the warehouse now. A bright torch burned at the corner. Squid gazed at Eppie in its light. "I won't forget that now. We were friends, right?"

"Aren't we anymore?"

"We can be more than that. Come on, you want to?" He grabbed her and kissed her roughly on the lips as a Cerean sailor passed. Eppie, shocked, took a moment to respond, but then she shoved Squid off.

"Get off me," she said. She yanked her dagger from its sheath and pointed it at him.

The Cerean turned around and laughed. He said something to Squid that Eppie couldn't understand, and Squid answered in their language.

Eppie backed away. The Cerean stayed, watching.

"He says Cerean girls know who's master, I should wait 'til we get there," Squid said. "I reckon he might be right. You sure you don't want to?"

In answer, Eppie brandished her dagger.

"I like that knife," Squid said. "But I should be the one holding it. C'mon, give it over."

Eppie shook her head. Squid moved as if to come closer, to wrest it from her, but then he glanced over his shoulder at the Cerean sailor. Another one was there too, watching them. He hesitated. He wasn't sure he'd be able to get it from her; that must have been it. She wanted to show him that he couldn't take it. Not now, not ever. She inched closer and he backed off.

"You look more like a girl now or something," Squid prattled. "I thought you might've changed your mind. You sure look different; dirt's just the same on you, though." He sneered, as if the insult could hurt her.

"You wouldn't know," Eppie said. The road was clear behind her, and she reckoned she was just as fast as Squid and his new Cerean friends. "I'm going back to the keep."

"I'll catch you in the morning!" Squid said cheerily, as if he hadn't just tried to take her against her will.

To Na's gullet with him! Eppie thought as she turned and ran up through the town. She was so angry and flustered that she had to backtrack twice to find the main gate. Once inside, she found her spot in the hay, and despite her trembling anger, she fell into a deep sleep, just as far from the Enomaean stable hands as she could get.

§

Eppie woke with a piece of hay in her nose. She sneezed.

"Shush!" someone said. He had his hand on her shoulder.

Eppie tried to pull away, but his grip was strong. Strong, but soft enough not to hurt. She came all the way awake in an instant.

"We can't talk here," the man whispered.

The voice was familiar, but just barely. "Thorat?"

"Bring your things," he said.

The prospect of leaving Tiadun Keep and getting away from Squid again was enough to get Eppie on her feet in a moment. She'd only just arrived, and although she'd expected to rest there a second night, she didn't like the place. She liked what she'd seen of Squid even less. Had he ever been a friend? Had some foreign demon possessed him since he'd been gone, or was he just trying to impress the sailors for some reason?

Thorat was different. He had nothing in common with Squid. He crouched beside her, facing away, looking down the long axis of the barn in case anyone approached. Eppie belted on her knife, threw her cloak over her shoulders, picked up her sandals, and tapped him on the shoulder. He led her all the way to where the three Enomaean horse handlers slept in their bunks, covered in furs as if the night were colder than it was. Thorat listened for a moment, then moved a bale of hay to one side. He ducked behind it and disappeared.

Eppie followed. He'd found a trapdoor or some kind of loose board that hid an opening big enough to slide down through. She followed, dangling from her arms and dropping down into the outer paddock with a soft thud. Thorat used his sheathed sword – a common one, not the one Eppie had brought him – to move the trapdoor back into place.

They crossed the paddock in silence, climbed over a fence, and entered a small wood. It was only then that Thorat stopped and spoke to her.

"Why didn't the others come?" he asked.

"The others?" Eppie took a moment to collect her thoughts. "Sovara's cough is worse and she won't leave the shrine. Sunna says she's pregnant, and just before your message came, Varin twisted his ankle. They said it would be all right after a half-moon or so, but meanwhile, they wanted you to have the sword."

"What about Garren, or even Raina?"

"Raina said she needed to find a wet nurse, and Garren said he'd be missed, he couldn't just disappear, and besides, someone had to look after Sovara."

"That's true. I should have sent for Ferrent."

That hung in the air for a moment. He didn't want her there. "Why didn't you?"

"He was offered a job here, a job no honest man would take, let alone a Defender. I trust him, but not Calar." Thorat ran his fingers through his hair and looked away to the west.

Eppie had only been in Tiadun Keep for an evening, but she'd heard Calar's name more than once. He was the prince's brother, and he made his presence felt in the stables and barracks, while the prince himself stayed in his tower, closeted with his mistress and his Enomaean priest most of the time.

"What sort of job was it?"

"The more you know in this place, the worse off you are," Thorat said, which was no answer at all. "You should go back to Anamat and continue your training. You made it here, so I'm sure you'll be all right to find the way back."

It was what she'd wanted to do when she first saw Squid again, but now it didn't feel right. Besides, Sovara had seemed half-eager to get her out of Anamat and had said that she should try to keep Thorat alive. She stared at him through the darkness.

"Go on back," he said. "You need more training."

"I thought you needed help," she said, piecing her thoughts together. She could do something, maybe. She'd rather try to than scurry away. "I'm sure the sword will help, but I'm here now. There must be something I can do. I was a pretty good fighter before I even met you and Sovara. I haven't gotten worse."

Thorat shook his head. "There's nothing for you to do here. I'm going to go to the gate, and I'll probably die there. Tiada's so faded that they might be able to kill her, too. Dragons aren't always strong. There's nothing you can do about any of it."

Eppie considered that. "I could sneak out and put holes in the Cerean ships so they can't sail off with the dragon stones."

"They'd only fix them or send for more ships –. Wait. How did you hear that they want the dragon stones? I suspected it, but I wasn't sure. They've been talking about going into the hills for timber, which is bad enough if you ask me, but they have more picks and shovels than a logging expedition needs. The last time Cereans tried to mine in Anamat's hills was before my time as a Defender. It was –"

A rustle in the underbrush stopped Thorat short, but it was only a small woodland creature.

"Maybe we'd better move farther away from the keep," Eppie said.

Thorat answered by leading the way through the wood, dropping the story of the Defender's last battle. As dawn was breaking, they crossed a field into another grove, near a farmhouse beside a small village that lay mostly out of sight of the keep, behind a low hill a short distance up the Anamat road. Another road crossed through it, leading up into the mountains to the west.

"I gave my notice at the keep, so they shouldn't come looking for me. If anyone stops us, we'll say you're my cousin – is that all right?"

"Sure," Eppie said. In the rising light, Thorat looked tired and disheveled, but he was still breathtakingly handsome. Not that it meant anything to her. "Look, I won't be completely useless. I can at least go into the villages ahead of you, have a look around. I'm no green-knee, but I'm not a mercenary guardsman, either. I could pretend to be a herder from the next village over."

Thorat considered that. "All right." He sighed, as if resigned to being stuck with her. "But when the others come, if they come, you should go back to Anamat."

Eppie nodded, even though she planned to stay until it was over, whatever "it" turned out to be.

"We'll need to send a message to Ferrent, or else I could send you." He seemed to be coming to terms with the fact that she wasn't leaving right away. "It's only another long day's walk from here to the border of Kiralun, and another two days or so from there. The Cereans will take longer than that to get to the gate. I have an idea of about where it might be, but it will be hidden and... I don't know how you'd find it, or if you should." He looked out across the stubbly field to the farmhouse.

"All right, then," he said. He dug in his pocket for a bead and handed it to her. "Ask those farmers if we can stay in their shed for the morning, and see what cooked food they'll sell us. Meet me back here."

Eppie nodded and took a drink from her waterskin.

"Na's blood," Thorat cursed.

"What's wrong?" Eppie said.

"I forgot my waterskin. Ask if they have one to sell." He handed her another bead. "We should find out if there are any minstrels around who can carry a message to Ferrent. I probably shouldn't send you out alone again."

Eppie shrugged. She'd never gone looking for a gate before, and might not know one when she saw it, but at least she'd seen Tiada. She went to make arrangements at the farmhouse, leaving Thorat frowning after her, as gloomy as marsh reeds in autumn, sighing all the time. He would be a dreary companion in a bleak province, but both the Enatel and the ambassadress were counting on him, and she was supposed to help somehow.

§

Chapter 9

It was folly to send an apprentice out with a charged sword, even if the others were all unable or indisposed, Thorat thought as he watched Eppie cross the field to the farmhouse. Maybe Varin had sprained his ankle, but Garren should have come. Surely, Raina could look after Sovara, or Sunna could. It was just as well Sunna hadn't come, though. He didn't relish the thought of bringing a pregnant priestess to a dragon's gate. There was no telling what would happen then.

He needed someone to fight at his side, not just a messenger to deliver a package. They could have sent a common courier and left the girl to continue her training so she could have some chance of passing her trials at Midsummer. A blade was only worth as much as the skill of the man wielding it, magic or none. His own blade would have been better than nothing. He'd brought it with him from the keep. Now he had two blades. He could let Eppie use his ordinary one, to see what she'd learned. Maybe they'd sent her because Sovara had decided that she probably wouldn't pass the trials, or because she thought that this mission—whatever it turned out to be—was doomed, and that it was better to lose an apprentice than a fully trained Defender. Or maybe it was all just bad luck and foreign curses.

Eppie disappeared into the farmyard. From where Thorat sat, he'd be able to see anyone coming long before they saw him, so he set down the package and began to unwrap the sword. He folded away the cloth, revealing a bronze hilt and a simple brown leather scabbard. The hilt fit his hand perfectly, just as his regular sword's did. The stone in the pommel was what distinguished it. Now far from the dragon, it looked flat and gray at first glance, but a closer look revealed delicate silvery veins within. The stone had come from that piece of the dragons' realm given to the Defenders, down by their buried world-tree shrine. The dragon would recognize it, he hoped. Perhaps Tiada would appear to him now, if she wasn't gone beneath the earth forever already.

He unsheathed the sword and felt its balance in his hand, letting it rest in his grip while he got used to the weight of it. Tiada's temples were neglected, and some of the shrines in the villages near the keep looked like they'd been abandoned entirely. The prince – or Calar – had raised the pay of the fighting men after Midwinter. He had also promised the farmers near the keep that if all went well with the foreign trade, the next year's taxes would be halved—not that that would do them much good if Tiada gave no more strength to the soil. Without the dragon in the skies, the armed men from the merchant fleet seemed a far greater force than Tiadun's hinterlands could muster.

Then there was Calar, the prince's brother. He wanted the throne, for all the good it would do him. Some men wanted power, no matter what its price. Or maybe he just wanted to bed the ambassadress, not understanding what that meant, not wanting to understand it, only lusting after her clear, pale skin, the perfection of her body, her – Thorat stopped himself. Could that have driven him to kill? He didn't think so. His own brother had been a lot more likable than either the prince or Calar, as far as he remembered. He'd even felt a little bit bad about saying that he was dead when the sword had arrived earlier.

He set the charged sword aside and inspected his common sword. It was a better blade than most, and after half a year of Sovara's training, the apprentice was probably better skilled than the average provincial guardsman. Whether she was skilled enough to make up for her lack of bulk in a fight was another question.

Thorat was still mulling over things when Eppie returned, surprising him out of a doze.

"You shouldn't go to sleep with that unwrapped," she said.

Thorat hastily covered it.

"It's all right; I saw it in Anamat," she said. "I got a spot in that shed for us, and there's a minstrel coming through the next village up the road tonight. The farmer reckons that if we set out after the midday rest, we should make it there before full dark."

"We'll probably die in this dragon-forsaken province." Thorat sighed and hauled himself to his feet.

"It's not dragon-forsaken," Eppie said. "I saw Tiada from the pass, up in the mountains."

"You did?" No wonder Eppie seemed so cheerful. If he'd seen the dragon, he'd have hope too, even with dozens of Cereans ranged against them. It seemed that the dragon was alive and had not left the surface of the earth entirely, despite her apostate prince. Thorat's heart lifted a little at the news.

"The bandits have seen her too, I think," Eppie said.

Thorat's cheer evaporated as suddenly as it had come. "Bandits?"

"I'll tell you all about it later," Eppie said with a yawn as she turned to the field again.

"No, wait, tell me here," Thorat said.

They stood under the trees while the day grew brighter, and Eppie told how she'd wandered off the road to find a place to sleep, and how she'd gotten away from the bandits with a hot meal in her belly and the almost-stolen sword besides.

"And they didn't come after you?" Thorat asked.

"Not that I could tell. I don't think they even unwrapped it," Eppie said, "and besides, they were drunk. I'm sure they could tell that it was a sword, but beyond that, they probably didn't know what it was."

"Except that they wanted it," Thorat mused. "I knew there were bandits in the hills, but not that... Were there many of them?"

"Less than a dozen," Eppie said. She seemed unworried. She should have been worried. Some of the more devout priestesses talked of going into the hills when they'd done their time in the temples. Maybe they became bandits, too, but it seemed unlikely. The surliest of thieves and black-blooded murderers went to Na's country to escape the city watch or a prince's reach.

"Here, take this," Thorat said, handing Eppie his old sword. He took the one with the shrine's stone in its hilt and tied its scabbard to his belt.

Eppie grinned as she took his old sword. "Thanks!" she said. "I haven't swung a sword since Anamat." She tied it on. It was a little too long for her, but not by much. For all that she was slender, she was tall enough. If she had any skill at all, she'd be able to make use of it. Speaking of skill –

"You'd better get back in practice," Thorat said. He looked out across the still-deserted field. "Let's go back to that clearing and see what you can do. We'll rest later."

All morning, Thorat and Eppie tried out their new blades, drilling through the old familiar exercises until their arms ached. Maybe it wasn't hopeless after all, but Thorat still wished that Garren had come instead.

§

They spent that night at the next village's tavern, where a halfway-skilled minstrel sang ballads until deep into the night. Eppie yawned in the corner while Thorat went to speak with the minstrel, then they took their small packs to the upper room, the last time they'd sleep under a roof for a while, Thorat told her. It was good to be away from Squid. She didn't care if she had to sleep in the mud, so long as he was nowhere near.

The next morning, they put more distance between themselves and the keep. They walked north on the Anamat road until they found a likely patch of woods, with a clearing big enough to swing their swords in. Eppie felt the smooth-worn hilt of Thorat's sword in her grip. It was far better than the practice swords she'd held so far. Despite her time away from the training hall, she felt the movements return to her, better than they'd been before, as if the sword itself carried some of Thorat's skill. For his part, he looked pleased enough with the charged blade, but not as if it made him faster or better than before.

"Why wouldn't your old sword do?" Eppie asked after they set out again. "This is a good blade, isn't it?"

"It's the stone in the hilt of this one," Thorat said. "It acts as a sort of homing beacon. It will help us find Tiada's gate, which I hope Ferrent will be able to find on his own. When we get there, she might recognize the stone and us."

"You mean she might know that we're with her? Wouldn't she know that already?"

"She might, and she might not. She has good cause to mistrust humans here, from what I've seen at the keep."

Eppie wouldn't trust anyone at that keep either.

"Why did they send the whole sword, then? Why not just the stone?" she asked.

"I don't know why. It's just what we've always done, I think." The Defenders seemed to have quite a few things they did out of tradition and for no other reason she could discern. "We can ask Sovara, if we get back to Anamat," Thorat said.

"I'll ask her when we get back," Eppie said, holding fast to the belief that she would return. "Is it hard to find the gate?"

"It usually isn't clear where they are. The dragons are shy, as they should be, but there should be some signs as we go along. Hopefully, we'll find it before the Cereans do." Thorat looked back over his shoulder, but they were between villages, and the road was deserted. "The prince or his brother will have a lot of angry guests if they can't find it, but it would be only what they deserve."

Eppie was puzzled. "But if it's hard for even you to find, how will they find it?"

Thorat walked on a few paces before answering. "The dragons are shy of humankind; they need to be lured out," he said. "That's what the priestesses are supposed to do, to meet them halfway between the realms, but sometimes they don't."

"Yeah, usually they just take the beads and -"

"There are still some true priestesses," Thorat said.

Eppie thought of the ambassadress. He was probably thinking of her too, resplendent in her marble shrine. Iola was a true priestess, if anyone was.

They might try to bribe a priestess to show them the gate, or threaten her," Thorat said. "I'm told that's how they found Lemira's gate, the last time. I think it's part of why Sovara hates priestesses so much, but I'm not sure."

"What happened there?" Eppie asked.

Thorat shook his head. "I wasn't there. The old Enatel died there, along with others of us. They say it hasn't been the same since, but it's all I've known."

They walked in silence for a while.

"I don't know if Sovara hates all priestesses. I mean, there's Sunna."

"Sunna's different," Thorat said.

"But do the priestesses even know where the gate is? Can they, if they're all dragon-blind?"

Thorat shrugged. "They could have handed down the knowledge, even if they never use it, but if they've lost it or keep their secrets, the Cereans have other ways."

"Like what?" Eppie asked when it became clear he wasn't going to go on.

Thorat looked both ways up and down the still empty trail. When he was satisfied that no one was coming, he took a stick and smoothed out a patch of bare dirt in the road.

"Suppose the gate is here," he said, marking a spot with an X. "It's a place where the dragons' realm touches the surface of the earth. All around it, there will be thicker growth, taller trees sometimes. If you were to dig – which no one should be doing in the mountains, but they can if the prince allows it – you would find veins of good earth or even of precious stones." He sketched a few lines radiating out from the X. "Follow those veins, and they'll lead anyone to the gate, even without dragonsight. The Cereans mined all the dragon stones from their land, and they have their own beliefs about the power of those stones. I think they've been wanting the ones from Theranis ever since they killed their dragons, hundreds and hundreds of years ago."

Eppie tried to imagine Cerea bare of dragons yet somehow still fertile enough to support the people who lived there. "So, you're saying that anyone could find the dragon's gate if they wanted to?" she asked.

"Anyone willing to wound the dragon's flesh to get her stones, if no one stops them," Thorat said. He threw his drawing stick into the underbrush and started walking again. "The keep mistress doesn't bow to Farseer, but the prince does. Maybe they think the Enomaean god can hold back

Calar's Cerean allies, but they'd have been wiser to stay on the side of Tiada."

"Why would Tiada favor them, when they're dragon-blind and they've let her temples rot?"

"The dragons don't only favor those who can see them. Look at you: do they favor you more than a skilled guildsman?"

"I guess not," Eppie said. "And there's another thing." She hurried to get the words out before she thought better of it. "Before I left Anamat, I had to find Sunna, and she was with the ambassadress. She wanted me to stay, to be a priestess. The ambassadress did, that is. Sunna said I didn't have to. I won't do it. I don't like being walled in like that."

Thorat went still. "I'm sorry."

"For what?"

He made a shooing motion, as if to brush off a fly. "It's nothing, it's just that... I wish Garren had come."

"Well, I can't do anything about that," Eppie said. "Look, at least now you can find Tiada's gate before the Cereans get there, right?"

"I won't be much use against them all alone," Thorat said, as if she weren't walking along right beside him.

"Oh, one other thing," Eppie said. "The ambassadress – she said to send you her love."

Thorat kicked a stone and cursed.

§

They traced the edge of the woodland, heading east along Tiada's spur of hills. Thorat was fairly sure that the gate would be in that direction – the villages he'd seen on his tax-collecting rounds had seemed a bit more prosperous that way, their temples less neglected – still neglected but not completely dilapidated. It would have been faster to travel on the roads and well-worn paths between the villages, but this way, they would be less likely to miss the gate. They slept and traveled at different times of the day, pausing whenever they reached a good clearing to practice their sword work. Eppie was quick on her feet and she trained with earnest desire to learn, but when she concentrated too hard on the angle of her sword, she sometimes forgot to mind her footwork and tripped over some small branch or stone. Still, she was good for a half-year apprentice. He hadn't been wrong to bring her to the training hall, but he did wonder why Sovara had sent her off into such danger.

Eppie was the one who went into the villages to buy supplies. She could still look almost young enough that a villager might still think that she was on her way to Anamat. Even as a young woman out of place, she would raise the villagers' guard less than he would, as an armed man with no clear allegiance.

On the third full day of walking, the gem in the hilt of Thorat's new sword warmed slightly. It was a subtle change but enough to assure him that they were getting closer. He rested his hand on the hilt. It tugged up deeper into the hills. They were approaching a village of some forty or fifty cottages, the largest they'd seen since leaving Tiadun Keep.

"You want me to go in there and get more bread?" Eppie asked.

Thorat considered. He could think and search better if he were alone, but Eppie was the one who'd seen the dragon.

"Let's climb up higher, see what we can see," he said. "I think we're getting close. I'd rather know more before you go into the village."

The low-lying land was on the cusp of early spring, with fresh green growth sprouting up in the meadows around the villages. They waded up into the underbrush, from the warm lowlands to the cool late winter of the hills. As they climbed, Thorat watched the ground for signs. Myril had once told him that each dragon had a plant that grew only in their realm. She'd said that the priestesses selected their novices by having them point out their home realm's particular plant. He didn't know what Tiada's plant was like, so he just looked for anything he'd never seen before. Soon, he spotted a tiny blue fiower with a bright orange center and spade-shaped leaves no bigger than a child's fingernail.

"Here!" he said with a smile. "This must be the plant that Tiada has as her own."

"Which?" Eppie looked down, puzzled.

"Tiadun's livery is blue and orange. I've never seen this fiower anywhere before, have you?"

Eppie shook her head. "I don't pay much attention to plants."

Thorat shook his head. Dragonsight or no, Eppie really wouldn't be make much of a priestess. "You should notice them," he said. "It may be part of priestess lore, but it's useful. Myril told me about it, and I'm sure she could teach you more if we get back to Anamat. Let's keep looking for these. We must be getting close."

Eppie raised a questioning eyebrow at Thorat's sword. He nodded. "It's warming, and no sign of Cereans or the prince's men."

"Yet," Eppie said.

Thorat forged on through the thick wood, looking for a break in the trees large enough for a dragon to fiy down through. The lush growth was a good sign for the strength of the earth, but he could find no sign that the dragon had been nearby, not in her visible form. In every clear spot, Thorat found the little fiowers, more and more of them as the sword hilt warmed until it was almost uncomfortable to touch.

He came into a tiny clearing, so small that he might have lain across it with his feet in the underbrush on one side and ferns uncurling over his head at the other. He pushed on through it and felt the sword for direction. It tugged him back.

Behind him, Eppie had stopped. She was looking at a spot on the hillside, where a gnarled oak's roots draped out over a sharp slope.

"There's a cave here," she said.

"It's too –" It was so small that he hadn't even seen it, far too small for a dragon to emerge from. "A dragonlet could come and go this way, but a realm dragon shouldn't be small enough to get through there," he said.

Eppie went over to the exposed roots, brushing the earth off them. "There's something here," she said softly, then she ducked under a large root and disappeared.

"Eppie!" Thorat's voice rose in panic.

"I'm just in here," Eppie said. "I think this must be it."

"It can't be; it's too small," Thorat said. He came closer, leaning in under the root. What he saw took his breath away. It was the dragons' realm, small, but as close as he'd ever seen it, so alive that he could feel its pulse thrumming in his ears, almost blinding his eyes. Eppie stood in the center of a small, round room. It was like the inside of a ball, or of a bubble of foam, luminous and delicate, made of living, glowing stones. They lit up with their own light, the lifeblood of the earth, of the dragons. They were dazzling. Eppie was dazzled. She took a step deeper in.

"Don't go in," Thorat said. "It's the other realm." He'd stood outside three of the dragons' gates up until now, but he'd never entered them. It was too dangerous, forbidden. As he entered the mouth of their realm, he could feel it drawing him in, like a womb that could take him back. No wonder Iola wanted to go there, again and again and again.

He grabbed Eppie and yanked her back out into the forest clearing, back onto the surface of the earth.

In the daylight, Eppie's face hardened back to its accustomed guarded expression. She frowned at him and rubbed her arm.

"You'd hardly know it was there from the outside," she said. "I never saw anything like it."

Thorat sat down on a fallen tree at the edge of the clearing, looking at those roots, the tree that masked Tiada's gate. "You shouldn't have gone in there," he said weakly.

The gate felt fragile, like a blown bubble of glass that might shatter at any moment. How could Tiada pass this way and not collapse it?

Eppie looked out into the woods, down toward the village. "Maybe they won't find it," she said.

"Or Tiada will draw herself down under the earth and close her gate."

"What would happen if she did that?" Eppie asked.

"I don't know. If she died, the land would be dead, with no life in it, no soul. She's the soul of the land. It's like a husk of itself already, though. I don't if anyone would notice or care."

"I thought the dragons could destroy the land, slough the people off. At least, that's what they told me when I was little, to scare me. That's why my mother always gave offerings at the shrine."

Eppie had never mentioned her home village to him before. He didn't pry further. "I think they can do that," he said, "but this opening still seems too small, too weak. Maybe she'll just go under the earth and come out again somewhere else. The gate might be closing already. They say that's what happened to some of the dragons of Cerea. In Enomae, they just killed them." Thorat sighed.

"How?"

"With magical hunting spears blessed by their eagle-headed god." Thorat beat his fist on the log he was sitting on. "The prince's priest probably has those."

A bird trilled from a nearby tree and a dragonlet darted out of the forest and into the cave, going right by as if they were invisible. To Thorat, the dragonlet itself was just a winged brightness against the backdrop of the forest and the flowers, but Eppie stared after it as if it were solid and wholly real. She said she'd seen Tiada, too. Was he becoming dragon-blind? He couldn't, not now, not ever. How could he defend the dragon if he couldn't see her? Maybe Sovara had given him up for lost, and his apprentice, too, but they had to do something.

"I guess the best we can do is to stop them from finding the place," Thorat said at last. "At least until Ferrent and some of the others come. I wish Garren were here."

"Or even Sovara," said.

§

Apart from the looming threat of an army of Cereans and the Tiadun prince's men coming to raze Tiada's veins from the land, that next long quarter moon would have counted as one of the happiest times of Eppie's life. It was only herself and Thorat, camping in the hills. They spent their first day near the gate, wandering around the nearby woods, looking for a camping spot. They settled on a place a short distance uphill from the shrine, under the boughs of a spreading rhododendron bush. A nearby clearing – wider than the one by the gate – gave them space to practice their sword work.

They soon settled into a routine, waking at dawn, eating a cold breakfast, then taking up their swords and rehearsing their drills. Every couple of days, Eppie went into the village to buy bread and other supplies, saying that she was from a nearby village and herding in the higher pastures. Thorat snared rabbits for meat and looked out for any signs of Ferrent or the other Defenders. They made a fire to cook the midday meal, rested, trained again, and as soon as it was dark, they ate a cold evening meal and settled down to sleep. Thorat taught her a whistle, subtly different from a bird's call, that they could use to find each other in the hills if they got separated.

On Eppie's fourth trip into the village, some news blew through the market square while she was waiting to buy some cheese. The cheesemonger was a staid-looking man with a pockmark on his chin, and at the cart beside him, a young woman sold billowing bags of carded wool.

"Did you hear what that messenger said?" the young woman asked.

"'Course I did," the cheesemonger said. "The chief got word that the prince and a whole hundred of Cereans will be coming up this way to hunt."

The young woman shook her head. "They shouldn't come when we're planting, but at least the lambs are born."

"The messenger said that they'll be here within the quarter moon. They've left the keep already." He turned to deal with his first customer of the morning, and Eppie took her place next in line. She sniffed at the cheeses, as if she were considering their different flavors and colors, but she liked the plainest ones best. When it was her turn, she indicated a round, hard cheese and wordlessly handed over the beads.

"It'll be good for businesses," the cheesemonger said to the young woman selling wool.

"For you, maybe. No use to me unless they packed their spindles along."

Another customer approached and jumped into the conversation. "Cerean fighting men? They probably don't even know how to spin."

Eppie listened a little longer but heard nothing more of interest, so she slipped back into the forest.

Back at their camp, she waited for Thorat's return and laid the fire, gathering dry leaves and twigs, then bigger branches into a cone in their makeshift fire pit. She struck the flint until a spark caught, just as Thorat returned, carrying two skinned rabbits, which he spitted over the fire. Eppie told him what she'd heard in the market.

Thorat frowned. "I can't find any sign of Ferrent. He should have gotten here by now."

"Would he be able to find us?" Eppie asked.

"He should be able to. I think it's time for me to go into the town and see if I can learn anything more." He took hung his sword on one of the boughs of the rhododendron. "Stay here and guard this," he said. "I should be back by sundown."

§

Thorat went into the village with only his short dagger bound beneath his tunic, out of sight. He had no intention of using it, but he was used to carrying it, and it made him feel a little more at ease. Outside the Anamat valley, small villages in Theranis were suspicious of strangers passing through, as they should be, with the Cereans looking for dragon gems to steal and bandits darting in from the mountains.

The woods above the village gave way to small orchards of olives and apples, then to fields of grain, gardens, and farmyards. Most of the cottages were thatched, but at the center of the village were several tiled roofs – the chieftain's house, the temple, and the tavern, most likely. People were emerging from their houses after the midday rest, setting out for their gardens and pastures. None greeted Thorat with more than a nod, and most not even that.

He found the tavern on the market square across from a white-walled temple with a dusty porch. The temple's door stood open, as if the priestesses were in residence but didn't care enough to tidy the porch. At least it wasn't utterly deserted. Thorat wondered if the priestesses knew that Tiada's gate lay so close to the temple, and if any of them could be persuaded to show it to some interloper. At Lemirun, one of the Defenders had tricked a priestess into showing him the way. Thorat wouldn't have thought a priestess would betray the dragon so, but it had happened and could happen again.

The tavern, on the other hand, was a fine building, almost half the size of the temple, and its porch as clean and polished as any tavern porch Thorat had seen in his travels, certainly cleaner than the dusty sanctuary across the market square. Tavern porches were rare in the north and west of Theranis, but here in the south they seemed common. The few late diners sitting there scarcely turned their heads to watch him pass. Thorat pretended not to look at them, either. They were three young men and an older one, carrying pruning saws and heavy leather mitts. They tipped their ales back before returning to the orchards.

Inside, the tavern was dark and deserted except for the barkeep and one lingering patron snoring in the corner.

"What are you after?" the barkeep said. "Stew's gone."

"I'll just have a bread and ale, then. Thirsty work, walking."

The thickset, gray-haired barkeep pulled a loaf of bread out of a fiat wicker basket and filled a tankard from his tap.

"You keep a clean tavern," Thorat said. "I've never seen tables with such a shine beyond the prince's high table."

"I like my place well kept," the barkeep said.

"A well-kept tavern is easy on the stomach," Thorat said as the man brought the bread to his table. It was still warm.

The barkeep gave a half-smile. For all that his tavern was as clean as a temple ought to be, he was a surly fellow.

Thorat ate in silence and sipped his ale slowly as the barkeep lumbered around the room, tidying up. A young man dozed in one corner, lying on a bench with a cap over his face. There was something odd about his clothing.

"Move on, there." The barkeep poked the young man as he came around that corner of the room. "If you want to sleep, you'll have to pay for a bed."

The young man startled up and sat, blinking at the man. "Apologies, sir."

"You should have gone back to the keep yesterday, or at least this morning."

"Sorry, sir."

Thorat recognized the young man. He was the Theranian sailor who'd been on the Cerean ships, the one who'd been skulking around Tiadun Keep, always underfoot in the kitchens. The maids had complained of him, how he'd taken on foreign ways and thought they should obey him only because he was a male and they were serving wenches.

"Come have an ale with me before you go," Thorat said to him, rolling a bead out onto his table for the barkeep. "I've a lonely road ahead of me and I'd like to hear some news." The boy might recognize him, but then, he might not. It was dark enough in the tavern, and he wasn't wearing guardsman's livery any more.

"I've got no news, just messages to carry," the young man said.

"Name's Gornen," Thorat said, hoping the young man wouldn't recognize him.

"Folks call me Squid," the young man said.

Thorat raised his eyebrows. "Strange name."

Squid shrugged. "What brings you to these parts?" he asked.

"Carrying a message to the keep," he said. "What might I find there?"

"You might as well rest here," Squid said. "The prince and all of them are coming this way, going to show their Cerean guests the hunting out this way. I hear there's boar in these forests, and bears, too."

"Is that so?" Thorat asked the barkeep.

"Boar, some; bear, no. You've got to go into Na's country for that. You've got to be a fool to go hunting there, what with the bandits and all."

"Bandits?" Thorat said. "Do they give you much trouble out this way?

The barkeep nodded. "Closer every day. They used to keep to the high valleys, but folks have been seeing the smoke from their fires in closer these days. Seems they're squeezing us from both sides, hunting out our winter meat." He scooped up a half-dozen tankards and disappeared into the back room.

"Friendly around here," Squid said. His cynical tone pulled Thorat up short. Anamat scrapplings were always disparaging the provinces, but this young man sounded more bitter than most.

"Friendlier at the keep, I hope?" Thorat asked, trying to mask his thoughts and to lighten the mood.

Squid shrugged. "Not much. Good luck to you there." He stood and downed his ale in one gulp. "As the man said, I'd best be going." With that, he walked out the door.

Thorat took his time with his bread and drank as slowly as he could, in hopes that some more helpful patron would come by, but no one did. The barkeep fidgeted, eager to be rid of him. So, he thought, the villagers thought that their smoke came from a bandit fire. Perhaps they should move farther up before the villagers raided their spot, driving them back beyond the pastures to the wild country, as if they were bandits themselves.

§

Chapter 10

Eppie hated waiting. She stirred the fire into sparks while Thorat went down to the village. At least she was with him, though, not sitting in Anamat waiting for him to come back only to fall into the ambassadress's alabaster arms. Maybe that was why she'd volunteered to deliver the sword to Thorat, to see him for herself again, to see if he was really all she'd imagined him to be after their brief meeting at Midsummer. He was still the handsomest man she'd ever seen, but he was also glum and wary, distant and not as charming as she remembered. From time to time, he would turn to the hills and gaze longingly in the direction of Anamat, with an expression on his face that reminded her of the ambassadress, who was always there, waiting for him like a jewel in a box.

She sat down in the shade of the rhododendron and picked dirt out from under her nails. Squid had joined the Cereans and thought that she was fool enough to trade with them, even though the first thing every green-knee girl learned was to keep as far from the foreigners as possible. She'd only heard of one scrappling girl being stolen away for sure, but there were rumors of more. Surely, Squid didn't think she'd become an utter idiot while he was away, did he? Or maybe he knew things she didn't, things that made the Cereans seem less bad.

Lost in her musings, Eppie didn't notice the villagers approaching until they were almost upon her.

"Where do you think they went?" someone asked loudly.

Eppie startled up, rustling the leaves. She stilled her jumping heart, then carefully crept back to the edge of the clear space, gathering up swords and gear as she went, moving as quietly as possible.

"That's their fire, all right. Should have come up when they had it lit. I'd like to get my hands on those bandits."

Bandits? Eppie thought.

"Stole two of my sheep only last week!"

"They're a plague on us."

One more voice: "I'm not sure –"

"What, that the bandits are a plague?"

"No, just not sure that this is a bandits' camp," the last one said. Eppie reckoned that there were four or five of them, all men. She peeked through the leaves. It looked like they were armed with heavy hoes and threshing flails. "There's not enough tracks around here for it to be a camp of bandits."

"Hmm. You're the hunter, but what else could it be?"

"Don't know. Any case, whoever it is can't be any good to us."

"What, are we going to wait for them to come back?"

"They'll hardly walk right up when we're all here. Best to come back after dark."

The one who'd questioned the nature of the camp spoke up again. "They might move on before that."

"Well, we'll make sure they do move on if we find them here tonight." The speaker chuckled, as if hunting bandits was has favorite sport.

Eppie held herself very still as the villagers crashed away back to their lands. Why couldn't they all just keep to where they belonged and not have these hunting and raiding excursions? For that matter, why didn't the foreigners keep to their own shores? Why did they come to hunt Theranis's dragons, when they'd destroyed their own? She missed Anamat, Anamat at Midsummer in particular, with its fat pockets and strong bridges, shelters that didn't rustle in the night winds like ghosts passing by.

Well, no gang of village men could stop her from going back. She only hoped that she could escape the Cereans and the prince's men, too.

§

Thorat took an ambling path back to the campsite, hoping to come upon some way of deflecting the foreign hunters or miners who were coming to raid the dragon's gate. Nothing presented itself. If he could find a priestess willing to lend him some dragonfire lamps and then find another small cave in the hills, he might be able to create an illusion of a gate that would be good enough to fool the prince's men and the Cereans until they dug deeper. An illusion could stall them long enough for the others from Anamat to arrive, not to mention Ferrent, wherever he was. He should have arrived already.

As he approached their camp, a wide swath of broken twigs and kicked-up leaves told him that they'd had visitors, hasty, rough visitors. He paused for a moment to listen but heard only the soft rustle of the forest around him. He ran the rest of the way to the rhododendron. The coals of the cooking fire had been scattered and trampled out by large feet. His gear was not where he'd left it, just under the shelter of the thick bush.

"Eppie?" he asked quietly.

A crunch of leaves came from deep in the undergrowth. Eppie emerged, dragging both swords and most of the rest of their gear.

"They came looking for bandits," she said. "Stupid villagers." She said it as if she were more annoyed than worried, but he could see by the flush on her face that her heart was racing.

"I heard some of them talking in the tavern, but I didn't realize they'd be coming so soon," Thorat said. "I should have come back right away."

"It wouldn't have made a difference," Eppie said. "They're planning to come back tonight, they said. Did you find Ferrent in the village?"

Thorat shook his head. "No. Now we'll have to move further away from town, into bandit country, just when the prince and his Cereans are about to arrive."

"Any other news from town?" Eppie asked.

"Hardly anyone at the tavern, just a messenger from the keep. He sounded like an Anamat scrappling, but he was wearing Cerean clothes. I'd seen him around the keep, but he didn't seem to recognize me without my guardsman's getup." Eppie was looking down at the ground, an odd expression on her face. "What is it?" he asked.

Eppie didn't look up. "Maybe I should have told you," she said. "I didn't think it would matter, but now that he's here, I know that boy. He left Anamat at Midsummer on a ship, and now he's here with the Cereans. Taking to their ways. He wanted me to go to their ships with him and sell the sword."

"This sword? He wanted to take it from you?" Thorat took it from her and cradled it in his hands. That would have been the end of everything, the death of his chances against the foreigners, the death of Tiada. They would have taken Eppie, too, probably.

"I couldn't believe it myself," Eppie went on. "What kind of fool does he think I am? Every green-knee girl knows about them!"

Thorat could believe that they wanted the sword, but he wouldn't have thought the boy capable of spotting it through its wrappings.

"Can he see dragons?"

"Never," Eppie answered. "Or if he did, he hid it really well. He used to tease me for staring out into nothing."

The young man had looked clever enough in his way but cocky, the kind of young man who came in droves to the tournaments, thinking that they could best seasoned fighters.

"I wonder why he went with them," he thought aloud.

"I don't know," Eppie said. "Maybe some of the same reasons I went with you to the sword hall."

"What?" Thorat recoiled at the comparison.

"No, no, not like that. You didn't make me go, and they didn't make him join them, but he thought it would be an adventure. We'd been on the streets a long time, and it was the first thing that came along that seemed better." Eppie paused and turned further away, so that he couldn't see her eyes. "He was my friend, but he was never the kind of boy you'd trust with much. He was always holding back a stash for himself, never sharing the best of his take. And he was completely dragon-blind, thought the priestesses were all just like the Cereans say we all are, the free-favored females of Anamat."

"And you counted him as a friend?"

Eppie sighed. "Sure I did. He was quick and knew his way around. He'd brag, but he told it like a good story. I still kind of miss him." She shuddered. "I shouldn't. I guess I just miss what I thought he was."

"I hope... Well, no use pining." Thorat looked at the trampled remains of their temporary fire pit. "We'd better move on," he said. "Let's see what we can find upslope."

§

"Ow!" Eppie's cry awoke Thorat from a deep slumber.

They'd camped under an overhanging rock. Despite the rocky bed underneath, Thorat had slept deeply. Before he could react, someone struck him over the head, hard enough to hurt but not enough to knock him out. He lashed out, but his reactions were sleep-slowed and clumsy. Two big men got his arms into their grips. They stank as if they hadn't bathed since last Midsummer, if then.

"You let that man have the sword, and you wouldn't give it to us?" It was a woman's voice, an old woman's voice. The crescent moon had set, and in the faint starlight he could scarcely make out the bandits' forms silhouetted against the sky.

Thorat tried to turn but the man on his left struck him again. Bandits. They'd gone into bandit territory. They'd have done better to take rooms above the tavern and let the cursed Cereans see them.

"It was sent to him," Eppie said.

"With you along to sweeten the package." The old woman spat. "And you so young."

"I'm not that young," Eppie said.

"She's just a messenger," Thorat said.

"Then why is she still with you?" one of the bandits grunted.

Thorat was flabbergasted. They thought that Eppie was his lover? Paid or coerced?

"It's *not* that!" Eppie said before he could answer the accusation.

The bandits took a moment to ponder that. "You're quite sure?" asked an old woman's voice.

Eppie grunted. "Yeah. Now let me go."

"Better come with us. Can't have lowlanders on our hills."

"The Cereans will be in the village by next nightfall, and may Na curse them," one of the men said.

"Taking us won't stop them," Thorat said. "We're no friends of theirs."

"No?"

"Don't listen to him, Vigda. They must be advance scouts, sent from Anamat."

"We're not working for the Cereans, that's for sure," Eppie said.

"What, then? For the prince?" the old woman said. "That's hardly any better."

Thorat willed Eppie to be silent until they could talk together, until they knew more. Whether she sensed his wish, or whether plain sleepy confusion muted her, she said no more as the bandits bound their hands behind their backs and marched them up the hills. Thorat heard his sword slide out of its sheath and saw its faint glow out of the corner of his eye. He heard the bandit's heartfelt sigh of appreciation. The bandit had it out for some time, then put it back into its sheath and wrappings. He knew something about swords, that bandit, because when he inspected Thorat's old blade, the one he'd given to Eppie to use, he merely grunted, "A good blade, this one," and re-sheathed it without further comment or wistful sighs.

Dawn crept in, cold and gray, as the bandits marched Thorat and Eppie up into the peaks on the border between Tiadun and Getedun. These mountains were not particularly high, but they were wild enough for Thorat to feel thoroughly out of his element. They crossed a rocky ridge, then suddenly a bowl of a valley spread out before them, dotted with hide tents that made a sort of village.

"Let's put them in with Forlan's brother," one of the bandits said.

The others nodded and grunted assent. They led Thorat and Eppie through the center of the circled tents to one on the outskirts. In front of it, a massive bandit slumped loosely at his post, eyes distant. He sat up when he saw the others approach, then his eyes lit on Eppie and he grinned.

"Hello, little scrappling!" he said. "Happy you came back." The big bandit's speech slurred a little, and he had an odd look in his eye.

"Hello, Forlan," Eppie said.

Thorat raised an eyebrow at her, but the men holding his arms wrenched him away.

"These are the...uh, the folks I met on my way into Tiadun," Eppie said.

"They are?" Thorat said. He didn't think Eppie could possibly be to blame for leading the bandits to capture them, but she seemed far too comfortable with them. They were bandits, as bad as the Cereans, maybe worse. It was well known that they made blood sacrifices, as if Na were like Farseer.

"Where will we put the girl?" one of the men asked.

"She can stay with me," said the old woman, Vigda. "Better, safer that way."

"Thorat's all right," Eppie said. "I can stay with him."

"Not under my nose," Vigda said. "Stick him in there and we'll all get some sleep."

"But -" Eppie protested.

"But nothing. Come on."

With that, the men thrust Thorat into the darkened tent and closed the flap behind him. Before his eyes had time to adjust to the gloom under the stitched pelts, he unceremoniously tripped over the tent's other occupant.

"By the eye!" the man cursed.

His voice was familiar. Thorat peered at his indistinct shape. The man sat up and looked at him, too. He pushed the hair out of his face, and then he laughed.

"Thorat?"

"Ferrent? What are you doing here?"

"Well, I was captured, as you can see. But other than that, it's a long story. How about you?"

"These bandits broke up our camp in the middle of the night. Now there's no one –" He looked uneasily over his shoulder.

"It's all right," Ferrent said. "It's only Forlan."

"That bandit?"

"Quiet in there!" Forlan roared, as if summoned by his name.

"He's my brother," Ferrent whispered.

"But how?" Thorat said.

"As I said, it's –"

The tent flap burst open. "Quiet! Sleep!" Forlan shouted at them.

"Very well, but – "

"Quiet! Sleep!" Forlan, whatever else he was, was very clearly dragon-touched, not to mention twice as big as an average man. Thorat was tired. Ferrent pointed him to a pile of no-doubt-flea-ridden bracken and furs. Lacking any better ideas, Thorat went to finish his night's interrupted sleep.

§

Ferrent seemed perfectly at home in the bandits' hide tent, despite the fact that he was a prisoner there. Thorat didn't want to ask too many questions, though, not with bandits circling them like carrion crows.

Near midday, one of the bandits came and announced that they would be allowed out for a short walk around the rim of the valley. He introduced himself as Gran. Forlan,

Ferrent's alleged brother, would also walk with them. Thorat hoped that he would be able to talk to Ferrent alone. Besides, his body felt stiff and sore after the night's disrupted sleep and the morning of confinement. He stumbled out of tent's shade into glaring sunlight, squinting to make out the too-bright forms in the valley below.

In front of one of the other tents, a few of the bandit men stood looking over a small pile of swords, while Eppie sat beside the fire, turning the spit. His stomach complained at the smell of meat. Vigda, the old woman, moved over from the fire to join the circle of men gathered around the swords. The charged blade was there, as well as the old one that Eppie had been using. The apparent leader of the men picked up the Defenders' magical sword and said something that seemed to conclude whatever discussion they'd been having. Vigda gave him a quick kiss, then went on to take the herbs to the stream for washing.

"I want my sword back," Thorat said.

Gran laughed at that. "You'll have to take that up with Larn and Vigda. I don't think you'll be getting it back."

It was an outrage, but Ferrent said nothing, only nodded sympathetically. Gran wasn't as big as Forlan, but he was quicker-witted. Ferrent still hadn't explained how his supposed brother had come to be with the bandits, or why he himself hadn't made his escape. They all seemed to think it perfectly natural to sit in this valley while the prince and his Cerean allies marched on Tiada's gate.

He looked back at Eppie when they reached the top of the valley.

"How long will you keep us prisoner here?" he asked.

"You yourself?" Gran said. "It depends on what you're worth."

"Not much, not to you," Thorat said. "I'm a townsman, not much good at hunting." *Or kidnapping scrapplings, or killing them, if it came to that.*

"That's not all they do here," Ferrent said, oblivious to his thoughts.

Gran nodded. "That's right. A man's worth is a man's worth."

Thorat had no idea what the bandit meant by that, and he didn't think any of them would give him a plain answer. "What about the girl, Eppie?" he asked.

"Oh, she's just like a scrappling. She can go back to the lowlands any time she wants, though I don't know why she'd want to," Gran said.

"She can?" Thorat asked.

Gran nodded. "She's too young for the hills, unless she's killed a man. Has she?"

"No," Thorat said slowly. "I don't believe she has. Is that... Do you require that for men in your band?"

Gran shrugged. "It's preferred, but for our priestesses, we want ones who know how to do what's needed when it's needed."

Thorat was thinking of asking what that was, and wondering whether the old woman was the one who made the blood sacrifices. The only other time he'd tangled with bandits, when they'd had Iola, he'd been quite sure they were preparing to kill her, or maybe just defile her first. The memory of that day still chilled his blood.

Ferrent nudged him. "It's not all bad, up here in the hills. Don't look so grim."

"But we have work to do!" Thorat protested.

Gran looked at him, puzzled, but Forlan made an echo.

"Work to do!" He started laughing his manic laugh, then jumped in front of Thorat, grabbing him by both wrists. Before Thorat had fully registered what was happening,

Forlan had flicked him up into the air with a twist of his hips. The mad bandit swung Thorat around in a circle, dancing with him as if he were a child's rag doll. Thorat scrambled to regain his footing, his mostly-empty stomach threatening to turn itself inside out.

"What was that for?" Thorat said as he landed on a bit of scree beside the path.

"Be still, my brother," Ferrent said quietly. To Thorat's surprise, Forlan listened. The mad bandit helped Thorat to his feet, then clapped him on the back so hard that Thorat coughed, but he didn't think he'd bruised any ribs, not quite.

Gran waited for him to recover, then sprang a question on him. "So, Forlan's brother's friend, have you killed a man?"

Thorat hesitated. "I haven't had need to."

"No?" Ferrent said.

"It was the year before I came to Anamat," he said, knowing that Ferrent would know what he meant. He'd been even younger than Eppie was now when they'd had that last pitched battle in Lemirun, the battle that had taken the old Enatel, Konnat. It had left Sovara as their leader, and nothing had been quite the same since, or so all the others said, the ones who survived.

Gran's steps slowed, and he looked at Ferrent and Thorat. "How long have you known each other?"

Ferrent counted on his fingers. "Close to ten years, I think."

Thorat thought. "That's about right. Maybe eleven."

"We'll walk back to the camp now," Gran said. "You still want to talk to Larn about that blade?"

Thorat nodded. "I want it back and for him to let us go back down the mountains."

"Don't go down the mountains!" Forlan said. He jumped, a sudden and awkward movement. "Mountains are for staying!" he said. Then he settled into a slow walk. Gran stayed beside him, letting Thorat and Ferrent walk ahead.

"Why didn't you come to us first?" Thorat asked.

"I was on my way, but I kept to the hills because I didn't want any trouble down below."

"You sound like them."

"You're the one who sent warning. In any case, when I saw Forlan, I wanted to stay. It's been a long time since I saw him."

"But you knew we needed you," Thorat said.

"I do, but I'm not sure I can face another Lemirun."

"How can you say that and still call yourself one of us?"

Ferrent shrugged. "Maybe I can't; I'm just telling you why I'm still here. Besides, I don't think I could fight my way out."

"No? But you must be a better swordsman than these..." Thorat gestured down toward the bandit camp.

"I wouldn't be so sure of that. I've seen Larn with a sword in hand, and he's not one I'd face lightly. The rest of them can fight too. Besides, when I came, they said I could stay as their guest, on account of Forlan being my brother."

"He's really your brother?" Thorat asked.

"My half brother, or milk brother, at least. He was a priestess's child; I was the second son of a fishing family. He was fostered with us. We were born around the same time and we always thought that we had the same father. That was what we told each other, though of course the priestess told us that it didn't matter, and our milk mother didn't want to hear about it."

"Of course," Thorat said. It was hard to imagine they had even one parent in common. Maybe they were cousins, though.

"He's not much like me; at least, he's much bigger. He always was, but we knew that we would both have to go to

Anamat, probably in the same year, so we stuck together. I could tell him when I saw a dragonlet, and our father said he didn't mind if we talked about those things, but not to do it where the rest of the village could hear. We did go to Anamat together, and after a short season on the streets, well, you know."

"And then a year of training?" Thorat prompted, looking back over his shoulder. The others were still some distance behind.

"He was good, better than me," Ferrent said. "Konnat tested our sword-work together a few days before Midsummer, then we took lots to see who would go down into the well first. I went first, and you know how it is; I wasn't sure I'd make it through, but then I felt the dawn come and Konnat came to bring me up. I was all right by evening, and I assumed that the same would happen with Forlan after he went in. I said my goodbye and good luck, and then I never saw him again until I came here. I don't know what happened after that, but he must have gone into the hills. Now here he is."

They both looked back at Forlan bumbling along with a strange skipping motion, as if he were trying to remember his child self in his oversized body.

"He must have been the last one who broke in the test."

"We haven't had many since," Thorat mused. "It's like what happened to Conn's son in the legends. Strange to think that none of the first settlers were dragon-blind."

"None that we've heard of," Ferrent said. "Maybe it's not the people of Theranis who are growing blind. Maybe the dragons really are hiding themselves."

Thorat thought of his long, dragonless sojourn in Tiadun. "I hope not. What do we have to fight for if they're leaving us?"

"The last blush of the dragons' favor, I suppose," Forlan said.

"If I can get that sword back, we can try. Do you think he'd return it if I won it in a challenge?"

"Larn? It's possible, but don't be too confident that you'll win."

"Anyone going into a tournament would be foolish to be so sure of himself, but this? They're bandits."

"They can fight. Wait until you've seen them practice, if they let you see."

Thorat looked sideways at Ferrent. Surely, he was just making excuses for the fact that he'd lingered too long in this valley. Then he looked back at Forlan. There was a resemblance between the two of them. He would have been glad to see a brother too, but not gone mad like this. No wonder Forlan had gone into the hills, but it was a great shame that he hadn't passed that test.

"Maybe the girl apprentice can find the others from Anamat when they come," Ferrent said. "Maybe they can do what needs to be done. I'm not sure I can face another Lemirun, myself."

"But we have to do it," Thorat said. Then he looked over his shoulder. Gran and Forlan were gaining on them. They needed to keep their secrets, and they needed so much more.

§

After a while, Vigda took her turn at the spit and Eppie rested her sore arms by shaping coarse dough into rounds and throwing them on the fire-warmed stones to cook. It would be a good meal and filling, but working the dough reminded her of Raina's cottage. She wished she were back there, or that Raina would find her here. Surely, together they could break out of the bandits' encampment in time to keep the Cereans away from Tiada's gate.

"You do much cooking there in the lowlands?" Vigda asked her.

"Hardly any," Eppie said.

"Then what do you do? I can see you're no priestess."

"Really?" Eppie said, oddly reassured that Vigda, at least, didn't share the ambassadress's plans for her. "How can you tell?"

"Well, first of all, you're out wandering unattended, and that man claims he hasn't touched you."

"Not that way," Eppie said.

"Secondly, you're making the bread all wrong. Here, let me show you." Vigda let the meat rest for a moment, picked up a bit of dough, and folded it over itself before flattening it, somehow making a round of it.

"It symbolizes the two realms, touching here," she said, pinching the rims together, "and folded into each other there." She doubled the dough.

Eppie tried to follow along but the dough stuck to her fingers, making a mess. Vigda chuckled. "Don't fret the dough too much. What you were doing, well, the men are hungry, so they'll eat it, but it's not priestess bread."

"This isn't priestess bread anyway, not with this dough. The flour they use in Anamat is lighter," Eppie said.

"Is it?" Vigda said. "Well, I've never been to Anamat, and I wouldn't care to go, but up here in the mountains, we're so close to Na, we can make priestess bread with any flour at all. Even if it isn't temple bread." She spat on the dirt and made a warding motion. Larn was coming across toward them. Eppie looked up to the hill to see Thorat and the others returning to the circle of tents.

"I'll finish this for you," Vigda said. "You go have a wash in the stream there. I've got to talk to Larn here before your lowlander comes back around. Shoo, go where you like."

"Go where I like?" Eppie said. "Does that mean I can go back down?"

"I wouldn't go back to the lowlands if I were you, not in Tiadun," Larn said as he took Vigda's place at the spit. "Awful lot of foreigners coming. Not safe for a young person, even if you were a boy, which I can see you're not. Sorry for rousting you out in the night like that."

"But why?"

"Can't have lowlanders in the hills," Vigda said. "You're not what we call full grown yet, though, so you can come and go if you like. Off with you."

Eppie went, still unsure that they would really let her go. She left the pair of bandits sitting companionably by the fire and went to find the stream, but she would not leave without at least talking to Thorat first.

§

Chapter 11

Forlan ambled, weaving back and forth across the path, forcing them to walk more slowly than Thorat would have liked. As they reentered the camp, Eppie walked away from it, alone. The old woman left her place at the fire too, leaving the bandit who seemed to be in charge alone there.

"There goes your apprentice," Ferrent said.

"She's not *my* apprentice," Thorat said. "She's our apprentice."

Ferrent looked after Eppie as she disappeared into a nest of low bushes. He frowned. "They haven't let me go to the stream alone once, and I've been here for six days."

Gran laughed, startling Thorat from close behind. "That's because you're a grown man," Gran said. "The scrapplings, when they pass this way, can come and go. Apprentice is nearly the same thing."

"And she's suffered nothing for taking back my sword?" Thorat said.

"Why would she?" Gran asked.

Ferrent laughed before Gran could say more. "Oh, it's your sword, now, is it? Not ours?"

"Well, it was sent to my care, so for now it is," he said, though Ferrent's point was correct. It was only his to use for the task at hand, if he could escape in time to do it.

"It's Larn's now, except that no one owns anything here," Gran said, gesturing to the man by the fire.

"Then how can it be his?" Thorat asked. Gran said nothing, of course. The bandits couldn't have any good answer to that question.

As they reached the fireside, Larn rose and extended his hand in greeting. "That's right," he said, "no one owns anything here. I hope that you slept well?"

"I was sleeping well enough before you woke us in the middle of the night, but apart from that march in the dark, yes, I slept well enough."

"It was hardly the middle of the night," Larn said. "It was almost dawn when we tucked you in."

"But not when you roused me," Thorat complained. "I suppose I can thank you for your hospitality, though, and for reuniting me with my comrade."

Larn was not quite as big as Garren, but he moved with almost as much practiced ease. Maybe Ferrent was right to say that he would be a formidable opponent in a fight. Larn ignored Thorat's complaint and passed around some coarse, misshapen lumps of bread.

A stolen and spitted lamb turned over the low fire, dripping with succulent juices. It looked and smelled far more appetizing than the charred lump of dough in his hand. He took a bite anyway, taking some time to chew it to an edible consistency while the other bandits gathered in from around their camp.

"I'd like to get my sword back," Thorat said after he'd finally managed to swallow his bite of bread.

Larn snorted. "I'm sure you would, but that's not possible. It doesn't *belong* to you."

Thorat hesitated. How did Larn know that? Had he somehow overheard it on the mountain? It hardly mattered, though. "It was entrusted to me," he said.

Larn peered at him. "That's no ordinary sword, and no second-rate swordsman should wield it."

Thorat's back bristled, but he took a deep breath and kept his voice even. "I am not a second-rate swordsman."

"Among the lowlanders, maybe not, but here? I'd like to see you prove it."

Grunts of assent followed Larn's statement as some of the newly arrived bandits leaned in eagerly. Eppie returned from her trip to the spring and stood just outside the circle, listening and watching.

"I don't mind proving it," Thorat said. "Shall we have a test bout, with the sword going to the winner?" Sovara would never forgive him if he gave that sword up to bandits. He shouldn't have to fight for it, but he wasn't overly concerned – he rarely lost a bout against anyone he hadn't trained with before.

Larn showed no signs of worry, either. "I'll let you try to fight for it, lowlander, if you dare," he said with a smile. "If you win the bout, the blade is yours to keep so long as you're here with us. If you leave, we might take it back. It pleases me, that blade."

"I'm sure it does," Thorat said. He didn't have any intention of staying with the bandits. He just needed to get the sword back. After that, he had some chance of getting ready to defend Tiada when the Cereans came, if he could get away with it.

"Do you have blunted tournament blades?" he asked, preferring to arrange the details of the match rather than argue about the prize.

Larn gestured around at their poor camp. "Why would we carry such useless things?"

"Ferrent tells me that you practice some."

"I've seen you," Ferrent said. "You've trained most mornings, these past few days."

Larn sighed. "Practice blades it is, then," he said. He gestured to Forlan, and the big madman ambled off into the brush surrounding the spring. Thorat was glad that Eppie was back. He didn't want Forlan—harmless as he seemed so far—to meet her in the bushes there.

"What are the rules of your tournaments?" Thorat asked Larn.

"We have no rules here; we're lawless, you know."

Thorat couldn't tell whether Larn meant that in earnest or whether he was making a joke.

"You can't have a bout without rules," Ferrent objected, finally speaking, finally coming around to his side. "When I've been in tournaments, we've had three kinds of man-to-man bout. You can have a bout to first wounding, until one man is on the ground for a half-count, or to disarming."

Thorat nodded. "First wounding is usually the quickest."

"So, let's not do that," Larn said. "No sport in it, really. Ground or disarming."

Thorat considered the choices. Getting Larn to the ground would be hard enough, if what Ferrent had said were true. He was big and quick. He'd have a better chance with disarming.

"To disarming," Thorat said.

"Let's change it a little," Larn said. "I won't play all the way by lowlanders' rules. Disarming or grounding, either one."

Thorat agreed. Larn could set any rules he liked, but at least these were clear enough that he could work with them and form some sort of strategy once he'd taken the measure of his opponent.

There was a long moment of silence, then Eppie came up and took a piece of the bread from beside the fire, knocking it against a rock.

"How do you like my bread?" she asked.

"This?" Thorat fumbled with the leathery piece of food in his hand. "I've had better."

"Now, now," Ferrent said. "I've had far worse, too. I think all the bread in Kiralun is as tough as this, some tougher."

"I never said I could cook," Eppie said. "So, where's this bout going to happen?"

Larn pointed to a fiat area halfway across the valley. "We train over there. I'll have Vigda go bless it against deceit. She'll have it ready by the time Forlan gets back with the practice blades."

"You hide them down by the stream?" Eppie said.

Larn frowned. "You can't have all our secrets."

"Sorry." Eppie took a piece of her misshapen bread and bit into it. "So, this is Ferrent?"

Ferrent stood and bowed, taking Eppie's hand in a courtly gesture. "At your service, lady."

"Don't call me lady," Eppie snapped.

"Now, there," Larn said. "Shall we have the scrappling call the start or the priestess?"

"Not me," Eppie said.

Thorat looked over at the old priestess. Though grizzled, she still had some grace about her.

"Our priestess's blessing might go to the victor, too," Gran said helpfully.

Thorat felt his face go hot.

Ferrent broke in with a laugh. "Still pining after the –" He stopped himself before naming the ambassadress, at least, but then he went on. "Thorat here has a, ah, a particular priestess he favors, a very particular priestess."

Thorat looked down at the ground, then looked up. Eppie was blushing too and looking down at her feet as if studying a loose thread on her sandal.

"That's not proper," Larn said. "But you know, I have one I favor myself. We all should."

"Nonsense," Ferrent said.

"Your farmwife?" Thorat said.

"That's different." Ferrent sighed. "She's not a priestess, and besides, she no longer favors me."

"I'm sorry," Thorat said. He was still half-jealous, though. "At least now you're here."

"Here in the barren mountains," Ferrent said with a wry smile.

Thorat grunted. Ferrent might be within his rights to feel jilted and bitter, but at least he'd had some time with his farmwife, far more than Thorat had ever shared with Iola. He would never have so many nights in Iola's bed, not while she was a priestess, and she would never be anything else.

Gran got to his feet as another bandit emerged from his tent, yawning. "There's Kendet," he said. "He brought in this fine sheep. The mountains may be no good for farming, but there's plenty of good hunting here."

Hunting of poor farmers' sheep, Thorat thought.

"And you're neither of you farming men," Larn pointed out, "and we've got a contest to fight."

They walked across to the fiat part of the dip in the mountains. Larn, Kendet, and Gran went ahead, while Eppie hung back with Thorat and Ferrent.

"Are you all right?" Thorat asked Eppie.

"Fine," Eppie said, looking away.

He felt that something was troubling her, but the bandits there seemed to be sincere about their prohibition against harming or holding scrapplings. The same code was held in the villages and Anamat, but it seemed to be weaker protection than it once had been. Maybe these southern bandits were different from the ones he'd seen in the north so long before.

"Are you going to leave?" Thorat asked her.

"Maybe, once I get a good share of the food," Eppie said. "I'm hungry, and besides, I'd like to see you –" Eppie stopped short of predicting the outcome of the fight.

"We should walk closer to the others," Ferrent said as Larn waved at them to hurry up.

"In a moment." Thorat lowered his voice. "Do you think you can find the others down near the village?"

"I hope so," Eppie said, "if they've come."

"If you do find them, tell them where we are. If there are enough of them to break us out of here, maybe we can get to the gate in time."

"Why not just tell Larn and Vigda what you need to do, or offer to help them keep the lowlanders out of the forests? If they don't like lowlanders in the hills, they'll like Cereans there even less," Eppie said.

"They only plague the villagers in their pastures!" Thorat said. They hadn't done him any harm yet, true, but he'd only been in their camp for a morning.

Ferrent clapped Eppie on the back. "We can't tell them who we are, but that's not a bad thought. I'd like to fight beside my brother again."

"I can't trust them," Thorat said. "Our order is too small already. What if they put knives in our backs? We can't let them destroy us."

"I don't think they would," Eppie said.

Thorat shook his head. She was too trusting. How had she survived so far? He worried that she would be taken in by illusions in her test at Midsummer and wind up like poor deluded Forlan, stumbling aimlessly around the hills, or maybe the priestesses would get her after all.

He shook his head clear. There would be time to worry about that later, if any of them lived. For now, he had a bout to fight.

§

The two men squared off on a levelish stretch of winter-beaten grass, with spring green sprigs just starting to brighten it at the roots. Eppie looked for signs of Tiada's small blue-and-orange flower but found none. Forlan presented each man with a practice blade, the weapons even more battered than the ones they had at the hall in Anamat. If the Defenders had once had a hidden, ancient relationship with the swordsmiths, it no longer stretched to new practice blades.

Vigda took the center of the field, holding up a crown of cedar boughs. "To Na, our offering," she said. Now she spoke with a voice that carried like city bells, not the common voice she'd used when they were talking around the cooking fire. "To Na, we pledge our swords, to keep the hills free of corruption and unbelief." Then she spread her arms, pointing one hand to each of the contestants. "To the victor, the blessed sword, to lead us to our duty."

Ferrent, standing next to Eppie, cocked his head. She looked up at him. "What is it?" she whispered as Vigda set the wreath down and walked back toward them.

"It's very like what we say back in Anamat, you know."

"I haven't heard it yet."

"You will," Ferrent said. "I think you will, if any of us live through this. Last time –" He stopped. Thorat and Larn were advancing toward each other with long, careful strides. Seeing them across from each other, Eppie was struck by how similar their movements were, how alike they looked despite their different clothes and Larn's thicker build.

"Now, that's interesting," Ferrent said, as if to himself.

Eppie wasn't sure what he was looking at, but he was staring very intently. "What?" she asked.

"I wonder if Forlan remembered more than we thought he would, and taught these –"

Thorat raised his sword slightly and made a quick, almost darting side cut at Larn's neck. Larn stepped back, parried, and returned the strike, which Thorat evaded by going to the side and making a long, low slice to the torso. Larn's blade dipped and caught it just before it landed, then sent Thorat's weapon flying up in a wide arc. Thorat managed to hold on to it, but even Eppie could see that it was a near thing. Both men were sweating already. Thorat retreated and began to circle.

"You know a thing or two, lowlander," Larn said.

Thorat gave a tiny nod in response, still visibly taking the measure of the bandit.

Eppie closed her eyes, hoping that Thorat would win back the blade. She almost missed the next move.

This time, it was Larn who darted in. Thorat's blade shot up to block the strike, then twisted. Larn's sword spun loose, but before the sword hit the ground, Thorat had lost his grip too. Larn got behind Thorat and, with his bare fist, knocked the sword to the ground. Thorat spun around, unbalancing Larn.

For a long moment, the two men stood locked in a human knot, held together by bare strings of tension, sweat beading on their brows. Larn got a leg loose, and the two men fell to the ground together.

"Draw!" Vigda's voice rang out.

The two men gave a muffled grunt. They separated, scrambled up, and dusted themselves off. Forlan retrieved the swords.

"You have the priestess call the match?" Thorat asked. The only priestess in Anamat who would be half knowledgeable enough to do that was Sunna, and she was only half a priestess.

"Who else?" Larn said. "Shall we fight again?"

"I know your tricks now," Thorat said.

"Not all of them." Larn waved for the swords but Vigda shook her head. Forlan stood still, holding them, looking back and forth between Larn and Vigda.

"The agreement was for one bout," Vigda said. "The lowlander has shown himself worthy of holding the charged sword, however he got it."

"He has?" Larn said, while Ferrent said, "How?"

Thorat looked puzzled, too.

"What about me?" Larn said.

"I knew you were good enough already," Vigda said, in her ordinary voice. She straightened up and spoke again as priestess and judge. "This is what I decree. The lowlander will stay in our camp for seven days and teach us what he knows, along with his companion, Forlan's brother."

Thorat's jaw flapped open. "I..."

Eppie knew that he wouldn't want to do that. She didn't know which was worse to him, the prospect of sharing the training hall's secrets or the fear of the Cereans creeping up on the gate while he stayed in the hills.

"I can't," Thorat said.

Larn clapped him on the back. "Think on it. Meanwhile, I'm hungry."

They all trooped back to the fireside and lifted the roast onto a board beside the fire. Eppie's mouth watered. Gran made the first cut, sliced it in half, and gave half each to the two contestants while Vigda passed around the basket of tough bread and Ferrent and Forlan went to the stream for water. Eppie wrapped a piece of bread around a cut of meat and some of Vigda's strange herbs, then went to sit beside Thorat.

They were not alone, but every man seemed intent on his eating.

"I can't stay here," Thorat said quietly. "They'll be at the – They'll be *there* in no time."

"If they can find it," Eppie said. "We almost couldn't, and you knew what to look for."

Ferrent returned from the spring. He raised his eyebrows as he sat down with them.

"The opening is small," Thorat explained, "as if she's retreating."

"But she's not gone," Eppie said. She took another bite and chewed on it slowly. The little valley had a peaceful beauty about it, even if it was in Na's wild lands. Joining the bandits seemed much better than being trapped in a temple if she didn't pass whatever test there was at Midsummer, or if she went mad. This place was a long way from Anamat, but they all seemed happy enough, if a bit fiea-bitten, and the men gave Vigda more respect than common priestesses in the city usually got.

"So, you'll go look for the others?" Thorat asked her.

Eppie nodded. "I'd half rather stay here, though. Better eating."

"This is good meat, but it's not that good," Thorat said. He sounded annoyed, even angry.

"Sorry," Eppie said.

"Look," Ferrent chimed in. "It's not that you have to go; it's that you're the only one who can. You can show the others the way to...to where we need to go, and we'll come when we can."

"They could come rescue us," Thorat said. "I think Garren could take them all on."

Ferrent shook his head.

"I don't think Garren's coming," Eppie said. "Maybe Raina and Varin, but Varin has that sprain."

Thorat hung his head, despair overcoming him, but Ferrent made him get to his feet, and they made a show of congeniality as they ate, though Eppie could tell that Thorat would rather have been almost anywhere else, anywhere he could do something.

§

Before Eppie left, Thorat made her rehearse the whistled signal that the Defenders used to locate each other in the hills. It sounded almost like a bird's call but not quite. He'd been caught out by it himself more than once, hearing the bird and following its song until he realized that the actual bird's call lacked the final trill, and that its calls came at closer intervals. Never mind, though; at least the apprentice knew it now. The others would only have to follow the small army of Cerean merchants and the prince's men to the village. Beyond that, he didn't know what they would do.

He had no desire to sit in the mountains, playing at swords with bandits, but they wouldn't let him leave, and he wouldn't be able to fight his way out if Ferrent wasn't fully on his side, or if any of the others were half as good as their leader. Ferrent didn't want to leave his half-wit brother, and said that Forlan was nearly as swift on his feet as the others once he had a sword in his hand, even if he seemed like a bumbling oaf the rest of the time. No, they wouldn't be able to fight their way out. Worse, Ferrent seemed to have taken Eppie's preposterous suggestion for far more than it was worth, as if the bandits might fight beside them at the gate.

True, the bandits didn't like lowlanders in their hills, and they took a dim view of villagers going too high up into the forest, but they also hated the villagers with a bile that reminded Thorat of his own dislike of bandits in general. This band seemed less inclined to skewer scrapplings, but their dragon, Na, would eat a man if he had the chance. He had to find the others, or rather, they needed to find him and get him out of this camp so they could all go down and meet their deaths at Tiada's gate, impossibly far from Anamat and Iola's embrace.

Vigda offered him her blessing, but he did not go to the rite with her and she took no offense at his refusal. He wondered if this was what Sunna might be like when she was older. He even missed Sunna. He missed them all.

The charged sword, with the piece of the dragons' veins in it, stayed out of sight, hidden in Larn and Vigda's tent. For most of the rest of the day, Thorat trained with their practice blades, ate their stolen meat, and thought he would go mad from being trapped under the unbroken dome of Na's blue sky.

§

They let Eppie take Thorat's common blade, saying that she would need a weapon if she insisted on going back down among the corrupt lowlanders. She set out along a faint path away from the bandits' valley. At the edge of the forest, she stopped to look back. None of the bandits were following her, but she almost wished they would, since they insisted on keeping Thorat. She'd gotten used to his company in the past half-moon, more than used to it. She almost turned around and began to climb back to rejoin him. Perhaps she could cheer him a little, and there would be nothing she could do at the gate alone. There seemed to be little chance that the others from Anamat would reach them in time to help. She would have to persuade Thorat and the bandits to come down, all together, somehow.

Then she heard the distant sound of a horn, far away down the hill. There wasn't time to persuade them. The prince and his allies had come. The least she could do would be to go and find out how many they were, and how well armed. It would be better for them to know that much before they came stumbling blindly down. There still wouldn't be enough time, but if Tiada kept her gate so well hidden, then maybe the interlopers wouldn't be able to find it right away. Maybe there would be time to find some way of stopping them.

The trees' shade closed around her, from tall evergreens to scraggly bushes pushing out their new spring leaves. Eppie lost sight of the track and navigated by following the downward slope of the land through the thinner parts of the underbrush. The horn blew again, closer this time, its call accompanied by the distant sound of crashing through the underbrush. Eppie hurried toward the sound, but when the horn blew a third time and the mad rush of crashing seemed almost upon her, she found a likely-looking tree and climbed into the canopy, her newly borrowed-again sword clattering awkwardly against her back.

The boar barreled through a moment later, chased by shouts and arrows. Eppie saw a finely dressed man on horseback fitting his arrow to the string. He let loose and the arrow flew in a sure arc, landing squarely at the back of the boar's thick neck but bouncing off its hide. She glanced back to the man on horseback just in time to see him fall forward on his mount as he careened in a circle under the trees.

"The prince!" someone called. "The prince fell! Come!"

The prince's horse passed below her perch, with the prince's arms wrapped around the horse's neck and a bright red spot spouting on his back. The rest of the hunters crashed up behind him, coming to a halt some place below the tree. She heard a thud as the prince fell, and the jangle of the horse's gear as it tried to get away. Someone swore and she heard more crashing.

Eppie couldn't see the prince, so she edged down and out along one of the tree's lower limbs to get a better view. Another finely dressed man dismounted and knelt at the prince's side. She held her breath and listened. She could just make out their words.

"Terenet," he said. "What felled you?"

The prince put a hand to his side and drew a ragged breath. "You know better than I, brother, you or your sons." He was bleeding fiercely, half his jacket stained red already.

"My brother, it was not by my hand."

"Only at your orders," the prince said. Then he fainted.

"Someone bind these wounds!" the prince's brother ordered.

Another man rushed up. Eppie moved higher into the tree as quietly as she could manage. For now, all eyes were on the prince, but if she were the prince's brother, she would be looking for someone else to blame. Who better than an armed scrappling up a tree, even if she didn't have a bow and arrow? If it were down to her word against that of the prince's brother, that would be the end of her for sure.

The hunters sent a messenger down to the camp right away, and soon after that, they'd bound the prince's wound and loaded him onto a stretcher. Eppie waited for the noise to fade, then she climbed down. She followed their trail, a wide swath of broken forest, as the shadows fell long and dark and the birds struck up their evening chorus.

She was almost to the edge of the grain fields when she heard the call, a snatch of birdsong that wasn't quite right, one note too drawn out, the interval too long. It was the call Thorat had taught her. She answered it.

§

"Sunna?" Eppie said when they came into view. "Why are you here? I thought you couldn't travel in...uh..." Sunna's belly might have been rounded, but its bulge was still small enough to hide under the fall of her unbelted tunic. Varin, beside her, was the one who looked thin and pale.

"Where's Thorat?" Sunna asked. "And what happened here?"

"Shouldn't we be trying to be quiet?" Varin said. He plunked down on a fallen log. The two of them had come up the trail along the edge between the field and the forest, the same one that Eppie and Thorat had followed almost a half-moon earlier on their first approach to Tiada's gate. The prince's hunting party was already far away across the field, trampling the new wheat as they went, a dozen men on horseback and about as many following on foot, a large party compared to what Eppie would have expected, but small enough that the prince's brother could probably buy the word of any man in it, to confirm that the prince had been shot by accident.

"We've just come from the Anamat road," Sunna said. "In the last village there, we heard that the prince and his foreign guests were coming this way, so we followed. I'm glad we didn't miss you."

"Well, you did miss Thorat," Eppie said. She explained that they'd found the gate, but that the villagers had driven them from their campsite, and then the bandits had broken up their new camp and dragged them into the hills. She also told them that Thorat had nearly been beaten in a tournament bout with the bandits' leader, and that Ferrent was with the bandits too.

"He wants you to come rescue him," she finished. "He was hoping that Garren would come."

Sunna shook her head. "Garren stayed back in Anamat. If the worst happens, if we're all killed, he thinks that maybe he and Sovara can train up the next generation of Defenders, if they can find enough suitable apprentices, not that they're likely to find them."

Varin sighed. "My ankle's no good, barely good enough to walk on, let alone fight."

"It hurts him," Sunna said.

"And Sunna gets tired too, on account of she was careless."

Sunna gave an exasperated sigh. "It's not carelessness; it's just that sometimes it doesn't work the way it's supposed to."

Eppie looked back and forth between them. They sounded like they'd had had this argument more than once before. She tilted her head and squinted. Sure enough, she could detect the slight thickening of Sunna's waist when she stood up straight. "I thought that you couldn't come, because of that."

Sunna shook her head. "I thought I couldn't, but after you left, Raina and I had a long talk. I couldn't very well attend the ambassadress like this, either, and Raina didn't want to leave her children. She said that I could carry mine with me more easily now than I'd be able to later, and that I should go when I could, that if all went well, I could stay to the back of the line."

"A line of three doesn't have much back to it," Varin said. "But if all *doesn't* go well, it won't matter, anyway."

Sunna nodded. "I don't think we're in any fit condition to rescue Thorat from a band of even half-skilled swordsmen, even if they do go around wearing furs and making blood sacrifices." She shuddered.

"I'm not sure about the blood sacrifices," Eppie said, "and what *I* thought was that maybe they could help us, but Thorat didn't agree. They don't like 'lowlanders' in what they call their hills, and I think the gate's close enough that it might matter to them."

Sunna shook her head. "No one trusts bandits. Why would they? They're bandits, even if they have a mad hermit priestess with them."

Varin gazed out at the field. "So, what happened with that hunting party, and why are you following them?"

"The only thing that hunt might have killed was the prince of Tiadun."

§

Chapter 12

They talked until the evening crossed into night, and Eppie shared some of the food the bandits had given her. The meat had gone cold and the bread was even harder than it had been at midday.

"If they've got more of this, I don't mind joining the bandits," Varin said, as if the bandit food were better than what they'd gotten in the villages.

"Well, I do," Sunna said.

"One of them used to be a priestess, or still is," Eppie said. "Ferrent said she can fight, too, but I haven't seen it."

"Interesting," Sunna said. "I've heard of priestess bandits. In the temple, sometimes they mention them along with the hermit priestesses, but I never heard of anyone meeting one. In Anamat, they're just a rumor."

"I think she hates Anamat, but she says that she's never been there."

"We might as well go to them," Varin said. "What other chance do we have against the foreigners?"

"I don't mind getting a bunch of bandits killed if we can persuade them it's their fight, too," Sunna said, "but I'd hate to be the one to have to tell Sovara about it after."

Eppie felt like she'd learned a lot since Midsummer, but she was still a long way from even Sunna's level of skill, and she wasn't ready to argue with Sunna's idea of what the Enatel would think. "I did tell Thorat I'd ask you to spring him from the bandits' camp," she reminded them.

Sunna took off her pack and rolled out her thin fur sleeping mat. "We'll go in the morning," she said.

Varin slumped down next to her, spreading himself out to sleep too. Eppie still felt wide awake.

"What about me?" she asked. "I could go up to the mountains tonight and tell them you're here."

"No, not yet," Sunna said. "Morning will be soon enough." She yawned. "Is the prince of Tiadun dead, do you think?"

"There was a lot of blood, and he looked pretty pale. I've never seen a man die before, but he sure looked done for to me."

Varin rolled onto his side and propped his head up. "I've seen men die, and I've seen men recover, too. You were up in the trees, right? Did you have a really good view?"

"Good enough to see that there was a lot of blood. He went kind of limp, too."

"I'd really like to know for sure," Varin said.

"So would I," Sunna said. "Maybe you could go into their camp and try to find out. I'd leave your sword here with us so it won't clatter around and get in your way, and so that if they catch you, you can say you're just a local herder or something, looking for a scrap."

"I could, but won't it be dangerous?" It was a foolish thing to say. Of course Eppie knew it would be dangerous. The journey had been easy enough, compared to what it could have been, but it was a far cry from walking into an armed camp or trying to overhear a prince's well-guarded business.

"This whole thing is dangerous." Sunna yawned. "And I'm almost asleep. We'll see you in the morning?"

"Sure," Eppie said, "or maybe I'll wake you when I get back. If I don't come back, try to find the bandits. They're camped in a nice valley just about straight uphill from here. Then if you can't find them, go east along the bottom of the hill until you start seeing this little blue-and-orange flower. Follow it along to where it grows thickest. The gate's small; there's a big tree over it. It doesn't look like much."

"Flowers?" Sunna said from under her blanket. "So, Thorat's been teaching you priestess lore. Very funny."

"Thank you," Varin said. "I'll remember that for next time he boasts about his manliness."

"I've never heard Thorat brag," Eppie said, immediately wishing she hadn't spoken.

Sunna yawned. "He doesn't need to, curse him."

§

The two of them yawningly wished her good luck. Eppie had eaten well that day, and she'd slept straight through from dawn until noon, so she felt ready to walk all night as long as there was moonlight to see by and it didn't rain. The prince's camp was only across the field and down the road a bit, close enough that she'd heard sounds from it here and there, when her conversation with the others lagged. The smoke from their cooking fires spiraled up, obscuring the stars.

She set off into the night, following the trail of the hunt across the field to the road then creeping up to the edge of the camp. She'd expected to feel uneasy without a sword on her back, but oddly, she felt more comfortable, as if she was a scrappling in Anamat again. She was a little too tall for the role, but she still knew how to melt into the darkness.

At the camp, armsmen and servants were still pitching tents. A gaggle of village children stood watching while the Enomaean horse handlers tried to shoo the most curious of them out of the way. That only prompted the rest of the children to giggle while the bolder ones imitated the strange sounds of the foreigners and their beasts. The Enomaeans had their own cluster of tents, near where the horses grazed and downhill from the main encampment, which the children were not quite bold enough to approach.

The main camp consisted of about a dozen circular tents surrounding a fire. Most of the Cereans crouched around the central fire, warming their hands. A boar roasted over the flames, and looked like it was almost done, which meant that at least some of the party must have ridden ahead of the tents. Nearby, a villager unloaded bread from her donkey cart. The fare smelled no better than the bandits' meal. Eppie lurked in the shadows, watching.

The men around the fire kept glancing over to a pair of tents at the uphill edge of the circle, away from the Enomaeans and their horses. A pair of armsmen stood in front of one tent, hands resting on the hilts of their swords. Every now and again, one or the other of them would leave his post and circle around the back of the tent. One of the Cereans, more richly dressed than the others, looked over to the guarded tent about twice as often as the others did. He was the only one sitting on a folding camp stool – the rest sat on logs or crouched on their heels.

Another figure entered the circle from the direction of the village, one with a familiar slouch. It was Squid with his foreign cap on. He went straight to the Cerean on the stool and said something in a low voice. It must have been too hard to hear even from nearby, because the men around them stopped whispering and strained to listen, then shook their heads. When he'd done delivering his message, Squid took a piece of bread from the cart, indifferent to the fact that no one else had eaten yet. That was Squid, all right. Eppie decided that she'd rather see what was happening in those tents than wait where she was, where Squid might spot her.

She made her way around the outside of the circle, keeping low and darting through the bright, fire-lit patches between the tents. She waited until one of the guards had made his circuit, then she stole up to the back of the tent. Creeping softly along the ground, her right pinkie toe came up hard against a rock. She sucked in her breath, trying not to cry out in pain, and teetered on her uninjured foot.

"What's that?" said one of the guards.

"Probably nothing."

Eppie stilled herself. A pile of gear lay at her feet, shovels, pegs, and empty sacks. She flattened herself to the ground between the pile and the edge of the tent. She wondered why they'd left it there, behind the prince's tent, but it was lucky for her that they had. By the time the guard made his second circuit to double-check about the noise, she'd managed to quiet her breath again. She listened.

"Do you think he'll wake again?" asked a woman's voice from inside the tent. The words, and the sound of her voice, were full of worry.

"Farseer gathers his warriors home to the clouds," said a man with a foreign accent. That had to be the priest of Farseer.

"I didn't ask you about Farseer! I want to know if he will wake again." Now the woman sounded like she was scolding the priest, and as if she had full authority to do so.

"We do not trouble our god with the failings of the body, not at its ending," the priest said in a patronizing tone.

"What good is your god, then?"

"Your prince was felled by an arrow, a fitting fate for a man," the priest said, as if the woman's anger meant nothing to him.

"I don't see *you* throwing yourself into battle," the woman said.

Someone came in through the front flap of the tent. "Stop your squabbling," the man said. Eppie thought it might be the prince's brother, the one who had claimed that he hadn't shot the prince with his own arrow, but she couldn't see him, so she wasn't sure at first.

After a little while, she peeked under the edge of the tent and saw the man's large feet walking across the rugs. There were none of the usual straw mats in this tent—it looked fit to be a prince's chamber, if only a temporary one.

"Will he wake again?" the man asked.

"Farseer doesn't concern himself with such things," the woman said bitterly. "Calar," she said, "as keep mistress, I command that you send for the village priestess. Surely, even a poor village temple has a healer better than this fool."

"I never claimed to be –" the priest began.

"Quiet, woman, and stay to your place," said Calar. That *had to* be the prince's brother.

"This *is* my place. Send for a priestess."

Calar stomped back out of the tent, his feet raising clouds of dust as he went, while the woman grumbled under her breath.

A weak croak sounded from the cot. "Stop talking about me as if I'm not here," the prince said. His voice wavered and there was a bit of a gurgling sound behind it, but he was very close, and the words were clear enough for Eppie to hear. "Thank you, Gallia, my love."

Eppie heard a rustle of cloth and the faint sound of a kiss. She was perilously close to the head of the prince himself.

The priest of Farseer cleared his throat.

"Yes," the prince said, in a voice that was now barely audible.

"Shall I prepare the altar to summon Farseer and his kin, to bear your soul to the clouds?"

The prince coughed and gave a cry of pain. The woman, the keep mistress Gallia, made soothing sounds.

"The clouds?" the prince said. "No, not the clouds. I am not Farseer's."

"But you are!" the priest said loudly. "You have been accepted at his altar and you are dying the good death of a warrior. You are a proud son of Farseer."

"Help me up a little," the prince said to his mistress. She helped him to sit, aided by another person, someone who had not spoken, probably a servant. The prince cried out in pain, panted a few ragged breaths, then spoke again.

"I'm not," he said.

"We will say the summoning," the priest said.

"No!" the prince roared, or as close to a roar as he was able to produce. A cushion fell off the cot and landed right in front of Eppie's nose. She would have scooted back, but the sound of clanking warned her that the guard was coming around again. She held her breath as someone picked up the pillow and replaced it on the cot, the hand so close that she could almost feel its warmth through the fabric of the tent wall. She should leave, she thought, as soon as that guard went away, but they were still talking inside the tent.

The keep mistress stood. "Go away, man." Her voice was sure and commanding. This time, the priest heeded her. He made an indistinct noise, then went out with a great fuss of shuffling.

There was a brief lull before the heavy fiap of the tent was pushed aside again.

"May Farseer greet you –"

"Go, man," Gallia said. "Leave these shores before the dragons' kin eat your eagle god!"

"Go," the prince echoed, though so weakly that the priest probably didn't hear him. When the tent fiap had closed again, Gallia sat down on the creaking cot. Eppie heard the sound of another kiss.

"Leave us," the keep mistress said, dismissing the servant. The prince and his mistress sat in silence.

"Thank you, Gallia," the prince said after a while. "I see them now, the dragonlets. As soon as that arrow hit me, I saw one in the wood, up in a tree. I didn't know what it was, but see, just there, by the chest? She is brighter now, now that the..."

"There's no need to speak his name."

"I never saw them before, not with you, but I love you."

"You saw them before, though?" the keep mistress said. "When? You never told me."

"I'm sorry. I should have. It was on the night my daughter must have been conceived, when I went to the Great Rite at the temple in this village. I should have known they would come back."

"Your daughter?" Gallia said. "So, it was I who was barren?"

"It doesn't matter now."

"It does matter!"

"I'm dying, and it's too late; I never knew her, not for long."

Eppie heard the tent flap open a little, but the prince and his mistress were too intent on each other to notice, it seemed.

"Is she dead, then?"

"I don't think so. She was in Anamat. She went there as a scrappling and became a priestess like her mother, but I think she left the temple, too." He sighed. "They didn't tell me where she went."

"We can find her," Gallia said. "I'm sure of it."

The prince shifted position. "She doesn't want to be found."

It was so quiet that Eppie began to wonder if the prince had fallen asleep, or if Gallia had somehow left without making a sound, but finally, Gallia spoke again:

"Why Farseer, then? I always counseled you against it."

"You were wise," the prince said. "I thought we needed some strong allegiance to work against the Cereans he called in, stronger than just our neighbors in Kiralun or Getedun. I did not think they would be so slow to back me, and after all, Farseer at least flies like the dragons."

"Not quite like them."

"No, not at all like them, but that was what I thought at first."

The tent flap closed, and this time, they noticed the sound.

"Calar. Curse him!" the keep mistress said.

"He'll rule, and it will be the final ruin of Tiadun." The prince sighed.

"I could challenge him."

"Don't. He'll only find a way to kill you, too. My daughter would have standing to challenge his rule, but no one else does. No one would be fool enough to do it."

"I'll find her," Gallia said.

"No, she wanted to run. I don't know why, but she's long gone now, and at least she'll live," the prince said. "Help me lie down again."

"I'll need help," Gallia said.

The prince took a long, ragged breath. "I'll have last rites at the temple," he said. "Offer my body to Tiada's flame in the village square."

"I'll see it done," Gallia pledged. She gave him another kiss, then went to fetch the servant.

Eppie could hear the hubbub at the front of the tent. It was as good a time to get out as any. The prince was dying, his brother had killed him, and he had a daughter in Anamat. He wanted last rites at the temple, and a funeral pyre there. Those were the main things. An easy enough message to carry. She edged herself backward until she could stand, but she stumbled on a spade and it clattered against the other tools in the pile.

"Who goes there?" gasped the prince.

Eppie didn't wait to see who would give chase. She ran straight out across the field to the nearest dark cover of hedges and trees. She dove into the forest, then crept back to the spot where Sunna and Varin lay side by side, snoring. She crept in between them and slept.

§

Thorat spent the afternoon with Larn, comparing fighting techniques and picking at the carcass on the spit. Gran and Kendet had gone hunting. Ferrent and Forlan went off on some expedition of their own, with Ferrent assuring Thorat that they would stay close by. Thorat had to admit that Larn was a strong swordsman, but Ferrent's sympathy with the bandits still galled him. Larn was cordial and politely curious, and shared a few interesting techniques he'd learned. No good could come of it, but Thorat slowly admitted to himself that the bandits seemed friendlier than Tiadun's lowlanders, certainly friendlier and more trust-inspiring than anyone in the keep had been.

As the day was growing late, Thorat finally decided to ask Larn one of the questions that had been troubling him.

"There's enough wild game in these mountains to keep you in meat, so why do you steal the villagers' sheep? It angers them and sets them against you. I always thought..." He couldn't quite bring himself to say it.

"Which province do you hail from?"

"Onarun, in the north," Thorat answered, wondering why it mattered.

"In Onarun, do they tell the story that we bandits eat village children as well as the lambs, and that we take them to Na's mouth and fiay them?"

"Well, ah, not in so much detail, no, but you do steal children and sacrifice them to Na, don't you?"

"We let that girl of yours go. We let all of them go."

"Not all bandits do, though. I saw some once who stole a girl and took her to a –" He stopped himself short. The thing he'd seen was a secret thing. As comradely as Larn seemed, he had his own loyalties.

"What, an altar?" Larn asked. He didn't wait for Thorat's answer. "True bandits don't have altars, but we see them spring up sometimes near a village where there's been trouble with thievery, usually to make the thieving look like the bandits' work, when half the time or more, it's the next village over. We always destroy those when we do find them." That was interesting but not what had happened.

"It wasn't an altar," Thorat said. He wasn't sure where to begin, or whether or not to begin at all, but the days stretched before them. He had plenty of time. "It was a gate, an open gate."

"Which one?" Larn didn't look as surprised as Thorat thought he should be, and he sat down on a smooth stone overlooking the campsite. He looked up at Thorat expectantly.

"It was near the border of Coradun, straight up from there into the bare mountains. I think it must be Na's."

"You know a fair sight about gates for a lowlander." Larn stood and walked away. He did not invite Thorat to follow. He disappeared into the tent he shared with the old priestess woman, Vigda.

Thorat considered the fact that he could have left the camp right then, but the bandits still had the sword and Ferrent was away with Forlan. He didn't know for sure where Eppie had gone, either. The bandits had kidnapped her, but they'd let her go because they trusted her for some reason, and she returned the favor. For himself, he still felt the echo of that time he'd first met Iola on the journey to Anamat, when the bandits – worse bandits than these, from what he'd seen so far – had kidnapped the future ambassadress. He couldn't trust them, not yet, but his fear of these particular bandits was slowly easing away. It might disappear entirely if he let himself forget, but he did not want to forget.

None of this musing and remembering would help him guard Tiada's gate, though. He went back down to the fireside, and there he took a stick and sketched a rough map in the ashes. If the Cereans came up from the village along the old, overgrown path to the gate, there was a chance that he, Ferrent, and Garren could pick them off one by one at the narrow gap between trees and thick brush a short distance down the hill, near the old shrine. It seemed, at the keep, that only a handful of the Cereans were fighting men, maybe half a dozen of the entire crew of the two trading vessels. The rest were just laborers and sailors. Thorat wondered if any of the fighting men, or even most of them, might have been left back to guard the boats. He hoped so. That would leave only the prince's guards to contend with. They were men he'd come to know, and though they weren't well-loved comrades, most of them were decent enough men in their way. He didn't relish the thought of cutting them down, but he could do it if it were in defense of the dragon. Then their numbers would prevail over his skill. It was a foolish errand. He wondered if the bandits would enjoy it. They probably would.

That night, he told Ferrent about his plan to stop the interlopers between the two big oaks just downhill from the gate along the path.

"But what if they come another way?" Ferrent asked.

"Well, I have that one plan, which is more than I had this morning," Thorat said. "It's probably hopeless."

"Lemirun," Ferrent said thoughtfully. "I wonder if that was the only time they'd gotten so bold as to come into the hills until now, or have they come and gone from other gates, with us knowing nothing of it?"

"I don't know," Thorat said. The battle to drive foreign miners from Lemira's gate had come just before his time. "What I do know is that we can't stay here, sitting comfortably up in the mountains as if we came on some kind of pleasure walk."

"It's been good to see my brother again."

"I know, but –"

"But what I saw there, in Lemirun – and I didn't see it all; you never do when you're in the midst of a fight – what I saw there and what I remember make me think that something unexpected will happen. We won't know what until it does. We can't plan for it."

"What was so unexpected at Lemirun?"

"Well, you've heard how Konnat, the old Enatel, and so many others died. Two of those who died were a priestess and a young Cerean man who saw the dragon. The dragon Lemira was so faded that even the village children could only see her as a ripple in the air. When the priestess and the Cerean saw the gate, they plunged in. They must have died. After that, Lemira was stronger. I know we helped to hold the Cereans back, to convince them not to come again for a while, at least, but those two who went in, who sacrificed themselves, did more than we did to save the life of the dragon herself. We can't do this alone."

"We can't this at all if we don't go down to the gate," Thorat said. "I only wish I'd seen Tiada, to know for myself that she still lives."

"You will," Ferrent said, lying back on his bedroll. "You will."

§

The others arrived after they'd breakfasted the next morning while Thorat was helping Vigda prepare a small deer for roasting. He spotted them coming over the ridge along the faint trail they'd walked the day before, their slender forms outlined against the sky. He could see at first glance that neither of them was Garren. Sovara would not have left the shrine, so neither of the slender forms was the Enatel, either. Ferrent leapt to his feet and ran to greet them while Thorat sat, waiting for them to come into focus. When they did, he saw that it was only Varin and Sunna, both of whom had been at the sword hall only a little longer than he had, neither of whom would be able to best Larn in an even man-to-man fight, or priestess-to-man in the case of Sunna. Sunna's middle had grown some. His heart sank at seeing it for himself. She was walking strongly, though, which was more than could be said for poor Varin.

"What's the matter, man?" Vigda asked Thorat. "Are these not your friends too?"

"They are," Thorat said, not trying to hide the disappointment in his voice. He got up and jogged over to catch up with Ferrent before she could ask him any more questions. She didn't follow, and he seized on the opportunity to talk to Ferrent alone again.

"We could just walk out of here now," Thorat said in as low a voice as possible.

Ferrent looked at him as if Thorat had lost his mind. "Is that how you repay their hospitality?"

"I don't call it hospitality when I'm hauled from my bed in the middle of the night and they have our swords."

Varin's sword hilt gleamed brightly at his side, but it was no blessed sword, only a very good common blade. Sunna's was blessed, but only with priestess magic, not swordsmith magic, and it was a little short, good enough in close combat but not when a tall man with a longer blade was coming at her. With only those two swords and Eppie's – if they could find her again – they would be slaughtered. They would probably be slaughtered no matter what they did.

"I don't like the idea of going in with fewer swords than men and women," Ferrent said, as if reading his mind. "There's a chance we can turn this to our advantage still, and I for one won't throw that away."

"Have you seen the Cerean armsmen?" Thorat said. "They're fierce enough, but there aren't many of them."

By that time, they'd come close enough that Sunna could hear them. She hurried to join them, with Varin limping behind. They exchanged quick greetings as they met.

"Eppie went into their camp last night," Sunna said. "She did a fine bit of creeping and listening. If I'd been there, I would have counseled her not to go in so close, but I wasn't, and it was a good thing. She learned more than I could have hoped for."

"Go on," Ferrent said. "It's good to see you again, but what's this?" He reached toward her belly but she backed away.

Sunna blushed. Thorat wondered if they'd been lovers, but even if they had been, Sunna would have fallen back on her priestess habits and told him to go on with his duty, and now it seemed she was carrying a baby in her belly.

"We've missed you in Anamat," she told Ferrent.

"Don't worry; I'll be back this Midsummer."

"If we don't all die here," Thorat said.

"I don't think it's all that glum," Sunna said, ignoring Ferrent's pointed glances to her midriff. "From what Eppie said, it looks like the prince's camp will be in some disarray, and not much better armed than we are. She only saw two Cerean armsmen, plus the prince's bodyguard and his nephews, who appear to guard the prince's brother along with half the armsmen. The prince is dying, probably dead by now."

"Eppie says that the nephews shot him, or some of their henchmen," Varin said. "The prince had turned away from the dragons, but then..."

"Then what?" Ferrent asked.

Sunna took Ferrent's hand and smiled. "The prince said that he saw dragonlets when he was shot, that he was seeing one as he lay in the tent dying. He sent the Enomaean vole-slaughterer packing, and says he wants his funeral at the village temple."

Thorat's jaw dropped. The fool. He'd thought that the prince was just a mild, ineffectual man. Now it seemed that he'd denied the very existence of the dragons when he'd seen them for himself, unlike anyone else in the province. The prince had turned his back on a dragon he could see. His ability to see dragons was far more shocking than the idea that Calar would arrange a hunting accident.

Vigda was halfway up to meeting them. "Come down and council by the fire!" she called. "The bread is warming."

Sunna gave the old woman a salute, but before they started to walk, she leaned in close to Thorat. "The prince also said something about having a daughter who he didn't know well, who was or had been a priestess in Anamat. Any idea who that might be?"

Thorat nodded. "Darna came from Tiadun, didn't she?"

"But she's no princess," Sunna said. "Oracles are often wrong."

Thorat would have asked what oracles she was talking about, but Vigda was close enough that she would hear everything they said now. They were still trapped in the bandit camp.

Thorat had been in Tiadun Keep for a season, and though he hadn't had much opportunity to observe the prince closely, he'd seen enough of him that he could find similarities between Darna and Tiadun's ruler. The prince had a strangely familiar scowl, the same slant of the jaw, and both of them had red hair. What had possessed Darna to flee this place if it could have been almost hers to rule? But then, the answer to that question was obvious. She wasn't a man, so she would have been sent to priestess training of some sort, then been married off to another prince or to a favored chieftain. If the prince had no sons, she might even bring the chieftain in to become prince, but she would only ever be mistress of a keep that was as oppressive as any place Thorat had seen.

Then there was Calar. Had he been plotting even then? Darna's uncle wouldn't have liked to see her installed as keep mistress, bypassing him. Even without Calar's traitorous ambitions, Darna would have hated the ugliness of Tiadun Keep. She would have longed to escape, to see Anamat and Anara. She also would have hated to be played as a piece in the prince's games. If there was anything Darna valued, it was her own freedom. She would never have had that in Tiadun, even if it wasn't such a dry province and lonely.

Darna must have seen Tiada – she wasn't dragon-blind at all, no matter what she said. He only wished that he had, more recently, but at least Eppie had seen the dragon. Maybe Tiada only appeared to young girls and dying men. The Cereans might cut through the dragon without even knowing what they were doing. They wouldn't want to know what they were doing, would they?

They'd reached the fire. Vigda was introducing Sunna to the other bandits, while Ferrent hovered protectively behind her.

"Now, what brings you out journeying like that?" Vigda asked Sunna.

Sunna gave her wry smile. "A friend told me that it's easier to come like this than with a babe in arms, that I should make my journeys while I can."

"Sensible enough," Vigda said. She looked as if she wanted to say more but knew her advice wouldn't be welcome. Sunna sat down with a small groan.

Varin elbowed Thorat. "What do you say?"

"To what?" Thorat looked around.

"Ferrent reckons these folks could help us," he said quietly.

Thorat shook his head. "We'd have to tell them who we are."

"Not necessarily," Varin said, "and who says they'll live to tell the tale?"

"There is that." Suddenly, Thorat found that he didn't relish the thought of leading the bandits into slaughter any more than he liked the thought of going in himself at such bad odds.

"What brings you to these hills?" Larn asked the newcomers.

"We've come to join our comrades," Varin said, gesturing to Thorat and Ferrent.

Larn looked at Thorat. "And what mission brought you here?"

There was a long silence. He wished he didn't have to speak. He felt his heart knot up, but then he took a deep breath and called on his minstrel training, however incomplete, and prepared to spin out a tale.

Thorat looked around the circle. The bandits, all eight of them, had come to the fireside. Fluffy clouds blew across the sky, promising rain before the next morning. Sunna sat companionably between Ferrent and Vigda. The women seemed to have taken the measure of each other and decided that they were comrades, and he hated arguing against Sunna.

She always got the best of him when words were involved rather than blades. Varin wanted the bandits' help, and Ferrent had his brother here, his long-lost and dragon-struck brother. He seemed to be alone in his unease, and so he set it aside, wondering how much he would regret this.

"Like you," he began, "we've come to guard the hills."

One of the bandits guffawed, but he went on. "We don't come to guard them from the people of Theranis, not from the ones you call lowlanders, but from the Cereans who've come again to try to steal the dragons' lifeblood. They're on their way to Tiada's gate; that's what I learned down at the keep." He took a deep breath. "Would you join us in defending it?"

Larn glared at him. He leaned toward Thorat then got to his feet. "Defending the gate?" he roared. "You corrupt those words, lowlander! No one can defend the dragons' gates if their whole land is not held holy! Only Na's land remains pure. That is what *we* defend."

Sunna stood next. Thorat forgot how tall she could look when she was angry. Now she towered over the chief of the bandits and grasped him by the shoulders, staring him down.

"Keeping the land sacred is the priestesses' calling, but they cannot do it if the gates fall closed, if Tiada disappears forever. Tiada has been seen, or at least her dragonlets have."

"By whom?" Vigda demanded.

"By our apprentice, Eppie, and by the prince of Tiadun himself, who is dying or dead," Sunna said, not letting go of Larn.

Vigda spat on the ground. "I'd feed him to Na."

Varin spoke next. "Eppie went into the camp and listened. She said that he asked for a funeral pyre in the village, so that Tiada might take him." He sounded like a boy. Varin always seemed so young, even though he was older than Thorat, even though he'd defended a dragon's gate before.

Vigda laughed bitterly. "The prince hasn't seen Tiada in a long, long time, not since I had my hands on him."

Thorat tried to catch Sunna's eye, but she was ignoring him. "He sent the foreign priest away," Sunna said, "but none of that matters, not to Tiada and the safety of her gate, not now."

"The Cereans have come. They want the stones of the dragon. They'll take her gate down if they mine there," Ferrent said. "I don't know if Tiada can die, or if she will only go under the earth, but it is our sacred duty to do all we can to keep her with us."

Forlan cocked his head, as if he were listening to something no one else could hear.

Gran spoke next. "We do not concern ourselves with the lowlands or their dragons. We belong to Na."

Sunna let go of Larn and stood over Gran, who was sitting cross-legged near the fire. "And if the lowlands fall, what then? How long will these hills be free?"

"As long as we can defend them," Vigda said.

Larn sat back down with a heaving sigh. "Go on, then. You may all go, and take your sword with you. We'll keep our own council without your lowland lies to pollute our ears. We will come - or not - by the will of Na."

§

Chapter 13

"I'm glad that they know why we're here," Ferrent said as they walked away from the bandits' camp. Thorat had the sword on his back again, but it wasn't enough to lift his spirits.

"I wish it hadn't come to that. We shouldn't have had to tell them. I'm still not sure it was the right thing to do," Thorat said.

"No, we needed to, and it was right," Sunna said. Ferrent and Varin nodded agreement with her.

"We're not even supposed to exist," Thorat said.

"You know, I carry a lot of secrets, not just this but priestess things, too. Sometimes, it seems to do more harm than good, and it wears me out. Besides, we could use their help."

"If they choose to give it," Thorat said.

"If it eases your conscience any," Ferrent said, "you might consider that Forlan knows what we are already, somewhere in his addled mind, so it was never a secret from him."

"And then there's the fact that our secret is safe enough with the bandits," Varin added. "After all, they hardly even talk to farmers, let alone the men in the keeps. If they cross paths with a few traders and tell tales, which doesn't seem likely, who would believe them? You wouldn't have."

"I probably still wouldn't," Thorat said.

"So the secret's only half out, and you haven't named the Enatel or said how many of us there are, or how few," Sunna said. "For all they know, we're just an ill-sorted bunch who took this on in the name of a forgotten legend. You've hardly led them right to our training hall in Anamat with the governor's men behind them to run us out."

"They know we're not like other lowlanders or they wouldn't have let us go so easily," Ferrent said.

"The fact that your brother happened to be in their camp, half mad or not, didn't hurt either," Thorat said.

They reached a point where the track split into several barely discernible trails through the forest, going in various directions down the slope. Thorat hesitated.

"Shall we go to the village or straight to the gate?"

"To the gate, I think," Ferrent said. "We might as well get the lay of the land and see whether or not the Cereans have found it. That's the worrying thing."

They all agreed on that. Thorat and Sunna looked for the little flowers to lead them in the right direction, but found none. Eventually, he spotted the upper branches of the rhododendron where he and Eppie had camped.

"There's our old camp," he said, pointing toward it. "I was there with Eppie before the villagers and the bandits fiushed us out. We might as well leave our packs there, especially now that the villagers are distracted by the prince's men and the foreigners, and the bandits have decided to let us go. It's as good a hiding place as any near here."

It had only been a few days since they'd decamped from the place, but Thorat felt a wave of nostalgia well up in him as if it belonged to a better time. Their fire pit was still there, only a little trampled by the villagers. When he'd last slept here, things had been bleak but simpler. He'd only been waiting for help from Anamat and for the battle to come. Now, with the bandits knowing their business, and with whatever was simmering between Sunna and Ferrent, things were more complicated.

They left their gear hidden in the underbrush and made their way along the hillside to the gate.

"You say there were flowers here?" Sunna asked.

"There were; I'm sure of it." He certainly couldn't find any now, but the contours of the land hadn't changed. They soon reached the old oak, its roots veiling the gate to the dragons' realm.

"Here we are," he announced.

Ferrent and Varin looked skeptical. "This is worse than Lemira's looked," Ferrent said.

Varin shrugged. "I never got a good look, but I suppose it's to be expected, if they're all fa –"

A flicker of motion caught his eye and the three men turned to look. The bright orange flash of a dragonlet darted by, visible for only an instant but leaving a streak of dragonlight in its wake which lingered for another heartbeat.

Sunna had stopped the abandoned shrine, and she looked up too late to see the dragonlet. "What is it?" she asked.

Thorat gestured to the fading trail of dragonlight. None of the rest of them spoke. Sunna took a small stone out of her pocket and laid it on the shrine. She went to join them, grouped around the all-but-invisible cave mouth, into which the dragonlet had disappeared.

"It doesn't take much to call them back," Sunna said after a while. She had a dreamy, faraway lilt to her voice, almost as if she were an augur, though she'd never prophesied before. Maybe it was pregnancy. Men sometimes sought out priestesses who had gone astray in the rite, whose bellies were swelling, to find where they'd gone off the dragons' paths themselves and how to rejoin them.

The gate looked small and forlorn, like a simple hole in the dirt.

"Eppie went inside before I could stop her," Thorat said. "It's real."

Sunna chuckled, now in her ordinary voice. "Well, that'll rouse Tiada if anything will. It was a real dragonlet?"

The others nodded.

"I haven't seen one since I left the valley," she said, looking up over the hills as if she could see Anamat beyond the forested mountainsides and the two provinces in between.

"Nor had I," Ferrent said. "I even wondered if only Anara had them now."

Thorat stared at the cave mouth. Varin paced.

"It shouldn't be hard to draw them off, to disguise this," Varin said.

Thorat shook his head. "We looked all over these hills. This is the only cave of any kind near here."

"We could almost dig one," Varin suggested.

"Or draw them into the dark under that bush at dusk and light a few lanterns?" Ferrent said dismissively. No one would be taken in by anything the five of them could construct in a few days' time.

Thorat began to pace a circle around the edge of the clearing. If the foreigners and the prince's men came up from the village or over from the camp, they'd have to find their way through the uncharted brush of the forest. That meant that the first two men would come slowly, pushing the brambles out of their way. They'd be easy enough to pick off one by one.

"I don't know if you should fight," Thorat said to Sunna.

"The Enatel said that I could."

Varin nodded. "She did."

"Fine." Thorat disliked the idea of Sunna fighting, but if Sovara had ordered it, that was that. "That means there are four of us, plus Eppie, who's bound to turn up sooner or later. We can pinch them at the head of the path, then two of us can flank the gate while the other two go up into the oak to come down on them from above. It helps that they don't have many spearmen."

"And we have to kill them all," Ferrent said. He and Varin looked at each other and shook their heads.

"Do you have any better ideas?" Thorat asked.

They didn't, so the four of them walked through the scenario a few times until dusk began to fall, then set out for their campsite.

Someone had lit a fire by the rhododendron. Thorat waved Ferrent forward to investigate.

"They wouldn't spend the night so close, would they?" Sunna asked.

Thorat shook his head.

"It's only Eppie," Ferrent shouted back. "Come on, we can toast our bread."

"You call that bread?" Sunna grumbled, but so did her belly, loudly enough to hear.

They gathered around the fire and exchanged greetings.

Eppie smiled at Thorat. "I lit the fire because I saw your packs. They're busy enough down below. I don't think they'll be looking up this way much."

"I guess it's all right," Thorat said. "What are they doing down there?"

"I slept a bit more after Sunna and Varin went to find you, but I don't think it was too long. I was back at their camp before the midday meal. It was quiet for a while, just servants and the prince's brother coming and going from the tent. That was Calar, the one who had him killed. I heard a raised voice every now and again. The mistress and one of the village priestesses were in there all day until late in the afternoon. Then the mistress came out and found Calar. They had some kind of argument, but I couldn't hear the words. Then Calar went back into the tent and came out. At the end of it, the mistress went to one of the common soldiers' tents and turned them all out. Servants brought her trunks and then Calar had his things moved over to the prince's tent. They sent out the order to the village men to gather wood for the pyre. They're supposed to work on it all night and keep it dry from the dew, too."

"So, he turned out the keep mistress rather than keeping her for himself?" Sunna asked. "That was stupid of him. He should have had her bless him as prince."

Eppie looked confused. "Why would she do that?"

"Gallia doesn't like Calar, and I'm sure he knows it," Thorat said. "She'd probably sooner stick a blade in his back than bless him for taking her lover's place. She really loved the old prince and hated his brother. I'm just a guardsman, but even I could see that much."

"Still, he might have forced her," Sunna said glumly.

Thorat tried to picture Gallia bowing to the man who'd murdered her prince or had him murdered. "That wouldn't be easy," he said. "She's her own force to reckon with. I wonder what will happen to her."

Birds were beginning to settle down for the night and the moon was rising. Eppie and Sunna passed the bread around while Varin unwrapped the meat the bandits had sent with them.

Ferrent broke the silence. "It's not our concern, what happens to the keep mistress. What we need to do is to keep those Na-cursed foreigners away from the gate, if they can even find it." He looked to Eppie. "Do you think they can?"

"I saw one of the priestesses talking to a Cerean. They might."

Sunna almost threw her meat into the fire. "Stupid provincial priestesses."

They ate the rest of their meal in silence, then Ferrent and Sunna went to get water from a nearby creek and took a long time returning. When they did, Ferrent hovered close to Sunna, all but putting his arm around her shoulders. He seemed to be oblivious to Varin's glares, and so did Sunna, but Thorat noticed them all. He'd been away for a long time, thought not as long as Ferrent. He wanted to know how things stood among themselves before moving in to do whatever they could do in the morning. Going in with two men pining after the same woman and her pregnant at that? They all needed clear heads. Eppie was sighing too, but he didn't know why. His own head was none too clear, but at least he wasn't pining after Sunna, only Iola, far, far away.

"Come on," Thorat said. "Let's go down to the gate and see what traps we can arrange."

Sunna stayed behind, but the rest of them went. Ferrent and Varin worked together easily – they'd done this before – and Thorat helped out where he could. Eppie lingered on the fringes.

"I want to go down to the village and find out what's happening," she said after a while.

"They usually light funeral pyres at dawn, but they could wait until dusk," Ferrent said. "See what you can find out, and get a better count of their numbers."

"Meet us back at the camp," Thorat said, "and stay safe. If we don't see you there before first light, we'll meet you down by the village at dawn."

"Sure, that's fine," Eppie said. The sudden sadness in her voice caught Thorat off guard. For a moment, he wanted to run after her, to call her back, but he stayed where he was. Of course she was sad. They were looking into the jaws of a fight that might be the end of all of them. She was too young to die. Still, there'd been a kind of longing in her eyes.

"Help me with this log," Varin said.

Thorat did, but then he made his excuses and went back to the campsite to talk to Sunna. When he arrived, she was shaking out their blankets.

"Be careful with Ferrent," Thorat told her. "He's just left a lover over in Kiralun, and I don't think he was happy about it."

"Who ever is?" Sunna said bitterly. "I don't care; it's just for old times' sake."

He should have known that she wouldn't want advice, but he bumbled on. "He won't want to be your lover for long, if I know him."

"I know him too," Sunna said. "He suits me well enough."

"Varin's jealous too," Thorat pointed out.

Sunna looked off into the distance, out at the first stars visible through the trees. "He has no right to be, you know."

"Let's get this log out of here," Thorat said. They rolled an old branch aside to make more room for everyone to sleep together. "Jealousy has nothing to do with rights."

"It's still not his right, and he knows that."

"He's not the father?"

Sunna snorted. "Hardly. It was probably a petitioner from Coradun, but it doesn't matter. I'm a priestess of Ara's Landing and at least I can keep to the old ways, even if it seems that no one else can."

"The ambassadress does."

"Only when you don't tempt her. At least you'll never come to me as a priestess."

Thorat grunted assent, but he had a sinking feeling in his gut about it. "It's not that I wouldn't," he said.

"Oh, be quiet, would you?"

She couldn't be angry about that, could she? Well, there was nothing he could do about any of it, it seemed. He hadn't even seen the dragon for himself. He wished that he had, to know if she would be strong enough to help drive the invading merchants back from her veins in the land.

They brushed the sleeping area clear, then brushed it again, as if they would be staying there more than a night, as if they might live through the coming day.

"Couldn't you have taken the herbs?" he asked her after a while.

"I did, but they didn't work. They often don't, especially if you don't try hard enough, if you don't really want them to work."

"But why wouldn't you?"

"I must have wanted to get away from the temple," she said, exasperated. "I didn't realize how badly I wanted to."

"Sovara could have sent you on assignment somewhere, couldn't she?"

Sunna snorted. "No, she couldn't have. Officially, she doesn't exist; don't you remember that? And your lover-girl there wouldn't let me."

"She's the ambassadress," Thorat said, "and she's not my 'lover-girl.'"

"She is," Sunna said.

Maybe it was true, but if the ambassadress couldn't fill her role, who else could?

"Anyway, it doesn't matter now, not here," Sunna said, shaking out the last of the blankets. "I got away from the temple, got a good dose of clear air around me, got to see the provinces again. She couldn't make me stay when I'm like this now, could she?"

"I suppose not." He wished that Iola would make *him* stay some year instead of having Sovara send him off to his likely death, but that was outside of her powers. He had to save Tiada, not only for the dragon and her realm but for all of the dragons and the people of Theranis, and especially to safeguard Iola on her journey to the other realm at

Midsummer, to make sure that the dragons all were whole and unwounded, even if they were retreating from the surface of the earth.

Varin and Ferrent returned, and they soon settled down to sleep, with Sunna between the two other men and Thorat on the end, waiting for his apprentice to return.

§

Eppie went straight down to the village, not bothering to find the trail, and arrived a little distance beyond the last house. The prince's men and the Cereans had transformed the village into a small town. Their camp loomed in the fields, their boots and horses turned up the road, and they lounged around all quarters of the village, making everything look rough and tired. Eppie kept to the bushes, not wanting to cross their paths.

At the edge of the village, she discovered that someone else had been at work too, probably the villagers or the priestesses. Little shrines had sprung up along the edge of the forest, made of hastily piled twigs and fieldstones surrounding crudely crafted figures of the dragons carved from wood or molded from still-damp clay. The villagers had left lamps and bread at the feet of the rough statuettes, and though Eppie didn't see the dragonlets themselves, she felt a stirring in the forest that hadn't been there before.

She entered the village down an alley between two houses, as wide as an Anamat street but the narrowest gap the village afforded. She wove through the shadows between the houses until she reached the central square. There, the bustle of activity had grown to such a pitch that it almost might have been a corner of Anamat on an ordinary evening, right down to the Cereans on the tavern porch, looking askance at the goings-on and leering at the priestesses, while the villagers labored to bring in wood and pile it high.

A priestess and the old keep mistress were standing on the temple porch, overseeing the construction of the pyre and consulting with one another from time to time.

Eppie watched from behind a rain barrel beside one of the houses, then crept around to a bush at one side of the temple. From there, she could almost hear what the priestesses were saying. Some years before she came to Anamat, there'd been a season in which the priestesses had ruled, in the moon rounds between the death of the old governor and the selection of the new one. The succession of princes was usually simpler than the selection of a governor, but it seemed that even here in the provinces, the priestesses had a turn at ruling, however brief.

A few villagers had gathered on the far side of the temple porch. They presented themselves two and three at a time and spoke to the older priestess there, who gave them short answers and sent them on their way. From the bits and snatches Eppie overheard, they were mostly asking the priestesses for advice and mediation in local disputes, or with personal problems, nothing to do with the Cereans and their plans, or even the prince.

Eppie was about to go across to the tavern, to see if she could hear anything useful there, when a hand landed on her shoulder.

"Word travels fast, huh?" said a familiar voice. "Where'd you get that sword? Can I have it?"

Eppie spun around to face Squid, fists ready. "What are you doing, creeping around here?" she said. "And no, you can't have it."

"I should ask you that; you're the one hiding in the bushes. I've been here for a good quarter-moon or so. Everyone knows I work for the Cereans. Who do you work for?"

"Everyone knows I'm a herder from the next village over, flocks on the high pastures already 'cause we haven't got enough rain."

"With that sword? Not much of a story."

"You tell them anything different, I'll show you what this sword can do."

"Ha, I'd like to see that!" Squid said.

Eppie glanced over her shoulder at the priestesses to tell Squid that they were making too much noise. He got the hint and led them back to a deserted area behind the temple.

"And I'd like to see them torch this thing at dawn," Squid continued as soon as they were around the side of the building, "but I got other things to do while the dragon's busy eating up the old prince. Nice snack."

"I wouldn't eat him," Eppie said.

"Cereans don't think much of this so-called priestesses' rule," Squid said. "They reckon just put Calar in charge so they can get on with it."

Even though he killed his brother? Eppie wanted to ask. Instead, she said: "Sure, 'cause Calar's the one they've been dealing with all along, isn't he?"

Squid shrugged. "I don't know. Looks that way. They didn't like the Enomaean priest any more than they liked the keep mistress and her priestesses, with all their meddling. Just look at it!" He waved back at the temple.

"I don't see anything wrong with it. Why not let them keep ruling?"

"Nope," Squid said. "They're going to hurry him back to the keep to get him stuck into the throne there, sure as anything."

Eppie's stomach lurched with hope. Could that mean they would let the gate be?

"So, they're just going to forget about the so-called hunting they came here for?"

Squid squinted at her. He might have been suspicious, but the urge to brag won out. "Nah, that won't take long now that the Enomaean isn't here to find out where to get the stuff."

Her stomach sank again. "So, they know where to get it?"

"They got a pretty good idea."

A whistle sounded from over at the tavern.

"I gotta go," Squid said.

He ran off before Eppie could figure out whether he was just bragging or if the Cereans really did know how to find the gate. She made one more circuit of the village. The people were bringing more offerings to their shrines in hope of seeing dragonlets at dawn. The Cereans were trooping out along the road back to their camp, making warding signs as they passed the makeshift shrines. They carried their picks and shovels on their backs, burnished like swords. Squid had said that it wouldn't take long now that the Enomaean was gone. How could the Enomaean priest and his bird-brained god have anything to do with it? Was he stopping the Cereans somehow, or did the Cereans believe in the Enomaean priest's curses in a way that they didn't believe in the dragons' power? More likely, it was as Squid said: they were just afraid that the Enomaeans would come in after them to take the dragon's gems.

Back at the campsite, she crawled under the thick-leafed boughs to find the others. The moon had given her enough light to find her way through the forest well enough, but its light couldn't penetrate the dense bush and she had to feel her way along, crawling on her hands and knees. She stumbled when she hit a foot.

Whoever it was sat up, grabbed her arm, and in a moment had her neck locked in a vise grip between his arm and body.

"It's just me, Eppie!" she gasped.

The grip released. "Sorry." It was Varin. "Don't like to be surprised in the night."

Sunna groaned. "None of us do, but you knew she was coming back. No need to go off like a Ganatean spearman."

Thorat cleared his throat. "Well, now that we're all awake, anything to report?"

Eppie rubbed her neck. It was sore. "Not much," she said. "They're going to burn him at dawn. The priestesses are holding court at the temple, and the..." She hesitated before sharing Squid's bit of news about the Cereans.

"There's room for you over here," Thorat said.

She felt her way along, now able to make out small distinctions in the shades of the darkness, but still not quite able to see enough to steer by.

"Is that all?" Sunna said.

"Not quite," Eppie said. "The Cereans were at the tavern, watching them build the pyre and the priestesses giving their judgments from the temple porch. I don't think the foreigners are going to hang around for the burning; they were already heading back to the camp."

"So, they'll go back to their ships empty-handed?"

"That would be more than we could hope for," Ferrent said.

"I don't think so," Eppie said. "But whatever it is, they won't take long about it." She decided to leave Squid out of it. "They looked impatient."

Thorat yawned. "Well, let's get some sleep now. We can go down to the village when the birds start their jabbering, see the funeral, then head back up to the gate."

"And get some provisions," Sunna said.

"But what if –" Eppie couldn't quite give voice to it. What if the Cereans didn't even wait that long?

"You don't have to go down to the village if you're tired," Thorat said.

"It's not that; it's just..."

"I'll stay up here too," Sunna said. "My feet are sore."

"Just what we need, one hand less," Varin complained. "My ankle's not great either."

"Stop bickering and get some sleep," Thorat ordered.

For a little while, Eppie heard only the rustle of the leaves above and the small noises of the others shifting to get more comfortable. The ground had been swept but it was still lumpy enough to make it hard to fall asleep. She felt a rock digging into her back, and it was cold even through the blankets. Thorat was at her side, radiating heat, warm and strong. She edged closer. They lay under the same blanket, with the second blanket beneath them. Even through the thick weave of their winter tunics, she could feel him. His legs were bare, and so were hers. They were almost touching. One of the other men was snoring, as was Sunna. She'd never get to sleep.

Eppie would have looked at Thorat's face if there had been any kind of light. Instead, in the near-pitch darkness, she reached out to feel it with her hand.

He made a small, sleepy murmur as his hand came up. She thought that he would brush her away, but instead he reached out and pulled her closer until their faces were almost touching. She could feel his breath. Tentatively, slowly, she leaned her chin in until her lips were over his. She brushed her lips against his, almost a kiss. He rolled closer to her, and their legs touched. She pulled his tunic up along the strong muscles of his thigh.

§

Thorat woke abruptly. He was not in the temple. He was not with Iola. He was on a rocky forest floor under a bush, and an untried apprentice girl was pulling him close to her. He rolled away, taking the blankets with him.

"Stop," he said.

Eppie sat up. He could just about make out the shape of her. She'd rolled away now, and she was holding her knees to her chest, breathing as heavily as he was, panting as if they'd just sparred.

"I'm sorry," he said.

"I wanted to," Eppie whispered. "I'm sorry. I don't know why. You keep saying that we might not live through tomorrow, so why not?" Her voice cracked.

"I can't."

"You could." She might have been right, but with the spell of sleep shattered, the moment was gone. Was that what she'd been sighing about these past few days?

"I was asleep," he said. "I wouldn't have, if I were awake."

"It wasn't much," she said.

"And a good thing, too."

"I'm going to take a walk." Eppie yanked the blanket away from him and took it with her as she stumbled out into the clearing. He heard her curse as she stubbed her toe, but then she set off again, rustling away through the underbrush.

He listened until he could hear no more of her. He lay awake for a long time, then fell asleep just as the birds started singing.

§

Chapter 14

"Wake up; it's almost dawn," Varin said.

Thorat cursed himself before he even opened his eyes. He should have known not to fall back asleep. He felt the spot beside him, on the other side. It was empty. He had one blanket wrapped around himself. The other, the one that had started the night on top of him, was gone.

"Where's Eppie?" he asked.

Varin yawned and looked around. "Don't ask me. She did come back from the village, didn't she? Or did I dream that?"

"She came back," Ferrent confirmed. "We were all awake. She said they were going to light the pyre at dawn, and something about the Cereans. I can't remember exactly what."

"She said that they were getting impatient, and that they weren't going to go to the funeral," Sunna said. "So, where did she go now?" She looked right at Thorat, rather accusingly. Had she heard them? That was the kind of thing she would hear.

"I don't know," Thorat said. "I think she said she was going to take a walk."

Ferrent pushed through the heavy leaves and went out to the clearing. Thorat strapped on his sandals and followed. It was getting light, but it was a misty dawn, good for hiding.

"Do you think she would have gotten lost?" Ferrent asked.

"No," Thorat and Sunna said together.

She was definitely giving him a disapproving look.

Thorat took a deep breath. "We'll find Eppie later, or more likely she'll find us. She knows her way around these woods better than any of us. She'll come back when she's ready, but right now, we need to get down to the town before they light that pyre."

They other two men followed him down the hill while Sunna stayed behind to pack up the camp.

§

Eppie fumbled her way along the forest path in the darkest hour of the night, following the line of the hill toward the gate, climbing trees here and there to get her bearings from the stars and from the faint outline of the hills above. At last, she saw the silhouette of the mighty oak ahead, the tree that masked Tiada's gate. She thrashed on toward it, not minding the branches lashing against her damp cheeks. That had been so stupid. He was in love with the ambassadress. Of course he didn't want her. How could he? She was just a rough-edged scrappling, barely even an apprentice. She wouldn't want to be like the ambassadress, anyway, all preened and perfect. She could never be that, even if she did want it, no matter what the priestesses thought. It was stupid to want him. She didn't want to die without having touched a man and drawn the energy of the dragons up from the earth the way that even commoners could. Of course, priestesses were better at it. She'd felt it beginning to stir in her, just for a moment, not enough to be a priestess, but still she wished she could have had more, but it was stupid to go fumbling around for it on the cold ground in the middle of the night when she didn't know what she was doing and when she should have been getting ready to die.

She climbed the slope above the gate and found a smooth rock to sit on, tucked in the vee between two roots of the oak. She leaned against its trunk, wrapped the blanket around herself, and waited for the bleak light of dawn. She laid the sheathed sword out at her feet and ran her hands along it. It was a good sword, his sword. She was just an apprentice to him; that was all. Why wasn't that enough now? Why had she even come?

She dozed lightly, woke to the birdsong, then slipped into stiff-backed slumber as the stars winked out above the trees. She woke again to the first red rays of dawn and the distant sound of men's voices, arguing somewhere far away down the hill. They sounded too close to be coming from the village, or even on the road to the village. They weren't bandits; they were city men, or at least some kind of lowlander, and not hunters, either, to judge by their lack of stealth. Why weren't they in the village, watching the prince burn up? She couldn't make out their words. At first, she thought that it was because they were too far away, but as they got closer their words got louder without becoming much clearer. They weren't villagers; they were Cereans.

Quickly, quietly, Eppie folded up her blanket and tucked it behind the tree. She slung her sword across her back and went down to the clearing in front of the gate. Sure enough, someone had been there in the night. They'd broken branches and trampled underbrush along the dotted line of old flagstones leading from the village to the gate, but they'd stopped short of the clearing in front of the gate itself. The marks of their travel only went as far as the little shrine, or what had been a shrine. It was broken now, its stones scattered on the muddy forest floor, its statue smashed, desecrated. It hadn't been like that when they'd all been there the day before, when she'd seen it with Thorat.

She yanked her thoughts away from him. Where was Tiada? Better to think of the dragon than of Thorat. Eppie stole back to the clearing and peered inside the cave.

When she and Thorat had first followed the scattered growth of flowers to this place, she'd seen the gate only as a gap in the hill, but that impression hadn't lasted long. Now she didn't see how anyone could miss it, even though its entrance was no taller than her shoulders, with dirt-clotted roots draped around it. From that first moment, when she'd stepped into the living vein of the earth, it had glowed with light for her. It glowed now, brighter than before, as bright as the morning sky in the east. No one could miss it, or could they? Could the dragon-blind see this light or not?

She hoped that they couldn't, for Tiada's sake, but she stayed and basked in it for a long moment, feeling Tiada's power surge past her like a wind, washing away the night's pains and worries, and all the pain of nights before, too.

She couldn't stay there long. The Cereans were getting closer. She was alone. The others were down in the village, too far away to call. Sunna was supposed to have stayed at the camp. Maybe she would still be there. Eppie climbed a little way up the hill to another tall tree and whistled out the mock birdcall. She waited. No answer. She whistled again. Still nothing. She hurried back to the cave mouth, careful to avoid a trap that Ferrent and Varin had laid. There was another one along the path, just this side of the shrine. If she sprang it, that might delay them a little.

They hadn't reached the shrine yet, but she caught a glimpse of one of them from above the cave. Definitely Cereans. She felt the earth hum beneath her feet and knelt down to touch it. It rumbled like an enormous purring cat. The dragon was coming.

Eppie went back and knelt in front of the cave, the gate to the dragons' realm. Although she was no priestess, she tried to reach out to Tiada with her mind. She imagined the dragon as she'd seen her in the distance when she first crossed into

Tiadun. It had been a moon-round before, but it felt like a lifetime. Even yesterday felt like a lifetime.

Holding the image of Tiada in her mind, Eppie begged the dragon to stay under the earth, not to reveal herself as her enemies came tromping up, crushing the blue-and-orange flowers under their feet, violating the peace of the hills. Eppie tried to reach her thoughts into the earth, but the threat at her back kept her mind rooted in her body. All she heard of Tiada was the purr of the earth growing louder and louder as she knelt. The sharp snap of a branch on the path below broke through her concentration. They were almost at the ruined shrine.

The day before, when the Defenders had set the traps, Eppie had admired their handiwork. She hadn't thought she'd have to spring the traps herself, and she wasn't sure she'd be able to, but at least she'd seen how they worked, and she knew where to cut the first rope, woven through the trees until it was all but invisible from the disused path. It would drop an old tree onto the interlopers if they came that way. She was glad she'd brought the sword. After that, she had no idea what she'd be able to do, except that she had to hold them back long enough to let the dragon fly.

The gate grew brighter, shining like the full moon on a Midwinter night, then like the red, distant sun behind a bank of clouds. The gnarled oak roots twined around and over it shook and shimmered like a curtain of lace.

One of the Cereans said something loudly. He was at the shrine.

Eppie left the gate and went into the woods to take her position. She brushed the camouflaging leaves off the rope and drew her sword out of its sheath.

The sun rose, its red rays striking the treetops.

The Cereans stopped their jostling and bashing through the trees. For a moment, they stood eerily silent, then they began to chant.

Eppie couldn't understand the words of the chant, but she could feel its rhythm like an axe on wood, hard and martial. The chant repeated itself, twice, three times, then shifted until it was almost like a song but tuneless, as if it had been meant to be sung but the beauty of it had been forgotten, as if the men here couldn't sing but only shout. It was loud enough that she almost missed the sound of one figure walking in a circle around them, not chanting or mock-singing at all. He was a slender young man, in an Anamat-style tunic. He was Squid. Squid had led them there.

She wanted to just curl in a ball and be sick at him, but there was no time. The Cereans broke their circle and one of them gave a command.

To Eppie's horror, rather than continue right up the path, they fanned out into the forest, each going three paces out from the shrine at regular intervals while one man stayed at the center. After they paced out, he gave an order, and each of the others dug their shovels or picks into the earth. There were about a dozen of them, all of the Cereans who had been in the camp. They seemed to have no idea what they were looking for, as each picked up dirt or ordinary stones and brought them back to their commander.

He ordered them off again and they paced out, six paces this time, again returning with nothing of interest. One of them was coming almost straight toward her hiding place. He'd covered half the distance between her and the shrine already. The sun was beginning to come down through the boughs above. She held her sword carefully behind her leg, hoping to keep it from catching any of the dots of sunlight now filtering down through the trees.

The men went back to their commander again and he ordered them out once more, nine paces this time. Eppie heard the sound of a pick striking a hard stone. It came from the man who was closest to the path to the cave mouth. The gate shone even brighter now, its orange veering into yellow from behind the roots but still as though the light was coming from far away. The Cereans didn't seem to see it.

The Cerean closest to the path, where the tree would fall if she dropped it, shouted. All of the others stopped their digging as the commander called back to him. They made their way toward him, wading through the brush to see what he had found only two short paces away from the place where the tied-up tree was supposed to land.

Sweat ran down Eppie's back in a rivulet, making her shiver in the cool morning air. She tried to ignore her racing heart. She stepped slowly, carefully into a better position over the rope and waited for them to move closer to the target. There was a great deal of arguing and pointing, but she ignored all of that, paying attention only to their positions.

The Cereans seemed to come to some conclusion. They sent Squid out first, to walk along the path that it had taken them so long to find. Squid sauntered forward, a city boy stumbling through the growing ferns and brush. He was out of his element, more so than she was. Even in the village, his step had been full of confident swagger, but the forest broke his stride, made him awkward, hesitant. He plowed on, eyes darting around, never quite landing on her hiding place. She could see him, though, which meant that once he did look in the right place, he would see her, too. He passed under the tree. Should she have dropped it on him?

The Cereans began to follow. Then, over all their noise, she heard a bird calling from the hill above, the trill a little longer than it should be, the gap between calls a little longer too. She answered in kind. The others were coming. She would not be all alone.

Most of them were now under the trap. She raised her sword, flashing in the sun – or was it dragonlight?

Squid saw her. He cried out.

She brought the sword down as swiftly and surely as she could. The rope snapped, all but one strand, and the old dead tree shuddered and shifted above. A few of the Cereans looked up and pointed.

Squid said something in Cerean and pointed at her as she swung again, slicing through the last strand of rope. The Cereans' leader was staring right at her as the many-limbed tree smashed down, trapping his sword arm in one tangle and knocking him to the ground, but not for long.

Squid was free to the side of the dragon gate. He was moving toward her. Eppie ran, glancing back over her shoulder once as she sprinted for the safety of the oak, the spot over the gate. It was high fighting ground, high enough to make up for some of her short reach. When she reached the tree, she looked back again. Two of the Cereans trailed Squid, with more at their backs, slowed down only a little by the tangled tree across what had once been a path. Most of the men trapped under the tree were struggling to get free, but two of them screamed, and one looked like he'd fainted or been knocked out.

A gong rang out in the village below, louder and clearer than seemed possible, the sound carrying all the way up to them on the mountain. The earth heaved in response, and the Cereans, all but the fainted one and the dumbfounded captain, clutched amulets against their chests. Suddenly, Squid was nowhere to be seen.

Then the gate exploded. Eppie lunged for the tree and wrapped herself around its trunk, making an anchor of it, holding on it as it clung to the shattering earth. Tiada erupted out of her gate, pushing the earth aside like the banks of a birthing canal. She tore into the clearing, her beating wings thrashing down against the too-close branches of the trees surrounding her. The dragon stretched, shaking off the dirt. She undulated like the rippling sea, like waves of ripe grain. She was golden-orange and blue, strong against the spring green of the trees, the ground beneath her feet. Her head swung around, taking the measure of the land.

Tiada's head swept around the clearing, searching for something, or someone, glancing over the heads of the confused Cereans, who were shouting at one another and pointing at nothing. Eppie could hear them as if from a great distance, but she only watched the dragon with her long neck and shining scales, her impossible wings stretching wider and wider. Tiada searched. Then she looked at Eppie and saw her, saw Eppie seeing her. Their eyes locked, girl and dragon. In those eyes, Eppie saw the whole land of Tiadun, all of Theranis down to the heart of the chambered earth, all the people in their places and out of them. She could see Thorat and the others in the village below as the priestess lit the pyre. She could see the bandits coming down the mountainside and Sunna rushing toward her. She could see the Cereans, some fainted, others holding on to their caps as a strange and sudden wind buffeted them. They could see none of the wings of the dragon but only felt the wind. She could even see Squid, creeping up behind her with his knife drawn. But mostly, she saw Tiada, she saw the dragon, soul of the earth, taking flight.

Squid threw his knife. Eppie ducked. The dragon screamed as Squid's knife landed in her neck.

§

Down in the village, Thorat, Varin, and Ferrent stayed at the back of the crowd to avoid notice. Varin stood on a barrel beside the tavern to get a better view of the pyre.

"She's coming out with the torch now," he said.

"Who is?" Thorat asked.

"The priestess, I guess."

"Are you sure it isn't the keep mistress?"

Varin shrugged. "How would I know? You get up."

Ferrent helped him down and Thorat climbed up. Thorat had worried that he would be seen and recognized if he went up there, but the guardsmen's eyes were all fixed on the temple porch and the pyre before it. The body of the fallen prince lay lifeless and pale on top of the dark brittle logs.

In death, the prince looked serene, far more serene than he'd ever seemed in life, almost as serene as Darna had looked for a flash of a moment when she'd washed up on the shores of Anamat harbor, before she'd woken up and resumed her disgruntled ways. Was it possible that this had been her father? The prince's body rested on a bed of logs, like a raft that would float on the flames as if they were water. He was wrapped in bright blue cloth with a sash around his middle of such bright orange that it seemed as if it were on fire already. The morning mist lingered in the valley, softening everything but the funeral pyre.

"Do you see the Cereans?" Ferrent asked.

Thorat looked around the square quickly, spotting nothing out of the ordinary except for a thin, gray-clad figure crouched in the shadows of one of the houses, as if he could make himself invisible there. It was the Enomaean priest, the priest who the prince had banished, now wearing a plain tunic rather than the golden robes of his eagle-headed god.

"They're not here. Maybe they're back at the camp? They don't like the priestesses, and it goes both ways."

The keep mistress stood beside Calar at the top of the temple steps. She held the torch, but he was trying to take it from her. It was a symmetrical tableau with the mistress and two priestesses on one side facing Calar and his surly sons on the other.

The murmur of the crowd obscured whatever Calar said as he reached for the torch, but then they stilled.

"It is my role," said Gallia. She knew the priestess's way of making her voice carry out as far as she willed. Everyone heard her.

"It will be your last role in my realm," Calar replied. He might not have meant that to be heard, but his words sounded into the silence. A flood of outraged voices surged after that silence and fanned out through the village. The villagers' voices stilled as the sun broke through the low mist, striking the temple's gold-tipped tower. Gallia shoved Calar aside and set the torch to the base of the funeral pyre. Flames licked up their ladder of logs as the sun rose over the village. The crowd shifted back, away from the heat, watching for the moment when the fire would swallow their prince.

It was then that the dragon screamed.

A few of the villagers looked up. The priestesses on the temple porch looked to one another. Only Gallia cried out in response. Calar gave a signal and the old prince's guards surrounded the keep mistress, as if to take her prisoner even though she was clad in priestess robes and mourning at the immolation of her lover and prince.

Thorat should have been looking at the sky, but he looked at the guards instead. He wanted to see the dragon, but what if he couldn't? He *could* see the men. They were well under Calar's power, and though they might not have liked what they were doing, they could see no one else strong enough to wrest the reins from Calar, especially if Gallia was gone. Gallia was looking at the guardsmen too, looking each man in the eye. They looked down, shamed by the accusation in her eyes.

Then the dragon cried again and Gallia looked up.

Thorat's gaze followed hers. The dragon fiew into the village square. As Thorat saw Tiada, the sword at his belt sprang to life, changing from an inert object into something that tugged slowly toward its dragon, like a lodestone. The blue-and-orange dragon fiew, but her wings were half faded to gray. Her blood dripped a rain of fire over the tavern roof. She landed on the prince, a burning dragon on the burning pyre. Tiada took him in her claws, in her mouth. She engulfed him like the fiame. The pyre collapsed.

The village youths leaped back to escape the burning logs and the guardsmen backed away too. Through a gap in their ranks, Gallia ran. She ran across the falling fire to the far side of the square, right past Thorat and the two other Defenders. All eyes turned to look at them. Thorat froze. He'd been seen and recognized. The dragon was fiying away already. She arched into the sky, still living, strengthened by this last rite.

A few of the guardsmen made a move to follow Gallia, but Calar barked and they clattered to a stop.

"Let her go!" he said. "Let her think she can challenge me. We have a pyre to burn. She can starve in the hills for all I care."

Calar went on shouting at the guardsmen and the villagers, but Thorat heard no more of it. While everyone's attention was fixed on the prince's brother and the hysterical priestesses on the temple porch, he jumped off the barrel and ran, with Varin and Ferrent at his back.

As he rounded the last shed on the outskirts of the village, he spotted Gallia disappearing into the edge of the forest.

"Are we following her?" Varin panted.

Thorat shook his head. "To the gate. Tiada's already wounded."

"But she looked so strong," Varin said. "Lemira never did, and she lived."

"She was bleeding," Ferrent confirmed.

They ran toward the path to the gate, not far from where Gallia had gone. A few days before, the path's entrance had been almost indiscernible in the line of the forest's edge, but now it was wide open, a broad lane of beaten-down bushes and broken grass.

"May their gods rain curses on them!" Thorat said. He ran as fast as he could, hoping that they wouldn't come too late.

As far as Thorat knew, the gate was utterly undefended. The sword tugged him onward. With the dragon flown, it would be wide open to the Cereans. They would be able to fill their bags and go, draining Tiada to the last drop of her life as fast as if they'd taken her on directly. She would return, she must return.

A dragon is only as strong as its land, as its realm, and the land is only as resilient as its dragon. The gate joins them, and when a gate collapses it breaks the bond. Only the body of the land is left, and the soul of the dragon goes down into the depths of the earth, far away from other living things, leaving the earth parched and dry. The fallen dragon will be shut off from humankind forever, shut off from the surface of the earth where all things grow, from the sun and the sea and the green fields rolling down from her mountain bones.

Behind him, Varin and Ferrent looked grim and determined. They'd done this before. He hadn't. They had so little time, they were so few, there was so little they could do.

§

Eppie watched the dragon go. She'd been so close that she could almost have jumped onto Tiada's back. She'd wanted to, but the desire had come too late, after the knife had flown and Tiada had cried out in pain. The knife had been aimed at her, right at her heart. She'd ducked, flattened herself, and rolled to the edge of the high ground, one foot dangling out over the warm cave mouth. She shouldn't have ducked. She should have let Squid hit her. Then the dragon might have flown unwounded. Eppie watched Tiada fly away. She was still alive, they both were, for now.

The earth rolled beneath Eppie like a living thing, or like the sea. She grabbed on to the roots to stop herself from falling into the bright cave mouth. She grunted and pulled herself up onto the solid ground. When the earth was firmly underneath her again, she got up on her knees to take her bearings.

Squid was standing on the slope above her, his back to the forest. He looked ill, as if he'd just woken up after a night of drinking Ganatean raki like it was Anamat ale. His hands hung down, limp where they'd stopped halfway to reaching for his second knife.

"What was that?" he asked as his eyes came into focus and settled on Eppie.

"Tiada, the dragon."

"But I thought they didn't exist." Squid stared after the dragon, far away now but somehow still visible. They saw her dip down into the village and rise again, brighter, satiated.

As the dragon flew off to circle her lands, Eppie turned to see Squid, gazing with blank-eyed wonder after the dragon. Dragon-struck. That was what he was. Behind him, a shadowy figure emerged from the forest, sword drawn. It was Sunna.

"Do you still see her?" Eppie asked.

Squid nodded, then he ran at her. He'd gotten his second knife. Sunna came up behind him and sliced down across his back. Eppie flattened herself against the tree trunk as Squid screamed as Sunna's sword bit into him, echoing the dragon's pain at where his own blade had hit. He fell into the blasting heat from the cave, which carried him down into the clearing below. One of the Cereans was standing there, and he looked up to see Squid spiraling like a blown leaf over him. The Cerean was not a servant or a merchant at all, but a fighting man. The blade of his shovel was as sharp as a spear, only thicker. How had they not seen that before, that the shovels were weapons? As Squid came down, the Cerean put his shovel up to deflect the blow and stepped aside with the practiced footwork of an armsman. The blade of the shovel caught Squid in the ribs and skittered sickeningly into his gut, then the Cerean fiung him aside.

"No!" Eppie shouted. She leaped down after Squid's empty body.

Her knees buckled with the shock of landing. That was the last thing she remembered.

§

Chapter 15

Thorat's thoughts dragged back to that moment in the night when he'd woken to find Eppie kissing him and pulling him closer. He'd admired the men and women who had taught him too, and that admiration was not so different from desire, but he simply hadn't noticed what lay behind Eppie's spells of wistfulness. Now she'd gone and it was his fault. He should have noticed, should have known. His waking mind kept jumping over that fact that she was a girl, treating her as if she were a boy apprentice, but in sleep, he'd felt her smooth skin against him, and for a moment of dreaming, he was back where he always longed to be.

Now he was racing into a fight he might not survive. Varin had begun to chant, and he joined in, hoping to drive the awkward night out of his mind, to focus on the fight ahead. He hoped Eppie was safe and far away, and Sunna too. The path blurred beneath their feet as they sped toward the gate. Ferrent joined the chant. It took breath but seemed to help them move faster, the trees blurring by as they pushed on. Would Sunna have fought the Cereans or run, if they found the camp? He didn't know. They drove themselves on until they reached the ruins of the little gate-side shrine. There, he slowed from a noisy run to a quiet walk and took in the lay of the land. The stone in Thorat's sword tugged him forward.

"Someone dropped the tree," Varin said.

Thorat nodded. He held a finger up and listened. "That's fighting, not mining."

They ran around the base of the tree, where they saw four Cereans still struggling to escape its branches, one still fainted away from pain or fright. That was one less to fight, until he woke again. From the sound of it, the rest of them were all in the clearing, fighting.

Nothing was quite as he'd expected—the others had been right about that. First of all, Sunna was there. She had her feet on the oak's trunk and was hanging on to one of its limbs with her left hand, while the sword in her right hand swept over the melee below, darting in and out while the Cereans moved their heavy shovels to block her point. Stretched out as she was against the trees, he could just see the rise in her belly. The Cereans' shovels were sharp and pointed. They were weapons as much as – or more than – they were tools. But they were still shovels, heavy and slow compared to Sunna's sword. She had the advantage over them for the moment.

Eppie was not so lucky. Somehow, she'd landed at the center of the fight, with four large men and their heavy weapons bearing in on her. A fifth man had staggered off to the edge of the clearing, holding his wounded arm against his belly, while one more was climbing up the slope, circling behind Sunna and her menacing sword. Unlike the others, he was armed with a throwing spear.

That one faced an ambush of his own as Forlan the mad bandit came crashing down on him with a heavy broadsword, a two-handed blade as likely to crush as to cut.

Behind Forlan came the rest of the bandits, all calling the altered snatch of birdsong Thorat knew so well. It sounded strange, in so many voices, and there was something not quite right about it, out of tune or off beat.

He took this all in in an instant, but the center of his attention stayed on Eppie. She had sunk to her knees and was snarling at the Cereans. One of them said something to the other, and he grunted, grinning briefly as he dropped his sharp shovel and grabbed Eppie's arms from behind.

"Help her!" Thorat said.

Ferrent was already on his way, but the man pinning Eppie was closer and quick enough to take advantage of the moment. Eppie struggled, but the big Cerean got her hands behind her and whipped a belt around her wrists, buckling it with one motion. He tried to kick Eppie aside while he took up his sharpened shovel again, but Ferrent knocked him off balance and landed a strike to his side, The Cerean crumpled.

Thorat and Varin were close behind. Varin positioned himself between Eppie and the Cereans while she tried to work her arms free.

"Took you long enough," Sunna gasped from overhead. She got her sword into one of the Cereans and he fell, blood spurting from the side of his neck. Sunna leaped down to finish the job and disarm him, but as she jumped, and as Thorat struck Eppie's wounded captor once more for good measure, Eppie wrenched her arm free only to roll right into the felled Cerean's sharpened shovel. She cried out and one of the other Cereans whipped around. He struck her head with the flat of his shovel and she fell to the ground, unconscious and bleeding from her twisted arm.

The four Defenders and the half-dozen bandits now outnumbered the standing Cereans. Vigda and Sunna sheathed their swords to drag Eppie out of the thick of the fight. As they got her away, one of the Cereans who'd been trapped under the fallen tree worked his way out.

"One of them went down for help," Gran said as he came up alongside Thorat.

Thorat grunted. "Thanks for coming." He was glad that they added to their numbers, even if he wasn't sure what they would do next.

"Separate," Thorat shouted. "One on one." Their swords had a better reach than the shovels, but not by much, and the shovels could break a sword quicker than the other way around. They would have to move quickly.

Varin, hampered by his still-sore ankle, didn't move quickly enough as two Cereans set on him at once. A shovel stroke felled him, cutting into his side just as Ferrent dispatched his attacker with a strong strike to the neck, killing him almost instantly. Ferrent stepped out of the way just in time to dodge the Cerean coming in from behind, and Larn jumped out of the bushes to get that one in the shoulder. Between them, they finished him off.

Vigda had her sword out now. Gray hair flying wild, she ran at a startled Cerean and skewered him, then pulled out the sword before he could strike back.

Thorat got in behind another shovel-wielder's guard, too close for sword work but in a good position to get his knife out.

One more Cerean, unguarded, ran to the gate. He dashed inside the still-glowing cave mouth. There was no disguising it now; surely they would know what they'd found even if they denied the dragon's very existence.

"One went in!" Sunna shouted. She followed him.

Someone cried out in pain and fell. It was one of the other bandits. Thorat heard Larn curse, and then at last he got his knife out of its sheath, but it was too late. He turned to take on the Cerean beside him, but the man had chosen to run rather than stay and fight. He counted three Cereans, including the one who'd gone into the gate. One of them shouted something and they all ran back down the now-well-trodden path to the village. Thorat started to chase after them, brandishing his sword, but Larn got in his way.

"Stop," Larn said. "They have more men below. You're winded."

Thorat opened his mouth to say that he was the commander of this mission, but all that came out was a gasp. His gaze went to Varin.

"No help for him," Larn said. "Come together."

Thorat looked around for the others. From inside the gate, he heard Sunna cry out as if she'd been stabbed. The earth trembled beneath their feet.

"She's returning," someone said. He looked over his shoulder for the dragon, but he couldn't see her, then he ran to the gate to try to rescue Sunna, but she was already staggering out into the clearing. She looked half-crazed and she was trailing blood. She had no visible wound, but there was a lot of it, and she looked deathly pale.

Tiada winged down, blocking out the sun. She was there, real but gray and thin against the brighter light of the sun. It streamed through the dragon as she circled, peering down at them. Thorat shuddered. She saw right through him, as if he weren't even there, just as he could look right through her. He felt himself fade, as if he might become nothing, as if he had never been. The sword in his hand grew heavy, too heavy to bear, tugging down into the earth, pointing the way to the dragons' realm. Tiada turned away.

Thorat stared blankly at the greening trees. The sword lost its unnatural weight. He heard someone breathing beside him and there was Larn, looking sick with worry. Ferrent had fallen to his knees, his head bowed in prayer. Varin and Eppie lay still. Eppie was breathing. Varin wasn't. Sunna stretched her arms out to greet the dragon.

How they'd forgotten about the spearman, Thorat wasn't sure. Tiada landed. Just as Sunna stepped up to touch the dragon's shimmering flank, the spear flew.

It struck Tiada in the neck. Her blood—what was left of it—came forth in a shower. Sunna staggered away, wiping it off as it smoked on her bare skin and burned through her

tunic, veiled now in smoke more than cloth. Tiada's eyes
dimmed, but only a little, and she gathered her strength into
her mighty scaled shoulders. She struck out, wove her neck
like a snake through the trees. She snapped her jaw around
the Cerean spearman, teeth running through him, then spat
him out. His shredded body careened through the air, landing
impaled on a small pine tree, his last scream cut short.

The dragon turned to Thorat and lowered her head. Now
she saw him again, her fading eyes focused on his still-solid
form, every ache and pain of his body magnified, rippling out
as he tried to reach for the dragon. He couldn't move. Did she
think he was friend or enemy? Did she think at all, or was she
simply motion and life without thought? What was the dragon
to him? He looked at Tiada fading like a mirage before his
eyes. Had she always been a mirage? No, she was there, and
real, he was almost close enough to reach her. The burning
blood rolling down her side was real, too. He thought at last of
Iola, how all her blessings had not been enough to save this
one dragon.

Tiada opened her maw and it was like looking into the
heart of the chambered earth. Her teeth shone like clear
crystals, her tongue like a carved ruby, too big, impossibly big.
Her jaw snapped shut within a finger's breadth of his face,
leaving her nose almost touching his. An orange blush flashed
along the length of her fading form.

I am dying, she said. *Take me back to the chambered
earth, my Defender.*

"As you wish." She might well have eaten him. He'd
thought that she would, hoped it, even. He wasn't strong
enough for this. As transparent as Tiada was, she was still a
dragon. "We will all have to carry you," he said.

Tiada looked right through his eyes again, but in a
different way this time. She recognized him in his soul.

Finally, she gave an almost imperceptible nod, then lowered her body to the ground.

The distant crash of the retreating Cereans had faded to nothing. In the forest clearing, the only sound was the labored breathing of the Defenders and the bandits, and the soft, hot drip of the dragon's blood leaking out onto the earth, where it burned the ground green, then golden, winter-gray then green again.

"She wants us to take her back in," Thorat said into the silence. "We'll all carry her."

§

Eppie's head hurt like a thousand too-early mornings all put together. She could hear voices, but she wasn't sure where she was. She was lying on a pile of leaves, or an old branch. A twig dug into her back and her arm felt like it was on fire. She tried to open her eyes, but the light hurt like knives in her brain. She tried again. Why did her arm hurt so much? On the next try, she managed to see it. Her arm didn't look so good. It was covered with blood, fresh blood, all of it hers.

She remembered dropping out of the tree into the midst of the Cereans, and then maybe there was some fighting but it all blurred together and the memories slipped past too fast to grasp in her aching mind. Using her less-wounded arm, she pushed herself up to a sitting position. The world swam sideways and churning bile lurched up her throat, then settled back into her empty stomach. Everything hurt. As she sat up, her guts twisted sideways but at least her spinning head settled out to level.

The dragon lay in the clearing in front of her gate, but paler than before and wounded. Eppie remembered that from before she'd fallen, or jumped, but now even more of the dragon's fiery blood fell. It dripped from her neck, and where the blood fell under the dragon's body, the earth was doing strange things, shifting and changing colors and making the world tilt around her again.

The next person Eppie saw was Sunna. She'd seen Sunna, too, just before it all went black, but now Sunna carried some sort of wound that didn't bear looking at, at least not with a woozy head. The Defenders and the bandits had gathered around the dragon. Sunna bent and touched her forehead to the dragon's nose, then stepped to one side, cradling Tiada's head, which looked almost as big as the priestess's body. Vigda took her position to the other side of Tiada's head while the men—Thorat, Larn, Gran, Forlan, and Ferrent—folded the dragon's wings in, almost as if they were swaddling her.

Eppie tried to get to her feet, but her limbs wouldn't hold her. She crawled forward. Gran noticed her and with a glance seemed to say "stay back," but Eppie kept crawling. The world juddered dangerously around the dragon and her gate was closing. As small as the way to the hollow earth had been before, Eppie could feel it shrinking as she watched, the earth turning in on itself, withdrawing the power that welled up from its heart. Tiada's gate held open but just barely. It wasn't big enough for the dragon herself, nor for the people who carried her, not for most of them, anyway.

Eppie crawled forward another pace, but her progress was even slower than the awestruck, horrified stagger of those carrying the dragon. A dead Cerean's body lay across her path, still warm with its lost life but cooling fast. She wouldn't touch it, couldn't, so she found it in herself to stand and step over him. Her head had steadied a little more when she stood, and she could see the dragon better.

Tiada's body had been weakened by her long estrangement from the people of her land, but she was still glorious, still a dragon in the flesh. Her new wounds had drawn out her already-too-weak blood, thinning her down nearly to her skeleton and making the bones of the land soft and riddled with fault lines. Eppie could see them reflected in the dragon's visible body, ready to shatter. Even as she approached the dragon, Tiada's distinctive blue-and-orange flowers withered around the edges of the clearing, right up to the shadow of the dragon's body, where they bloomed more fiercely for blooming their last.

They had the dragon sideways to the hill. Sunna and Vigda looked to each other, then took the lead, trying to bring Tiada's head to the cave mouth.

Tiada jerked her jaw from the priestesses' grasp, knocking Sunna down. Sunna rolled over and came up on her feet again, dusting the earth from herself, shaking.

I would see this world until the last, Tiada said.

"I never thought I'd touch a dragon in the flesh," Vigda said softly as she reached to draw the dragon's head back to the cave.

They hadn't heard her.

"There's someone coming from downslope," Gran said, jerking his head toward the village.

Eppie opened her mouth, but she felt too small to make a sound. When she tried again, her voice came out clearly, like the voice of some soothsayer in trance, only not quite as polished.

"I think she wants to go in tail first," Eppie said. "To see the land and sky."

Thorat turned and saw her then. He looked like it was the first time he'd actually *seen* her since that first time they met. They matched each other's gaze for a moment.

"We'll do that, then," Thorat said, breaking the connection.

Larn looked as if he were going to object. He glanced back and forth between Eppie and Thorat, then nodded.

Something else happened then; it looked like a dream. First, Larn the bandit seemed to transform and Thorat changed, too. They grew thinner and nearly transparent, like the dragon. They began to turn her around, to guide her into the hill. They caressed her scales, just touching the long fierce spine of her back, molding her wings down until their stiff lace of veins turned fluid again. Thorat led the tip of the tail into the cave mouth. For a moment, it glistened with a fire that answered the sun. After that, it answered only its own riddles, and only to the dragons, closing in on itself.

Gran said something, but no one heard his words. They were transfixed by the sight of the dragon backing into the gate. It folded around her, the living stones becoming part of her flesh as the wounded moving soul of her, her visible form, melted into the earth.

I will come again, the dragon seemed to say, as though that were possible.

You're dying? Eppie thought.

I cannot die. You can.

But if you can't die...

I can go under the earth forever and join the deepest stream.

Eppie failed to understand how that was different, but apparently, the dragon thought so as she flashed out of sight, leaving a shower of stones in her wake, like a gift glowing with her fading power. Despite knowing better, Eppie felt herself reaching for them. They reminded her of the dragon, but she coveted them; she felt she could have one for herself alone as if it had nothing to do with the power of the land and the dragons who guarded it. She reached for a stone but stopped short of touching it.

"I think we should leave these here," she said as she noticed that the others were reaching for them too.

They hesitated, all but one of them. Gran had not reached for the stones at all. He had released the dragon, not being able to quite grasp her somehow, and was facing the village.

"They're coming closer, more of them now," Gran said. "Leave the stones; we need to save ourselves."

"We need to guard the gate. If they take these, they'll come back for more!" Thorat said, stepping up to Gran.

"We should drive them back to the flatland," Larn said.

Ferrent shook his head but said nothing. They could hear the villagers, and the prince's men, or Calar's men now. From the sound of things, they were coming with horses and carts, rumbling over the hollow and dry earth. It trembled ever so slightly.

Sunna and Vigda conversed in quick undertones, then Sunna spoke. "Tiada is gone," she said. "She's gone where they can't hurt her, where no human can ever reach her. If she emerges again, it will be long after our lives and our children's lives are gone and forgotten. Leave them the rocks; their power will fade. Gran's right; we must save ourselves now."

"Go, then, if you want," Thorat said. His eyes were on fire with something Eppie hadn't seen in him before. He looked as dragon-touched as Forlan, who was now coming down from the slope with the body of the Cerean spearman draped over his shoulders like a sack of grain. The tree must have shaken the body off. Forlan dumped it across the path.

"Go to the hills!" Forlan said.

Thorat turned to Eppie and stared at her. "Will you stay and fight?"

Eppie wanted to say that she would, that she would fight for him, but Vigda took her by the arm. "You're wounded," Vigda said with the authority of a woman who'd seen some battle wounds before. "Come back up to the camp."

"Sovara would say to go back to camp," Ferrent said.

"Come on," Larn said. He laid a hand on Thorat's shoulder and pulled him away. "The women are right. Back to the camp."

Thorat slumped under his hand and nodded. "I don't like it. We shouldn't retreat," he said, but he followed the bandit chief's lead.

They left only a splatter of blood and of course the dead Cereans. The dragon's gate closed in on itself and her stones went cold, some turning into common pebbles, others into gems of a thousand colors, clear like the sky or deep like the sea, red like blood and green like the life of the land. What prices would they fetch in the markets of Calandria? It didn't matter to the dragon or the dead land she'd left behind.

Eppie almost looked right past Squid's body. She wouldn't have seen him at all except for the flutter of a bird nearby, looking for morning worms. He lay on the forest floor, an expression of surprise frozen onto his face, staring dead-eyed after the place where he'd seen the dragon. Eppie broke away from their sorry, bleeding group and went to close his eyes, then she followed the others on up the hill, taking Thorat's hand and tugging him on when he looked back one last time.

§

"We should have fought," Thorat said tiredly. "There were enough of us."

"They were better prepared than we were, and most of them unwounded," Larn said. "Quiet now."

Thorat had so much more to say, but he needed the silence, too. What had just happened? Had the dragon died? They'd all seen her at last, even touched her. That touch was the strangest thing. Part of him had gone into the dragon, had animated her, but when the gate swallowed her, he'd felt himself come back into his own body, but he felt stronger, even while he knew that he was still winded from the fight. Some of the light had gone out of the sword in his hand. Its power, the power it had borrowed from the dragon, was fading away into the land. They could have beaten back Calar and his henchmen; he was sure of it. He knew their strengths and faults to a man, but too many of the Defenders were wounded and the rest were spent, in no condition to take on any kind of fight.

And Varin was gone, dead, his body left there in the wreckage.

"I have to go back for Varin," Thorat said.

Vigda, the old priestess-bandit, stopped. "What would you do with his body?"

The others waited for his answer. He had to tell them. He wasn't sure that he should.

"If the gate were still open, I would leave him there. Is it too much to ask for a funeral pyre?"

"These mountains are on the border of Getera's realm," Sunna said. "Maybe she would come." Tiada had come for the prince, after all. The dragons still did come sometimes.

Ferrent was shaking his head. "It's too late," he said.

Larn held up a hand. "I believe I may understand you, but it's a strange thing for city men to ask. Our Kendet fell, too. If we bring them away from the gate, away from the lowlanders, then maybe we can carry them between us to the eye and build them a pyre there."

"Offer them to Na?" Ferrent looked as horrified as Thorat felt.

"But Na's eye is so far away," Sunna said, "nearly to the far end of Theranis. It would take us a moon round to reach it going through the mountains, maybe more. Getera is closer."

Vigda shook her head. "Getera is fading, too. Her gate is as close to their keep there as Tiada's was to the village here. The prince and his men would take notice, and they wouldn't like to see a bandit, or even an Anamat guardsman, burned like a chief." She paused. "And Na has three eyes. I take it you don't know the one near the border of Helanum?"

"No, I didn't," Sunna said slowly. "How far is it?"

"We could reach it from our camp in about five days," Larn said. "The air will be cool on those trails."

So, they could hope that the bodies wouldn't stink too much.

"I didn't take a wound," Thorat said. "I'll go back down for them."

"I'll go with you," Vigda said, "for Kendet." She turned to the rest of them. "Those of you who are able, go to the camp and bring back stretchers. We'll carry the bodies two by two."

"Four of us will come back down," Larn said. "We'll take them in turns."

Vigda left Sunna's side and beckoned to Eppie. "Look after her," she told the girl. Eppie had lost some blood, but she was strong, she'd survived. She'd done a good day's work, too, from dropping that tree on the Cereans and holding them off until the last. The apprentice had survived. Unlike Varin, who'd been apprentice at the last battle like this. Sunna was still on her feet, but not by much. Her wound, whatever it was, seemed to have shrunk her to half her height and strength.

Eppie propped Sunna up as Vigda came down and took Thorat by the hand. She smiled up at him in a way that didn't match his grim mood or the wrinkles on her face. "Come with me," she said. "I'll show you the way and maybe we can pick off a few more with those clever traps of yours."

Thorat had wanted to wade back into the fight not so long ago, but now the prospect of lifting his sword again made him feel empty, defeated. He felt as if the fight had gone out of him. His heart yearned for peace, no more battles. All he wanted to do was to bring back Varin's body and see him laid to rest, preferably in the dragons' embrace. Then he would limp back to Anamat and home with whoever could trail after him.

"We won't let them take the stones, at least not much," Vigda said as they walked. Her wrinkles deepened as if she were amused by it all, not as if the heart had just been ripped out of this piece of the land. "Don't worry," she said, as if reading his thoughts. "Na still lives."

"Na?" Thorat said. That was small consolation, if any.

"Na will outlive them all; just you see."

How could Na, the untamed dragon, inspire these bandits so much? And was that really what they were? Bandits?

"I hope I don't live to see that day," Thorat said.

Vigda, old priestess that she was, stilled herself. All the world around seemed to slow at her command as she gazed beyond the ordinary. "You will, boy; you will," she said in a prophetess's tones. Then she snapped back into herself and scratched behind her ear.

"Where were we, now?" she said.

"Going back down to the gate so the prince's men—or rather Calar's—can't wonder where those two bodies came from, or what they had to do with the Cereans. You wanted to stop them taking the stones, though I don't see how we can." The thought of facing more Cereans was almost enough to make him turn around and go back up the hill.

"Ah, yes, but I can," Vigda said. "And let's not get our own heads stuck onto those nasty Cerean spears." That didn't make it any better.

"I think the spear was Theranian," Thorat said. "It's a lot like the ones they use for boar hunting in the north." Rather than hit a boar, this one had struck the dragon with a final blow, like the spears of Enomaean legend. "I wonder how they saw her."

Vigda huffed as she climbed over a log. "She showed herself, that's how. I don't know why she did it. Maybe she was just tired." Vigda spoke in her ordinary voice, but this too had the ring of truth to it.

Thorat wasn't even sure that the dragons had reasons anymore. The silence of the forest was too deep. It felt oppressive. "Why did you go into the hills?" he asked.

"Me?" Vigda said. "Plenty of reasons, none of which I'd expect a man to understand. Mostly, though, it was that I stopped being able to hear the dragon within temple walls. So I left. It happened in temples all over Theranis around that time, even in Anamat, or so I hear."

The girls must have been able to see the dragon when they were in the temple, but they'd never said that they could.

"When did that happen?" he asked.

Vigda shrugged. "Before you were old enough to swing a sword, I'd say. Maybe ten or twelve years back, maybe more, maybe less. I don't count the years anymore."

If her count was close to right, that would have been around the time of the clash at Lemira's gate, around the time he went to Anamat as a scrappling and before the girls joined the temple. He would ask them about it when he returned to the city. If he returned to the city.

Vigda slowed. "We're almost there."

"So are they." Thorat could see past the leaning oak clear down to what had been the shrine. Vigda had chosen a good route.

"Shimmy up that tree like a good lad and tell me what you see," Vigda said.

Thorat looked up. It was a good climbing tree. "Gladly," he said. He grasped the lowest branch, then the next, clambering up. He was relieved to see that it wasn't the tree that had impaled that Cerean spearman. That one was only a stone's throw away and still dripping with guts. Thorat shivered. It was Garren who had told him the story from Enomae, of how one of their so-called heroes had driven the last of the dragons down into the sea, with a spear very similar to that one.

The first person he saw and recognized was the Enomaean priest of Farseer. He'd changed his clothes. Now he was dressed as a Cerean, and Calar was pushing him toward the remains of the dragon's gate.

§

Chapter 16

Eppie gave Sunna her good arm to lean on, but even that effort tugged and pulled at the hastily bandaged wound on her opposite shoulder and arm. She would have begged for a stop, but Sunna and Ferrent limped on, looking even worse than she felt. Sunna was deathly pale and still bleeding but more slowly now, as if there wasn't much more life to wring out of her. Eppie half wanted to ask if it was the baby, the pregnant belly gone out of her, but she couldn't spare the energy to speak, and if she couldn't, then neither could Sunna.

Gran was holding Ferrent up, and whenever they had to step over a log or a rock or go sideways, the two of them sounded muffled complaints about their catalog of wounds. Ferrent's forearm was ripped. He kept it as still as he could manage, but he winced with every step. Gran had hastily bandaged his thigh and he held a wad of cloth to his side. Forlan and Larn seemed not to have sustained any damage worse than bruises and small cuts. Rather than prop up the wounded, they guarded the front and back of the train, looking out for danger and making sure that no one fell behind.

They halted for a rest after a while, then they went on and halted again. They were just getting up from their second rest when Larn stopped halfway through his command and looked down the slope, his jaw dropping.

Eppie turned to look. The forest was moving, the trees bowing in a long, silent wave as the earth rippled beneath them. A hard, jangling sound followed the quake of the earth, like the breaking of a brass harp-string, harsh, echoing off the strings around it, suddenly thrown out of tune.

The movement in the trees subsided. They stood back up in their accustomed places. There was silence, then a birdcall, then another. The ground rumbled once more, then it was still.

The sound of the broken chord jangled away into emptiness. Larn turned back to the track and they all followed, as silent as the earth around them and feeling just as empty. They rested and walked again until Eppie felt that the trudge back to the bandits' camp would last forever.

The skirmish at the dragons' gate had ended shortly after dawn, and even with all the halts and slow progress, they reached the bandit camp by midday. Someone had lit a fire, and there were more people around it than they'd left behind, including a half-dozen bandits Eppie hadn't seen before. They were mostly men, plus one woman. The woman – she was even older than Vigda – took one look at Sunna and Eppie, then spoke to Larn.

"Give them your tent," she said. "Vigda can help them."

Eppie started to protest that she was all right, but she didn't even have the breath to say the words. Sunna looked too tired to even think about being polite.

"Where's Vigda?" the old woman demanded.

"Gone to gather the dead," Larn said. "Send your men with stretchers, two of them."

"Who fell?"

"Kendet," Larn said. "I'm sorry. They're at Tiada's gate."

"Not a gate anymore," Forlan said.

The old woman squinted at him and grunted something about mad prophecies.

Forlan picked up his brother and carried Ferrent over his back to the nearest tent.

"Who's that?" the old woman asked.

"Forlan's brother," Larn said.

The old woman turned to Eppie and Sunna, still rooted where they stood. "Go on, you! I'll be tending you. Who's the other dead?" the old woman asked, tight-throated.

"A lowlander," Larn said. "Friend of Forlan's brother there. We said we'd take him to the third eye and burn him with Kendet."

"What fool are you?" the old woman raged. "To take a lowlander to the eye? To burn him?"

"I pledged it," Larn says. "You can go your way or stay here if you want no part in it, but bring the bodies up and we'll be in your debt."

A crow cawed as it fiew over.

"I'll send my men," the old woman said after a pause, "but if any of them take a wound or worse, it's on your head."

Eppie didn't hear Larn's response as she helped Sunna toward the tent, but halfway across the circle of tents – three more of them now – Sunna balked.

"I want to go wash first," she said with a sudden burst of energy. "Where's that stream?"

Eppie led her there, and before long, the old woman appeared with a bundle of stained and worn but still-serviceable linen. They were soft with wear and dried them much better than the furs would have. Back at the tent, the old woman re-bandaged Eppie's shoulder and arm, tut-tutting over it. She found more cloths for Sunna and examined the back of her head, where she found a bump of some sort. Eppie watched her through half-closed eyes while she prepared poultices for that and Eppie's wound. Someone brought them bowls of broth and rounds of the rough bread, and they ate as much as they could before falling into exhausted sleep.

§

The Enomaean priest looked ill at ease in his Cerean robes.

"I'm glad we caught you before you set sail," Calar said. "It would be a shame to lose the one man who could banish the old god from this place."

"I never said I could do that."

"Of course you can," Calar said. "Only invoke your Farseer and we'll be safe enough."

"I won't call my god to this cursed land." The priest spat and turned as if to go, but Calar's henchmen grabbed him by the arms and lifted him.

"You will," Calar said. "Or call the Cereans' god; I don't mind as long as we can get them their goods and go back to the cleared land."

Calar's men carried the priest into the clearing, but they went haltingly. They had to step over the body of one of the Cereans on the path, and they averted their gaze from the other Cerean bodies on the ground. They looked at the pile of gemstones lying by the dragon's collapsed gate. The priest, to his credit, did look at the fallen.

"You think the dragon slaughtered these men?" he asked.

"Don't question me, man; just do your work," Calar said. He was keeping his distance from the clearing, the dead men, and whatever might be left of the dragon.

One of the armsmen finally let go of the priest and looked down, himself. "That's a sword wound," he said.

"But look over here," another of the men said. "I never seen anything like that." He pointed at the ground.

"It's strange, all right."

Calar took a step closer. "You say these men were cut down by swords, not the dragon?"

"Mostly, my lord," one of the men said. When Calar didn't speak immediately, he went on. "I'd say it was the ghosts, the ones who haunt the dragons' places."

"Nonsense," Calar said. "Ghosts can't carry swords."

"I don't know," the guardsman said, hanging his head, "just that it's said that they do, that they cut down any –"

"Enough of that!" Calar said. "It must be bandits or some such. We'll scour these hills and pay them back, but first take these bodies and bury them. They brought shovels; use those."

The men hesitated.

"Go!" Calar ordered.

They bent to pick up the shovels, and a pair of guardsmen moved the fallen Cereans farther away from the gemstones. "I wouldn't think bandits would have such good swords," one of the men muttered.

"And you," Calar said, turning to the Enomaean priest. "Say some banishment for ghosts, too. The men are getting as skittish as lambs."

The priest sighed. "I suppose the Cerean men can have their death rites, as far as I know them. Will that do?"

Calar scowled and returned to his position at the edge of the clearing. "Do what you need to do; just say some banishment so my men will be willing to carry those rocks away. Fools, to be afraid." He said it loudly, as if that could banish his own unease as he got as far as he could from the bodies.

The priest looked grim. "Bring me three torches from the camp and a blanket made of wool," he said. "Also a clay tablet, still wet, to write their names in."

One of the Cereans, not from the group who'd been there to fight at dawn, came up the path. He had two tablets and offered one to the priest. "We will make torches here," he said, stumbling over his words. "A linen bag can open for blanket. Not back to camp."

"Good. Hurry up with it." Calar glanced anxiously at the gate and retreated to the ruined shrine.

§

Thorat watched from his perch in the tree, not daring to make a sound. Vigda waited below. The armsmen and foreigners followed Calar's retreat to the shrine, arguing about where to bury the Cereans. Thorat scaled down the trunk and reported.

"I don't see how we're going to get in there," he said. Varin's body was off in the underbrush and Kendet had limped away from the gate before breathing his last, but they weren't far away and the men from the keep would find them soon. To be buried under Cerean rites would be worse to them than not being laid to rest at all.

Vigda listened to his report, chewing her cheeks pensively. "I have an idea," she said. "The old guardian tree's loose on its roots. Wouldn't take much to get it to tumble."

She was right; the old oak *was* leaning farther out than it had been the day before, but there were simply too many armed men around. He'd seen Vigda wield a sword, out of the corner of his eye for a moment in the earlier fight, but he wasn't sure of her skill and they faced a dozen armed men. He shook his head.

"It would hold them off for a bit," Vigda said.

"Hold them off from what?" Thorat asked.

"From coming to find our camp, you flatlander."

There was that. He should be glad that Calar blamed all this on menacing bandits and that he dismissed the stories of the Defenders' ghosts, but he wasn't.

"We'll never get out of here alive, never mind with the bodies," Thorat said.

Vigda just chuckled and slid soundlessly down the hill.

Thorat followed. She gave him no choice, really. Vigda kept to the cover of brush, circling around out of sight of the clearing. When they came back in sight of the oak's leaning trunk, Calar and the Enomaean priest were standing in front of the pile of stones at the gate.

§

"Your brother would not have robbed from the grave of your fallen dragon," the priest said.

"No?" Calar said. "My brother was a fool, nearly the death of our line. His mistress was barren, and he would not take another."

"That is a worthy choice. Farseer's faithful do not care too much for descendants, rather more for honor."

Calar gave a dismissive snort. "Would you not take these, then?"

"They are beautiful," the priest said. "And these, more than anything before, tell me that your dragons are true gods, even if your temples are for women."

"You're wrong; they're for men. Strong men."

"Then where are –" The priest cut himself short of asking whatever had been on his mind. "I must prepare for the Cerean rite of passage as well as I'm able."

"Fools," Calar muttered again, still trying to convince himself.

Vigda whispered in Thorat's ear, "Now!" She rushed forward in a heedless crash of leaves and branches and threw herself against the trunk of the oak as high up as she could reach. With surprising agility, she clambered out along one of the lower limbs until her body dangled and the oak began to tilt.

It was suicide. Calar looked up, of course.

"A madwoman!" he said.

Calar's men were some distance way, back at the ruined shrine. Thorat rushed forward, trying to reach Vigda before she fell onto Calar, or onto the pile of Tiada's stones. The forest blurred around him as he ran, and the earth began to tremble and shake as if Tiada *did* still have some life in her, even though what was left of her was trapped under the earth. Calar blanched. The Enomaean priest fell to his knees. Vigda just fell, fell slowly, pulling the oak down with her as she went. Thorat rushed in to catch her, and then they were trapped as surely as the Cereans had been tangled in the tree Eppie had dropped on them at dawn.

Calar looked around for his men. Rather than wait for them or take up his own sword, he ran back toward the shrine.

"Coward!" Vigda screeched after him.

Her voice froze the forest. For a long moment, everything was still, and then Thorat shook himself free of the tree, dragging Vigda out after him.

"Let me go!" she said. "This is my place to die."

Thorat could hear the confusion of the men from the keep and the foreigners. They weren't ready to mount an attack.

"I know that man," one of them said.

"He's just a –"

The priest's voice rang out as strongly as Vigda's had. "Back, away! Go or you gods will strike you down!" The priest of Farseer believed in the dragons, even now that Tiada was gone. How strange.

A hum rose in Thorat's ears. Whether it came from inside of him, from the earth, or from something else, he wasn't sure. The earth of the hillside slid over the stones, burying the glistening drops of the dragon's life under common mud as the tree's roots snapped and something else broke too, deep beneath the surface of the earth, sending a dissonant chord up out of the depths. He could only just hear Calar screaming for the men to follow him, to kill the bandits, but no clatter of armed men coming toward him followed the command. Their screams faded into the distance.

The next thing he knew, he was lying on a jostling stretcher with the stink of a half-dozen bandits and their unwashed furs to wake him fully to his senses. He struggled to roll, the jostling slowed, and he retched the bile of his empty stomach out onto the forest floor.

"You didn't kill him," said someone in a rough voice.

"He got in my way." That was Vigda, and she wasn't happy with him.

"What happened?" Thorat asked, his voice coming out slurred and groggy.

"Landslide. We dug you out."

"Could've left me there," Thorat said. It would have been a long sight more comfortable under the earth than this was. His body hurt, inside and out. Maybe Tiada would've taken pity on him, if she was still in any way alive, and carried him down to the dragons' realm to see Iola.

He tripped back over his thoughts. "Stop," he said.

With a little grumbling, the men carrying the stretcher set it down. Thorat sat up and looked at Vigda. "I need to talk to you. Alone."

The other bandits stepped back a few paces. They were carrying another stretcher and Forlan carried a body over his shoulder.

"I can walk," Thorat said, hoping that it was true.

"We're most of the way there already," Vigda said. At her direction, Forlan dumped the body of Kendet on the stretcher. Thorat staggered over to Vigda, his knees wobbling a bit, but they steadied enough that he could walk almost normally except for a sharp pain in his ankle.

Vigda was an old priestess; that was what the bandits said. He had no reason to think that she wasn't, but she was no ambassadress. He stood close to her and lowered his voice but didn't look directly at her.

"Were you trying to get in?" he asked. She would know what he meant: into the chambered earth, into the dragons' realm, into that other world.

"If I was, who are you to stop me?" Vigda said.

He would have liked to say that he was a Defender of the Dragons, and the lover of the ambassadress, and that she was the only one who had the right to go down, but how could he say that? He wanted to go down into the dragons' realm as much as any man could, more than he had right to want.

"I think you were too," Vigda said.

"Maybe. I'm not sure."

"Your sword is gone," she added. "We looked for it for a while, but the lowlanders were coming back. It was a good sword."

"It was more than a good sword," Thorat said with a sigh. "But never mind; we can get another, and a common sword is almost as good in the right hands."

Vigda stepped away and spoke more loudly. "You must tell me where you think you can get another," she said. "Meanwhile, back to camp. I'm hungry."

§

It was almost dark when Eppie woke, and it took her a moment to remember where she was and how she'd gotten there. There had been the battle at the gate, in the clearing; there had been the fading dragon telling her things, then carrying Tiada into the hill, where she would join the deepest stream. Then they had stumbled back to this camp, where the furs didn't smell especially clean but at least there were not too many fleas. She'd slept deeply.

She sat up, or tried to. Her arm hurt so much that it felt like it was going to collapse under her. She prodded it, clenching her teeth against the pain. The sting was mostly on the outside, closer to the skin than the bone. She leaned on it again, which didn't hurt any more than just moving it. Sunna was asleep beside her, and someone was opening the tent flap.

"I'm only come to see that old Gennie patched you up well enough," Vigda grumbled.

"You're back," Eppie said. "Is Varin all right?"

"Dead," Vigda said.

Outside, people were shouting and arguing. The fire crackled, sending out flashes of light. Thorat's voice came through as clear as anything. "How was I to know she wanted..." he said, but the rest got drowned out.

Eppie sat up a bit more. It felt like someone was shooting arrows through her upper arm. Everything else hurt too, only with more of a dull ache.

"Come out and let's have a look at that," Vigda said, dragging her out of the tent.

"Not bad," she pronounced. "See, they would have done well enough without me." She dropped Eppie's arm and returned to the group around the fire. Eppie wondered if she should follow.

Sunna groaned from inside the tent. "Is there any water in this place?" Her voice sounded as if she were trying not to cry. "Is anyone here?"

"I'm here," Eppie said. She tried to count the figures around the fire, but between the smoke and the moving around, it was too hard to tell exactly. The others who'd arrived while they were down at the gate were still there.

"There's a bunch of Vigda's band by the fire, and some others I don't know," she told Sunna. "I'll look for the water. It's dark."

"I can tell that much." Sunna sounded none too pleased to be alive.

Eppie found a pile of gear stacked outside the tent, including a full skin of water and another one full of sour wine. She brought both in to Sunna, handing her the water first.

"Is that wine there?" Sunna said, sniffing. "Hand it over, would you?"

Eppie took the waterskin and drank from that herself while Sunna adjusted herself into more of a sitting position and downed a gulp of wine. "Wretched stuff," she pronounced. "Everything hurts."

"You killed him," Eppie said.

"Killed who?"

"Squid. He was a friend of mine, or used to be."

"That boy who was throwing a knife at you?" Sunna asked. "Some friend. How in Na's crotch..."

"Shh," Eppie said. The sounds of shouting outside had crested and subsided, and she'd missed whatever they said.

"He was a friend of mine. We camped together for three years. Then this Midsummer, right before Thorat found me, he took work on a foreign merchant ship. I saw him again at the keep, at Tiadun, and –" Eppie shuddered at the memory. "I don't know if he'd changed or if I was just always wrong about him."

"I don't know either," Sunna said. "I don't know anything, but what I do know is that he was trying to kill you. Like I said, some friend."

"Then I ducked and he hit Tiada instead. It's like I killed her."

"That's ridiculous," Sunna said. "She was already fading."

"I could have stopped Squid, at least. I should have realized."

"What, with a knife coming at you like that? How?"

"No, before that, at the keep, maybe even a long time before that, back in Anamat."

"Thorat could have stopped him at the keep too. Thorat wasn't his friend. He could have done a lot more, I reckon."

"Thorat's path wouldn't have crossed Squid's much, if at all," Eppie said. "He wouldn't have known, not with everything else that was going on there."

"Anyway, none of us can change it now. There's nothing to be done," Sunna said. "I've gone and gotten these furs all bloody, too."

Eppie poked her head outside to look up at the stars. "Sky's clear. Maybe we can wash 'em tomorrow."

Sunna sat with her knees tucked up against her chest. She looked like a lump of rock there in the darkness.

The shouts from around the fire subsided for a moment, then flared again.

"What are they arguing about?" Sunna asked.

"How should I know?" Eppie said.

"Never mind; I don't even think I care. Anara's left knee. I should have stayed in Anamat and let the temple healers have their way with me. It's too late, but there it goes."

"You lost the baby?" Eppie said.

"Wasn't a baby yet. Wasn't even kicking. I'm so tired."

"Me too, but -"

"I was just trying to stop him from killing you, and you are still alive."

"It cost too much."

"She wouldn't have died from that one knife thrown. It wasn't just him killing her."

"Everyone said she was weak already, but I saw her, and I just didn't believe it, didn't believe she could go like that," Eppie said. "Do you remember when the bond she had with the earth broke?"

"What?" Sunna said.

"That jangling sound, on the way up here."

"How did you know what it was? That's priestess stuff."

"I don't know how; that's just what it seemed like to me," Eppie said. She got up and went to the tent flap. "I can't believe he was trying to kill me. I mean, I knew he was selfish and mean a lot of the time, but he wasn't that bad, not before the Cereans got whatever they are into him. And he was dragon-blind, right up to the end when all of a sudden he wasn't. Kind of like the prince, I guess."

"Did he – that boy – ever see Anara?" Sunna asked.

Eppie shook her head. "He *said* that he didn't, but he might have been lying. He lied about everything else."

Sunna shifted and heaved herself up into a crouch. "We've all been wrong about men, or boys sometimes. I was only trying to stop him from killing you."

"I know," Eppie said. "Thanks."

"Thorat should have been paying more attention. If he'd stopped him at the keep, turned him away from the Cereans, it might not have come to killing."

"I don't think Thorat knew," Eppie said. How could he have? She hesitated at the door of the tent. "At least that's one man who honors the priestesses."

"For all that's worth," Sunna said, "and it's really only the one. Waste of a man."

"Sure is," Eppie said.

Sunna clapped her on the back and it was all Eppie could do not to scream with the pain as it pulled on her bandages.

"Sorry," Sunna said. She changed the subject. "What by Na's teeth *are* they arguing about?"

"I'll go find out." With that, Eppie staggered out of the tent, with Sunna following at her heels. They limped over toward the fire together.

The number of bandits in the camp had more than doubled with the arrival of Gennie's band, so despite the loss of Kendet and Varin, the group around the fire looked like a crowd. Larn stood at the center, waving his arms and talking in tense, clipped tones while Gennie faced him, hands on her hips.

"You can't take a lowlander to Na's eye," she said.

"They pass by there on the trail all the time," Larn said.

"But they don't stop."

"He died defending Tiada's gate!"

The bandits roared at one another, pointing and shouting. Eppie wanted to cover her ears and crawl back to the tent, but Sunna was pulling her forward, right toward Thorat. He didn't seem to notice them until they were at his shoulder. There, Sunna abruptly let go of Eppie and leaned into Thorat.

"You're up walking?" he asked.

"Just barely. What are you all arguing about?"

"Whether they're going to let us carry Varin's body up to Na's third eye to make a pyre."

"Varin?" Sunna's brow wrinkled and her jaw dropped. Her voice came out in a whine. "But I thought he was just wounded."

"Not just wounded, no," Larn said, coming over to her. "You should be resting."

"I'll go back to the tent," Sunna agreed.

"We'll send along some broth and bread. You have to eat," Ferrent said, his voice gentle.

"I'll help," Thorat offered. He took Sunna's arm, leaving Eppie to trail behind, feeling invisible. He handed Sunna into the tent with great care and Eppie went to follow. Finally, he spoke to her.

"How are you?" he asked.

"Mostly all right," Eppie said, looking down at the ground. "That one big cut, otherwise just bruises and sore, I think."

"You did well, there. I'm sorry about...the other night. It was just last night. I just can't. Maybe you'll understand when you have apprentices."

"Me? I'm never going to have apprentices." How could she? The dragons were dying. They were all going to die. Squid was dead, and curses on him, too.

"I think you will," Thorat said. Then he thudded her on the back, a little bit like Squid used to do when they'd first come to the city, only without the veiled threat in it.

She just nodded. If she tried to speak, she was probably going to cry. Inside the tent, Sunna was sobbing again already. Around the fire, the bandits' shouts had tapered off to grumblings punctuated by a staccato back-and-forth between Larn and Gennie. She didn't want to let them see her cry. She could hold off until after they'd eaten something, maybe. Ferrent was bringing it. After that, she could cry all she wanted. Varin, too. It just wasn't fair. Squid was rotting.

Thorat returned to the fireside, pausing halfway there for one quick look back over his shoulder. She went into the tent and joined Sunna, not bothering to hold back the tears any more.

§

Two days later, Thorat and the others said farewell to the valley encampment. Sunna was not quite ready to travel—anyone could see that—but she insisted that they go, and that she would be no bother. They wove along the narrow mountain paths to the third eye of Na, stopping to rest a little more often than they really should have. Gennie's band stayed in the valley over Tiada's gate, or what had been Tiada's gate.

Ferrent asked a few careful questions, ascertaining that the bandits knew the location of all the gates in the southern half of Theranis, even if the priestesses had forgotten them or been made to forget.

"Lowland priestesses," Larn spat. "They're closer to the princes than they are to the dragons. We chase them off when they come too close, at least since we got word that some of them were stealing stones."

"Priestesses, stealing stones?" Thorat asked.

Larn nodded. "They probably gave them to the princes, who only want them for trade goods these days. We wouldn't stand for it."

"I wouldn't have either," Thorat said, "but what can the ones who are devoted to the dragons do?"

"They can come join us in the hills or find another way," Larn said. "If there are any true priestesses left, which I doubt."

"There are true priestesses."

"Like there's hen's teeth."

"It's better in the hills," Vigda added. "They were afraid, most of them. Look what happened to me: I never went back. I died up here. I'm a ghost to the ones back in the temple, like I should be by now." She frowned at Thorat, still angry that he hadn't let her follow Tiada down.

It was a small party, only the five bandits and the four remaining Defenders – if Eppie even counted as one of them – to carry the two bodies. Thorat and Eppie trained a little when they had a chance, joined by Ferrent and sometimes by one or more of the bandits. They reached the burning grounds just before the moon turned.

Na's third eye was a clear lake nestled in a rocky dip between the mountain peaks. It looked like a mere pool, but it was so deep that no one had ever plumbed its depth. There were few trees of any size nearby, but the bandits kept a stack of timber hidden a little distance off the road. Larn found it for them and they hauled what they needed back to the lakeside.

Ferrent stood beside his half-mad brother. Now that he'd gotten used to Forlan, Thorat could tell when his moods were going to shift from mostly rational into a faraway state where no two thoughts could meet. When he was in one of his more settled moods, as he was now, his resemblance to Ferrent was undeniable.

"What do we need to do?" Thorat asked Ferrent.

Ferrent shook his head. "Right now it's just a matter of building up a pile. I've only done this once, and I was barely more than an apprentice then. Varin *was* an apprentice then."

"I'd rather not have to do this more than once," Thorat said.

Forlan spoke suddenly. "Ah, you'll have to, though," the madman said. "You'll outlive us all."

Ferrent looked at his brother, laughed, and nodded. "You'll outlive the old ones, anyway. You and that girl."

Eppie trailed behind them, pulling a log of her own along. "Who's going to outlive who?"

Thorat looked back at her. He certainly hoped that she would outlive the older Defenders. She was young, after all, and that was the way things should be.

"Forlan here says that you and I will outlive the rest," he said.

"I don't want to think about that," Eppie said.

"Neither do I," Thorat said. They were building a funeral pyre. What else was there to think about but death?

There was one more thing to think about, though, and that was the matter of their return to Anamat, of what would happen when they got there, and of whether Larn and his band, or even all the bandits, might help the Defenders in their mission to drive back the invaders, to turn the tide of foreigners that threatened to drown the dragons in its greed for the treasures of the verdant hills of Theranis.

§

They lit the funeral pyre at dawn. It burned through the day. Na did not come when the sun rose, or when it set, but in the middle of the night. As the half-moon's light washed up onto the mountain peaks, the surface of the lake rippled. There was no wind. Waves built up but never overspilled the dry banks, not even when a soundless, invisible thing burst forth from the water in a fountain.

None of them saw Na, but they all felt him pass in the night, rippling the air overhead, changing something.

In the morning, they crushed the last of the coals into ash and set out for Anamat.

§

Chapter 17

Larn led them along the ridgeline, where the bandit tracks overlooked the traders' trails in the valleys below. They only spoke to discuss immediate, practical needs. Forlan said nothing at all for days on end, but Thorat didn't notice his silence at first. They usually made camp in the late afternoons, sending Ferrent and Vigda out to forage for roots while Thorat and Larn hunted. Forlan set up the camp and started the cooking fire while Sunna lay down and gazed into nothingness, exhausted.

"Now I know how the ambassadress feels," she remarked one night. They were sitting around the campfire, scraping the last drops of a rough meal from their makeshift trenchers and resting their feet on the warm stones around the fire.

"It's only losing a baby," Vigda said. "Lots of women do."

"It's not just that," Sunna muttered, but Vigda didn't hear her and went on.

"It's a wonder you didn't just lie down right there and turn yourself over to the village temple."

"I'm more priestess than that!" Sunna said.

"So, your priesstesshood is what gives you honor now?" Larn asked.

Thorat considered stepping in to speak up for Sunna, but he could hardly draw breath before she came back with her own retort. "There's still truth in the rite, even if some can't see it," Sunna said. She sounded angry and more like her old self than she'd been since Tiadun. "The lesser temples aren't much to be proud of these days, but even there, we have our dignity." She winced as she tried to get up. Thorat got to his feet to help her, but Eppie was quicker. Sunna gave him a wry smile, then turned back to Vigda. "I've seen women who've lost a baby, and even if they don't want to move from their beds for days, they can and usually do. It's been longer than that now."

"It's hardly been a half-moon," Vigda said.

"There's another part," Sunna said. "I was only in the gate for a moment, but I was in there, in the other realm."

"It was longer than a moment," Thorat said.

Sunna shook her head. "It wasn't long, but I've been feeling it pull at me ever since. The tide was wrong, all coming out of the earth and not going into it. I felt myself tugged against it with the spring of the year coming out at me, crushing me between it and the heat of the sun bearing down, even though it was only dawn. I still feel crushed like that, compressed, all the time, and as if something's still missing."

"The seed blossoms and goes to harvest," Vigda said.

"Maybe so," Sunna said, as if she knew what Vigda was talking about.

"I felt it too, a little," Eppie said.

"How were you inside the gate?" Sunna asked.

"When we first reached it, me and Thorat, I just went in."

"I pulled her out," Thorat said. "I only reached my arm in, though." He hadn't felt whatever Sunna was talking about, but Eppie and Vigda were both nodding along as if it made perfect sense, as if they'd felt the same.

"I might have gone in further otherwise," Eppie said.

Vigda's face lit up with a broad, wrinkly grin, but Sunna looked at Eppie in horror.

"You'll have to tell her. If you want to take her place –"

"No."

"Tell who?" Vigda said. "This is a matter for the hills, not the city or its priestesses. Besides, that gate's gone, and she's just a child."

"I'm not a child!" Eppie said. "I don't know why you all think I am! I'd be a priestess by now if I'd let them take me when I first came to Anamat, or nearly so, and girls my age in the villages have their own babies now, some of them."

"You're not like them, though," Sunna says. "You have more to learn than most of those girls will ever know exists, as much as the ambassadress herself had to learn, I'd say."

Thorat finally spoke. "You already know a good bit of our work." He paused to look uneasily at the bandits. "You don't have to go to the ambassadress if you don't want to."

"What's the ambassadress want with this girl?" Vigda demanded.

Thorat and Sunna looked at each other. "You say," she told him. "You're the one who promised."

"I shouldn't have," Thorat said. "It wasn't my promise to make. The ambassadress says that Eppie was the last dragon-seeing scrappling in Anamat. I hope that isn't true, but she wants a successor, and..."

Eppie was shaking her head. "She told me, and I told her I wouldn't go."

"You can change your mind, but you should still tell her yourself. We'll go with you when you talk to her," Sunna offered.

"I don't want to. Nothing's changed. I don't need to go talk to her."

Thorat wished she would, though. "You could do both, like Sunna."

"Like I used to. I'm done with going back and forth," Sunna mumbled.

Thorat wasn't sure that Sunna could just leave her role as go-between, but he didn't need to tell her that. The Aralel could, or the Enatel. "You can still become one of us," he told Eppie.

"She already is," Ferrent said. "She was at the gate. The rest is just ceremony." He glanced at Forlan. That "mere ceremony" had broken him, but Eppie had been inside the gate already, and she sat there by the campfire as if not much had changed. In any case, she hadn't gone mad, not that any of them could see.

"It's not just ceremony," Sunna said. "The first year isn't even over, and then there's a lot of training still to go. The –"

Larn leaned forward, frowning. His furs hung loose around him and his face was hard in the firelight. "You're keeping secrets from us. We've shown you our hills, even our funeral rites. Tell us."

Vigda laid a hand on his arm. "We have a few secrets left too, and these are our guests. Besides, the funeral rites weren't new to them."

It was true; the bandits had built the pyre almost exactly as the Defenders did. They hadn't heard the words of each others' prayers, but they'd come to exactly the same points in the ceremony and followed the same rhythms. Sovara might not like the idea that the bandits shared their ways, but maybe if she met them, she would see the advantage of having more skilled, living swordsmen beside them at the dragons' gates along with the old ghosts.

"It'll have to wait until we get to Anamat," Thorat said.

"More shame for you, to take orders like that," Vigda said with a yawn. "With my tired old feet, it had better be worth the journey."

"At the least, you'll get to see Anamat," Eppie said. She spoke with nearly as much eagerness as Thorat felt. Anamat, crown of Theranis. Home.

Vigda gave her characteristic half-snorting chuckle. "I've seen half the keep towns in this land. I hear the city's not what it used to be, anyway." She spat on the ground. "I'll stay to the hills."

"Enough for tonight," Larn said suddenly. No one argued with that. They swept the ground, stretched their sleeping rolls and blankets out in a line, and turned in for the night.

§

A few days later, the Anamat valley stretched out before them at last, its green fields, orchards, and villages rolling down the long low slopes to the city perched on the edge of the bay, its wide wall encompassing almost everything Thorat held dear. He prepared to set off into the cultivated lands with his two old companions and their new apprentice, leaving the bandits behind.

"We stop here," Larn announced.

Vigda nodded. "We'll wait for you to return. If you're not here by the next quarter-moon, we'll go our ways."

That gave them five days. A day and a half to cross the valley each way, two days to convince Sovara that it was worth coming to meet these so-called bandits.

Ferrent looked at his brother and began to raise his hand in a gesture of farewell, but Forlan, who hadn't spoken once since they'd left the funeral pyre, stepped up suddenly and spoke.

"I'll go with you," he said. "I'd like to see the old hall." His voice was clear and calm. The manic light in his eyes seemed to have slipped away. Something had changed during that long silent walk, or maybe just now as they stood looking out toward the city. Thorat peered at him.

"Are you sure?" Ferrent asked. He also seemed to be reassessing the ground he stood on. "I don't think we can take you back to the hall," he said.

"Then I'll meet the others down at the tavern, whoever's left," Forlan said with a smile. "I think I'm seeing clearly now. How many years is it that I've been gone?"

For a couple of heartbeats they all stared at him, dumbstruck. "About ten," Ferrent said at last. "Maybe twelve."

"He's been with us for at least eight," Larn said. "I never heard him speak so clearly, not for so long."

Forlan shook his head. "I scarcely remember the time. Eight years, you say? I do remember a little. It's fine, high country in the mountains. I got lost there, I think. I must thank you for guarding me, watching over me. I'll repay you."

"There's no need," Vigda said, blinking back tears. "I don't know why we didn't bring you back here before."

Forlan gestured to the valley below. "That's where my madness began, and that's where it will end, but I don't think coming here sooner would have helped. Not without my brother and his companions here. I'll go with them now, but I pledge that I'll return to you."

"Do you remember everything?" Ferrent asked.

Forlan shrugged. "Not everything. Maybe I'll remember more later, or forget it all again, but whatever happens, we'll walk into the city together again."

Vigda ran forward to embrace Forlan. "Na's blessings on you, and Tiada's, if she has any left," she said. Then she shooed the lowlanders away, and she and Larn retreated into the woods.

As they left the wild lands behind, Thorat wondered how it was that the Defenders hadn't learned about the bandits before. Perhaps they'd been too intent on hiding to notice anyone else doing their work, or maybe it was just that they were city people who shared his reflexive hatred of the bandits. It wasn't much worse than what the bandits thought of the flatlanders, except that at least the bandits knew something of the rest of the world, while flatlanders knew next to nothing of the mountains. Even if many or most of the bandits were thieves and murderers, there were some like this band, and they were worth knowing.

If the Defenders and the bandits worked together, might they be able to drive back the Cereans? It was a full moon before Midsummer, and already the harbor was crowded with Cerean ships, with more on the way. When he'd first come to the city, there would have been only three or four foreign ships in the harbor at a time, even just before Midsummer. More came every year, and the foreigners might already outnumber the bandits. They certainly outnumbered the Defenders. The foreigners might have strength of numbers, but the bandits and the Defenders knew the terrain, and they knew the dragons. Maybe that would be enough to stem the tide, or even turn it back.

But one dragon was gone already. Tiada had faded into the earth. At least, that was what it had looked like to him. Would she still exist in that other realm? Iola would know. She was above the earth now; she would be waiting for him. For the first time in days, he stopped worrying about what Sovara would think.

§

The gates of Anamat at last. Eppie didn't realize how much she'd missed the city until they hit the outer edge of the West Gate market and she got the smell of it, felt the press of marketers against each other, their dusty sweat and the donkeys' manure drying in the sun. She smelled sweet steaming bread, the sharp tang of new onions, and the bright wet reeds of a woman weaving baskets. It smelled like home.

"I don't think Sovara will agree to let him back," Sunna said.

"She'll have to," Ferrent said. "There are so few of us."

"Right now, I don't care if the Enatel lets me join in again or not," Forlan said. "I can't imagine an Enatel other than Konnat. Certainly not Sovara."

Ferrent smirked. "It took some getting used to, but believe me, she's the Enatel now, and I don't think she's any worse than Konnat was, maybe better."

"I'll see for myself, I hope. Meanwhile, it's good to see Anamat. I'd almost forgotten what it looked like."

"The memories do slip away, some of them," Ferrent said, as if he'd forgotten as much in two years as his brother had in a decade of madness.

Eppie looked back over her shoulder at Forlan, who wore an expression of awestruck wonder. If he hadn't been standing half a head taller than any other man in the crowd, she would have taken him for a green scrappling. Ahead of them, the crowds thickened, so she moved in beside Sunna, who'd been walking strong again since the edge of the valley. Maybe the sight of the city had given her strength, or maybe it was just time and healing.

At the West Gate, Thorat greeted the watchman as if he were an old friend. The watchman smiled as they went past, even though they looked like a pack of bandits. They stopped at Garren's shop, where Forlan took his leave, not being officially allowed to return to the training hall.

"You can't give away your secrets, so I'll find the place on my own if I can," Forlan said. "If I can't find it, I'll leave word with Garren of where I'm lodging."

"I don't want to lose you again," Ferrent said.

Forlan brushed his concern aside. "Go see the Enatel. I'll find you there, or if not there, then where it really matters, in the hills and at the gates."

The brothers embraced, the bond between them almost palpable. If Sovara didn't accept the bandits' help, she'd be likely to lose Ferrent to the hills. Sunna might go too, if only because the Aralel had no authority in the bandits' country.

They walked up the palace road through the west quarter of the city, through another square, and down the quiet lane. The little gate was still there, and the short tunnel under the narrow house, and then the steps up into the sunny courtyard. The old geraniums on the landing were gone, but someone had set out a new pot with a few green herbs poking up over the rim. The stairs looked more rickety than ever.

Ferrent paused. "Now I see how no one ever finds us here," he said. "It's....it's shabby."

Sunna shrugged. "It is what it is and the steps are still safe, I think. Come on, laggards." She sprang ahead and fairly ran up the steps, with Thorat just behind her. By the time Eppie and Ferrent walked into the hall, Sovara was already emerging from her lair.

In the dim light, she looked the same as she had the summer before, maybe a little thinner, maybe a little grayer, but standing just as tall. For a moment, no one spoke.

"We're back," Eppie said.

Sovara looked them over. "Ferrent," she said with a nod. She looked at Sunna, gaze lingering on her belly, and behind her, to the place where Varin didn't stand. "But not all of you."

"No," Thorat said with a heavy breath. "Varin was burned in a pyre in Na's realm. I'm sorry."

"And this one is gone down beyond the other realm with Tiada," Sunna said, one hand on her belly. "What there was of it."

"I am sorry, but at least you four have returned."

"And one other," Ferrent said.

"Leave it for later," Sovara said. "Put down your packs and take up practice swords. Show me what you've learned, or forgotten."

Thorat jaw flapped a little as he bit back all his long tales of the battle and the bandits, but Sunna elbowed him and he followed Sovara's direction. Eppie set down the practice sword she'd borrowed from the bandits.

"Where did that come from?" Sovara asked. "Never mind. Keep it for now and use it in the training. It's as good as the others."

With that, Sovara strapped on her own sword and went to bow before the shrine doors. She opened them with one smooth movement, revealing the statue of Anara, as golden and lifelike as the one in the ambassadress's own chamber, if a little smaller. She lit the incense and then they began, rehearsing cuts and parries, moving in the old familiar space with the old familiar sequence of movements.

It felt like home, like a home Eppic hadn't even known she'd missed. She glimpsed Ferrent, blinking his eyes to push back the tears, and Thorat, throat bobbing as he swallowed. Sunna smiled for the first time since they'd left the gate.

They had been tired when they began, and when Sovara finally bowed before Anara's statue again the four of them were limp with exhaustion.

The Enatel had just closed the shrine doors when they heard a clatter on the stair outside.

All eyes turned to the door as they rose from their bows. Forlan leaned against the doorpost, looking like a bigger, rougher version of Ferrent.

"Forlan was with the bandits," Ferrent said.

"As madmen often are," Sovara said. "Welcome back, apprentice."

"I'm not an apprentice in the hills."

"You are here." Sovara's voice was stern, but she almost smiled. "I've never heard of anyone coming back from the hills, from the breaking. You'll have to take the test again, with the young one, but this time you will pass. You'll both have to."

"Yes, Your Grace," Forlan said. He gave Eppie a nod and looked around the hall, letting out a pleased sigh as he gazed at the shrine doors, the high rafters, and the dusty sword racks. "I suppose I'll have to stay in Anamat a while, then," he said. "It's very crowded, after the hills, and I don't remember so many foreigners."

"There weren't so many then," Thorat said. "There are more and more every year."

Sovara nodded slowly. "I understand you were with the bandits."

"I was," Forlan said. "They say it was for eight years or maybe more. I don't know what I did before then, or really even during that time. I have a few memories, but most of those are from the past moon or so, since Ferrent found me."

"Were you looking for Forlan?" Sovara asked.

Ferrent shrugged. "I was looking for Thorat, and the bandits captured me. I wouldn't have gone willingly, but I'm glad they found me."

"Your training must have gotten rusty in the provinces."

Ferrent opened his mouth to speak but Thorat cut in first. "It didn't, or at least he got no rustier than I did in half a year as a guardsman. We fought at the Midwinter tournament. He's as good as he ever was, I think; it's only that some of the bandits are better."

Sovara raised her eyebrows.

"I wouldn't say that Larn is much better," Sunna put in. "But he did have three other trained men on his side, not to mention Forlan."

"I see." Sovara went to the table and poured herself a cup of cold tea. "Tell me about the gate and about these bandits." She sighed. "I don't like it, but I do see that they've returned Forlan, so let's hear it."

"Should I go fetch water?" Eppie asked.

Sovara gestured to a tall jar standing beside the table. "Raina brought some this morning, so we have tea already. You can pour."

Eppie took the cups down off the shelf. They were dusty from lack of use, all but the two dirty ones on the end. She found a rag that was cleaner than her tunic and wiped them out before she poured. The tea had gone cold, but it had honey in it, and it was wet.

Once they all had their cold, sweet tea, Thorat took a deep breath and began. "The bandits were at the gate too, and there would be fewer of us here if they hadn't been with us, on our side."

Sovara looked skeptical, but Thorat went on. He made Eppie tell how the prince had been killed on the hunt one day, and then Thorat explained that most of them had been in the village, watching the funeral from beside the tavern, when the Cereans had gone up to find the gate.

"But I was there, at the gate," Eppie said.

Sovara looked at her as if to ask why, but then only asked what she'd seen. Eppie told her, and told Sovara how she'd sprung the trap and done as well as she could, and how the others had come just soon enough that she'd lived and returned, and that Sunna had been there first, before the others.

"Tiada was already injured when she flew down to the funeral pyre," Thorat said. They'd left out the part about Sunna killing Squid. Eppie thought that Squid wouldn't matter to Sovara, and besides, she still didn't want to talk about it. Thorat carried on with the rest of the story, with

Sunna and Ferrent filling in details here and there. Sunna didn't say much about her time inside the gate, or the injury she'd gotten there, but Sovara patted her on the hand when they reached that part of the story, and Eppie looked away. The maternal gesture seemed strange: Sovara wasn't like that; she was cold and stern, harder than all the men of Anamat put together, except when she wasn't.

Thorat told how they'd all gone back up to the bandit camp, and gave a quick summary of his return to the gate with Vigda, to get Varin's body back to safety.

"A bandit priestess," Sovara mused. "And you lost the sword."

Thorat nodded.

"But most of us came back alive," Ferrent said.

Sovara turned to Eppie. "Look here, girl," she said, and she spoke with the authority of the Enatel. She wasn't just an old woman who just happened to be the most skilled swordmaster in Anamat. Enat's heir gazed right into Eppie's soul. After a long moment, Sovara broke the locked gaze and nodded to Thorat.

"She went in," Sovara said. "Came out with wits intact, too. She'll do, I think."

"I will?" Eppie said. It was not what she'd been expecting. She'd done all right, they all said she had, but the Enatel saw things differently, and she hadn't been there. Eppie's heart lifted. She hadn't realized, until that moment, how much she'd been dreading coming back to Anamat only to be judged lacking, fearing she'd have to go to the temples after all, fearing that she wasn't good enough, that her scrappling days would be all she could remember of Anamat before they made her go to the hills. Thorat, Sunna, and Ferrent had tried to reassure her, but they weren't the Enatel; what they thought wouldn't count in the end. "I can stay?" Eppie asked. "You won't give me the drink of forgetting?"

"I don't think it would work on her, anyway," Forlan said.

They all laughed, a bit nervously, but they laughed.

"Two nights before Midsummer, you'll go down to that part of the testing. It still needs to be done. Forlan will go after. The practical tests will come before, for both of you. I expect you to be here training twice a day until then."

"Yes, Your Grace," Eppie and Forlan said together.

"Meanwhile, about these bandits. Are you suggesting that I leave Anamat and go into the hills to be ambushed by them?"

"To meet them," Ferrent said. "I don't think they'll ambush you."

"They'd better not," Sunna said, "and I don't think they will."

Sovara made Thorat and Ferrent show her some of the new techniques they'd learned from Larn, a variation on a parry which had caught Thorat off guard, and a feint followed by a thrust, which had been new to all of them.

"I think I saw Konnat do something like that once," she mused. "I'll think about it and go down to sit vigil in the shrine tonight." She looked to Thorat. "You'll keep watch above," she said. "If I don't come back, or if I come back without my wits, you're to take my place."

"Me?" Thorat squeaked. "What about Garren?"

Sovara shook her head. "Garren's stronger, but you'll last longer. Besides, there's the ambassadress to consider."

Forlan looked puzzled, but Sovara leaned over to whisper something in his ear. He smirked.

"But you've been sick," Eppie said, remembering how gray Sovara had looked before she'd gone off to take the charged sword to Thorat. "Are you well enough to go to the edge of the valley?"

"I'm well enough if I want to be, apprentice," Sovara said. She frowned. "Now go down to the tavern and bring back supper."

§

Chapter 18

Thorat waited for Sovara, yawning but still awake as the first morning light brightened the clerestories. In his meditations, he'd faced only his own memories and conscience, not the shimmering signs of the dragons Sovara was confronting. Still, it had been a long night full of doubts. *Had* he done the right thing? Could he have done anything else? He tried to imagine how it might have played out if Sovara and Varin had broken him out of the bandit camp. In all likelihood, they would have failed in that, but even if they'd succeeded, Ferrent would have stayed behind or would have argued all the way. They would have lost him.

Even if he'd come with them to the gate, the five of them would have been no match for the Cereans, wounded already from their fight with the bandits. One or two of them might have been able to run for the hills, to throw themselves on the bandits' mercy, but then would they have been let free again to return to Anamat? No. Not at all likely. And in the end, it had become Vigda's mission more than his. He felt unseated, and yet he was alive. He would live to see the dragons again, and to see Iola.

Sovara emerged from her vigil as dawn was breaking. She settled the hatch over the opening in the floor before she turned to Thorat and nodded.

"I suppose you'll have to come with me to meet this bandit and his priestess –"

"Vigda."

"– whatever her name is. The rest of them will have to stay in Anamat. Sunna has to go back to the temple. She can tell the Aralel what little she needs to know about Tiada's death, and I know nothing of what's happened in the temple since she left. I'm not bringing Ferrent or Forlan, either, or the apprentice, for that matter."

Thorat nodded. He was tired but not too exhausted to walk at Sovara's pace. The higher price was that he wouldn't be able to see Iola for almost another quarter-moon.

"Put on your sandals. I have all the beads we need and Raina will give us waterskins," Sovara said, as if they would leave immediately.

"Sleeping rolls?" Thorat asked.

"We're in Anamat valley. We have inns here, and taverns," Sovara said.

The others began to wake, and by the time Sovara had conveyed her orders and everyone had gotten a bit of bread, the morning was halfway gone. When they reached Raina's house, it was almost midday, so they stopped for a meal and a rest. Raina woke Thorat, shaking him by the shoulder.

"I'm coming too," she said.

"What about your weanling?" Thorat asked, yawning.

"It's only for two nights," Raina said. "I can leave her with the others that long now."

"Good," Thorat said. "Sovara's none too pleased about this. You'll be better company."

Raina grunted. "Sure. And I'm not the Enatel. I've been tethered to this farm too long."

When Raina was young, she'd gone to the gates with the rest, but since then, she'd been caught up in growing her brood until some of them could run the farm for a half-year at a time.

Thorat felt better for having rested, so he ventured a question as they set out. "What made you decide to come meet them?" he asked. "I thought you might not."

"Well, I don't like it, but you didn't like bandits any better than I do when you set out, and now you've changed your mind. Besides, when I look at the world tree, there's so much of it that I don't understand. There are missing threads, parts of our lore that Konnat either didn't have time to tell me or didn't know himself. The chance to learn any more of that, well, it's even worth talking to bandits."

"They can help us, too, if they will."

"I'm not so sure about that, but I'll meet them."

They walked until well after dark that night and slept at a tavern more than halfway to the valley's edge. They walked through midday the next day, coming to the meeting place partway through the following afternoon.

At first, Thorat thought that they'd left, because he could see no sign of their camp, but after a while, he heard the far-distant trill of a bird, or rather, the imitation of a bird call.

Sovara did nothing, and he followed her lead, but Raina returned the call. It sounded again, louder. Raina called back once more, then they waited.

Moments later, Larn burst out from behind a rocky outcropping, sword at the ready. Sovara drew her own sword – a practice blade – as she stood to face him. Larn was smiling.

"So, old priestess."

"I'm nothing of the sort."

"It's not an insult here."

Sovara snorted. "It's not what I am. Show me what you can do, old man."

"You call me old?"

"Nearly as old as I."

They circled each other as they spoke. Vigda came out from her hiding place and watched, arms crossed in front of her chest.

"He's a bit like Garren," Raina observed quietly.

"Not as fat," Thorat said, "but Garren smells better."

The swords came down at the exact same moment, and though Larn's held the center, Sunna's was quicker to recover. She moved with a practiced ease, a precision that the bandit leader echoed more slowly, with his longer, heavier limbs.

They did not fight to wound but only to take the measure of each other. They circled, cut, and parried. Half of what they did were drills Thorat knew well; the rest was new to him or subtly changed in a way that could tip the balance.

"Enough!" Vigda declared after a while.

Sovara stepped back and lowered her blade slightly but did not take her eyes off Larn until he nodded.

"And are you the one that Forlan's brother would not name?" Larn asked.

Sovara raised her eyebrows at Thorat before she answered. "I suppose I might be," she said.

"Are you the leader of these flatlanders who say they defend the gates?" Vigda asked, coming closer.

"For a little while now, I have held that office."

"And what do you call yourself?"

"I prefer not to use my title outside our hall, beyond our shrine. What is yours, bandit?" she asked Larn.

"Guardian of Na, or at least, one of the guardians of Na."

"I see," Sovara said. "And there are many of you? You have no one leader?"

"Not since the last Enatel died without naming an heir."

"There has been an Enatel in Anamat this past hundred years or more," Sovara said. She hesitated, then she reached under the collar of her tunic and drew out her medallion, the mark of her rank that Thorat had only glimpsed once or twice in ceremony. It was inscribed with, and echoed, the world tree that mapped the links between the dragons' realm and the surface of Theranis.

Larn looked at it for a long time. "Do you even know what that represents?"

"I certainly do."

"It has been gone a long time."

"It is right where it was left. It doesn't move, but it is hidden now."

They were talking about the shrine, the deeper part of it below the Defenders' hall. Vigda looked on, curious.

"There are other things that have been lost. Our histories, for one."

Sovara nodded. "Those are lost."

"Histories?" Thorat broke in. "Written histories?"

They turned slowly to look at him, frowning, disapproving. They both nodded.

"I have a friend who is a chronicler. I can't imagine the priestesses or the chroniclers destroying written histories."

"They destroy plenty," Vigda said.

"Still, it might be worth looking?" Thorat said.

Larn jerked his head at Thorat. "I see that the Enatel does not command absolute respect any longer."

"The Enatel, as you know, does not exist outside the walls of our training hall," Sovara said, not acknowledging Thorat. She slipped the medallion back under her plain, coarse-woven tunic.

"But the Defender of Na does," Larn said. He sat down on a rock and invited the others to rest on a fallen log nearby.

"Tell me, then," Sovara said with a half-smile, "why does the untamed dragon need your sword?"

"Why should men fear what they cannot see, a creature who can never frighten them without destroying him? We keep these hills clear for Na. And you?"

"It is the same with the gates, when there are enough of us," Sovara said. "But we are only ghosts in these hills."

"As we are," Larn said. "As we all will be."

Raina had brought a bundle of bread and a jar of still-warm stew from the tavern where they'd had their midday meal. They shared that as a supper while the sun went down over the mountains. Larn and Sovara talked long into the night, comparing the stories and techniques they'd learned from those who had come before them. Most of the stories were familiar to both of them, but each had a few the other had not heard.

At midnight, Sovara yawned despite herself.

"I am an old woman, and it is late," she said. "We will go, to return to the shrine."

"I'd like to see this shrine of yours, but –" Larn looked over his shoulder to the mountain peaks, dark against the starry sky. "My place is here in the hills; I'm pledged to stay here. Are you pledged to stay there always?"

"Someone must tend the shrine," Sovara said. "But no, we do go where there is need."

"Perhaps we will meet again, then," Larn said.

Thorat cleared his throat. "Perhaps it would go better if we knew one another next time we met," he said.

Raina and Vigda nodded.

Sovara let out a long breath. "We can meet. Send us a messenger when you are near, and we can come for five days to the valley by Na's eye, all except for one or two who will stay behind to guard our way to the shrine."

"I am glad to hear that the tree still burns," Larn said. It was hard to see his face in the darkness, but it sounded as if he were smiling. "We will come in the moon-round before next Midsummer."

"And now we will go back to the city," Sovara declared, getting up. "The apprentice needs further training before she's tested. Your Forlan, too. He's still a bumbling apprentice, for all his age."

"But he came back from madness," Vigda said, shaking her head in wonderment.

"He did. I never thought we'd be grateful to have such an old apprentice, but we are. So few with dragonsight anymore."

Larn nodded. "Even in the hills, we have some. I am pleased to learn that the dragons can still be seen from the lowlands. I'd thought it was impossible too."

"Just as this is impossible." Sovara bowed to him, and with that, they took their leave.

§

It was almost midnight again and two days later when Thorat finally set out for the temple. The full moon rose over the tiled roofs of the city. He kept to the shadows, down the alleys and across the cobbled streets, like a thief dodging the watch. He scrambled down the canal bank and ducked into the hidden tunnel. Once he was out of sight, he slowed his pace. The tunnel didn't smell as rank as it usually did. It was then that he realized he hadn't bathed since he'd left Tiadun Keep almost two moon-rounds before, apart from a hasty splash in the mountain streams. He stank. He considered turning around and going to the public baths, but he was too close now; he couldn't bear to be apart from her any longer.

The carved marble grille that barred the entrance to the bath was unlatched. Sunna must have told her he was coming. The bath lay silent and still, its waters dark as ink and the white marble dome above glowing dimly in the twice-reflected moonlight. Thorat let himself in. She must be alone; he was sure of it. Otherwise, it would not be so quiet. It was too quiet. Was she not here?

He should have asked Darna or Myril to make sure that Iola would be here, and alone, before he came. Instead, he'd rushed in, still stinking like a bandit, too impatient to wait. He crept over to the door of the ambassadress's main chamber.

A single lamp lit the shrine and the golden statue of Anara arching over the empty offering place. An embroidered cloth covered the platform, telling him that no petitioner had hastily departed and none was expected soon. Everything was in perfect order except for the shadowed corner next to the sleeping nook where he'd rested once or twice. There, a wooden box sat on a table with its lid ajar. A parchment beside it had been hastily tied into a scroll, the knotted string around it coming undone. He wondered if he should leave and come back in the morning. He looked again at the parchment, wishing that he could read and write, to leave Iola a message of his own. He should have Sunna teach him, or maybe Myril, if she didn't think it was too late to learn.

He caught a whiff of incense, then of himself. Again, he regretted not going to the public baths first. The outer gate clattered.

"I don't know what to make of it," said a female voice, an old woman's voice.

"Well, if you don't know, I certainly don't." That was Iola; he was sure of it. He retreated into the bathing chamber.

"Ask Anara," the old woman said.

Iola sighed loudly.

Thorat took a bead and tapped it on the marble wall three times, a sharp, high sound.

"What's that?" the old woman asked.

"Nothing," Iola said. "But I do find I'm hungry all of a sudden. Have Lena bring me tea and cakes, maybe a little wine, too."

"Didn't you eat at the palace?"

"The governor's food doesn't agree with me." Iola yawned. "Tell Lenasa to leave it on the step. I'll be bathing."

"And so would I, too, if I'd been up to the palace and back," the old woman said. With that, she tottered away.

Thorat heard Iola come in and take off a heavy cloak, throwing it onto the bench in her sleeping nook. She came to the entrance to the bath chamber in a cloud of perfume, her silk robes rustling.

"Is that really you?" she whispered.

Thorat stepped out into the pale light. "It is," he said.

She hurried toward him but stopped short. "You've been in Tiadun." She sniffed. "No, bathe before you tell me about it. I'll join you." Her voice was tense with worry. "The cold bucket is over there."

Thorat followed her direction and went to bathe at last. His clothes had grown thick and heavy with the dust of the road and the sweat of his journeys. He peeled them off and threw them into a pile by the wall, feeling much lighter without them. He found a rough square of cloth by the bucket —probably meant for scrubbing the floors—and used it to help slough off the dirt and dead skin. Even without lamplight, he could see the grime of the water that poured off him and snaked across the clean floor to the drain. He washed it down with the bucket, shivering under the blast of cold water but feeling some of the wear of the journey begin to fade. He had failed to save Tiada, but at least he had returned, unlike Varin. He said a silent prayer for him, poor, ever-youthful Varin, and went on washing. Maybe he should have been the one to fall by the gate, if not the first time, then when he'd returned with Vigda on her suicidal mission.

When he set the cold bucket's ladle down for the last time, Iola was waiting in the bath. He hadn't heard her come in, and she was watching him.

"Come in," she said. "Tell me what happened."

Thorat touched his toe to the scalding hot water of the soaking tub. "It's too hot."

"It isn't," Iola said. "It shouldn't be. Just ease your feet in."

Thorat hesitated, then sat at the edge of the pool opposite and lowered his feet in tentatively. It was still too hot, so he pulled his feet out again.

"Interesting." Iola slid away from her perch and swam over to him. She reached up from the water and ran her hand down his leg to his foot. Her touch was hot but not scalding, and when she reached up again, her hand felt merely warm.

"Try again," she said.

This time, the water only felt warm, the way it was supposed to feel. He felt the burn again only when his rising cock got wet, but then only for an instant. He longed for Iola, but first, he had to address the dragons. He sank all the way into the bath, letting the water close over his head. Their currents swirled around him and pulled him down, but it was a gentle tug, not like the irresistible power that had drawn Eppie, Sunna, and that hapless Cerean into the gate. When he pushed away to get back to the surface, back to the air, it let him go.

Breaking back through the surface, he swept the water away from his eyes and looked up to the dome. He felt too rough to be in such a beautiful place. Iola was still looking at him, her lips rising into a little smile.

"Do you ever think of going to the hills?" he asked her.

Her smile came alive then. She looked up to the dome above them, as he had done. "More and more lately," she said. "Even if there are bandits, it could hardly be worse than some of the princes these past few years. I love the temple, but I'm starting to see that I can't go on like this much longer."

"I need to tell you about Tiadun," he said. He made his way across and sat on the underwater bench beside her. He held her hands in his and told her all about it, everything he could remember, and even the things about the bandits. The only thing he left out, and he wasn't sure why, was the thing the dying prince had said about having a daughter in Anamat.

Iola shuddered when he told her about the prince and the Enomaean priest. "Voles," she said. "So, he was following the cult of Enomae's eagle-headed god, but he saw dragons? I never heard of such a fool." She shook her head. "It's a wonder that these princes have ruled for so long."

"They can't all be fools. The one in Getedun isn't bad."

Iola nodded.

"So, will your apprentice girl come to be a novice here?" she asked. "She could study here and train in your sword hall. I know it's hard, but Sunna did it, and it would be easier than all this chasing around the hills, with foreigners and even an old friend trying to kill her."

Thorat thought of Eppie and shook his head. "She won't come to the temple."

Iola sighed. "I'd hoped she might have changed her mind. She could be like Sunna."

"I don't think even Sunna can be like Sunna any more. She says she's worn out from it. She lost the baby in Tiada's gate."

"She was... I didn't even know! Is that why she left?" Iola looked horrified but didn't rail against Sunna's lack of devotion as he'd feared she would. "She didn't tell me. We have the infirmary here. We could have managed it."

"It might have been easier than losing it in the dragon's gate as she did, but that's not what she chose."

Iola's arm drifted up and traced circles on the water. "Your apprentice wouldn't have to stay inside the temple all the time until I can't fly anymore."

"And how long will that be?"

Iola shrugged. "I will fly this year. I don't know if I'll return."

"Don't go." Thorat let go of the edge of the bath and turned to face her. He pulled her into the circle of his arms. "Come to the hills with me."

The bath felt too hot again.

"I'm tired," Iola said. "Let's go to bed." She slithered out of his grasp and raised herself out of the bath, a shadowy sprite in the moonlight, shining. Thorat followed.

"Not to the rite?" he said.

"No, just to bed. Let's go to the hills."

She didn't mean it as he'd meant it, though. She only meant that she would cast aside her calling for a little while, that she would welcome him as a woman who wanted to lie with a man, a particular man, and not as a priestess embodying the path to the dragons for her petitioner.

As dawn approached, Thorat fell into a deep sleep.

He woke because someone was shaking him.

"You have to go," Iola said. "The Aralel is coming."

Thorat clenched his eyes shut against the bright morning light. "Come with me?" he said.

"You know I can't," Iola said, pulling him up to sit. "Go get your clothes on and go before she finds you here."

"What if another gate closes and you can't return?"

"Anara's gate won't close." Iola spoke as if Anara were beholden to her, as if only Anara mattered, and as if the dragons alone had the power to keep their gates open. "Try to stop the others from closing, if you can."

Thorat got to his feet and started back toward his secret passageway. He stopped at the doorway into the baths.

"I'll keep my apprentice, then. She may not be able to take your place as ambassadress, but at least she can help us keep the hollow earth from closing in on itself while you're with the dragons."

Iola looked down. She nodded. "Take her, then. I will fly again, as long as the winged ones will have me. Maybe I will be the last."

"Maybe you will," Thorat said. "Maybe you will."

§

Thorat drilled her for a quarter-moon straight, with Sunna taking up the slack. Forlan sweated alongside her. He was stronger than she was, but his memory of his time with the Defenders was foggy, and he remembered only snatches of his training in the hills. Eppie didn't know half of what he did, but she learned as quickly as she could and everyone seemed satisfied with her progress.

That didn't ease her nerves much as she sat beside Forlan on the training hall floor and Sovara called Garren out to test her. Everyone else was watching from the side of the room. Sunna looked like she wanted to lean over and whisper something to Thorat, but she held herself back.

Eppie rose to her feet, took the proffered practice sword from Thorat, and squared off across from Garren.

She almost missed the first parry, and he didn't hesitate with the second strike. Was he trying to make her fail? Her heart hardened against him. She would not fail.

A few swings later, she caught the glint in Garren's eye. He'd made her angry on purpose. Now that she was in the flow of the mock fight, though, she kept going, matching him strike for strike, blow for blow.

Sovara sounded the gong. Garren withdrew. Eppie returned to her place, and Forlan got to his feet to face the Enatel herself.

For a moment, it looked like he would fall, but Sovara made a subtle adjustment in her stance, which gave the former bandit just enough time to regain his footing. He rallied. They'd both passed.

The Defenders celebrated with a meal of roast duck and pea soup, with bread Garren had made for the occasion. They also had a cask of better-than-usual ale, but Eppie only had a sip. Her real test still lay ahead.

"I wasn't going to let you fail," Garren said.

Eppie jumped like she'd been spooked. "I wouldn't have wanted to pass if I wasn't ready," she said. "Sovara wouldn't have let me."

"Maybe not, but you were ready."

Eppie looked at the spot at the front of the room, the door that would lead her down below. Garren followed her gaze.

"So, you already know where it is?"

Eppie nodded. "I saw you all coming out after I brought the message from Thorat."

"Hmm. Clever of you. You'll be fine," he said, but his voice lacked conviction.

"I don't know," Eppie said.

Sunna cut in. "Of course you'll be fine; you went into the gate."

Eppie shook her head. "That was only for a moment; this is all night."

"But it's not the same," Sunna said. "It's longer, but it doesn't burn so hot."

Eppie hoped she was right, but she didn't feel any more confident when Sovara gave her the nod and got a torch to lead the way down below.

"I'll take you down, and I'll come back for you at dawn," the Enatel said. "What you see there is between yourself and the dragons. We just take your measure."

Eppie gulped. "I'd like to say my farewells to everyone now, just in case."

Sovara didn't offer her any false assurances, and Eppie was almost grateful for that.

"That's prudent of you. The dragons dislike overconfidence."

So, Eppie said goodbye to Thorat, Sunna, Garren, Raina, Anot, and Harron, who'd come back from the north, and finally to Forlan.

"You'll come back," Forlan said. "They told me so."

She gave him a weak enough smile in response, but that reassurance meant more to her than Thorat and Sunna's backslapping had. Forlan was still half-mad. The dragons still talked to him. They'd never talked to her, not like that. Would they now?

Sovara lit the torch. It was time. She lifted the hatch from the floor and made Eppie go first, down onto the slippery, dank stair, down past the neighboring buildings and into the last remains of the old temple of the Defenders that had once stood proudly at the center of the city, for all to see. Now it was a secret within a secret, dark and full of ghosts.

She even thought that she heard Enat himself whisper to her once on the way down. She'd survived a moment in a mouth of the dragons' realm, but a whole night?

Sovara let her into the inner sanctum. The torchlight faded away up the stair, leaving Eppie in total darkness. She stood in the center of a space she could feel but not see. She could hear the echo from the walls around her. It wasn't a big room, no bigger than the front part of Garren's shop, but it did feel a bit like it belonged to that other world.

Sovara walked too softly to hear, and she didn't hear the hatch close, either. Time slipped by. She wasn't sure how much, with only the irregular drip of water from the walls to mark its passing. She closed her eyes, but she couldn't sleep. If she slept down there, she might never wake.

After a while, she took a step forward. Nothing changed. A second step took her to the center of the room, and then things did begin to shift, first with a dull glow in one low corner of the wall, like a dying firefly, then like a firefly coming to life and calling to its fellows. The light spread, a long pale branch spreading diagonally up. That was Na. She said, "Na," and it brightened. The next thread was Anara's, followed by Corana and the fluttering pulse of Lemira. She didn't recognize the others, but they came anyway, all of the realm dragons and three sea dragons. That is, all of the realm dragons except Tiada. She would have known Tiada, too, but she wasn't there, not anymore, not for human eyes to see.

All night, Eppie watched them flow through the land, ribbons of fire singing together in the heart of the earth, touching each other but never joining, always changing, yet also so strong that she would have thought them immortal. They were immortal. What wasn't immortal was their connection to the surface of the earth. She felt a shift. They began to fade. Dawn was coming.

The room was black again when she heard the hatch open above and saw the torchlight approaching. Sovara looked at the room and raised an eyebrow. Eppie nodded. Sovara smiled and led the way back up.

When she reached the surface of the earth again, Eppie was whole and an initiate of the brotherhood of Enat, the Defenders of the Dragons.

Would she ever have apprentices of her own? If she did, it would be a long time coming, and for now, she didn't care. She smiled to Forlan. "You'll be fine this time."

"Na's strength is with you," he said.

§

Epilogue

The two apprentices had passed their technical test with ease, but Thorat scarcely slept the night Eppie kept her vigil at the shrine. After she emerged, wits intact, Sovara decided that it was high time one of them ventured up to the palace to volunteer for Midsummer guard duty. Thorat drew the short straw. He was passing through the palace hill market when someone hailed him from a tavern.

"Ho, Thorat!" the man said.

Thorat looked around and raised his hand to return the salute. It was one of the guardsmen from Tiadun Keep. He went over to exchange greetings.

"Come sit for a minute."

Thorat racked his mind but could not recall the man's name, or come up with a good excuse to hurry away.

"I thought you'd be off at your farm now."

Thorat shook his head ruefully. "Well, it didn't turn out as I thought it would," he said. "By the time I got there, one of my cousins had started to till for the spring planting already, and said he had first claim on it." He'd practiced the lie just in case, but this was the first time he'd had to tell the story. Fortunately, his former fellow guardsman was well on his way to a bellyful of ale already, and not the most inquisitive of men to begin with.

"Did you not have the right?" he asked.

"Oh, I did," Thorat said. "I just decided that it wasn't worth the fight, not this year, at any rate. I've got another good season or two of sword-wielding in me, and besides, I prefer Anamat women to villagers any day."

"Not me," the man said. "These girls run too quick for me. Ah, well, here we are again, then. It's a pity you had to leave when things were just heating up. We could have used your help. One of the fellows said he thought he saw you, but he must've just been wishing for your sword against those bandits. Still, it was good for those of us who came down from the hills alive. The new prince, that's the old prince's brother, he's paid us all more than we'd seen in years."

Thorat nodded, trying to look more interested than angry. "Is he the prince, then?"

"The governor hasn't confirmed him yet, but what else could he be?" The man, oblivious to Thorat's reaction, leaned in closer and lowered his voice. "And there's more," he said. "The new prince says the old prince had a daughter, and that she's somewhere here in Anamat. He wants her out of the way. It's a nasty job, but he's offering the man who does it half the territory west of the dragon's gate, may she rest in peace."

Thorat scrambled for words. "That barren land? Who'd want it?"

"Barren now. Wasn't when the dragon fiew," the man said. "It'll be good again, and there's lots of it. A choice of a bride, too, from the chieftains' daughters, if you want one."

Thorat nodded. "That's a high price he's offering," he said at last.

"So, will you try?"

A land grant like that would tempt almost any guardsman. Thorat tried to look pensive even as panic gripped him. "I'll think about it. As you said, it's a nasty job. I wouldn't like to do that kind of thing. I prefer an open fight, with an equally matched swordsman."

"Ah, you're good at that, I remember. But just think: you'd be a chieftain."

"Indeed." Thorat took a swig from his neglected fiagon of ale and set it back on the table. "But I was on my way with an errand to the palace now. Maybe I'll see you back here another night."

"Until we meet again," the man said, "and good hunting to you."

Thorat waved farewell without wishing the man any kind of luck at all.

He would have to warn Darna. The palace could wait.

§

Author's Note

This book has been through more drafts than anything else I've ever written. When I began to write it, I was practicing aikido several times a week. My martial arts practice and the people I knew at various dojo inspired some of the aspects of this story, but the cues I took from real life soon got lost in the story-building process. Now, all of those characters and practices stand entirely within the realm of fiction. That said, I want to acknowledge the late Sioux Hall, without whom I never would have gotten as far as I did in aikido, or with this story. Her tireless dedication to her students and the art of aikido was an inspiration. I'd like to dedicate this book to her memory.

I would also like to thank the people who helped me in the very long process of writing this series. I brought an early version of the beginning of this book to the Viable Paradise workshop in 2003, where Steven Gould (another aikido person, as well as a science fiction writer), Laura Mixon, and several others gave me professional feedback on the early chapters of this book. Jess Taylor provided a manuscript assessment on a mid-2000s draft of this story. Other early readers included the aforementioned Sioux Hall, among others.

Laura Ann Gilman wrote up a helpful manuscript report early this year, after which I revised the story substantially. Pris Nasrat and Victoria Goddard reviewed the next version, followed by another round of adjustments. Finally, Richard Sheely acted as copy editor.

Several other friends and writing acquaintances did final "oops detection." Any remaining errors are my own.

Finally, my thanks go out to you, for reading this story. I hope that you enjoyed it. If you'd like to come back for more, you can find the rest of the series or sign up for my mailing list at:

http://www.ameliasmith.net